Entice

Praise for Embrace

'Jessica Shirvington sets up a delicious romantic triangle.'
USA Today

'Addictive. Add to your must-read list.'
Entertainment Weekly's Shelf Life

'Shirvington's debut is smart, edgy and addictive.
A must-read for paranormal fans young and old.'
Kirkus Reviews

'Shirvington has a terrific story to tell.' *Los Angeles Times*

'One of the best YA novels we've seen in a while.
Get ready for a confident, kick-butt, well-defined heroine.'
RT Book Reviews

'Fans of otherworldly stories will likely enjoy this edgy,
suspenseful romance.' *Booklist*

'Has an abundance of crowd-pleasing elements: an
appealing main character, hunky angels and angel hunters,
and unrequited love.' *School Library Journal*

'The Twilight set will embrace this opener of a YA trilogy.'
New York Post

JESSICA SHIRVINGTON

ORCHARD

For
Mum and Dad,
who have always made it so easy to
have someone to look up to and are
a constant inspiration in both my
life and work.

Thanks for always being there.
I love you.

ORCHARD BOOKS
338 Euston Road, London NW1 3BH
Orchard Books Australia
Level 17/207 Kent Street, Sydney, NSW 2000

First published in Australia and New Zealand in 2011 by Hachette Australia
First published in the UK in 2012 by Orchard Books

ISBN 978 1 40831 482 1

Text © Jessica Shirvington 2011

The right of Jessica Shirvington to be identified as the author of this work has been asserted by her in
accordance with the Copyright, Designs and Patents Act, 1988.

The author and publisher would like to thank the following for permission to use
copyright material: State University of New York Press, Albany, for a quotation
from *Jung and Eastern Thought* by Harold G. Coward; University of Tennessee
Press, Knoxville, for a quotation from *A House of Gathering: Poets on May Sarton's
Poetry* by May Sarton and Marylin Kallett; Estate of C.S Lewis, for a quotation from
Miracles by C.S. Lewis © C.S. Lewis Pte. Ltd. 1947, 1960; Estate of C.S Lewis,
for a quotation from *Perelandra* by C.S. Lewis © C.S. Lewis Pte. Ltd. 1944;
Princeton University Press, Princeton, for a quotation from
The Archetypes and the Collective Unconscious: Vol 9 by Carl Jung.

The author and publisher would also like to acknowledge the following works
from which the author has quoted: *Douay-Rheims Bible*; *English Standard Version*;
The King James Bible.

Every endeavour has been made on the part of the publisher to contact copyright
holders not mentioned above and the publisher will be happy to include a full
acknowledgement in any future edition.

A CIP catalogue record for this book is available from the British Library.

1 3 5 7 9 10 8 6 4 2

Printed in Great Britain

Orchard Books is a division of Hachette Children's Books,
an Hachette UK company.

www.hachette.co.uk

I form the light and create darkness.
I make peace and create evil:
I, the Lord, do all these things.
Isaiah 45:7

PROLOGUE

'No one takes my life away from me.
I give it up of my own free will.'
John 10:18

The angel had been ordered to make his choice. It had to be of his own free will. But what they asked of him carried a high price. He would most likely never return. Most likely be destroyed. Or worse.

And no one would ever know the truth.

'You have decided, then,' a voice said to him.

I felt each moment as he did – the obscured version of time in what had to be an otherworldly place – but could see nothing. It was surreal; no visible people – just their presence or maybe auras.

It wasn't a question, what was said. They knew the moment he'd made the decision. They probably knew before him. He could sense them all around, the mighty Seraphim. Supreme knowledge lent them a powerful presence, but it was bitter this day.

'When the first of your tasks is complete you will move on to the next. You must not reveal yourself or seek companionship

with anyone, especially exiles, unless for the purposes of fulfilling your objectives.'

'I understand.'

'You will spend three years before the day on which you must act arrives. He has his role to play. It is not possible without your actions first.'

'I understand.'

And he did – understand. He had made this decision of his own free will, despite the sacrifice, for he knew it had only been asked of him because he was the perfect choice.

He felt the universe around him, the freedom of unfettered dominion over space and realm, and wondered when he would again feel this, if ever.

'Take a name of the times when you are there. Now go.'

And so it was. He made the transition amidst images of mobs and anger. To his destiny. To death. The flash of a kiss. All things to come.

A fog cleared around me and my surroundings came into view. I was suddenly in my art studio. Standing by the window was a figure I recognised. The one I suspected was my angel maker.

'What's your name?' I asked, still amazed by the way my words seem to float through the air in these dreams, as if they had their own physical presence.

'It does not matter. But you may call me Lochmet if you require a title.'

'What does that mean?'

'Warrior.'

I swallowed, suddenly nervous. The way he said it – with such force and confidence – made him seem so powerful.

'Why did you show me that angel? I don't get it.'

'Not yet. But you will. It is but a strand of one existence, from a very long time ago.'

'No, please don't... Just tell me.'

He turned to face me, his shoulders squared, and I struggled with conflicting urges. One drawing me towards him, the other, to cower away. I was sure he could see it, see right through me, which only made me more vulnerable.

'We all have the capacity to find the will to do what must be done – even when that which we must do terrifies us most. Remember this.'

'That's it? That doesn't explain anything. Who was he? I thought it was against angel law to exile to earth. How come the Seraphim asked it of that angel?'

He considered me for another delayed, vacant moment before his head tilted towards a painting beside him. The vision of a sandy beach with a midnight-blue sea crashing against rocks seemed to affect him. He stretched his arm out and brushed his fingers lightly across the textured ripples of the oil-painted canvas. For just a moment, the silence between us was almost comfortable.

But when he looked back at me I knew: he wasn't going to tell me any more about the angel he had shown me.

'Be mindful. A traitor is within your fold,' he said.

'Who?'

He shook his head and turned back to the window.

'You must walk your path, leave the footprints as evidence of your journey. I cannot take it...or change it.'

His voice held the first hint of emotion – a small, almost undetectable, quiver.

'But you did help me,' I started. 'Two years ago, in that classroom...' Even in my dream I felt the sickening memories and the lump in my throat willing me not to go on. 'It couldn't have been anyone else. You sent that teacher across the school to intervene.'

I swallowed hard, fought to hold onto my train of thought, not detour to that day, to that teacher holding me down while I struggled beneath his heavy weight.

'You interfered,' I said, then dropped my head. 'Thank you.'

His silence was all the confirmation I needed. I looked around the room, unsure what to say next. My paintings surrounded me, but, unlike before, they now included those that I had only planned. Envisaged. Somehow, this room held the paintings of my imagination.

I shuddered.

From behind me, I heard a roar. The deepest rumble, so strong it reverberated up my legs and into my spine.

'My lion,' I whispered.

I spun around, in dreamy slow motion. There was nothing there. I turned back to the angel. He was gone. Sprinkles of rain spat in through the crack in the window.

I stood, waiting.

And then everything around me exploded in a flash of colour that settled to nothing. I was nowhere, all alone apart from the rain, startlingly cold, stinging my face with every sharp landing.

Shards of ice.

Cold enough to wake me up.

CHAPTER ONE

*'In nature there are neither rewards nor punishments;
there are consequences.'*
Robert Green Ingersoll

I held the dagger in my right hand. The hilt heavy and intricately carved, the blade long and slim. The sharp point made an impression into the tip of my index finger – just enough to sting and stir the memories. Choices had been made and now the consequences were mine. Although I'd do it all again, although I knew now that there was something I had to do that was more important than anything else, the truth was – I mourned the life I'd left behind. I twisted the hilt slowly and watched the point pirouette on the pad of my finger.

My dagger – the dagger I killed myself with.

I put it down beside me – not wanting to touch it any longer, but unable to hide it away. I tried to snap out of it. Focus on the positives. For one – I got my period earlier in the week. Never had I been so happy for an emergency dash to the pharmacy.

Everything I had once believed in was shattered. It was still humiliating, knowing I'd been so naive under Phoenix's influence. I really *thought* I could trust him – so much so that I'd lost my virginity to him and unwittingly created some kind of emotional bond between us. A connection he exploited to destroy my already fragile friendship with Lincoln. Throw in jumping off a cliff, nearly being killed by a bunch of over-the-top psycho exiles, discovering that Phoenix was in fact the son of the first dark exile, Lilith, and that he tricked me into becoming one of the Grigori and, well, condoms hadn't been the first thing on my mind.

Shaking myself free of the memories – and questions – was hardest when I was on my own and as I'd learned a long time ago that Dad was more comfortable at work, where he could hide from his own memories, this was a problem. Solo time made it impossible to ward off the persistent whispers of my past.

I headed into my art studio and started to lay down some fresh paint – I'd just picked up a new supply of iridescent colours and had been playing around with them since I got home from school. My phone beeped.

I'm outside – where r u?

I blew out a breath and caught a glimpse of myself in the mirror. I'd lost track of time. Now I was late and looked like crap. My long dark hair was twisted into a matted knot and the loose strands falling around my face were splattered with red and grey paint. I hadn't even bothered to put on make-up this morning. Although I didn't really need foundation – most were too dark or yellowy for my creamy complexion – mascara was a must for my otherwise lacklustre hazel eyes. But the only thing I had time to fix was my clothes.

Be down in 5.

I ran to my room, stripping as I went, and threw on my most reliable jeans, the only option when pressed for time, and the first T-shirt I could find – boring black, but clean. I tried and failed to rescue my hair, finally just tying it up in a new version of the same messy knot and gave up completely on my paint-ridden hands. After a hurried attempt at applying at least a layer of mascara I grabbed my dagger and was out the door, pulling my trainers on between steps.

The mirror in the lift may as well have laughed out loud.

Shit.

By the time I reached the front doors of my apartment building, I'd completely forgotten about my appearance and unconsciously but predictably refocused on Lincoln. Sick anticipation crept through me, circulating and intensifying with every breath.

Yeah, I have it bad.

If possible, I had it worse than ever.

There was a time when I thought my love for Lincoln was unrequited, but now… Well, it's more complicated than ever, but the vibe – the crazy wired vibe that sparks between two people who are dancing around each other while simultaneously champing at the bit, *that vibe* – was one I was walking, stumbling, hacking through a thicket of, whenever we were near each other.

'Hey. I know it's cool to be late, but could we at least keep it to a fashionable ten minutes?' Lincoln asked, a smile in his tone. I felt his eyes take me in and quickly remembered my very average appearance. I tucked my hair behind my ear and he gave a quirky grin. He knew me too well.

'You know, when you talk like that, you really show your age,' I quipped, as I slid my swipe key into my pocket.

Lincoln's eyebrows shot up.

Good job, Vi.

Less than a minute together and I'd already made things awkward. The issue of our age difference had definitely taken on more significance since I'd found out that although he only looked twenty-two at most, he was in fact twenty-six. As I was only seventeen, it increased the gap to a hefty nine years. Then again, as Grigori, neither Lincoln nor I were confined by the normal parameters of life expectancy. Unless we got ourselves killed along the way, we would likely live well into the hundreds, the ageing process slowing the older we got. So the age difference in the end meant little. It was the *other* parameters that were our problem.

'Where are we going, then?' I asked, keen to change the subject.

'Griffin just called. He got a tip-off. Exiles have been spotted a few blocks from here. If we go now, we should catch them. You up for it?'

Lincoln wanted me to be good. He wanted me to be strong and capable. That was one of the things I loved about him. He didn't want me to hide away and not be able to protect myself, but at the same time, I could hear the concern in his voice.

'Yeah, let's go,' I rallied, trying to sound as sure as I should be.

Since becoming Grigori, my life has taken a sharp change of direction. I am, for all intents and purposes, a warrior. In many ways, that suits me fine. I like being strong and having extra abilities by way of supernatural enhancement is a-OK with me. I have learned the hard way that exiled angels do not belong among humans. There is a very good reason we are divided by realms of time and space and angels were simply not made to cope with the emotional extras that come with having a corporeal form.

Humans are born with the ability to feel, touch, smell, to experience both love and pain physically. Angels are not. Becoming human is just too much for them to process. In the end they go insane and most of them are vindictive monsters well before that.

Yet despite knowing this, there is still a part of me that struggles with the concept of killing them. Technically, that's not what we're doing, since we are only stripping exiles of physical forms when we return them to their realm for judgement. But…

And as if that wasn't enough, since embracing my angel half in the desert – plunging my own blade into the image of myself – I haven't been able to use my dagger, though I rarely go anywhere without it. It sits in a sheaf, carefully 'glamoured' so it cannot be seen by normal humans (weird to think I am no longer one of the *normal*), and whenever I train or head out for a hunt, like now, I have every intention of using it should the occasion call for it.

'Are you sure you're OK? I could call Griffin and he could go out with some of the others.'

'And who's going to go with him? Magda isn't back for another couple of days and everyone that can be active is already out doing something.'

Lincoln dropped his head. I nudged his shoulder as we walked on. 'I'll be OK. And anyway, practice makes perfect, right?'

He took a steadying breath, stood a little taller and ran a hand through his golden-streaked brown hair. He knew there was no talking me out of it and at some point he had to get on board. It wouldn't help either one of us if we didn't work together.

'Right,' he said, with a finality that made me smile. With that, he segued into a tactical pep talk to which I listened intently. I was learning to be Grigori, to be a warrior, but Lincoln had already travelled well down that road. Under his nice-guy facade was a mighty champion.

CHAPTER TWO

'. . . What? Shall we receive good at the hand of God
and shall we not accept evil?'
Job 2:10

The streets around the bridge were dodgy. Homeless people congregate around the massive stone pylons, using them as buttresses for their provisional squats.

The area is fairly sheltered and since it's well known as a homeless hang-out, residents are pretty much left in peace to haul out their shopping trolleys and tarpaulins at night. Most of them clear away during the day. A fact that confounds Steph. She struggles with the concept of anyone fitting all their belongings into one lone shopping trolley. Last time we'd gotten stuck down this end of town she'd speculated no end as to where all the shopping trolleys and their loot are hidden away during the day. I mean, she has a point. You don't see dozens of homeless people walking around during the day pushing trolleys. They must go somewhere.

By the time we turned into a small side street, the last of

the daylight was gone and there were no streetlamps. The evening was clear and there was a bite in the air but the absence of light always unnerves me and, of course, exiles, whether once of light or dark, prefer to play in the lee of night.

Entertaining themselves with the pain of humans was high on the to-do list for exiles. They have the power to infiltrate imagination and pretty much put whatever horror movie takes their fancy inside someone's head. Some of them use it just to taunt and frighten, while others use it as a kind of strategy. Over time, according to Griffin, they've used this ability to throw humans off their tracks entirely.

Apparently, that's where the myths of vampires, werewolves and other things creepy come from, even fairies and elves. If exiles sense that their supernatural power has been detected and they are not able to eliminate the problem using their preferred method of slaughter, they simply reveal themselves as something other than human, anything but what they really are.

It makes sense. People, I was learning, were, on the whole, more at ease with the virtual reality of vampires and intergalactic visitors than the troubling prospect of a biblical Armageddon of one-time angels, equally once of light and dark, who were now exiles driven by vengeance and power living among us. Yes, we are naive by choice.

I looked down the narrow street as far as my eyes would allow. It was littered with homeless people lying on flattened cardboard, the lucky ones wrapped in torn sleeping bags, the rest burrowed in piles of old newspapers. I scanned the dark red-brick walls, which ran at least five storeys high on each side. The protection they offered was part of what made this strip so popular.

Lincoln walked slowly beside me, his hand going to my elbow for a moment – a silent reminder that I needed to be alert. I tried to move myself quickly through the flush of heat that came whenever I felt his touch.

I stopped walking and he looked at me, a question within his features. I smiled into his emerald-green eyes before I could stop myself.

'I think I can sense them,' I said.

I didn't *think*, I knew. I'd been tasting apple for the past couple of blocks and the sound of birds flying, smashing through trees, was not one shared by others nearby. These were my angelic senses. Most Grigori had one. Some, like Lincoln, had two. Lucky me, I had all five and I seemed to feel them more acutely than any other Grigori I had met. Great to be special and all, but having an extra five senses can be, well, overwhelming.

'How long have you been sensing them?'

I hesitated. He saw. 'Violet… How long?'

I was worried Lincoln would judge me – that the fact I could sense them from so much further away would be a form of supernatural condescension and alienate me. 'Not long. Maybe one street back,' I said, awkwardly.

Lincoln raised his eyebrows at me.

'Three streets back.'

The corners of his mouth curled. He was holding back his Cheshire. I was a fool – he was proud of me.

I rolled my eyes at his twinkling expression. 'They're in the street. There are two of them,' I said.

He nodded, now refocused. 'I can smell them.' His primary angelic sense was smell, though he could also hear.

I returned his nod. Morning and evening or, more accurately, the power that created them, flashed before my eyes as the fragrance of sickly sweet flowers flooded the area so strongly it even overpowered the stench of the street.

He took half a step in front of me and I let him. I might be able to sense them from further away but Lincoln could size them up and pick the strongest much faster than I could.

They emerged from the darkness, looking human, but not at the same time. Both were dressed casually, although one had blood stains all the way up his right arm like an abattoir worker at the end of a long day. I had an awful feeling I knew what that meant. Exiles had a habit of indulging in the internal physical torture of their victims. It prompted me to again take in my surroundings.

While still keeping sight of the approaching engagement I cast my eyes quickly over the sleeping bodies lining the street. Why hadn't anyone said anything to us, stopped us, when we clearly didn't belong here, from entering into their indisputable territory? I took in one, then two, then three figures tucked into their sleeping bags, unmoving. Energy hummed through my body and a cruel thrum worked its way up into the base of my ribs.

I had let it once before – had allowed the energy to take over my body, forcing me to the ground, paralysing me in the pain of others. I grabbed Lincoln's arm. He didn't look back but I had his attention.

'They're all dead. They've killed them all,' I said, all too aware that the exiles were moving closer by the second. Agents of death.

'Linc, should I…you know?' I whispered shakily. He

knew what I was suggesting. Just after becoming a Grigori I had found myself in the unpleasant position of being surrounded by exiles while mortally wounded. It was then that I discovered that I could do more than strip an exile's powers or return them to the angel realm for judgement. Grigori rely on physical contact with an exile, through which they can incapacitate the exile for long enough to return them. It appeared I didn't need that contact and in fact could extend my power to include multiple exiles at the same time.

'No. Your power's spiking all over the place. Are you OK?' Lincoln replied quickly under his breath. They were getting closer.

The senses were on the edge but I had them under control... Just.

'I'm OK. I could try.'

'Stay focused. Stick to the plan,' he whispered back. But his tone left little room for discussion.

Great. The plan. The one that has me all dagger happy.

Except I'm not.

Lincoln and Griffin had insisted that I still had to enter combat the same way as all other Grigori. That it wasn't enough for me to rely on my power to get me out of everything. In theory I agreed. But at this very moment – standing smack bang in the middle of a slaughter zone while two over-stimulated, decidedly unhinged exiles moved in on us – it seemed extreme.

The exiles stopped in front of us, smiling. They were assessing us the way only otherworldly creatures can. A flick of the eyes, showing a defensive mechanism, and hunger at the same time. Exiles, whether light or dark, hated Grigori and loved killing us above all others. We were their greatest – their *only* – threat. If exiles were successful in eliminating us, there would be no hope for anyone else.

'You are a little late,' said the shorter of the two, the one with the bloodied arm, like he'd been waiting for us.

Lincoln had already positioned himself level with him, not that I needed the heads-up that this one was the more derailed of the two.

'It's a pity. We would have liked to have kept a few to tear apart in front of you. I prefer an audience. But we got bored.' He smiled, perfectly white teeth, pink full lips. Had I not been so sure of the senses I would have sworn he was a sixteen-year-old jock. That was the thing about exiles – they all looked healthy and strong, all in their prime.

'You knew we were coming?' Lincoln asked, twisting his body a little more, shielding me.

The exile laughed. 'I have a message for you.'

'And I thought your days as messengers were over.'

The jock-looking exile licked his lips, barely restraining himself. 'The reward of getting to kill you,' he glanced at me, 'and her, is sufficient incentive.'

'Well?' Lincoln said, showing no concern.

The exile's smile broadened and he spoke slowly. 'Nahilius said to tell you he's coming for what's yours.'

Lincoln stiffened. The exile cackled loudly.

'Make your choice,' Lincoln growled. There was no denying that when he went into fighter mode, he was lethal. But so were they.

'Choice?' The jock boy laughed. 'So kind of you to offer. I think I will choose decapitation for you and something a bit more…fly-by-the-seat-of-my-pants for her.' He looked to me, his buddy laughing away. Then I saw it. It was gone as quickly as it had come, but it was definitely there. Recognition.

He could sense me, could sense my power. Of course, given what he could sense and what he'd probably heard I could do to him, he should have run. Instead, true to exile form, he lunged towards me, relishing the challenge.

Lincoln was ready, his arm out, intercepting the exile, coat-hangering his forearm into his opponent's neck, breaking his speed and redirecting his attention. That was all I had time to see before my own creepy once-was-angel started throwing punches in my direction.

Why is it that they all know how to fight?

Exiles seemed to come to earth, take human forms and although none of them had great technique, they all knew how to hit. Hard. Luckily for me, thanks to many hours of training and some angelic augmentation, so did I.

We exchanged blow for blow. I'm not short for a girl, he was tall for a man, so he had that over me. He got in a few good knocks to my face, but he really favoured his right side so I just kept moving towards it, getting nice and close so he couldn't gain any leverage against me. I was getting on top of things, a series of kicks to his legs had left him shaky. I hadn't landed one in that magic spot that would blow out his knee, but he was stumbling.

A glow of colours lit up to my right. I knew what it was, but I looked anyway. Lincoln had the jock in a headlock and as I turned, I saw him plunge his dagger into the exile, returning him. What I *failed* to see was the tall exile's fist heading straight for my ear. It was a sucker punch, but then these guys had no morals let alone fighting ethics. I was caught off-balance and could feel the warm wetness that could only be blood seeping down the side of my neck as I fell, now completely aware of the exile coming down on top of me.

My hand went instinctively to my dagger, my fingers wrapped fiercely around the hilt. There was an opening. I was going down, he had launched himself over me, but I had time. If I hadn't hesitated I could have got it out, I *could* have returned him.

Instead, my shoulder smashed into the gravel road and I rolled onto my back quickly in an attempt to evade him. He collided into me so hard I felt the top of my spine being ground into the road and screamed. I punched him in the face twice, but he was too close now and had taken the advantage. He drove his knee into my stomach and drew back a clenched fist for what I knew was going to hurt, a lot.

But it didn't. He never got his chance.

All I saw was Lincoln's dagger coming through the exile's chest, the glory of his power's colourful mist and then, the exile was gone.

Lincoln stood above me, strong and ready for anything. I looked into his fighter eyes and they took a moment to soften. He put his hand out and helped me up. It was warm and real, and he pulled me into him and wrapped an arm around me to help me walk.

'I couldn't.' I wanted to explain, to give an acceptable excuse. I was letting him down by not stepping up. I wasn't just putting myself in danger but everyone else as well.

We walked away from the scene. The bodies of the exiles had disappeared but we were still surrounded by a killing field of homeless, dead people no one would claim and barely any would even notice gone. It had been too easy for the exiles to torture them. I felt bad walking away, like I was being disrespectful, but there was no option. We'd inform the police anonymously later. We couldn't risk getting pulled into murder investigations we could never explain.

'You did great. I can't sense any more of them,' he said, looking around. 'Can you?' He sounded unusually anxious.

'No,' I said, looking down. 'Do you know what they were talking about? Who's Nahilius?'

Lincoln hesitated. 'Just a troublemaker. No one for you to worry about.'

'Oh,' I said, keeping my eye on him as he looked away.

Lincoln tightened the arm he had around me, supporting me. 'It's just going to take some time. What you went through…in the desert. It's OK that you need some time.'

'You're upset with me, I can see it,' I said, wincing at the pain in both my ear and the back of my neck.

'What's the first rule in combat, Violet?' He spoke in his training voice. This time my cringe wasn't at the pain, but at the stupidity that I was about to have to admit to.

'Never take your eyes off your opponent.'

'Exactly.' We walked on. He didn't need to say any more. We both knew, this one was all on me.

When we turned the corner, out into a busier street, he pulled me a little closer, protectively. I loved being tucked in his arms, wrapped in his warmth, and wished we could have our chance to explore what we were to one another.

'We need to get you away from here so I can heal you.'

A drunk man dressed in a suit of rags slumped against the wall by the roadside and as we passed, his almost empty bottle fell from his hands, clinking into the gutter and making me look down. I stopped walking. I could feel something. Not the senses, something else. It was...stale. A lingering shadow of something...

I reached down and picked up the bottle to hand to the derelict, but I hadn't thought it through and as I straightened paid the price with a wicked head-spin followed by the throb of all throbs from my neck right up to my temples.

I shut my eyes briefly and took a slow breath. Lincoln steadied me.

'You dropped this,' I said, holding the bottle out to the drifter.

The man looked up.

So many things happened within a split second. First, the effort of reaching out made the man lose balance and his upper half joined his lower half on the ground again. Second, I gasped. Third, Lincoln pushed me behind him and pulled out his dagger in the middle of a busy street.

Then...Onyx burst out laughing.

CHAPTER THREE

'But we all are men, in our own natures frail,
and capable of our flesh; few are angels…'
William Shakespeare

'Finally! I've been waiting for you,' he hiccupped through a series of wet chesty coughs, 'to come kill me with your little knife!'

He lay back on the ground, arms splayed. 'Go ahead! Anywhere you like! Just make it count but not my face.' He closed his eyes and laughed again while he started to sing a tuneless ditty, 'Finally…finally…finally…they have come for *me!*'

'Oh my God,' I said, pulling up to stand beside Lincoln.

There are a great many things to fear out there, even when you are supernaturally strong and fast, and although the memories of what Onyx had done to me – how he had filleted me through the back unrepentantly and smiled as he watched life drain from my body – were fresh, there was little doubt that this man was a mere shadow of what had once been a very formidable, frightening enemy.

'What are you doing here?' Lincoln asked, not nearly as steady as usual. I realised he might be remembering his own near-death experience at the hands of Onyx. My hand flinched, instinctively wanting to comfort him, but I stopped myself. It wasn't cool to show weakness – even less cool to expose someone else's.

Onyx opened his eyes into slits and wheezed some more. 'Christ be damned! You haven't come to kill me, have you?'

'No,' I said.

'I suppose you were after that lot down the road. Noisy ones. No finesse.' Even through slurred words the sounds of contempt and longing were clear. 'I see they had some fun with you, though,' he said, looking at the blood dripping from my ear.

'So much fun they're no longer with us,' I sniped defensively. Although I could hardly take the credit.

'Lucky bastards.'

'You can still sense them?' Lincoln asked.

'In a way. Not that I needed to. Would've been more subtle if they'd come in with tanks. If you haven't come to kill me – go away.' He snatched the bottle that was still dangling from my hand and shuffled back to the wall.

I glanced at Lincoln. He looked appalled by the sight and stench of this man. I was sure his reaction was mirrored in my own face. 'What are we going to do?' I asked.

'What do you mean? We're going to get out of here and get you healed. Come on.' He motioned for us to move on, yet his eyes didn't leave Onyx.

'Have you, umm…seen one like this before?' I swayed a little, the pain becoming unbearable. The shock had held it off till now.

'No,' he said, hiding his concern with impatience. 'You're losing too much blood.'

I shook my head and recoiled. 'I know this is going to sound crazy, but I can't just…Could we at least get him cleaned up a bit?' I held my breath.

Lincoln pulled me a few paces away from where Onyx was in the process of finishing the dregs of what looked like a bottle of bourbon.

'Violet, are you forgetting what he did?' he asked, in a hushed but frantic tone.

'No, I just…'

'This could be some kind of set-up. He said himself he could still sense them, he's probably working with them.' He shook his head then looked back to Onyx again. 'It's too risky. Especially the state you're in.'

'We don't have to take him anywhere private. We're due to meet with Griffin in a minute. Maybe we should just take him to Hades with us?'

Before we could talk any more, Onyx pulled himself up to stand, using the wall for balance. He looked over to us and then…*spat*.

We watched as his lougie hit Lincoln's boot and simultaneously turned back to Onyx, who had started swinging the now empty bottle, making it clear that it would be the next thing headed in our direction.

'Filthy Grigori,' he slurred.

'Right,' Lincoln said, turning to me, 'can we *please* go now?'

We left Onyx by the side of the road with his empty bottle and little else.

It probably wasn't the best idea going straight to a club with an open head wound, but we really were late to meet Griffin and I'd insisted I was OK, much to Lincoln's distress. Apart from the fact that my ear had suffered a massive trauma and was not up for the thumping bass sounds that go hand-in-hand with any good club, my face, neck and shoulder were also caked in blood. I was glad I couldn't see all the damage.

The bouncer opened the massive swing door that had changed recently from a glossy black finish to an equally polished burnt orange. After a good look up and down, it was only once Lincoln had slipped the guy a twenty, while promising we were only stopping in for a minute to collect someone, that he let us in.

Griffin was sitting at the bar. He always looked awkward in his uniform of black pants and navy shirts. He was old-fashioned in style, but I was beginning to think that might be the best thing about him. His loyalty was old-fashioned too.

He was talking to a man we both recognised as the owner of Hades. Neither Lincoln nor I had met him before but we were aware of him and that Griffin believed he was more than human. It was obvious that whatever Griffin was saying to him had the owner looking seriously annoyed.

'Should we give them a minute?' I asked Lincoln, as he

helped me through the press of party-goers. My head was exploding.

'What? And miss out on the fun?' He gave me a wink. I smiled and my heart fluttered as his eyes stayed on me for that moment longer than 'only friends'.

Griffin saw us approach and quickly took in the state of me. 'Do I need to ask?' He spoke with a fatherly tone that I'd learned not to baulk at. Griffin was technically eighty-four and since everything that had happened – the way I'd embraced and then faced Onyx and Joel – I'd earned his confidence.

He rolled his eyes when I didn't respond. 'It looks like reinforcements couldn't arrive soon enough.'

I nodded. He wasn't going to get any argument from me. Two tutors and three students from the Grigori training centre in New York were arriving in two days and I couldn't be happier. I was going to be able to learn from the experts and have people my own age to train with, something I really needed. I was sure with their help I would be able to get over whatever it was that had been holding me back. Not to mention the other reason their services were required: the Scripture that can decipher the identity of all Grigori, even those who have not yet embraced and are therefore defenceless, was never far from my mind. I would not stand by and watch it fall into the hands of exiles. If they found the key to destroying Grigori and gained the upper hand the slaughter would not stop until all humans knelt before them, worshipping them as gods.

'See!' yelled the owner over the music. 'This is exactly what I mean. You people can't treat this place as some kind of drop-in centre. I'm running a business. I don't want to be involved in this...this... I mean, *Christ*!' He gestured sharply in my direction. 'She looks like roadkill!'

I looked at Lincoln.

'You do look pretty bad.' He smiled.

'I'll go to the bathroom and clean up. I'm sorry,' I said to the owner.

'Well, shit. Don't go into the girls' bathroom looking like that.' He ground his jaw. 'You can come upstairs.'

I looked at Griffin and Lincoln suddenly feeling a different type of uncomfortable.

'Yes, yes!' he jumped in, before any of us could say anything. 'You can all bloody well come.' He stormed off down the long side of the bar and through an unmarked door at the end, sparing us a *Hurry the hell up* glance.

We trudged up the stairs to a short corridor with three doors, Griffin filling us in as we walked. 'His name is Dapper. He's some kind of Seer. I'm still not clear on the details, but I do know that he can see what we all are. He seems to be able to see auras that surround people. I think he can pretty much identify anything supernatural.'

'That's handy. Who's he playing for?' Lincoln asked.

Griffin clicked his tongue. 'Well, that's the problem. He's a bencher with no intention of changing status.'

'Could be worse,' Lincoln said.

'True.'

Lincoln eyed me again. 'You holding up?'

'I'm good,' I said, my vision blurring.

'She's lying,' Griffin said, without even turning to look at me.

'Hey,' I protested. It was bad manners to use our powers against each other unless it was a must.

'Sorry,' Griffin said.

'Now who's lying,' I mumbled.

'Come on!' called Dapper impatiently, standing in an open doorway. He took up most of the space. I struggled to categorise Dapper in his manicured presentation of pants and black shirt, slightly at odds with his rough mannerisms. But the thing that really threw me; his belt was diamond-studded.

He led us into his apartment. Hades was elaborately decorated with lashes of rich colour and lots of sparkle so it shouldn't have surprised me to see the overtly feminine, elegant decor upstairs, but still, I marvelled. Dark wooden floorboards were covered with fluffy cream shag rugs and heavy modern furniture that could only be Italian – being the daughter of an architect meant only one type of magazine on the coffee table at home. I came from a world of interior design. It was immaculate and warm at the same time.

Dapper flicked switches, lighting up the living room and hallway to reveal a narrow walkway lined with books. All hardcover. All old. None that I recognised. He stomped his way down the hall directing me to the bathroom, while Griffin and Lincoln lingered by the doorway arguing in hushed tones. I was about to walk back to them and find out what was going on, but then they both looked at me. Whatever they were disagreeing about, it had something to do with me.

Great.

I turned back towards the bathroom and Dapper.

'Who else lives up here?' I asked, accepting the fresh towel he handed me.

'No one,' Dapper said.

33

'But the other doors?'

'My office and a flat.'

'No one lives in it?' I thought he wasn't going to answer as he looked at me like the very unwanted house guest I was, but he did.

'It's just for the bar staff. Sometimes by the time they finish work it's too late, or they're too drunk. I let them use it. It keeps them out of my space.'

Lincoln came up behind Dapper and motioned to pass by. 'Do you mind?'

'What? You need to go in and hold her hand?'

Lincoln laughed. 'No, but I would like to go in and heal her.'

Dapper looked at me, then to Lincoln. 'Yeah, right,' he scoffed, walking away. Lincoln laughed again. I went pink.

I balanced on the edge of the oversized bath feeling nauseous and nervous. The line between what was caused by injury and what was self-inflicted was rapidly blurring. Sharing bathroom space with someone was sacred.

'I've never had to heal anything this bad before,' he said, sitting beside me. He sounded a little uneasy too.

My eyes took in my reflection in one of the three full-length mirrors in the king-size bathroom. Dapper was totally vain.

'Oh,' I said, looking at my bloodied face and neck. My ear was still trickling fresh blood and when I twisted to try to examine the back of my neck, which had been pummelled into the gravel, Lincoln stopped me.

'Trust me.'

'Oh,' I said again. Then, refusing to look too weak,

I shrugged it off. 'OK, well...do your thing.'

'You know I won't be able to heal these completely,' Lincoln said, looking down at his intertwined hands and twisting his fingers. 'Griffin...'

When he didn't elaborate, I raised my eyebrows. 'Griffin what?'

'He suggested that...' He blew out a breath. 'He thought it might be best to see if you can...' but he couldn't find the words and was starting to look like he might up and bolt.

Then I realised why he was looking so impish. *Oh. My. Days.* I flashed back to the one time I had healed Lincoln. To the way we connected, the feeling of my power working its way from my body into his. How together we healed.

Together – kiss together.

'You want me to...' I danced a finger between us.

'It might help you. When you healed me after Onyx, it seemed like you healed your own injuries at the same time and since your abilities are so much stronger...'

'Yeah,' I agreed, forcing nonchalance. 'I mean...we should try. I think it might work...' Actually, I had no idea.

He gave a pained smile. 'I want you to be healed and I think this will help but I don't want you to do anything that...Griffin doesn't understand.'

He was right about that. No one but us knew how deep the feelings went. How impossible they were to resist.

'So...you don't think we should?' I asked, now feeling the blush of embarrassment.

'No. I think we should. If it means healing you and...if you're *OK* with it.'

I couldn't speak.

My mouth had gone dry and I was already panicking

that it would be too dry to kiss – if that was what was about to happen. But then I got it.

He was making sure I wouldn't go all schoolgirl on him – because in the end, we still couldn't be together. But just the idea of having a moment of closeness with him – even if only for medicinal purposes – was too tempting to deny.

'Don't panic, Linc. It's hands-on doctoring – nothing more,' I said, trying to muster a believable smile. *Liar, liar, pants on fire!*

Lincoln's eyes nearly burned a hole in me. He was looking to see if I was telling the truth and for a moment I thought he looked a little disappointed.

He reached gently for my face. 'OK,' he said, already moving towards me. His eyes were cast down until just before our lips met and then, as if he couldn't stop them, they met mine...and locked. Eyes are the windows to the soul – they can say so much in just a brief moment.

His lips smoothly met mine and gently his hands went to my shoulders. I couldn't stop my eyes closing. As if I had to close myself away from the world – just him and me.

Do you close your eyes when it is for healing? When it isn't meant to mean anything...but does?

I could tell he was concentrating on his power, working hard to heal me. I tried to clear my head and do the same. I stopped thinking about his delicious lips that fitted perfectly with mine, pushed aside the feeling of heat rising from him and of sharing the same air and found my power, tucked deep within me, simmering gently.

At first, my power seemed to reach out to Lincoln, searching for any sign of injury or malfunction. Once satisfied, it turned inwardly to me. I could follow it independently, even though it was part of me. When it found Lincoln's power already within me, the two joined forces and became one, accelerating the process, healing me almost instantly.

I felt Lincoln's sharp intake of breath. I pressed nearer, drinking in our rare closeness, craving more. Just a few seconds more, a few precious, stolen moments.

He pulled back a fraction: 'Violet.'

'Hmm,' I murmured, just wanting him closer again.

He jolted back, away from me. 'Violet, stop! You're healed.'

'Oh,' I said, as if it were news to me. I shuffled back, averting my gaze, even though I so desperately wanted to look at him and search his eyes. I needed to know why it had been so easy for him to pull away when it had proved so impossible for me.

The quiet in the room amplified each of my heavy breaths, leaving me so…exposed. Eventually, I couldn't stand it.

'Could you feel how…' I started.

'Our powers joined?' he finished.

I assessed myself in the mirror. All sign of injury was gone, bar the dried blood.

'Yeah.' I chanced a glance in his direction, hoping my face wouldn't give away everything I was feeling.

He nodded and smiled at me, showing a little awe.

'It's amazing. I feel completely…fresh.'

He stood, but then sat back down and ran his hand through his hair.

'You know,' he went on, 'we can't.'

'What?'

'The kiss. It was healing, Vi, and soon you'll learn

37

how to heal without needing to… It wasn't, you know… It doesn't count.'

His words were like a sharp slap across the face. I dropped my head. 'Yeah. No…I…I…' *Shit shit shit.* 'I didn't think it… No…I don't want it to…I…'

But before I could talk myself into more of a stupor, his hand went to my face, silencing me. His thumb smudged my cheekbone with just the right amount of pressure to make my heart gallop and my breath catch as it only ever did for him.

He was absolutely right.

The healing kiss doesn't count *at all*.

I bit down on my lip as he looked at me, my hazel eyes so inferior to his brilliant green, which now seemed unable to hide his desire.

Bang, bang, bang!

'If ya haven't fixed her by now – she's broken for good! Get out of my bathroom!' Dapper yelled.

Lincoln dropped his hand from my face and looked horrified with himself. I swallowed back the pain and feigned sudden interest in my fingernails.

'Vi, I…' He stood up, then spun back quickly to look at me. 'You see! This is why! Griffin doesn't understand.' He turned on his heel and all but flew out of the bathroom.

I just sat there in my front-row seat.

I wanted to scream when he closed the door behind him.

Why can't *we be together?*

He'd always said that Grigori partners have no future together. He told me it's not allowed – that it weakens us or something. The thing is, for all the times he's said it,

I couldn't fully believe it. How could I possibly feel this way about one person and there not be any hope? Was it really that easy for Lincoln to just deny what we both knew was there? Then, I caught sight of myself in the mirror and cringed, tugging at my blood-caked hair.

No wonder he'd run.

CHAPTER FOUR

*'Guard yourself from lying; there is he who deceives
and there is he who is deceived.'*
Sextus 393

By the time we got back to Lincoln's place, it was
almost midnight, which was much later than I had
planned. Not only was it a school night, but it was also
past a reasonable hour to get home and though Dad
was spectacularly efficient at being oblivious, I didn't
particularly love going behind his back. If he knew half of
what was going on in my life, well – he'd already had his
share of heartbreak.

Dapper, it turned out, hadn't warmed to us at all. After
letting us use his bathroom and a brief conversation in
which he pointed out – in clear and offensive language – he
was not about to get involved in our wars and if an exile
came into his bar looking for a drink, then that was exactly
what they were going to get, he threw us out.

According to Dapper, that was that.

I tended to agree. I didn't revel in the idea of him being

involved either, but Griffin still held out hope for some reason. He saw an important place for Dapper and he was the boss, after all.

I changed into the spare set of clothes I now kept at Lincoln's for nights like tonight. Sadly, not for the mornings. This change of clothes revolved purely around the not-wanting-to-be-seen-by-my-father-and-neighbours-covered-in-blood premise. Lincoln tried but failed to get me to eat some toasted sandwiches he made while I was changing. I was still too cross with myself for my earlier failings, still too sick to my gut with fear that I may never be able to use my dagger. And too embarrassed that I couldn't stop replaying our kiss in my mind. But I did gratefully accept the paracetamol. My headache was returning.

Lincoln seemed distracted, too. I couldn't put my finger on it, but something had had him on edge since the fight and I knew whatever it was, he didn't want to talk about it. When we were about to get into his Volvo four-wheel-drive for the ride home, he rushed me into the car and looked around as if he were expecting something to happen.

'Linc? Everything OK?'

He pulled himself away from whatever he was straining to see in the dark. 'Fine. Just want to get you home. You have to be up for school in a few hours.'

I let it go. If there was one thing I knew, it was that we can't always say everything when others want it. If he had something to say I had to trust that he'd tell me soon. *Unlike last time.*

'Don't remind me,' I cringed, hoping the few hours' sleep I was going to get would be enough to stop my pounding head.

Lincoln and I had turned over a new leaf. It hadn't been easy. Forgiving him. But then, he had a lot to forgive me for, too, and despite anything else I knew I needed him in my life. The few weeks we had gone not talking to or seeing each other had felt like surviving without lungs.

When I got home, I went through the all too common process of slowly turning my key in the lock, trying to avoid the loud click. Once inside, I started to sneak quietly down the hall. Then I saw Dad's bedroom door was ajar and his light was on. I knew what that meant. But still, for a moment, I pretended. I held my breath, let a little fear of discovery seep into my chest. I slipped out of my shoes and then headed to my room, my socks sliding along the wooden floor. If Dad caught me coming home at this hour I would definitely be busted and I couldn't afford that, not now.

As I passed the crack of light that escaped his door I slumped and blew out a breath. Of course, I'd known he wasn't really there. Probably not even home from work yet. I let my mind wander for a moment, fantasising like I used to when I was younger. I imagined coming home from school, Mum greeting me at the door wearing an apron and the smell of home-baked chocolate-chip cookies filling the air. Dad would be sitting on the couch, feet up, in jeans and a shirt because he'd already been home from work for a while and had showered and changed. But now, as I tried to pull on an age-old fantasy that I'd played over in my mind thousands of times, it was blurred and out of focus.

Knowing what I now knew about my mother, well…Even if she hadn't died, that fantasy would have been pretty much impossible. There would have to be this cloud in the room with us. Somewhere to hide the lies.

I shook my head roughly, forcing myself back to the real world. I didn't need to go there right now. I just had to accept Dad and I were both leading double lives. He was happier that we didn't overlap. Safer, too.

The next day basically consisted of one long headache only made worse by starting off with double chemistry – which for the life of me, I have no idea why I chose as an elective subject. I spent close to two hours pretending that I cared about the different elements that combined to give precious stones their unique characteristics. Miss Stallad was running around the room like this was the most exciting lesson she'd given all year. She buzzed about, explaining that she'd had a wave of inspiration that morning and had daringly diverted from the standard textbook for this class. She was on some kind of high, almost euphoric. At least PE was after lunch.

Normally, I love PE. Despite my supernatural qualities, unlike Steph, I'm not equipped with the genius gene. Art and PE have always been my favourites, and I've always done well in them. But staring out at the red Mondo track that had been set up with a full four hundred metres of hurdles I felt light-headed.

On the surface, Lincoln and I had jointly managed to heal me. No one would ever know I'd been sporting a horrific flesh wound just last night. Yet, whether it was the blood-loss still causing side effects or just my psyche lagging behind the speedy recovery, I wasn't feeling up to par.

When Lydia Skilton pranced past me in her baby pink velour tracksuit with matching face cloth draped over her shoulder sipping her water bottle, as if she were lining up for the race that was going to set her apart or something, I forced myself onto the start line.

It wasn't just me. No one liked Lydia and I suspected she preferred it that way. In any case, she wasn't going to beat me.

Hurdles were a bad idea.

After PE, I sat in the changing rooms and tried to swallow back the lactic acid, which normally didn't even affect me these days, and tried to move through the competitive guilt.

Steph found me there after I didn't turn up for English class.

'Scale of one to ten?' she questioned, not bothering with anything else.

'Four,' I said, then waved a hand through the air. 'Three.'

'I'll take that as an eight. Vi, you aren't superwoman, you know.' There was a loaded pause. Then we both burst out laughing, which kind of hurt more. 'OK, maybe you are in a way – but this armour you insist on having up all the time is going to cost you if you keep forcing every point, even Lydia Skilton.'

I grimaced. 'You heard.'

'What? That you kicked her ass three times in a row and she basically ran off the field crying?'

'It wasn't that bad,' I said, sure Steph was over-exaggerating.

She waved a finger at me. 'Hey, no one enjoys watching Lydia have to take a bit of her own medicine more than me.' It was true. 'But not when it leaves you in this kind of mess.'

I put my head between my knees. I knew I'd feel better after a rest.

'You know what's wrong with you?'

'Concussion.'

'No. Honey, you have buyer's remorse.' And, she was right. Lydia was annoying, but I could've let her win one. I had drawn on my Grigori strength to one-up her. I *should* have let her win one.

Steph dragged me to last period. At least it was art.

By the time I walked out of the school gates, I was feeling a little better. Art always helps – gives me some time out, an escape. And when I saw Lincoln leaning against the tree across the road, waiting for me, I felt better again.

And then worse.

He was holding my training bag. *Shit.*

I said goodbye to Steph, who was heading off with Jena Powell so they could work on their chemistry assignment, and crossed the road to Lincoln.

As I got closer, my power stirred, recognising him as it always does and my heart skipped a beat as *it* always does. He ran his hand through his hair and I wondered for a moment whether he felt it too – either one.

'Hey,' I said. 'I didn't think we were hunting today.'

'We're not. We're running,' he said with an intense determination.

'Oh. I kind of already went for a run today.' I really didn't want to have to back up again.

'Not like this. We're going cross country, out of the city. We've been spending so much time on combat training and hunting lately that we've been forgetting the basics.'

'And what are they?' I asked, looking at the ground, willing myself to pull it together.

He waited until I looked up at him and then he held my eyes. 'How to get away.'

When did Lincoln become concerned with getting away? We were the stay-and-fight type.

He started walking towards his four-wheel-drive. I just followed.

What else are you going to do, Vi? Tell him you're not up to it? Not likely.

We headed to the outskirts of the city, to a national park. I changed into my running gear in the back seat when we stopped. Lincoln grabbed a couple of bottles of water and waited by the front bonnet, not once turning in my direction until he heard me get out and close the door behind me. Then we were off.

It was pretty crazy terrain. Not like running on a track or even a path of some description. I knew that was why

Lincoln had chosen it. It's not like you get to choose your surface when an exile is running after you, but then again, if an exile is running after you, generally the best thing you can do is stop and fight. They're almost always faster than us.

Half an hour into our unnaturally fast run I could feel myself sweating and my heart racing. Before I knew what was happening I tripped over a rock and went down. Lincoln, who had been cruising a few paces ahead, stopped and was at my side in an instant.

'Are you OK?' he asked, putting his hand on my back only to then quickly move it away.

'Yeah,' I mumbled, brushing myself off, trying hard not to remember the last time I found myself lying face-down in the bush.

Lincoln's eyes went wide, as if seeing me in a different light. 'You're not well,' he said, putting his hand on my forehead, upset with me.

'I'm OK,' I lied, but I couldn't slow my breathing enough to be convincing.

'Why didn't you say—' But then he stopped, remembering who he was talking to. 'You're still feeling the effects of last night.'

I stood up, but had to lean on him a little. My arm and shoulder rested into his chest and I wanted to sink even further, to let myself go. He supported me, as always, but I could feel he was keeping a distance.

Because of the kiss.

I closed my eyes briefly then took a step away.

'I'm good, just a little tired. I can go on, just give me a minute.'

He studied me for a moment, before giving me a small

smile. 'You know, I forgot the New Yorkers are arriving tomorrow. We've probably done fifteen k. That's enough for today – they'll want you fresh for tomorrow. How about we grab some dinner and I take you back to yours? I'm starving anyway.'

He was giving me an out. I didn't have to admit I wasn't feeling good, or that I wasn't up to it. I nodded, unable to say it out loud, knowing my agreement was still a semi-admission. Of course, he didn't push it.

As we walked back to the car Lincoln paused at regular intervals. He mixed it up, stopping to do up his shoe or have a drink. Once, he even said he wanted to look at the view. Every time I knew he was doing it to give me a moment to rest.

We detoured on the way back to mine to get dinner supplies. When Lincoln says we'll just grab something on the way – he means grab something to cook. He isn't big on takeaway and knows there is zero likelihood of finding anything edible and in date at my place – other than coffee and milk, that is.

Dad wasn't home when we arrived, which was no surprise to either one of us. Lincoln set about organising his ingredients and the kitchen. I think he's actually the only person who's ever cooked a proper meal there. Dad and I are useless.

After I had showered and changed into clean sweats and a T-shirt I felt much better and sat down to a plate of grilled fish and vegetables with a lemon butter sauce. Lincoln, who had changed into a pair of jeans and fresh black T-shirt, poured me a Coke and grabbed himself his second beer.

'So I guess Griffin doesn't need you tonight,' I said, watching as he raised the bottle to his lips, the silver finish of his wristbands glinting under the down-lights. He never took them off any more. He saw no point now. I was jealous he had the choice.

It was unlike him to have a second beer. Usually, he is so restrained. Just in case we got called out or something. He turned his full attention to me for the first time since I'd come back in the room. Something flickered across his face, his eyes staying on my wet hair.

'No. I think we're all clear. He's out of town tonight anyway. He's gone to pick up Magda.'

Oh, great.

I just gave a nod. 'So, did you tell Griffin about those exiles last night? About what they said and stuff?'

Lincoln took another sip. 'Yeah, I filled him in on what happened. How's your fish?'

'Good. Thanks.'

Lincoln talked me through a few exercises he wanted to do over the coming weeks, if we could fit them into the schedule around school, the new Grigori timetable and hunting. I nodded, happy to do whatever, as long as I would get to be around him.

I yawned when we started clearing away the plates and Lincoln took that as his cue, grabbing his keys. 'You need to rest.'

But before I could tell him not to leave, or he could say he was going, my phone rang.

'Hello?' I answered.

'It's Dapper,' he snapped, gruffly. His hostility actually came through on the phone.

'Oh. Hi.'

Where did he get my number?

'Listen, you wanted me to tell you lot when there was a problem – you got it. Get your asses down here. Now!' He hung up.

I pulled the phone away from my ear and looked at it in horror.

'Who was that?' Lincoln asked.

I sighed. So much for rest. 'Dapper. We have to go back to Hades.'

CHAPTER FIVE

'Change is not made without inconvenience,
even from worse to better.'
Richard Hooker

When we walked into Hades, I didn't escape another look of disapproval from the same bouncer who had been there the night before. Clearly, I wasn't dressing to his standards. I wondered what he would do if he were actually able to see the big-ass dagger hanging from my waist. Actually, by the looks of him, he'd probably smile.

We made our way to the bar, which wasn't easy. It was peak time and the place was packed with party-goers, who had already been drinking for a good few hours. Dapper was behind the bar serving. He was chatting to some random, having a laugh. When he saw us, his smile vanished and I actually heard him grunt.

Lovely.

'I'm too busy for this,' he said to us, looking down to the other end of the bar that appeared surprisingly quiet. 'I called your boss man. He gave me your number.

You made him, you deal with him. Whatever you do, do it somewhere else.'

We went to the quiet end of the bar and quickly discovered what was keeping it desolate. I'm not sure if I smelled his foul smell or heard his foul words first. Either way, it wasn't the first time that I had experienced them both. I looked at Lincoln. He rolled his eyes and went over to where Onyx was sitting. The closest table had two girls sitting at it and one of them was crying. I figured there was a good chance it was Onyx's handiwork.

'Onyx, you have to leave,' Lincoln called over the music.

Onyx looked up for a very brief moment. He was so drunk I didn't know how he was managing to balance on the bar stool.

'Onyx!' I yelled, trying to get his full attention.

'You! You did this to me,' he slurred.

'What?' I asked.

'Made me *this*. Nothing. Why didn't you just send me back?'

The truth. At the time, I had no other choice. I was injured and I didn't have my dagger. He was going to kill me, so leaving him powerless had been my only option. But now, knowing the dagger difficulties I'd been having, the answer didn't seem quite so simple. Maybe I wouldn't have been able to kill him, even if I'd been armed.

'Onyx, you're human, not nothing. You got away with doing a lot of *really* horrific things. You should be in jail or something, but you're not. You should be happy to have another chance.'

He said something obscene under his breath.

When I turned to Lincoln, he was already watching me.

I tried to stay neutral, but he saw through me. I could never get anything past him.

'If you blame yourself for this, you're crazy, Violet.' He put a hand on my shoulder.

'I don't blame myself, I just know that he was supposed to be entitled to a choice. I took that from him. He wouldn't be here now if it weren't for me.'

'Neither would we.' He watched me for a moment longer, then we both looked over to Onyx, the problem we seemed to have inherited.

'You're not going to be able to walk away, are you?' Lincoln asked, but as he looked back at me, tilting his head slightly, he didn't need my answer. Instead he just nodded.

'Come on,' he said, heading back towards Dapper.

'What are you going to do?'

He smiled. 'Just watch out for flying glasses.'

He wasn't wrong. When Lincoln suggested to Dapper that Onyx spend a couple of nights in his staff flat, more than glasses were thrown. His ammunition consisted mostly of words, but there were also half a dozen limes, a pestle (without the mortar, thank God!) and half a bucket of ice. By the time he'd finished, the area around Lincoln had cleared to a good five-metre diameter, which was a fair space in a bar so full. Nearby, girls were squealing while guys were cheering Dapper.

'It'd only be for a night or two,' Lincoln tried to reason, brushing ice shards out of his hair and patting down his clothes. A girl standing near him started to help, brushing her hand down his back. Lincoln turned around and she smiled sweetly. I rolled my eyes.

'Ah, thanks, I've got it,' he said, stepping out of

53

her reach. He turned back to Dapper and I was sure he purposely avoided my eyes. 'We have nowhere else to send him. He'll behave himself. Well, at least you'll be able to close him away upstairs. And…we'll owe you one?'

I didn't think Lincoln had a chance when Dapper grabbed a cloth and started cleaning down the bar, ignoring him. I turned to walk away but Lincoln grabbed my hand. 'Just wait a minute,' he whispered in my ear.

I nodded, totally preoccupied with his hand that was still holding mine and was somehow burning a hole through me. Just as quickly he let it go without looking at me again. I bit my lip.

I didn't think they could, but things are getting harder.

Sure enough, a few minutes later Dapper returned his attention to us.

'Two nights, no more. If he's in the bar, he has to pay and if he gets drunk he has to go upstairs and…Two nights! That's it!'

Stranger things have happened, and to me, but this was impressive. It seemed Dapper had a soft spot after all and it was the lovely Lincoln who brought it out in him. Steph was going to have a field day theorising this one.

We helped a very ungrateful, but thankfully unaware, Onyx upstairs and into the staff flat. It was a studio with a sofa that folded out to a bed and a little kitchenette. Plain but nice. The staff clearly didn't use it much since everything was still in good condition.

Lincoln and I contemplated trying to get Onyx into a shower or at least undressed for about a millisecond before we both held back the gag reflex and dropped him on the fold-out bed. There are some things that even the best of us cannot do.

As we made for the door, Onyx flopped over onto his back and laughed his high-pitched cackle. 'He'll come for you, you know.'

Lincoln spun around so fast he was back beside Onyx in a flash. 'What are you talking about?'

'Not talking about you.'

I had a bad feeling about this. '*Who* is coming for me?' I asked, staying by the door.

'Last time I saw him, he was only interested in two things. Funny, I think between the two of you, they are also the two things that interest *you* the most.'

'When did you see him?' I asked, not needing clarification. The hairs on my arms prickled and a thrill ran through me. I didn't know if it was dread or anticipation. Phoenix.

'Just before he left. He found me, brought me some whisky.' He gave an over-exaggerated nod and almost rolled off the bed.

'What did he want?' I asked, my throat tightening with each word.

'To know what I knew about the Scriptures, and…you.'

I took a step towards him. I wanted to know more. But Lincoln pulled me back.

'You're insane, Onyx.' Lincoln looked at me. 'He doesn't know what he's talking about. He just wants to upset you. Phoenix is gone. Let's go.'

I nodded for Lincoln's benefit and let him lead me out even though I felt like our exit was premature. Before I closed the door, I turned back to see Onyx watching me, grinning stupidly.

Why are we helping this guy again?

CHAPTER SIX

'We learn that there are in the Creation, Beings –
perhaps very numerous – both good and evil.'
Richard Whatley

In the morning, I wiped the steam from the mirror in
the bathroom only to wish I hadn't. By the time Lincoln
dropped me home it was close to 2 am and since I needed
to be at the airport by six to welcome the new Grigori, my
sleep time had been seriously cut short. Plus, what sleep
I did actually get had felt restless with a familiar dream.

Dressed shabbily in the only school clothes I could
find – that is, from the floor – I set about making my first
coffee on what promised to be a high-caffeine-content
day. I gulped the first one down and was in the process
of making a second cup, simultaneously wringing out my
still wet hair, when Dad came out of his room dragging
a large suitcase.

'Morning, sweetheart,' he said, as he parked the
suitcase by the front door and came over to give me
a signature kiss on the top of my head. His face was warm

and soft – just shaved. 'Is that for me?'

I looked down at the coffee I'd just made. 'Sure,' I said, handing it over and setting about making another. 'I didn't think you were leaving until tonight.'

Dad was flying out to visit his international clients. He goes on the same trip every year, which is almost more flying than anything else, travelling from Tokyo to Dubai to Paris. It used to take about three weeks but he'd gradually been scaling back. Last year, he was home in a record ten days. This year, he'd managed to schedule the trip into one week. Given the chance, Dad would prefer to remain locked in his office where he can actually keep the rest of the world away, but certain clients insist on face-to-face dealings.

'I'm not, but just in case I get caught up at work I...'

I nodded. He didn't need to say any more.

'So,' he said, changing the subject and putting on his responsible parent voice.

I wondered if maybe he had heard me sneaking in this morning, or noticed I wasn't in bed last night. I glanced at him watching my hands as they gripped the frothing milk jug. I double-checked that the markings on my wrists were covered properly by the silver bracelets which were now a permanent fixture. I still didn't know why I had the new improved version compared to the leather wristbands all other Grigori received. My markings were wrapped around my wrist in a swirl of silver, like a tattoo or something, and when I used my power they reacted, churning like a river of mercury, reflecting different colours. Steph says I'm my own walking mirror-ball and swears one night she'll talk me into putting them to the disco test.

I won't.

'We should probably run through the house rules.'

'Oh. Sure,' I said, letting out a breath of relief that also held some disappointment.

'Same as always, really,' he went on. 'If you have any trouble, go next door. I've told the Richardsons that I'm going to be away and they've given you an open invitation for dinner and to come and see them if you need anything. I'll call you every night. At different times,' he gave me the, *I was a teenager once, too* look, 'on the home phone and no overnight guests other than Steph. I'll be checking with the doorman. OK?'

I gave Dad a military nod. 'Yes, sir.'

'Very funny. Just look after yourself.'

But actually it was funny. It was going to be harder to do whatever I wanted while he was away than when he was at home.

Yeah, we're a totally functional family.

'I always do,' I said, finishing the longest conversation I'd had with Dad in about three weeks. He didn't even realise, of course, which made it even harder. I wanted to be mad with him, tell him to pay attention, but I knew deep down, now that I was a Grigori, it was for the best.

The airport was packed with early-morning travellers.

Who'd want to go anywhere at this time of day?

All I wanted was to crawl back into my bed and pass out for a week, maybe more.

At least Lincoln will be here.

I looked at the information screen. The flight in from

JFK had already landed. I headed towards the arrivals area, keeping an eye out for Lincoln, but there were too many people. In the end, I gave up and just looked for our link. Our bond as partners. I can always feel him when I try. It's like searching out something that shines brighter than anything else.

But before I had a chance to zero in on Lincoln, I got a kind of flash of the whole airport. It reminded me of looking at one of Dad's blueprints, but instead it was driven by the senses. Somehow the shades of morning and evening were drawing me a map and then a buzzing energy focused in on some areas. It was just a glimpse and I didn't have any idea how I did it *or* how to do it again. The strangest part was, I sensed something that I couldn't put my finger on. The taste of apple was there but it was faint, more like a memory stimulating the flavour. I smelled flowers, but again they seemed distant. It felt like an exile, or exiles, but it also made me feel numb, like my insides had gone to sleep. I had no clue what it meant.

Maybe that I'm seriously not getting enough sleep!

I pushed the senses aside, unable to draw any rational conclusion. I found Lincoln quickly after that – could feel him – and started in his direction.

My heart skipped a beat when I saw him. I should have guessed – he was buying coffees.

'Good morning,' he chirped, passing me a fresh cup as soon as the barista had put them on the counter. He looked exactly like the man of your dreams is supposed to look first thing in the morning. White shirt, sleeves rolled up neatly, blue jeans, faded just enough. His light brown hair was ruffled, the streaks of sun-bleached blond haphazardly thrown about. The only noticeable sign of a particularly early morning was that he hadn't shaved. I had to work hard not to stare wide-eyed and was grateful for my hot drink keeping my hands firmly engaged, preventing me from reaching out to touch the stubble, which made the perfect accessory.

'Good timing,' I said, my voice telltale catchy. 'Are they here yet?'

'Just getting their bags. Should be out in a few minutes.' He put his hand on the curve of my lower back, guiding me closer to the arrivals gate.

Just breathe, you idiot.

But the problem was every touch, every moment with Lincoln was so intensified that his hand on the small of my back was all I could concentrate on.

Which is probably exactly why Grigori are never meant to be together!

'Hey, do you know if there have been any exiles returned around here lately?' I asked after we took up a spot near a side wall.

His eyebrows lifted. 'No, not that I know of – but that doesn't mean they haven't. Why?' He started looking around, unsure if he should be on the alert.

'It's probably nothing – I just feel a bit off this morning,' I reassured him as I leaned against the wall and blew on my scalding coffee. I hate it when they make them too hot. I slumped a little as I let my head hang back and decided to wait until we were outside the airport. Then I would try again to see what I could sense.

'Not much sleep?' Lincoln asked.

'No. You?'

'Enough.' He shrugged.

I stood up straighter. I wasn't going to come off as a wimp – if he could be tough, so could I.

'Where's Griffin?' I asked, ignoring the smirk he was giving me.

'Right there.' He pointed through the crowd and sure enough, Griffin was walking towards us.

'Good morning,' Griffin said, narrowly avoiding two peroxide-blonde girls manoeuvring backpacks that were bigger than them. I couldn't hold back the giggle when one of them spun around and he had to duck.

Griffin gave them a foul look before redirecting his attention to me. 'I hear you had an unexpected end to last night.'

'Yeah, did Linc tell you about Onyx?'

'Yes and I'm amazed he's resurfaced. I'll give it some thought. Maybe we can get him to a halfway house or something.'

'What do you normally do?' I asked, blowing through the little mouth-piece on the lid of my takeaway cup. There must be some kind of plan in place for these things.

'Violet,' Griffin said, raising his eyebrows, 'Onyx is the first exile I know who has become human and then resurfaced.'

'What? I...I don't understand. Surely others have chosen to be made human along the way?'

He just gave his head a little shake. 'There have been a few, but they never reappear afterwards. We'll talk about it later. Your new tutors should be out in a minute and I need to brief you.'

'OK,' I said, not entirely sure I could concentrate.

Was being human really that bad?

I remembered only a month ago when I would have given almost anything to have kept my boring human existence.

'Right,' he said, kicking back beside us like any ordinary twenty-five-year-old – something he rarely managed to pull off. 'So, Nyla and Rudyard are the tutors. They're both old friends of mine and they've been partners for almost four hundred years. Actually…'

'Hang on!' I butted in. 'Four hundred *years!*'

Yeah, just kicking back talking about his four-hundred-year-old buddies.

'Yes, almost. Probably closer to three hundred and eight-five, but when you get up that high I believe it is acceptable to round up to the nearest fifty. Don't you think?' he asked, smiling.

Lincoln laughed.

'Ha, ha, very funny. I'm glad you find me so amusing. I mean, I know you said we would live for hundreds of lifetimes, but it's different when you start, you know, meeting people that will soon be celebrating a quad-centenary.'

'Technically, they're over four hundred and two years old. They weren't always Grigori,' Lincoln said, enjoying himself as well.

'What about the other ones? They're my age, aren't they?' Suddenly, I was freaked out that I was about to be surrounded by a crew of ancients.

'Yes, give or take a year or two. I believe they're bringing three with them. A partner set and one in waiting. I don't know their names,' Griffin explained.

'In waiting?'

'Partner hasn't come of age yet,' Lincoln said, his tone flat.

'Oh,' was all I could muster.

Lincoln hitched one shoulder and looked around casually, even though it wasn't casual at all – not for him. He'd had to wait nine years for me, which was a long time for Grigori. Mostly partners only had to wait months or maybe a year for each other. No one knew why Lincoln had had to wait so long for his but I knew it mustn't have been easy for him during that time. Even Grigori who lose their partner are usually offered a new one within a year and even though some refuse – choosing instead to help in other ways, like the clean-up crew, or some just opting for retirement, though apparently that rarely panned out well – at least they have a say in the matter.

Griffin was watching the flow of people coming through arrivals. It seemed obvious when the wave of New Yorkers started. They didn't seem to notice the people standing beside them, or in front of them for that matter – they just walked at their own pace, which was faster.

I nudged Lincoln, 'I wonder what they'll look like?' I whispered.

When someone is more than four hundred years old, they would have to look weird, right?

I didn't have to wait long and when the group of five came over to where we were standing and two of them started hugging Griffin, I was shocked.

The people, whom I was assuming were Nyla and Rudyard, looked no older than Griffin. I mean, maybe a year or two, but there was nothing in it. Their skin was rosy and youthful and they were wearing normal, young-people clothes. Their jeans and T-shirt selections were more 'in' than any of Griffin's, who only occasionally ventured away from his reliable navy-blue button-down shirts.

The three standing behind were obviously the students. They all looked about my age. They stood back while the reunions took place. I felt their eyes burning several holes in me. I started fidgeting, unsure where to look, until I felt a hand smoothly brush my back. In one brief touch, support, confidence and power that could only come from my Grigori partner.

Only from Lincoln.

Once the hugging and amusing 'You haven't changed a bit' comments were finished – I mean, they probably hadn't seen each other in decades – Griffin turned to us.

'Lincoln and Violet, this is Nyla and Rudyard.'

We all started to shake hands. I greeted Nyla first. She was beautiful. She looked a bit Egyptian, with black hair, cut short around her face – Cleopatra style – bronze skin and a tall slim figure that made her look strong and athletic rather than fashionable or skinny. When I said hello she lit up with a beautiful warm smile of perfect teeth framed by deep currant-coloured lips. I liked her instantly.

Rudyard seemed more reserved. He took my hand, but didn't shake. He smiled briefly out of courtesy and inspected me with well-mannered eyes. I could see he wasn't sure of me.

Then I felt a twinge. First at the back of my neck but then it stretched out like an electric current, both up into my head and down into my body.

I yanked my hand back, but he didn't let go. It didn't

hurt, but it was really uncomfortable. Something was pushing against my power from inside. Something that wasn't me.

My eyes, urgent, flickered to Griffin. He seemed to be watching me with interest, not alarm.

Damn it. They're doing something to me. Testing me.

I fought off the urge to shudder at the unwelcome intrusion and instead started trying to put up the barriers around my power, protecting it and myself. It reminded me of when I had done the same thing with Phoenix not so long ago.

It took a lot of concentration and I lost control a few times and had to start again. I was still tired from the last couple of days and by the time I was getting command of the situation I was more angry than anything else.

Once I had my power protected I pushed what I realised was Rudyard's invasive power out from within me. I didn't bother with being polite.

He released my hand and stumbled back a few steps. Nyla had her arm out to steady him before he even moved. When he looked up at me, his eyes glistened with wonder and he smiled so widely it almost touched his ears.

'Impressive,' he said with a nod as he looked to Nyla again, who also gave a small nod. I watched as their hands automatically linked, fingers intertwining delicately as if the grooves between them had been moulded to each other over time.

What the…?

Both Rudyard and Nyla seemed overly interested in something as their eyes went back and forth between Lincoln and me. Strangely, it didn't seem as if they were looking at us as much as the space between us. I was feeling exhausted and increasingly uncomfortable as I shifted my weight from one foot to the other and was on the verge of a toilet excuse when Rudyard just snapped out of it. He gave Griffin a slap on the back, at which point I was free to deliver a death-stare to both Griffin and Lincoln, neither of whom had stepped in to help me at any point.

'I'm glad you called us, old friend,' Rudyard said, hoisting a bag onto his shoulder.

Griffin beamed. I was glad he was happy while I was still panting like an idiot.

Lincoln put his arm around me to help me stay upright. I shrugged him off and shot him a look. He knew better. Especially in front of the newbies.

'Violet, I am sorry for Rudyard's intrusion into your power base, but sometimes exploring the first impressions between one power and another is the best way to gauge strength. Not always the best ice-breaker, mind you…but efficient in its own way. He did not mean you any harm and we give you our word, such an intrusion will not happen again without your consent,' Nyla said softly.

I didn't say what I wanted to, just made a mental note: *no way is that consent ever coming from me, lady!* First impressions had been made on both sides.

Lincoln shook hands with Nyla and Rudyard and we all said hello to the three students, who up until that point had remained silent.

Probably part of the 'Check out her power' sabotage.

There were two guys. Salvatore – an Italian who didn't seem to speak much English but looked very kind with his thick curls of dark brown hair, bushy eyebrows and broad shoulders. The other guy, Spence, shook hands vigorously, his sandy-blond hair flopping forward over his face and green eyes that darted everywhere. They were a nice green, but no match for Lincoln's. He seemed happy to meet everyone – everyone but me, that is. Lincoln told me I was being paranoid when I whispered as much to him, but I definitely sensed the negative vibe when Spence glared at me.

Great to have new friends.

The girl's name was Zoe and she seemed...pissed off. She had that emo look that I didn't really get. I mean, does it mean you're gothic or emotional? I don't know. She was tall, though she slouched, and under her short spiky brown hair with peroxide tips, her eyes were heavily rimmed in midnight-blue eyeliner. But the thing that struck me the most about Zoe was that she was completely comfortable in her own skin. Standing there in a dark grey tight T-shirt, black pleated short skirt and army boots, she didn't care who had a problem with it. I envied her. All I had seen of her so far comprised her picking up her bag and slamming it down on the ground again with a huff on a number of occasions. I wondered if she had been dragged along and would rather still be in New York. *She probably already hates me.*

But when we were finally introduced, she explained right off the bat.

'Hi, I'm Zoe. I take it you've met my idiot partner, Salvatore.'

I looked over at Salvatore, who was standing next to Spence. Compared to the icy welcome I'd received from Spence, Salvatore seemed positively welcoming.

'He can't speak English so don't even bother talking to him,' Zoe went on. 'Can you believe it – stuck with the mentally challenged for like, ever.' She looked at me, genuinely horrified. Obviously this partnership was very new and *obviously* no one had ever explained to her that just because someone didn't speak fluent English that did not make them mentally challenged.

I stifled a laugh and shook her hand. 'I'm sure it'll get better with time,' I consoled.

She rolled her eyes.

When we left the airport, I remembered that I wanted to see what else I could sense once we got outside, but in the end I was just too tired from Rudyard's games.

CHAPTER SEVEN

'In all the chaos there is a cosmos,
in all disorder a secret order.'
Carl Jung

Steph was waiting for me, pacing near the top of the school steps when I jumped out of the taxi. As soon as I saw her face, I could see something was plaguing her.

'Hey. You didn't need to wait, you know. I could have met you in class.'

We turned and walked up the last few steps and into the school corridor together.

'Don't be ridiculous. I was hoping you wouldn't make it so we could skip it altogether,' she lied, flicking her hair at the same time so she could look in the other direction. I stuck to best friend code and didn't say anything else. 'You look like crap, by the way.'

Yep, friends for life!

'No wonder you haven't managed to wriggle your way into Lincoln's arms yet. Girls aren't the only ones who look at someone and imagine what kind of kids they would produce.' She waved her hand up and down at me.

'That's not the reason we aren't together, Steph.'

She raised her eyebrows. OK, so she was right to a point. I'd barely brushed my hair this morning and my school uniform, which was daggy enough on its own, had been taken straight off my floor and hadn't come within a peep of an iron.

'Seriously,' Steph said, giving a deliberate nod. She rummaged in her bag as we walked towards our first class. 'Here,' she passed me her pint-sized make-up bag – I knew from experience that it held absolutely everything a girl could possibly want from a cosmetics range in miniature form. 'You're going to need this.'

'Thanks,' I said sheepishly as we headed into history at a brisk pace. We were only a couple of minutes late, but Mr Burke had a particularly nasty reputation for locking kids out of the classroom if they were more than five minutes late. You'd think that it would actually encourage kids to do just that and avoid class altogether but, perversely, when threatened with losing the right to the education they usually feel forced into, kids flock.

'Wait for me after class, I wanna hear about the God Squad,' Steph said.

'God Squad?'

'Yep.'

The class turned out to be about as tepid as expected, even worse after I checked my timetable. Today was a double. I was stuck in there for almost two hours listening to

Mr Burke talking about the greatest villains of all time. He asked the class to shout out names of history's most notorious betrayers. I had no idea. I just put my head down and tried to take notes to stop myself from falling asleep.

Juggling school, training, hunting and now these new Grigori – the 'God Squad' according to Steph, who still couldn't separate the angel issue from the broader God dilemma – was wreaking havoc on my down-time. It was starting to feel like there just weren't enough hours in the day. But I was determined to prove to Griffin that I could manage a normal life and school while still doing my job as a Grigori.

The other option, finishing school at the Grigori training centre in New York, sounded like a terrible idea. Even if Lincoln could go with me, I wasn't prepared to leave Steph behind, or my Dad, and well, school mattered, too. All my art classes were here and I would start my scholarship course in four months. I'd worked really hard to get the spot and I had every intention of making the most of it. As far as I could see, the art programme at the Academy was lacking to almost non-existent.

'Any more names?' Mr Burke yelled out particularly loudly in my direction.

Whoops. I'd been dozing.

I sat up tall. I'd heard some of the names – Marcus Brutus, someone Arnold, Bernard Madoff.

'Violet?' Mr Burke was standing at my desk. He expected me to answer. *Great.*

'Um, well…' Blank.

'How about a hint, Ms Eden. Perhaps if I start you off with…the kiss of…'

'Ah, Judas, sir?' I offered hesitantly, not knowing if the name had already been said.

'Excellent,' he said, condescendingly, already walking away and returning his attention to the rest of the class. 'Judas is perhaps the greatest betrayer of all time. Death in a kiss – it doesn't get much worse than that. Anyone else?'

By the time Steph and I emerged from class my brain was fried. Steph, as usual, looked as if she had been revived for the day.

After she pushed me into the bathroom to fix up my dishevelment, I filled her in on the newbies – who I refused to refer to as the God Squad – while sifting through her cosmetics bag-of-everything.

'The Rudyard guy sounds weird. You should be careful, Vi. Just because they're Grigori doesn't give them a free pass down Trustworthy Street.'

I nodded while attempting to comb out a stubborn knot and was once again glad to have Steph on my side. For all her banter, she made solid points and was always in my corner – a true friend. One of the very few.

'Yeah. I guess I'll find out more this afternoon. I start training after school. You wanna come?'

Steph looked a bit unsure. 'Do you think I'll be allowed?'

I put my hand on hers for a quick second. 'Steph, you're my best friend. I don't care what they think. If you want to come, they'll have to deal with it.'

She beamed at my reflection in the mirror. 'Are you sure, Vi?' Then she handed me the mascara.

I smiled back, even though there was a part of me

that worried. Who was I, to bring Steph into this world of immortals and eternal wars? She had no power to defend herself. Getting her mixed up in it all was selfish and I knew it, but I couldn't push her out of my life. I needed her. She was one of my people.

'Hey, how's Marcus?' I asked, suddenly realising she hadn't run off to meet him or even mentioned him today. The two of them had been joined at the hip for the last few weeks. I was sure it would be any day now that they made their relationship 'official' – if they hadn't already.

'We broke up,' Steph said, heavy on the blasé.

I put down the make-up bag and gave her my full attention, wide eyes and all. 'Why? Are you OK?'

'Yeah. I was the one who…did the breaking.'

'Oh, well… Why?' I didn't understand. Steph thought that Marcus was the perfect guy. He ticked all the boxes. He was preppy good-looking, mega smart, came from a socially 'in' and highly funded family *and* he worshipped her.

'Let's just say, I learned a thing or two when I saw what you went through with Phoenix. I mean, I just figure…I don't want to do something that… You know…'

'That you'll regret,' I finished for her, looking down at the grubby bathroom-floor tiles.

'I'm not saying you should regret what happened. I…I just mean… Seeing how that all affected you…helped me make a few decisions of my own.'

'So Marcus wanted to…' I raised my eyebrows.

She nodded. 'It was fair enough, too. I mean, I thought that was what I wanted as well, but in the end I just knew although he was good on paper, I didn't love him.'

I was surprised. Steph rarely expounded. She was a 'doesn't explain, doesn't complain' girl. I wasn't sure what to think. I was glad for her, that she felt confident to make the right choice. Marcus was a nice guy, but if she wasn't with him for the right reasons then I was relieved she hadn't done something with him that she would have regretted. I knew all too well how that felt after what had happened between me and Phoenix. I still felt the residue of the connection it formed. And although that had broken, I wasn't entirely sure if the price for that one bad decision had been fully paid. Seeing Lincoln's reaction when Onyx raised the subject of Phoenix last night made me wonder if Lincoln would ever truly get past it.

Could I ever really ask him to?

The afternoon got better, marginally. I zoned out in religious studies and finished the day with art and a study period, which actually gave me a chance to catch up on homework. Within twenty minutes of last bell Steph and I were getting off the bus near Lincoln's place.

Since Lincoln had the biggest space, it had been set up as a kind of command centre for the time being. I was grateful to him for so quickly volunteering the warehouse. We had even pushed back half of his furniture to set up the training arena.

Steph and I walked up the few steps to his front door and I got the same exhilarating buzz that I always did when I knew he was near. I knew it was partly the angel in each of us recognising the other, but to me it was mostly human. I wanted things to work out for us so much even though I knew it went against Grigori code.

There had to be a way.

Griffin let us in and didn't spare me the disapproving look when he saw Steph. 'This isn't a social gathering, you realise. Your training is already limited by your hours at your other school.'

'Steph is a part of my life. She has a right to see this and understand it. It's not like I'm bringing in cheerleaders, Griffin,' I said, giving him a tight-lipped smile.

He wasn't impressed but stood aside so we could enter. Steph, unfazed by Griffin's concerns, brushed straight past. 'Hello, Grandpa,' she quipped.

I couldn't help but smile when I saw Griffin's expression.

My eyes scanned the room quickly. Everyone was there, right at home it seemed.

All except one.

Nyla and Rudyard were sitting close together on one couch.

Too close for just friends or Grigori partners.

Spence and Salvatore were on the other couch, engrossed with the PlayStation. Zoe was in the kitchen pouring herself an orange juice.

After I got through the introductions with Steph and had relaxed a little when Rudyard didn't try any more power tricks on me, I turned back to Griffin.

'Where's Linc?'

'Talking with Magda. She got back last night. I think they're in his room.'

'Oh, OK,' I said, starting to walk in that direction.

'Hey,' Griffin snapped. 'We start in two minutes. Zoe and Salvatore spar first, then you and Spence.'

Wow, it will be weird sparring with someone other than Lincoln.

'All right. Two minutes,' I echoed.

I went to Lincoln's room. Magda had been away visiting an old friend. She'd been gone almost two weeks. I could see Griffin was glad to have his partner back. I just hoped Lincoln wasn't *too* excited himself. Magda wasn't exactly subtle at hiding her feelings for him, or her dislike of me. If it hadn't been necessary for me to become Grigori to save Lincoln's life, my guess was that she would have preferred it if I hadn't embraced.

I was about to push the slightly ajar door open when I heard them talking. I couldn't help myself from pausing to listen.

'Are you sure?' It was Lincoln. 'Absolutely sure?'

'Yes,' Magda said, sounding forlorn. I could see the back of her shoulders through the crack. She was sitting on the bed.

Lincoln wasn't sitting. I could hear him pacing around the room, the heels of his loafers clicking against the wooden floorboards. I opened myself up to him for a moment and through our link I could sense his panic.

'How? How are you so sure?'

'Lincoln, I followed all the steps. I know how to be sure.'

'So he wasn't lying, then.' I could hear him mumble, could almost see his hands over his face.

What's going on?

'Doesn't look like it. What do you want to do about it?'

Magda asked, sounding so unsure, so unlike her.

'I don't know. Maybe we should tell the others?'

'Do you think it's the wisest idea to involve everyone else – people could get hurt, Linc.'

'You're right.' Lincoln sighed. 'What do you think?' he asked.

'I don't know, maybe I'm wrong. Maybe we should talk to Griffin and Violet.'

Well, there's a good idea.

'No, you are right. I don't want them to know about this, especially Violet.'

WTF! I felt myself tensing with every word.

'OK. If that's what you want, we can keep it quiet for now. Just you and me – like old times.'

'Yeah, the others don't need to be involved. Thanks, Mags,' Lincoln said, softly, the last two words slightly muffled. I was sure they were hugging.

I heard footsteps.

Oh no, no, no.

I quickly moved away from the door and took a few hurried leaps back down the hall to see Griffin walking towards me.

'Come on!' he said. 'We're ready.'

Lincoln's door swung open. He and Magda both emerged. He looked so tense and I could see him trying to hide it from me. Even if I hadn't overheard their scheming, I would have known something was upsetting him. People who are scared of getting found out all have that same deer-caught-in-headlights look. I should know – I was trying to hide a similar guilty expression.

He forced a smile and glanced worriedly at Magda.

They were both wondering if I'd overheard anything – though Magda didn't look worried so much as satisfied. Actually, she looked annoyingly elegant. Her long, blonde hair rippled softly around her face and down her back, a baby-blue sweater showed off her tall, mega-slim figure and to top it off a stunning sapphire hung from her necklace, perfectly positioned to make everyone's eyes go…there. Everything about Magda screamed expensive. Suddenly my oh-so-average presentation became all I could think about and Magda, of course, was looking right at me as if that was all she was noticing too.

'Hey,' I said to them both, throwing up a lukewarm wave before spinning on my heels to face Griffin. 'I'm ready, let's go,' I said, in a way that made it sound as if it had been me waiting for him. My attitude wasn't lost on him, but thankfully he let it slide.

I sat next to Steph, who, as it turned out, had found herself a new friend. I'd forgotten that she could speak Italian. When she and Jase, her brother, were younger, their father used to take them on some of his business trips to Italy. I think she even spent a year there when she was about twelve.

Salvatore looked as if he had died and gone to heaven. Clearly, being deprived of any coherent conversation had taken its toll. I did a double-take when I saw the unusually eager look on Steph's face.

'Salvatore!' Zoe said, clapping her hands in his face. 'Come! Time to fight,' she yelled, while she mimicked boxing hands as if he was deaf and dumb.

Steph looked appalled.

I watched in a bit of a daze, Lincoln and Magda's

conversation replaying in my mind and Rudyard and Nyla in my peripheral view – *joined at the hip*. Nothing made sense. Had Lincoln been lying to me all this time? Had he really just been making excuses for why we shouldn't be together? Nyla and Rudyard were clearly more than just partners and if they could be…

Zoe fought like a cat. She leapt and darted with economy of movement but freaky speed. Salvatore had a more reserved and calculated approach. Not as flashy but you could see instantly, he was to be respected. It was all over fairly quickly. Zoe won the spar, getting Salvatore into a potentially lethal hold. But I was highly suspicious that Salvatore had let her win.

'You're up,' Steph said and then gulped loudly beside me. When I looked at her, all the colour had drained from her face.

'It's OK, Steph. It's just training. Remember, we are a lot stronger than normal people,' I said, still completely preoccupied with Lincoln. He and Magda had only just joined everyone else. Clearly they'd had more talking to do.

Not again. Please, not again. Lincoln promised no more lies.

'Violet – your turn against Spence. Nyla does a lot of the combat training at the college, but since she hasn't watched you fight before she will only observe tonight and then plan a programme for you tomorrow,' Griffin said in his umpire voice.

'OK,' I said, making my way onto the mat to stand opposite Spence.

We hadn't really had a chance to talk since first meeting at the airport. 'You ready?' Spence snapped at me as if I were holding up his life.

Oh, this is going to be great.

'Yep,' I said. Punching him in the face was going to be my pleasure.

Out of the corner of my eye, I saw Magda lean in and whisper something into Lincoln's ear. Her hand rested on his shoulder and I was sure she glanced at me, looking for a reaction.

I didn't even see Spence coming. It wasn't that he'd done anything extraordinarily stealthy, I had just been pathetically distracted. I took a jab to the gut as punishment.

I tried to pull myself together. I knew this was important. Rudyard already had his first impression of me but I knew this would be Nyla's. Not to mention that everyone was watching to see what all the fuss was about.

Barely three minutes later I was flat on my back. I'd managed to get in a few good moves, but Spence had fought fiercely – at times even a little underhanded for a training session – and I never had a second to get myself together.

'See?' he barked. 'This is stupid! We come all this way to train with this chick and she can't even last long enough to make me sweat.' He stormed over to Nyla and Rudyard, leaving me sitting on the ground. 'It's not fair. I'm a good fighter – I should be allowed to hunt! I shouldn't have to wait for my partner.' He flung a hand back towards me. 'She doesn't even know how to handle herself against me and she's allowed to hunt.'

Steph stood up, hands on hips. 'Hey, macho man. Have

you ever disabled more than half a dozen exiles in one go? While you're lying on the ground dying?' Steph had a nice way of getting to the point.

'Who are you, anyway? This isn't a spectator sport, you know,' Spence spat at her.

'I'm the one who's going to explain to you two very important things. First, you need deodorant...like now. Second, if you thought beating Violet in a bit of sparring and then boasting about it like a total idiot would somehow make you look like some kind of under-appreciated hero-in-the-making, you are *so* out of luck it's almost funny.'

Spence looked around the room as if he were waiting for someone to drag Steph out and throw her on the street.

Rudyard stood up and put an arm out for Nyla to join him.

'We are finished for tonight. We're going back to the hotel. Zoe, Salvatore and Spence, we expect you for dinner.' Rudyard gave Spence a brief nod. 'Strong fighting.' Then he turned to Steph. 'You, Stephanie, are welcome to watch any training sessions Violet invites you to. I find your approach...effective.'

As they walked out the door, Rudyard looked back at Lincoln and Magda and then lowered his gaze towards me and winked, stirring something in me. It made me feel vulnerable, as though somehow he saw through me, somehow he knew why I'd fought so badly and was letting me off. But he couldn't know. He couldn't have overheard Lincoln and Magda. And he sure as hell couldn't see my heart twisting itself into an ugly knot.

Salvatore put a hand out to help me up. It seemed like it was obvious to everyone that Lincoln hadn't approached.

I could see his disappointment. I'd fought badly and I knew that since he'd been responsible for all my training to this point, I had let him down, too. Things were just getting worse and worse.

I needed some air and made for the door. I still had my rules: no running and no quitting. I thought being Grigori might make me consider them less, but I found I was still having to seriously resist the urge to take flight at times. Like now.

Steph raised her eyebrows as she saw me walking out. She was offering to join me but I just shook my head. I knew she wouldn't push it.

I walked a little down the street and sat on a neighbouring fence. Although Lincoln lived in a busy area, his street was only short and relatively quiet. It used to be entirely old warehouses, but now there wasn't one building that hadn't been converted into a trendy home.

'Hey, you taking off?'

I looked up to see Spence. He had his hands in his pockets and looked uncomfortable, like he wasn't sure he actually wanted to be talking to me – which made two of us.

'No,' I said, defensively. I didn't like the thought that someone would assume I'd just run away like that – even if he had completely slaughtered me.

'OK,' he said, smiling a bit with his hands in the air. 'Don't shoot. Look, I just wanted to say…I… Anyone could see you were off your game and I… Anyway, it was poor form. Not my usual style. It just pisses me off that they won't let me out to hunt with everyone else. I thought if they saw…'

'If they saw you take me down they would overlook the fact that if you're hurt by an exile you can die?'

'Yeah. Put like that it makes me sound like an idiot, but I had to try.'

'I get it. It wasn't your fault anyway. Like you said, I was…distracted.'

'By Lincoln and Griffin's partner, Maggy?'

'Mag*da*,' I corrected.

'She causing a problem?'

'No. Yes. I don't know.' A couple walking their dog cruised by and smiled at us. All I could think was – *They have no idea.* And I was envious.

Spence hoisted himself up and got comfortable beside me.

'Well, why don't you start by telling me what happened to make you fight like a girl?'

I laughed. 'I am a girl.'

'Yeah,' he shrugged, swinging his legs out, 'but no Grigori worth their salt fights like a girl and I've heard you've got skills.'

'Thanks.'

'So?'

'I don't know,' I said, but Spence just waited and eventually I gave in. 'I overheard them talking. She told him something that had him freaking out. He kept asking if she was sure. Then, when she suggested they tell Griffin and me, Lincoln panicked and made her promise not to tell me. I don't know what it is, but it's big and it's bad and he swore he would never lie to me again.'

And for the life of me, I have no idea why I am confiding in this stranger who has just pummelled the crap out of me. I guess

it's true what they say – physical combat can be as emotional as
any other major connection.

'Wow, that sounds bad. So you and Lincoln have history? You know that's not really on the cards for partners, don't you? I mean, someone's explained…'

'Yeah, yeah – we can never be together like that. I got the memo. It's complicated though, I thought we…I just didn't think he would be…'

'Right, I get it. And Lincoln and Magda? It sounds like she was telling him something major – something personal. Do you…?' He held a kind of frozen cringe.

'I know what you think. That's not it,' I said quickly, shutting him down.

'OK. But if they had a history before you two, I'm just saying, is it possible?'

'No. I…I don't know. He never told me if they were… are,' I said, looking down, holding back the tears. I didn't want to cry in front of Spence. I barely knew him. It was bad enough I was spilling my guts to him.

'OK, no stress. Well,' he nudged me, 'if you want to find out, we could always follow them.'

I looked up to see Lincoln and Magda coming down his front steps and walking in the opposite direction. They hadn't seen us.

In that moment, something clicked and I was suddenly very glad Spence had come into my life.

'Let's go,' I said, jumping down off the fence.

CHAPTER EIGHT

'Everything we call a trial, a sorrow, or a duty; believe
me, that Angel's hand is there.'
Fra Giovanni Giocondo

Following people through the city is tricky. Especially when they have a special connection to you that means if you get too close there's a good chance that they'll become aware of your presence.

It was still light at least, so we could hang back a bit and keep them in sight when there weren't too many people blocking our view.

Spence was like a pro sleuth. I was totally impressed and glad to follow his lead. We tailed Lincoln and Magda for several blocks and just when I was starting to think we should give up, Spence ducked into a shop doorway and pulled me in, too.

'What?' I whispered.

He smiled. 'You don't have to whisper.'

He was right, they were almost a hundred metres ahead of us. 'What?' I repeated in a normal tone.

'I think I know where they're going.' He pointed out the doorway.

Magda and Lincoln were walking towards a small hotel. Spence watched quietly while I held my breath. Sure enough, in they went.

A hotel.

I bit down on my lip and tried to hold back the tears.

How could he do this to me? To us?

But really, that was my answer.

There is no 'us'.

The part of me I would rather ignore taunted me from within.

You never had him in the first place.

Spence, who had been standing silently beside me while these thoughts raced through my mind, grabbed my arm. 'Come on.'

'What? Where?' I asked.

'Over there.'

'I'm not going over there. Let's just go.' I turned and motioned to walk away. Spence folded his arms and shook his head.

'Look, I get it, you're in a bad place, but right now you're thinking worst-case scenario. There's still a chance it's something else. Let's go find out. It can't make things worse.'

He pulled me back onto the street and marched on towards the hotel. I shuffled reluctantly after him. This was not a good idea.

As we came closer to the doors, my angelic senses started going off like a metal detector.

'Spence,' I said cautiously. 'Spence – something's not

86

right. There are exiles in there.'

I tried to calm the senses. To swallow away the tartness of apple, drown out the sound of birds crashing into branches, move past the cloying aroma of so many overlaid floral scents. I blinked away the flashes of morning and evening that flickered beneath my eyelids and tried to calm the sting of heat coursing through my entire body. Normally, these days, I had this process well in hand, but it could still be overwhelming when I was dealing with multiples.

Spence steadied me. 'You all right?'

'For now. But I don't know if we should be going in there.' I was already starting to back away.

'We should *definitely* be going in there.' He bounced on the spot. 'I mean, Lincoln and Magda are already inside. What if they're in trouble?'

'I don't think so. I'd sense it if Lincoln was in danger.'

'Yes, but can you sense it if he doesn't realise it himself?'

Good point.

'OK, but let's not get into anything we don't have to.'

Spence was checking his dagger. Luckily, we had to wear them when we did training sessions so we were used to fighting with them on. Though not as awkward as a sword, Grigori daggers were on the larger side with a forearm-length blade. Spence looked so excited. I looked down at my own weapon. *Damn it*, I wasn't excited at all. At best, I was going in there to fight with exiles when I was still too much of a chicken to pull out my dagger. At worst...I didn't even want to consider the other possibility.

When we entered the lobby, the hotel was surprisingly

large. From the outside it looked quite boutique, but although it was narrow it was actually very deep. There was a marble bar down the far end and a reception area by the entrance with armchairs and tables scattered in between.

I scanned the room quickly. In the heavily male-dominated lobby, the few women were dressed expensively but provocatively. On some, the fabric between the Manolos and designer blouses was so scant that little was left to the imagination.

'Ew,' I said.

'Yeah,' Spence agreed, though he didn't sound all that grossed out, and when I looked at him scanning the joint I just rolled my eyes.

'What?' he asked in response.

'You're such a guy,' I said, moving us towards a more discreet position behind one of the large marble pillars.

Men in suits, some wearing wedding rings, huddled at small tables with girls. A sense of deception emanated from the place. It felt tainted and dangerous.

'I think we should make this quick,' I whispered.

'Yeah – some of them really need to get a room,' Spence responded in all seriousness and although I was a little disgusted by his comment, I agreed. PDAs can be cute at the right time and in moderation but this was…

I spotted Lincoln and Magda at one of the small tables near the bar.

'They're over there at the back, sitting with someone else,' I said.

Spence looked at me with a screwed-up face and looked away. 'Guy or girl?' he asked, cringing.

'Guy. Why?' I replied, confused.

'Oh…well, that's…' he said, unable to finish, increasingly appalled.

I caught on and smacked him on the shoulder. 'Spence! Get your mind out of the gutter and concentrate!' I hit him again. 'They're with an exile and there are more at the tables on either side of them. I think you were right. They're in trouble.'

The man sitting opposite Lincoln was unprepossessing and kind of weedy-looking for an exile, which made me think he was hidden by some type of disguise. All I could see was a manila envelope moving over the table from him to Magda and then a white envelope sliding back from Lincoln to him.

'Catch that?' Spence asked, now the one whispering.

'Yeah.'

'Any ideas?'

'Not one.'

'Well, this is good, isn't it?' he said.

I felt a spike in the room as a familiar, unnerving feeling washed over me, sending a shiver down my spine. I started to look around, a different set of nerves playing on me now. I was just about to take a step towards where it was coming from when two menacing-looking exiles appeared with lightning speed and stood like a brick wall in front of us.

'I wouldn't exactly say *good*,' I answered Spence.

'Hmm.' But he was still smiling.

'This is a breach! You Grigori – lying, despicable humans,' said one of the exiles.

'We were just leaving,' I said, as Spence and I – understanding the very immediate need for departure –

spun around to face the exit. But we spun right into another three exiles who had come up behind us.

'No pass, no protection,' said one, who looked as if all his Christmases had come at once. Then his fist went squarely into Spence's face, sending him flying into one of the marble pillars with a thundering smack.

Lincoln and Magda were there in seconds, shocked to find me surrounded by a pack of angry exiles. They didn't even hesitate. They jumped straight into action. As did I. Before I knew it, we were in full combat, Lincoln and Magda each fighting off two exiles. Spence recovered quickly and took one from Magda, while all I heard was Lincoln yell, 'No daggers! Just put them down and get out!'

Fine by me.

Making sure I didn't make the same mistake I had the other day, I blocked everything else out and focused on the ginger-haired, polyester-wearing exile who was coming at me with venom. Luckily, he was sloppy, which made it easy. With a few well-placed kicks I was in control and I beat him down until he stayed there. I turned in time to see Lincoln knocking out his second exile, slamming his flattened palm right up and into his opponent's nose – one of his favoured moves – quick and efficient. Magda was already at the door and Spence was still going fist to fist with the burly exile who had first hit him.

I was about to step in and help when Spence took a running jump at the exile and somehow catapulted himself to land in a sitting position on the exile's shoulders. From there, he grabbed his head – taking the time to look at me and wink – then gave it a sharp twist. There was a loud snap and the exile fell to the ground. A broken neck wouldn't kill or return him, unfortunately – a Grigori blade was needed for that – but it would hurt like hell and keep him down for a while.

Once outside, Spence and I kept a quick pace, following Lincoln. We both knew he simply expected us to do so. When he stopped a few streets away, I went straight up to him. I didn't know what was going on but right now, I just wanted to know he hadn't been hurt. It had been stupid to go in there when we knew the hotel was filled with exiles.

'Are you OK?' I asked.

'No!' He spun round to look at me, his green eyes angrier than I'd ever seen. 'What the hell were you two doing in there? You could've gotten yourself killed!'

I took a step back. Spence came up to stand beside me as Magda stepped up to Lincoln.

'Linc, I'm sorry. We thought you might be in trouble.'

'How did you even know we were in there?'

'We...I...' I couldn't answer, couldn't admit to my childishness.

'You followed us!'

'Actually, it was me,' Spence said, stepping forward.

'What?' Magda jumped in.

'Yeah. I saw you guys going off and it looked like you might be going hunting. I thought I might be able to get in on the action. Sorry about that.'

I closed my eyes briefly. Spence was saving me, big-time.

'You *both* should have known better,' Magda said, not about to let me off the hook. 'You're not even allowed on active duty, Spence. I doubt your tutors will be impressed when we tell them you ruined a meeting we had with a source. Plus potentially threatening one of the only ones we have left. It was a mutual set-up – we declared our numbers and agreed not to cause them any problem if they met with us. We were there to get information, not to fight!' Magda looked as if she were enjoying this mess as much as Lincoln looked ashamed of it.

Does he really think so little of me? Am I such an embarrassment to have around now that Magda's back and he can hunt with her?

'Well, maybe *someone* should have told me,' I sulked, directing my words at Lincoln, who would now barely look at me. 'And maybe *someone* could have told me where he was going while he was at it, since he's supposed to be *my* partner after all. This isn't all on us, you know. What were you seeing that exile – source – for, anyway?'

'Nothing. It's just an old case I offered to help Magda with,' Lincoln said, looking at his feet.

'What? You're not going to tell me?' I asked in disbelief.

'No.' He looked at Magda, who tilted her head as if to direct him to go with her. 'Look, this doesn't involve you, Violet. Go home, get some sleep. You barely had any last night.'

Spence looked at me, smiling ear to ear and even gave his eyebrows a waggle. I ignored him.

'You and…Spence, will have plenty of time to hang out later on. I'll see you tomorrow,' Lincoln said, also absorbing Spence's expression.

With that, Magda and Lincoln hailed a taxi and were driven away. I guess they figured they'd be harder to follow travelling at high speed.

I buried my face in my hands. 'Oh my God. I want to die.'

'What do you mean?' Spence started, running his fingers through his hair and then ruffling it all up again. 'That. Was. Unbelievable! Did you even *see* that – I *leapfrogged* onto his damn shoulders and snapped his neck!'

I looked between the fingers over my face. 'That was pretty cool.'

'Cool? That wasn't cool – that was historic!' He gave me a nudge and I laughed as we started walking back. 'And it wasn't that bad. At least they weren't in the penthouse with champagne.'

'*Spence*, you're disgusting, you know that, don't you?'

'Yes. But you have to admit, not a bad result compared to the alternative. Mind you…'

'What?'

'Well, Magda *was* looking a little…you know…bloated. Maybe…?'

'No.' I took a deep breath and squared myself to face him. 'No!'

'Enough said.' He gave a nod and I knew he wouldn't mention it again.

'You do realise they're going to tell on us,' I went on as we started walking again. 'And when Griffin, Nyla and Rudyard find out – we're busted.'

'Yeah, but it was worth it! *Right on to his shoulders*…like a *freaking* acrobat!'

By the time I finally got home to an empty apartment, I was so exhausted I passed out on the couch for the night after briefly wondering how Onyx was going with Dapper.

I should have gone to check on him tonight but with everything...I promised myself I would go straight after training the next day. Just as my eyes became too heavy to resist closing, I felt a breeze cross my face. Strangely, it wasn't cold and I didn't feel so alone.

CHAPTER NINE

*'Fairytales are more than true; not because
they tell us that dragons exist, but because they tell us
that dragons can be beaten.'*
G. K. Chesterton

Steph didn't stop talking about Salvatore all morning, even
during class, she sent me notes – something Steph simply
does not do.

He is soooo nice!
He walked me home. Did I already tell you that?
I feel so bad for him, all he wants to do is be part of
everything and not slow things down. It's not his
fault he can't speak English yet. Zoe is such a bitch
to him but he just wants her to like him. But just as
friends – he isn't interested in her – I don't think.
What do you think?
S xxx

I wrote back, assuring her that I didn't think Salvatore had
any interest in Zoe romantically, reminding her, somewhat

bitterly, that Grigori partners are not allowed to be romantic together anyway – even as I was reflecting more and more on Nyla and Rudyard and how close they looked.

I told Steph all the things she wanted me to say – that she should help him out, maybe give him some extra English lessons – all the stuff that would bring them closer together. I didn't mention my concerns – that getting close to a Grigori in a romantic way could spell disaster and that maybe she should consider keeping a distance. I didn't know if that made me a good friend or a bad friend.

By the time the end-of-day bell rang, I was dying to get back to Lincoln's. I needed to see him, to clear everything up and get back on track. Plus, I had to make up for my lax performance yesterday and do better in training. In between notes from Steph I managed to mentally talk myself out of all my crazy theories, especially the – *I can't even believe I'm thinking it* – baby one. Of course Magda and Lincoln weren't having a baby. Just because it had sounded like a couple's kind of conversation – there simply had to be more to it.

Steph came with me again and I could see that as long as Salvatore was around, she most likely would be too. When we arrived, training was already in full flight. Salvatore and Zoe were both glistening with sweat and looked as if they had gone about ten rounds with one another.

Spence was in the corner using Lincoln's weights. In a singlet and shorts, he looked quite tall and showed off a fit body. For the first time, I really looked at him and saw that beneath the shaggy blond hair that gave him a kind of surfer look, he had gentle lines on his face that made him not boy, not man, but someone with a whole lot of potential.

When he saw me, his face lit up with a devilish grin and I found myself grinning from ear to ear and wondering how much trouble this new friend of mine was going to get me in.

'Hey! Where is everyone?' I asked him as Steph edged away from me. I knew exactly who she'd be making a beeline for.

'Well, Zoe and Sal have been going all day. They're just warming down. Your buddies told Nyla and Rudy about our little error in judgement last night, so we're not even allowed to spar today.' Spence dropped his hand weights on the floor mat and grabbed his water bottle. 'Griffin, Nyla and Rudy have been out most of the day looking into this Scripture thing you're all after. They said to tell you they'd be back in time to give you a theory lesson later.'

'Oh. OK. Sorry you got in trouble. I shouldn't have involved you in my mess.'

'Hey, don't apologise, I'd do it all again in a heartbeat.'

A thought that truly worried me.

'So um…where's…'

Spence raised a brow. 'Lincoln and Bitchda?'

My eyes quickly darted around, scared we were being overheard. No one was close enough to hear. I relaxed. 'Yeah.'

'Don't know. Lincoln dropped in at one point, said something to Griffin, grabbed a few things and went back out. Haven't seen Maggy. Not much love lost between you two, hey?'

'Not much.'

The door opened and in walked Nyla and Rudyard. Their arms were linked. Almost every time I had seen them they had been holding hands, or touching in some way, as if they were drawn to each other. Moths to flames.

'They're amazing,' I said to myself.

'Yeah. Rarest thing around,' Spence said.

I looked at him. 'What do you mean?'

'They're the real deal. Less than one in a million…or more.'

'I don't understand – what are you talking about?' But even as I asked, I felt my throat tightening because I knew; this was crucial.

He looked at me as if I had taken a stupid pill but before he could answer, Nyla was standing in front of us with a look that made Spence stop in his tracks. My eyes darted between them.

'Violet, it's time for your lesson. I believe since Zoe, Salvatore and Spence have finished for the day, we will have the place to ourselves and can have our lesson here.' She turned her attention to Spence and the others and gestured towards the door. 'We will see the rest of you back at the hotel.'

Spence mumbled something under his breath about the unfairness of it all and grabbed his bag along with the others, leaving me alone with Nyla and Rudyard.

I reached to get a notepad and pen out of my school bag. It was obvious Nyla was the fighter so I wondered who would be giving the theory lesson.

Rudyard called out from the kitchen. 'How do you work this thing?'

I dropped everything and bolted over to him.

'Don't!' I said, throwing myself between him and my baby. 'Ah, I'll make you a coffee.' No one touched the espresso machine except for me. It had been a birthday gift from Lincoln and since I'd waited two years to finally be able to have a good coffee at his place, I wasn't about to have Mr Four-hundred-plus, who probably missed the entire discovery of the espresso bean, mess with my well cared for and appreciated machine.

'Thank you,' Rudyard said, smiling at my reaction. He pointed to my notepad and pen on the bench. 'You won't be needing those. This isn't the type of lesson you will need to document, Violet. Nyla and I thought it was time you understood more about life as a Grigori and about your history.'

'OK,' I said, suddenly feeling a little nervous. I passed him a black coffee and after I made a latte for myself and Nyla poured a juice, we all sat at the table.

'First of all, both Nyla and I believe it is only right to disclose to you some things about your mother.'

My hands gripped my cup and I froze. 'Did you…know her?'

I heard the smile in Nyla's voice even though I couldn't look at her. 'She was a good friend for many years.'

'Oh.' I was sure there were a million things I could have said. But not one came to me at that moment. I never knew my mother. The only things I had ever received from her had been left for my seventeenth birthday a couple of months ago. I always feel uncomfortable when people talk about her. It's like they expect me to know her, to have some bond with her even though we never met, some kind of filial connection. I don't know. I don't have it. All I have is the knowledge that before me, she was Grigori and somehow, she knew it would be my destiny too. She left me one of her wristbands and a cryptic note. Bottom line – it all left me feeling pretty cheated. I figured since she knew what was coming she could have done more to give me the heads-up.

'She lived in New York with us for about thirty years, before she met your father. Rudy and I were her teachers when she first became Grigori and then later she herself was a tutor at the college for some time. Her partner's name was Jonathan. They were together for one hundred and twenty-eight years.'

I lifted my head. Nyla's smile softened.

'Grigori partner, nothing more. They were like brother and sister. Fought like cat and dog but loved each other dearly.' I noticed her voice dropped off at the end.

'What happened?'

'Jonathan and Evelyn had a single overarching assignment. Together they were responsible for only one exile of unparalleled power. It took them one hundred and twenty-eight years to defeat her and cost Jonathan his life.'

'Lilith,' I said, choking on the word.

Rudyard and Nyla both looked shocked. 'How did you know? Griffin said you hadn't been told of your mother's history. He doesn't even know himself.'

'When I embraced, my guides told me some bits, the rest I just kind of pieced together.'

'Well, that's impressive. I am sorry you had to work these things out on your own. Especially given your... previous involvement with Phoenix.'

I looked down, blushing. It seemed everyone in the world knew about that one stupid decision I'd made.

'That is part of the reason Rudy and I wanted to be the

ones to come here, so that we could tell you about her.'

'So what happened?'

'We don't know exactly. The battles with Lilith were legendary. She was very strong, very clever and had many followers. Jonathan died in their final confrontation, protecting Evelyn. It was Evelyn who discovered how to defeat Lilith. That last battle cost her greatly. She never forgave herself for Jonathan's death. After that, she refused a new partner and stayed with us at the college, training new Grigori. Then she met your father and found a new happiness. I'm ashamed to admit, that after she left, we lost contact. I think that was what Evelyn had wanted.

'She hoped she could have a normal life with James – as much as possible, anyway. We didn't even hear of her death until a few years after it happened and we certainly didn't realise that she had borne a child or that her child had been given an angel essence. If we had, we would have kept a better eye on you. It would've been the least we could do. When Lincoln first embraced and was told your name, no one in this city knew of your mother and since you went under your father's name – Eden – you were off our radar.'

'She left me her box with one wristband...and a letter.'

'Just one?' Rudyard interrupted, looking confused.

I nodded and his look morphed into something I couldn't decipher as he glanced towards Nyla.

'She knew she was going to die.' I had suspected it for some time, maybe even known, but it was the first time I had truly admitted it aloud.

Rudy nodded. 'It makes sense. She was talented, Evelyn. A dream-walker. She could converse with angels in her dreams – if they wished for it. Grigori made by the Seraphim, like Griffin, can be fed information in dreams, told things they need to know – like the names of the first of a partner set – but nothing like what Evelyn could do. I imagine she may have known for some time before you were born that this would be the outcome. I also imagine she may have played a hand in the decision.'

'I don't understand,' I said, shifting in my chair, increasingly self-conscious. It's one thing to wonder if your mother gave you up to this life – another thing for outsiders to confirm it.

'It's only speculation, but given her history and her power – I believe she would have been offered a choice.'

'In her letter. She asked me to forgive her…' and like pieces of a puzzle, one more snapped into place. 'That's why. She chose to die – to make me this.' I tried to blink back the tears that started trickling down my face. 'She left me.' My voice dropped to a whisper. 'She killed us both.'

Nyla's hand touched mine. I pulled mine away.

'What do you mean? You're alive and well, Violet.'

I didn't respond. How could I even begin to explain?

'She loved your father dearly,' Nyla continued. 'She never believed she would discover a love so strong, especially with someone…so normal. I know she would've been so excited to have a child with James and it would have been the hardest thing she ever had to do – leaving you both. She knew, better than anyone, the sacrifices that a Grigori must make. But she would not have chosen this life for you if she believed there was another way.'

'Yes,' agreed Rudyard. 'And that's the other reason we are here. For Evelyn to have made such a choice – to have committed her daughter to a life as a Grigori – we know the reason must have been... Well, she must have felt that it was critical and there was no alternative. We believe she was made privy to information, information so cataclysmic that it led her to believe it was only through you that it could be stopped.'

'Stopped how?'

'That, we do not know.'

'Do you think it has something to do with the Scripture?'

'Perhaps. We certainly need to find it before the exiles do. We have people in New York looking into it. The problem is, we just don't know the original thread to track it.'

The feeling in the room had become so charged that when the front door opened we all jumped.

Lincoln walked in. 'Hi. Where's everyone else?' He glanced at me and gave a small smile and I let go of the breath I was holding. I hadn't known what to expect from him after the previous night.

'Everyone finished a little early today so we could talk with Violet,' Nyla responded.

Lincoln's eyebrows went up. 'Oh.' Then he quickly added, 'Do you want me to leave?'

Nyla stood. 'No. Not at all. In fact, this is perfect timing. Rudy and I were hoping to talk to you as well. Would you mind?' She gestured to a seat.

Lincoln tentatively sat down. I wasn't much help, I was still absorbing everything else.

What now?

'Lincoln, though you trained in New York, we did not get a chance to get to know you well, unfortunately.'

Lincoln nodded and spoke for my benefit. 'I wasn't one of Nyla or Rudyard's students. It's a pretty big facility. We only met a couple of times.'

'That's right. So there are some things that you do not know about Rudy and I that probably were not explained to you during your training.'

'Such as?' he asked, while I looked up, more interested now.

Rudy answered, 'There are some things about being Grigori that others do not think important to teach. For Nyla and I, we believe in it more because it affects us directly.'

When we didn't say anything else, he went on. 'Have either of you known another pair of Grigori like Nyla and me? Who are not only partners in work but in life?'

I froze.

Did they just admit they were together–together?

Lincoln looked over the table at me. I could see his mind working, trying to see where this was going. 'No. Grigori aren't compatible. I've been meaning to ask you how… I mean, you still have power, but…'

'I believe you have only heard one side of the possibilities, Lincoln – and with good reason, I dare say. What Nyla and I are – we would be what you would call an exception as opposed to a rule.'

'Sorry, but I'm not following,' I said, trying to remain calm.

Rudyard looked to Nyla, who nodded him on.

'In a nutshell, Grigori partners often – usually fairly early on in a new partnership – have an inclination to explore…possibilities. When we realise that we are bound to one person for a very long time, it seems logical that if we could be partners in life as well as work, that would be a good outcome. However, history has shown us that the compatibility of Grigori is almost non-existent. Often, when partners explore the...'

'Physicalities,' Nyla offered, the corners of her mouth lifting.

I couldn't stop the quick glance at Lincoln. He was sitting very still, looking at his hands laid flat on the table as if he were about to push it into the ground.

'Yes,' Rudyard smiled at her, '*physicalities* of a relationship they quickly discover there are some very severe consequences. Many believe it is a type of fail-safe system the angels put in us to prevent emotional bonding that could distract us from our duties. Others,' he smiled again at Nyla, 'believe it has more to do with the angel part in us interfering, because angels are independent beings – they do not partner the way humans do. Either way, it has become apparent making a...physical connection is not something to be done without all the information.'

'But, you two are together?' Lincoln said, still not looking up.

'Yes, we are.' Nyla looked at me, a soft knowing smile settling on her lips. 'It is generally seen as a rule, a guideline to being Grigori, that we must all accept that partners are not compatible...as mates. Do you know why that is, Violet?'

'It weakens us.'

'Lincoln?' Nyla pressed.

'Sometimes we can lose our powers altogether,

sometimes just one partner does, sometimes both are left without defences.' Lincoln concentrated on his hands, inspecting his now splayed fingers on the table. 'It's always a bit different, but ultimately, the partnership is altered and weakened overall. Partners that…get involved…reduce their chance of survival.'

'Very good, Lincoln. I can see you have considered this,' Nyla said kindly, though it seemed to upset him and he threw his hands down and twisted his body in the chair away from us.

'Right,' I said, starting to realise the enormity of what they were saying. 'So, if partners are ever…'

'Physical,' Rudyard offered again.

'Yeah. It's…bad. I mean, really bad.'

Nyla's look turned to one of sympathy. 'It is a likely consequence. But as we said, it seems Rudy and I are the exception. With all things in life there are always different ends to a scale. We are the very opposite.'

Rudyard reached over and closed his hand over Nyla's. 'When Nyla and I first became partners, we fell in love quickly. But unlike many others, though we tried, it was simply not an option for us not to explore our love. It was part of us, and in the end, no matter what the cost, we believed in that love. When we first became intimate, instead of it pushing us apart, it brought us together – completely. Nyla and I are partners through our angelic essence and as Grigori, but we are also partners through our human souls, linked in every way.'

My eyes went to Lincoln. He had turned back towards the table and was already staring at me. I knew what we were both thinking and my heart started thumping so hard I was sure everyone could hear it. Remembering when we had kissed on my birthday, the way our bodies *and* souls had seemed to intertwine so perfectly. The way my healing always seemed to work through a physical connection.

'And your powers?' Lincoln asked, not taking his eyes off me. It was as if he couldn't.

'Fully intact – and through our connecting souls they are in fact amplified within one another.'

'I...I don't understand,' Lincoln said.

'It's hard to explain. The best explanation I can give is to ask you to imagine a tunnel. Like there is an invisible tunnel between Nyla and myself and we can each, at any time, walk through or reach through that tunnel to one another. So can our powers. We can always feel each other and each other's powers.'

And then...I got it. 'You're soulmates,' I said, my voice trembling.

Nyla nodded and squeezed Rudyard's hand and I felt the stirrings of something very, very dangerous. Hope.

'Are there other Grigori like you? I mean...is it possible that...' I asked, quietly.

'That you and Lincoln are kindred souls?'

'Yeah,' I said, blushing that I had to ask this question in front of Lincoln.

'It is,' Rudyard said. 'When I felt your power at the airport, it seemed to gravitate strongly towards Lincoln's essence. I have not seen one person's powers pull on those of another so strongly since...' He looked at Nyla. 'But it is more likely – you are not. In all our years, we have never met another set of partners that have been bonded in soul. And, if you are, while it is amazing, you should know, it is greater than any other kind of commitment. Greater than any kind of marriage in any culture, so think carefully before you…explore.'

Oh my God, this is the weirdest sex talk ever!

'OK. Well thanks for the heads-up.' Lincoln stood, clearly sharing my awkwardness. 'I'm going to make some dinner. Would you like to stay?'

'Thank you, but no. We're a little worried Zoe may try and put Salvatore back on a plane to Italy if we don't get back to them soon.'

'Yeah. Poor guy,' Lincoln agreed.

'Zoe's a good girl, she just had expectations for her partner – Salvatore was not it. But I believe she will be surprised, in time,' Nyla said, as she and Rudyard stood and instinctively wrapped an arm around each other.

Now that I knew they were soulmates, I could see every little movement was somehow catered for by the other. They truly were connected and when they looked at each other, although it was only brief, their eyes mirrored each other. Perfect love.

And look at me and Lincoln, we can barely look at each other. Every time we get close, something gets in the way. Would that happen if we are meant to be?

Just Lincoln and me – for the first time in what felt like ages. He set about making dinner. I didn't bother offering to help. We both knew unless it involved the coffee machine there was little point.

'I'm just going to throw on some steaks and make a salad. That OK?'

'Yeah. Great,' I said, feeling more uncomfortable than I had since I first found out about being Grigori. I walked around the massive open area that was now cluttered with gym equipment, the floor strewn with mats. I started putting some bits and pieces away in the buckets that sat at the base of my wall. I'd been trying to paint a mural on one of Lincoln's large blank spaces, but I hadn't got very far. It was a time issue, more than anything. That, and I'd hit a block. Every time I thought I knew what I wanted to paint, something changed my mind. Right now there was a huge sheet covering it.

'Here you go.'

I jumped a little, caught in my thoughts I hadn't noticed Lincoln come up behind me.

'Thanks,' I said, taking the glass of Coke he held out.

'I'm sorry, about last night,' he said. 'I shouldn't have gotten so angry.'

'I'm sorry, too. We should never have gone in there. It was stupid.'

'True,' he said, smiling now and appearing just as relieved as I was that we weren't headed straight for an argument.

I rolled my eyes but then got serious again. 'Linc?'

'Hmm?' He was walking back into the kitchen.

'Um...' I was going to ask him about Magda, but I couldn't. 'We should go check on Onyx tonight.'

'Yeah, I know. I'll do it.'

He said it casually, but it was a brush-off.

'Can't we go together?' I pushed.

He glanced at me then took a bite of raw carrot. 'Not tonight. I have to go out in a bit and there's no point in you waiting around.'

'Where are you going?'

'I'm…just helping Magda with something.'

'Magda?'

He raised an eyebrow at my tone. 'Yeah.'

'And you're not going to tell me what it is?'

'Vi, I just need to do this thing myself. It's…personal.'

I actually took a step back. A slap in the face would have been kinder. 'Personal? For Magda or for you?' Because the way he was talking didn't seem like it was Magda's problem alone.

Lincoln closed his eyes and rested a hand on the bench as if trying to find the strength to deal with me, which just pissed me off. 'Violet, just trust me. I don't want you involved in this. You're…a distraction.'

My jaw clicked to the side while I tried and failed to remain calm. 'But Magda isn't,' I said between deep breaths, unable to look at him.

'No. She isn't.'

'Great. Well, you and Magda have fun.' I handed him back the glass of Coke and started collecting my things.

'Violet, you're acting like I'm out having fun without you. This exile we're tracking, *he*—' But he stopped mid-sentence.

'He what?' I snapped.

Lincoln looked away. 'He needs to die.'

'You mean, be returned.'

'If that's the best I can do,' he said, his voice distant and rigid.

I stared at him, trying to hear what he wasn't saying – what I was clearly missing.

'So, just you and Magda.'

'Yes.'

'Well, I'll leave you to it then.'

'What are you talking about?' he asked as he watched me grab my bag, and head for the door.

'You and Magda obviously have things under control and I just remembered Steph is staying at my place tonight, so I should probably get back there and have dinner with her. I might see you tomorrow.'

'Wait. Violet!'

I slammed the door on my way out.

CHAPTER TEN

*'The heart is perverse above all things, and
unsearchable. Who can know it?'*
Jeremiah 17:9

Steph came round after I called her, and begged for company. After her afternoon playing with Salvatore, she'd been planning on popping into Hades to see her brother, but after I pulled the best-friend card she promised to be over in twenty minutes.

Steph brought pizza and got comfortable for what she knew was going to be a long night of me retelling the evening's conversation and analysing why Lincoln would suddenly only trust Magda.

'Vi, you don't even know if something is going on between them.'

'Yeah, well, he didn't even mention what Nyla and Rudyard had said about the soulmate thing after they left.'

It was even harder to understand since I was sure Lincoln had seemed genuinely intrigued, and even excited.

'From the sound of it, he didn't have a chance.'

'Steph!'

'Sorry. I think he was totally in the wrong and you have every right to be pissed off with him. And no one likes Magda anyway – she's a cow.'

I threw a pillow at her.

'What? Too much?'

I was just getting up for more ice cream when I heard a thump outside on the balcony.

'What was that?' Steph asked.

'I don't...' But I didn't get a chance to finish my sentence before someone (or something) was knocking on the glass doors.

'Steph, get back! Behind the couch!' I ordered, slipping into fighter mode.

'What's wrong?'

I raised my eyebrows. 'Apart from the fact that someone or something is knocking on the balcony door to my apartment that is *twelve* storeys high?'

Steph's face paled in the same time it took for her jaw to drop and to catapult herself behind the couch.

I switched off the lights, pulled out my dagger and moved to the wall beside the balcony door. In one quick movement I yanked the curtain back. My heart leapt into overdrive and I let out a squeal when I saw the figure standing outside the glass doors.

'Jesus Christ!' I yelled, jumping up and down to shake out the fear as I opened the sliding door, frowning when I realised it wasn't locked.

'Nope, but you're not the first to make that mistake,' Spence said, grinning mischievously.

Steph stood up from behind the couch. Spence burst out laughing.

'Seriously. Girls.'

'What are you doing here anyway? *How* are you here? I mean, did you scale the walls or something?' Steph snapped.

I bit back a smile. Not many people throw Steph off-balance.

He shrugged, 'It was easy, and anyway I'm here to collect you, Violet. In fact, we were hoping you might both be here. It saves the extra trip. You're just lucky it was me that came up. Zoe wanted to use the tree outside as a slingshot.'

'We?' Steph's eyes lit up. 'Who else is here?'

'Slingshot?' I asked, a lot more interested in how that could have worked.

Before he could answer either one of us there was another thud on the balcony. Spence groaned and spun around.

'I thought I told you to wait!'

Zoe pranced in, hands on hips. 'You were taking too long. Plus, you're not in charge.'

'You know, I do have a front door,' I offered.

'Aw – that's no fun, and anyway, Steph told Salvatore you were under military watch or something,' Spence said, shrugging as both he and Zoe laughed. They knew Steph's description of the doorman keeping an eye on things had been lost in translation.

I looked at Zoe. 'Did you *slingshot* up here from a tree?'

'From *the* tree, you've only got one outside, and yeah. I would've landed sooner but I overshot. Had to drop down from the roof. The guy in the penthouse looked pretty freaked.'

'Where's Salvatore?' Steph asked.

I looked at her with wide eyes.

Did she just miss what Zoe said? She flung herself onto the roof! THE ROOF!

Zoe's eyes narrowed in on Steph. 'He's waiting downstairs like a good puppy. You're welcome to go hold his lead.'

'We're going out, we came to get you,' Spence butted in. A good decision, if the look on Steph's face was anything to go by. 'Anywhere good to go around here?' he continued, exploring the living room, taking time to look around the corners and down the hall, checking out my place.

'What about Nyla and Rudyard, won't you get in trouble?' I asked, half expecting theirs to be the next dramatic entry.

Spence shrugged as he walked back. 'We slipped out. They don't really expect us to be in bed by eight every night, they just...prefer not to know, you know.'

'Oh, well, I can't go. My dad's away but he calls every night at a different time after ten. It's the only rule he has but I have to stick to it. I barely made it home in time last night. But Steph can go,' I offered. I knew Steph had wanted a night out anyway and judging by the eager expression she was flashing the entire room, I wasn't wrong.

'What number does he call you on?' Spence asked, walking up to the phone that hung on the wall. 'This one?'

'Yeah,' I replied suspiciously.

'Do you have a mobile?' he asked, condescendingly.

'Yes,' I said, getting aggravated.

He lifted the receiver from the wall, started pressing numbers, then looked up, 'mobile number?'

'Huh?'

'mobile-phone num-ber, Brains?'

I gave it to him and watched him punch in some more numbers. He hung up with a dopey smile on his face, 'Let's go.'

'What did you do?'

He rolled his eyes at me. 'I diverted your home phone to your mobile. When your dad calls you can just go somewhere quiet and pretend you're at home. Easy.'

It *was* easy. I couldn't believe I'd never thought of it before.

'Great!' Steph called out, already at the front door. 'Let's go to Hades. I've being wanting to go there all day. I'll go and wait with Salvatore.' She slipped out the door and that was that.

Spence and Zoe seemed to agree with her suggestion. We were going to Hades. I guess I'd get that chance to check in on Onyx after all.

Zoe sauntered into Hades as if she went there every night and claimed a table right by the dance floor. Steph and I spotted Steph's brother, Jase, who was working in the DJ pit. He's four years older than Steph and works the bar scene all around the city, but he was at Hades as much as he could manage. The DJ pit there was a fit-out to the extreme.

He gave us a sly look that melted into a smile when we approached, but he was mid-set and couldn't really stop.

He motioned for us to wait for five and I think, yelled 'Hi', but Steph blew him off. She wasn't about to wait that long to get back to Salvatore.

When we made it to our table Zoe was enjoying the music and Salvatore jumped up to get more seats. He really was sweet. Steph beamed every time she looked at him. I noticed that he seemed equally smitten.

Oh well, good for them.

'Where's Spence?' I asked.

'Getting jugs,' Zoe said, bopping in her chair.

'What?'

'Drinks. Jugs of shots.'

'Oh. It won't work. The bar staff here are pretty by the book and he's still seventeen, isn't he?'

'Yeah, but the boy's got skills.' Zoe gave me a wink and went back to watching the dance floor. I didn't imagine she would stay sitting for long.

Sure enough, Spence came back balancing a stack of five shot glasses and a jug of something that looked so naughty I caught myself grinning stupidly. I'd forgotten how much fun it could be to just do something normal. And when that annoying voice from within cried out – *That's because you're not normal!* – I tuned it out.

'How?' I asked.

Dapper was a strict licensee. It was an all-ages bar and restaurant, but he kept a pretty good eye on things. The only luck we'd ever had at drinking alcohol there was by smuggling it in.

'Glamour. It's my thing.' Spence waggled his eyebrows. I laughed.

'Speaking of which,' he said. 'We,' looking at Zoe and

Salvatore, 'were thinking it's time to introduce ourselves properly. We figure since Steph already knows about you, we're OK with her knowing about us too.'

I saw Salvatore nodding – he clearly understood most things – as Zoe just rolled her eyes.

'OK,' I said, not sure where this was going.

'All right then, I'll start.' Spence mockingly put his right hand in the air. 'Hi! My name is Spencer and I am an angel carrier.'

Zoe wacked him on the arm so hard it would have broken if he weren't Grigori. Spence rubbed his shoulder and looked at her ruefully. 'You know I do bruise and I am still breakable until I have a partner, as everyone keeps reminding me, so careful with the merchandise.'

Zoe motioned as if she were about to hit him again.

'OK, OK,' Spence said, smiling but also shifting away from Zoe. 'I'm from a Dominations Angel. I'm lacking in the parent department since they gave me up when I was born so I don't know which one died, not that it matters. I have all the normal gismos, my sense is taste – and I'm never going to eat an apple again – plus I can "glamour". So far, just myself and things that I can touch but I'm working on pushing it further.' He laid his arms wide to finish.

I couldn't agree more on the apple comment. I didn't think I would ever like them again either, which was a shame since I used to love the apple pies from McDonald's.

'See, was it so hard just to get on with it?' asked Zoe. 'I'm from an Archangel, I'm minus a father and haven't seen my mother in over three years. I have normals, my sense is hearing, plus I have an affinity with nature. I can manipulate it to assist me, mostly with motion.'

Wow, I'd never heard of that. 'That's how you used the tree as a slingshot?'

'Yeah. I'm still ironing out some of the kinks, but that's the general gist.'

I was surprised to hear that neither Spence nor Zoe had parents. I'd thought things were tough for me with Dad, but at least he was there and I knew – as dysfunctional a family as we were – that he loved me.

'So, I guess I'll fill you in on Romeo, here, as well,' Zoe went on.

Steph put her hand up. 'Wait! He can speak for himself. I can translate for him.' She looked at Salvatore and he nodded.

I was starting to gather that he could understand most things he heard in English. His difficulty was mainly just speaking it himself.

After he spoke for a moment to Steph in Italian – which sounded lovely, just hearing him speaking comfortably and in a normal tone – Steph turned back to the rest of us.

'Salvatore is by a Virtue Angel, his father died of…' Steph's eyes opened wide as Salvatore went on. 'Oh, I'm sorry,' she said to Salvatore before looking back at us. 'His father died when he was five days old in an aircraft crash – he was a pilot. He has all of the normal gifts that come with being Grigori, his sense is sight and he is a…seeker of lies. He says it is like what Griffin can do, but where Griffin is totally in tune with truth, in identifying its presence and delivering it, Salvatore is dialled into lies – to the layers of deceit that construct and surround them. Eventually, through his gift, he will be able to see the threads of one lie that has led to another and another.' Steph looked to

Salvatore nervously and he nodded in approval of her explanation.

'So to sum up,' Zoe said, rolling her eyes and pointing at Spence, 'Glamour.' To herself, 'Nature.' Then to Salvatore, 'Lie detector.' Then she looked to me. 'So? What's your deal? We already got the inbuilt wristbands figured out – what about the rest?'

I suddenly had stage fright. Not because I was scared to say but because I now had to admit that I didn't know.

'Well...I...I still don't know much about my angel giver. My guides didn't...*wouldn't* tell me. Griffin says I may never know.'

I didn't go into the other option Griffin and I had discussed – the possibility that I had come from an angel so high in rank that its identity could be withheld at its wish.

'I...well... My mother died giving birth to me. She was Grigori, too.' I swallowed through the lump in my throat. 'I have all five senses and I can sense exiles from a long way away if I'm trying,' I said self-consciously, aware that I was editing as I went along. I hadn't even mentioned to Lincoln and Griffin that on a couple of occasions, the airport most recently, I'd suspected my senses extended to something else. The night Onyx and Joel had attacked at Hades was the other time I'd felt it. The only person who knew about that was Phoenix.

Salvatore moved forward in his seat, straining to understand everything I was saying. Zoe gave Spence an 'I told you so' look.

'And,' I went on, 'as for gifts, some of that is still a little unclear too. I seem to be able to stop exiles from a distance – put them into the kind of lock most Grigori require contact for – more than one at a time, and when I was injured and didn't have my dagger, I…I was able to strip an exile's powers even when he did not will it.'

Zoe, Salvatore and Spence exchanged glances. Steph's gaze, like mine, was flitting between them, trying to work out what they were thinking. She was nervous for me, too. Spence poured the lethal concoction from the jug into the five shot glasses and slid one out towards each of us. He looked at Zoe again and she shrugged and grabbed hers. We all followed.

'Well,' Spence said, 'fuck me.' He drank.

With one more shrug from Zoe and a sigh of relief from me – we all drank…and drank.

CHAPTER ELEVEN

'For I have sworn thee fair, and thought thee bright,
who art as black as hell, as dark as night.'
William Shakespeare

When I spotted Dapper working behind the bar, I excused myself. From the moment we'd entered Hades I had sensed at least one exile. He wasn't as obvious as most and I got the feeling he was trying to be inconspicuous. The others hadn't said anything, so I wasn't sure if they could sense him.

On my way up to the bar, I walked right past the exile. He had ginger hair and a slim frame hidden beneath a well-worn leather jacket and was lounging on one of the sofas. I tensed instantly, bracing for the fight that should have been guaranteed, but the exile just watched me walk by and didn't even flinch. In fact, he didn't seem surprised to see me at all.

By the time I reached Dapper, I was a bit stunned. 'Dapper!' I called out, waving him over.

He rolled his head back and sighed when he saw me.

I leaned over the bar. This wasn't the kind of stuff you wanted everyone to hear. He moved marginally closer after a moment.

'Have you had many exiles in here lately?' I asked.

He shrugged, moving back a bit.

'You *do* realise there's one in here now?'

His eyes darted out towards where I'd seen the exile. He knew exactly who was in his bar.

'There have been a few lately,' Dapper admitted. 'They don't bring their troubles here and I don't cause them any either. You make sure it stays that way!' He moved back, but not before adding, 'And if I catch you drinking in my bar again, I'll take pleasure in barring you.'

I gave him a sheepish grin and decided I could pick up this conversation at a later, more sober, time. 'I'll, umm…' I started retreating.

'You *and* your friends!' he called out after me.

Unexpectedly, I was actually starting to like Dapper. Even stranger, I had the distinct impression the feeling was mutual.

Who would have thought?

I made my way back through the press of drinkers and past the ginger-haired exile again, still sitting back, sipping his drink. I couldn't work out why he didn't attack. I wondered if he was playing a game or if he had sensed the other Grigori in the room and decided the odds were too strong in our favour.

Or…maybe he's just out having a drink.

But I didn't believe that. There was something else, something I couldn't put my finger on.

I considered approaching him, but fear of Dapper following through on his threat saw me return to our table instead. Spence was sitting alone, throwing back another shot. When he spotted me he wiped his mouth and smiled.

'Just in time,' he said, lining up another.

'OK, but last one,' I said, increasingly woozy. 'Have you sensed that there is at least one exile in here?' I asked.

Spence nodded. 'Was just about to mention that,' he said, slurring a little himself. 'You wanna hunt?'

I shook my head. 'We have an agreement with the owner, no hunting on his property without life-and-death cause and,' the part that had me so baffled, 'the exile didn't look like he was here for trouble.'

Spence shrugged. 'We have a few places like that in New York. They're called "Sites of Neutrality".'

I turned around to check whether the exile was still on the sofa, but couldn't see him. I pushed my senses out and felt them drifting further away. He'd gone.

'Where is everyone?' I asked, refocusing on our table and realising we'd been deserted.

'Zoe's gone to hit on the DJ. She has a thing for musicians.'

'Oh my God,' I said, laughing. 'Does she realise the DJ is Steph's brother?'

Spence, who was knocking back another shot, burst out laughing, spitting it all over himself. I jumped back to miss the splash.

'No way!' he laughed, wiping himself down. 'Oh, this is so great. You couldn't have planned it better.'

I had to agree.

'How about Steph and Salvatore?'

Spence didn't answer, he just looked towards the dance floor, then to me.

'Good God,' I said as we gave each other a sorry nod.

Steph and Salvatore were already out there doing the dance of drunk rhythmless monkeys. They really were a match made in heaven.

'C'mon, you need to break loose!' Spence stood and headed for the dance floor. I didn't need asking twice. I loved dancing.

We laughed and joked and then got into the music. We were having the most fun I'd had in ages. Spence made it so easy to just relax and I was glad to have a new friend. We danced and jumped when a new song came on that we both approved of – only making us laugh more, to learn that we shared the same taste in music.

Then I felt it.

Not all of a sudden, but slowly creeping up on me.

I should have stopped. But I was hazy from the alcohol, so I wasn't sure – or maybe I just didn't want to be. I looked at Spence to see if he was feeling it too. He was definitely feeling *something*. As I looked at him, I lost my way, remembering things I had told myself to forget. Touches and sensations that had taken me away from reality and enveloped me entirely. My whole body reacted, dismissing common sense, thrilled instantly by the sense of possibility.

Enticed.

Before I knew it, Spence had me in his arms, or I had him in mine. Both, I think.

Our hips moved together and we kept dancing as we

closed the distance, but I wasn't really moving closer to him – it was someone else I was drawn towards. His lips met mine and when I kissed him back, my body exploded, electricity coursing through it, lust, lust and... Oh...

I couldn't control myself, couldn't stop myself.

Spence had his hands all over me. In my hair, down my back. Further. I tried to shut down, to find myself, even though part of me screamed to pull him closer. It took a few moments, but the second I did, I pushed him away so fast he stumbled back a few steps. When he caught his balance he looked at me, confused. He was himself again too. But I didn't have time to explain.

I found him instantly – everything now fitting together.

I *had* felt him back at the hotel. I had known it deep down. I'd just tried to ignore it. I'd even felt him before things went crazy with Spence, I just wasn't quick enough to admit it to myself.

He was sitting at the bar. Wearing all black. His dazzling hair, reflecting light that was not there. Our eyes met and the corners of his mouth slowly moved up as his eyes looked past me and beyond.

I turned – but I already knew.

Lincoln stood at the edge of the dance floor. Magda beside him, sporting a similar smirk to Phoenix. His green eyes shone, even from this distance. He had seen the kiss. I took a step towards him, desperate to explain. All I had time to see was his drink fall to the floor and he was gone. Magda too.

Well, if he wasn't already in her arms, you just pushed him there, Vi.

I spun on my heels. Everything had happened in a few

seconds. Spence had only just reached me.

'What was *that*?'

I didn't stop to talk. I stormed right up to Phoenix. 'What the hell do you think you're doing? Are you so screwed in the head, that this is how you get your kicks? By hurting me?' I screamed.

Phoenix looked at me calmly. Patronisingly. He smiled. 'I've missed you. Your naivety more than anything else, I think. But that's not to say I haven't missed…other things,' he swept his eyes over me.

'Oh my God, you're demented! How did you do that?'

'How does it feel, Violet – to watch someone run away from you? Shoe's on the other foot now, isn't it?'

Phoenix held an empty glass up towards the waitress behind the bar. The girl practically fell over herself, dodging another guy and tripping over an ice bucket on the way to top up his red wine.

Still likes red wine.

I wanted to slap myself for even having the thought.

He took a sip and I knew it wasn't just for show that he took a moment, savouring the taste. He always had… enjoyed experiencing human pleasures. Red wine had been one of his most valued.

'Just because our emotional bond is broken, Violet, doesn't mean you are not susceptible to my talents. Even through another person, it seems I am strong enough to break your defences. It is easier, of course, that you so wanted me to.'

'*What?* I did not!'

His smile deepened and his eyes narrowed. He leaned in closer and with people standing all around us, I couldn't move back. 'I know you felt it, lover. I felt your memories, your longing to go where I took you. I can even feel how you want to taste my wine, knowing I've tasted it – to press your lips against the glass,' he rolled the stem in his fingers. 'Exactly where my lips have been.'

'You make me sick,' I said, and meant it, even if he was partly right.

Spence pushed up beside me. 'Who's he?'

'Phoenix,' I said, not taking my eyes off him.

'Shit,' Spence said. Apparently further explanation wasn't required. 'Do we fight?' Spence asked me. I didn't answer. I didn't know.

'There is nothing for you here. The bond is broken!' I carried on, as if Spence hadn't spoken.

'Is it?' Phoenix stood up from his bar stool. Somehow he didn't struggle to find space to move. 'I told you before I left, lover, when I healed you, I gave you something.' He grinned.

I was about to yell at him again – tell him not to call me lover – when I felt a searing pain in my stomach. I screamed, the pain building so fast, faster than any I'd felt before. My hands went to my stomach as I looked at Phoenix to see if he was holding a weapon, then to my hands that were now covered in blood. My blood.

Phoenix shook his head and leaned forward. 'Tsk tsk, did I forget to mention? I can take it back.'

That was why the pain was so familiar, so frightening. He had given me back the injury Onyx had inflicted with his sword. The injury Phoenix healed.

I swayed, Spence's arm wrapped around me to hold me up while he screamed towards Salvatore on the dance floor.

Phoenix turned to leave. I was losing consciousness, but I heard him say to Spence, 'She is intoxicating, isn't she? I wonder, was it as good for you as it was for me?'

Then I felt the gust of wind I knew was his departure.

'I'll ask you the same question when I run my dagger through your heart!' Spence called out too late.

I dropped to the floor as Salvatore and Steph arrived. Spence knelt down beside me, his supporting arm never leaving me.

'Violet! What's he done? What do I do? Oh man, you're bleeding everywhere!' he wailed.

I couldn't answer. Black smoke played in the corners of my vision, blurring my sight. My legs, which had been prickling with pins and needles, went numb. Just as I thought I was going to pass out, somehow I sucked in a deeper breath than should have been possible. Almost instantly I felt considerably better. I looked down and pulled up my top. The wound was closing.

'What the...? Are you doing that?' Zoe had joined us.

'No,' I answered, my hands shaking as they touched the almost healed wound. 'It's not me. It's Phoenix. This is the wound he healed in me a month ago. Somehow Phoenix is doing this. When he left I...I...'

'You started to heal,' Steph finished, grabbing my hand tightly. 'This is bad, Vi. Bible bad.'

Yep.

I glanced around, suddenly aware of my state in the middle of a bar. But to my surprise, no one was even looking at me, bleeding to death on the ground. I scanned the area, dumbfounded. 'How?'

Spence gave me one of his winks. 'Glamour. No one

can see you, honey. You just stay there until you're good and ready.'

'Oh. Good one,' I said, mustering a smile despite the undeniable knot of guilt and all-round panic about what that kiss had meant to Spence.

Just to prove us wrong Dapper came over and put out a hand. 'Jesus Christ. Are you alive?'

'Yeah. I'm OK.'

Spence looked from Dapper to me, wide-eyed. I just hitched a shoulder.

'Good. Well, get up and stop bleeding all over my floor,' Dapper said, shaking his head. 'Why are you always covered in blood?'

It was a mighty fine question.

'I knew this would happen. Bringing your damn problems into my place.' He kept shaking his head, but I was sure I could see just the slightest amount of concern as he looked down at me. 'Ah hell, go upstairs, you know where everything is.' He put a hand out and pulled me to my feet. 'I'll be up when I can.'

'Should I ask?' Spence enquired, as we watched Dapper stomp off.

'No.' I was simply too tired to explain.

I led the way towards the unmarked door that went upstairs. Spence stayed close the whole time, keeping a hand under my elbow. I knew it was out of kindness, in case I keeled over again and he needed to put up another glamour, but I still wanted to shake him off…just in case.

Lincoln's gone. With Magda. She smiled – I'm sure of it.

As I felt the stirrings of a tear, I heard a chuckle I recognised from the end of the bar.

'Just when I was about to leave, the entertainment begins. Had I known I would have arranged closer viewing.'

'Shut up, Onyx,' was all I could muster.

'Now, now. Is that any way to treat the *person*,' his face scrunched when he said the humanising word, 'who can enlighten you as to what just happened?' He raised his eyebrows and displayed the kind of grin that only came with true joy.

I bit my lip and relaxed my instinctively fisted hands. 'What do you know?'

'No, no, no. The *first* question is – what do I want? A question that has a two-part answer. Part A is a bottle of bourbon. Trisha behind the bar knows which one I like. Part B I will explain upstairs.' He stood and disappeared through the door without so much as a glance to see if we were in agreement.

'Shit.'

'Sal!' Spence called out. He handed my arm to Salvatore. 'Help her upstairs.' He pointed to make sure he understood and Salvatore gave a nod and smiled at me.

'Where are you going?' I asked Spence.

'To get the bottle of bourbon. I'll meet you up there.'

I was about to argue, but what was the point? We all knew, even Steph, who already had the door open for us, that Onyx had us over a barrel.

'Come on, then,' Zoe pushed ahead, starting up the stairs. Steph glared at her but I suspected Zoe was going first to stop her. She was protecting her, though she'd never admit it. Once again, life as a Grigori was exposing my best friend to danger.

I was beginning to understand more and more why so many chose to not tell their loved ones the truth.

CHAPTER TWELVE

'Suddenly he saw a vision of a seraph, a six-winged
angel on a cross. This angel gave him the gift of the
five wounds of Christ.'
G. K. Chesterton

We passed by Onyx's flat. The door was open and the place was empty, apart from some haphazardly scattered possessions, signs of someone who has absolutely no level of regard for anything. We kept going down the hall to Dapper's. I walked slowly, using the time to regenerate my strength. The wound had healed, but once again, blood-loss and trauma were taking their toll.

The door was open and Onyx was reclined on the couch. He had his feet up on the coffee table and seemed almost at home.

'Well?' he asked, when we all crowded through the doorway.

I wanted to turn around and walk back out. Instead, I gritted my teeth.

'Spence has gone to get your bourbon. He'll be up in

a minute,' I said, moving myself away from Salvatore's supporting arm to stand alone.

'Good. Well, you may as well get cleaned up. As much as I like the image of you covered in blood,' the corners of his mouth twitched, 'Dapper wouldn't appreciate you ruining his lovely chaise longue.'

I crossed my arms and made no move, but Onyx just smiled and made a walking motion with two of his fingers.

'It's all right, Violet, we'll watch him,' Zoe said, stepping closer to Onyx. There was little I could do. He was in control – for now. After giving Zoe a quick nod I served Onyx a foul look and stormed off to the bathroom, pulling Steph along with me.

Steph let loose as soon as the door clicked.

'Vi, is this a good idea? He... He's the one that... You know...'

I did know. Unfortunately, I'd had more than a vivid reminder of what Onyx had done to me when he impaled me with his sword, nearly killing me. Knowing now that Phoenix appeared to have the ability to reinstate the wounds – *the terror* – at any time was... I swallowed and clenched my jaw.

Hold it together, Vi.

There are moments in life where there is nothing you can do. Information lands in your lap and you just want to scream and scream until there is only emptiness. It's when I feel like that, that I know I have to close down, shut it out – compartmentalise. Like now.

'I remember, Steph. But if he knows something...' I picked a spot on the floor, a crack in one of the dark grey tiles, and focused on it. I studied the hairline and its jagged edges as I tried desperately to block the flow. I refused to open my mind to everything that was going on. To Phoenix, Onyx, the possibilities of what might happen. Worse, right now, opening myself would only start the stampede on my heart – Lincoln.

It's always Lincoln. He'll never forgive me.

The last time I'd been in this bathroom we'd almost...

Every time we get close, somehow it's ruined.

I jumped when my phone started ringing and fumbled as I fished it out of my blood-soaked pocket.

'Hello?' Then, remembering that Spence had diverted the house phone to my mobile, quickly added, 'Eden residence.'

'Hi, honey. Just ringing to check in before you go to bed.'

I could hear fingers tapping away on a computer. Probably Dad sending emails. He always left them till the end of his day, or night, I should say.

'Hey, *Dad*,' I emphasised, looking at Steph, who nodded, understanding instantly. 'How's your trip going?' I asked, trying to keep a steady low voice so it didn't echo too much in the bathroom.

Steph moved silently and put an ear to the door, checking that no one else was going to barge in.

'Lunches and dinners with clients every day – it's driving me up the wall but it has to be done. Anything happening there? Is Steph staying over?'

'Um... Yeah. Well, no. I mean, no nothing's happening and yes Steph is staying over. We're just doing the usual. Pizza and movies,' I said, trying hard to recapture some composure after such a rocky start.

'Sounds good, honey,' Dad went on, oblivious to any

problem. 'Listen, I've got to get going. I'll call you tomorrow.'

'Sure, Dad.'

He hung up. I looked down at my phone and pressed the end button. 'Love you, too.'

Although I knew it was irrational, at that moment I was angry with him. For not knowing me, who I was, what I was going through. I knew it was unfair, that it was me who hadn't told him, but all the same... *Why can't he hear the fear in my voice?* Sense the way my world had changed? I had to sense *things* every day for the rest of my life, which would possibly be a very long time, and all I wanted was for him to be able to sense me. *Just me.*

'Vi – you OK?' Steph asked, watching me as she quietly moved to the sink and started rinsing blood from a towel we'd been using. She wrung it out and motioned gently to me to continue mopping up. Without a change of clothes, it was the only option, but it was pretty useless.

I wiped away the tear that had escaped down my cheek.

'Fine,' I said in response. 'Just...' But I didn't have an explanation. There was a lot going on. I couldn't put the feelings of desperation and foreboding, and all-round sick-to-the-gut sensation into words.

I spotted a bathrobe hanging on the back of the door and grabbed it. I pulled off my T-shirt. I didn't bother with my jeans.

'Hey,' I said, trying to rally as much as I could, 'do you think you could rinse this out and throw it in the dryer? I saw a laundry room back down the hall a bit?'

Steph took the T-shirt and looked at me, unconvinced. 'I know what you're doing. You can't deal with everything on your own, Vi.' She adjusted her focus down to the bloodied top in her hands. 'I know you think I shouldn't be involved in this stuff, but here's the thing – you made your choice when you told me the truth. Now I've made mine. You're my best friend, Vi, don't push me out because I'm not all "super". We stick together. That's that.'

Steph's expression looked so adamant but also... desperate. It wasn't just me who had a lot on the line. This world that I was now stuck in mattered to her, too. In her own way, she was just as stuck as me. We're best friends, after all – where one goes the other follows.

'I don't want to see you hurt,' I admitted.

She smiled wryly. 'How about you just worry about yourself?'

I smiled back. She could be right.

She bundled the T-shirt and the worst of the bloody towels together. 'I'll go take care of these.' She paused at the door, as if she couldn't help herself, and turned back to me, a small twinkle in her eye. 'Did you see all those books in the hallway?'

I wondered when she'd mention she'd just entered a version of geek heaven.

What was I doing?

What I *wanted* to do – badly – was run. I knew deep down that this was all my fault. Letting myself get close to Phoenix in the first place, letting myself believe that he was good, that he cared.

No. I'm more culpable than that. I let him believe that I was good.

I sucked in a few deep breaths and avoided looking at myself in the mirror.

Am I just as guilty as Phoenix?

Looking back, he probably never cared for me. He just wanted to control me, have me as some kind of trophy. But had I been any better?

Running was what had gotten me into this mess. Running from becoming Grigori, from my feelings for Lincoln, from the truth about my mother. It had all led me to Phoenix. I couldn't run any more. And quitting wasn't an option. I couldn't even hide. I was out in the open and Phoenix could find me anywhere.

He was a predator and…

I was his prey.

When I was confident the red blotches on my face had settled enough, I headed back out to where everyone was waiting. Spence had returned with a bottle of bourbon in his hand. He, along with everyone else in the room, cracked a smile when they took in my appearance – wrapped in a gigantic bathrobe. Everyone, that is, except Dapper, who had also made it upstairs.

'Oh, great,' he snorted. 'Just make yourself at home. Can I get you some slippers as well?'

I could see Zoe and Spence shaking, holding back laughter, and had to look away from them. Crazy how even when things are life and death, friends can make you see a funny side.

'Sorry, Dapper. You've been really kind. Steph is just

washing my top and while we talked I thought she could try and dry it. It won't take long.'

He grunted and made for his minibar.

He threw a glass out towards Onyx, who caught it easily. It made me wonder if Onyx and Dapper were becoming friends – the way they seemed to comfortably ignore one another but still be in some kind of weird sync.

Onyx set about opening his bottle of bourbon and pouring himself a drink. 'Thank you for this. I won't be offering any of you a drink.'

Not that anyone wanted one, well maybe Zoe…and Spence, but Onyx's words were a clear reminder of how much he hated us.

Dapper, however, finally cracked a smile. He grabbed a stash of small Coke bottles from his fridge and started offering them around.

Once we were all seated and Onyx had downed two large glasses of bourbon, he looked up at us all and there it was, the old Onyx. A part of him, anyway. It sent a shiver down my spine to see him come alive. This was his favourite thing to do – tell stories of doom and in particular *my* doom. It made me uneasy to remember the way he got such a thrill out of seeing other people's pain.

'It's a consolation prize I had not considered. Poetic really. That we've all potentially destroyed each other. Don't you think, Violet? That *you* destroyed Phoenix's humanity by teasing it out of him in the first place, that my attempt to eliminate you released your discovery of power, which in turn curtailed my greatness, leaving me with detestable humanity. That now I may still – indirectly, obviously – be the cause of your downfall through Phoenix himself. How deliciously bittersweet.'

'Onyx,' Dapper said, sternly, 'tell them what you know or leave them be.'

Onyx paused, but only momentarily, to consider Dapper before his smile returned. 'Dapper, I am glad you are here. The second part of my condition involves you.'

'Here we go,' said Dapper, rolling his eyes.

'As I have already mentioned I *was* prepared to leave, but it appears things have just…taken a turn. I will tell you what I know… *Some* of what I know,' he corrected, turning his smile on me, 'in exchange for ongoing accommodation.'

Onyx poured himself another large bourbon, the sound of ice cubes clinking the only noise to fill the uncomfortable silence in the room. Spence, Zoe and Salvatore tried to look busy staring at their Cokes. Even Steph, who had just walked back into the room, knew now was not the time for comment.

I looked at Dapper, who had picked up a cloth and was rubbing down the already-clean minibar.

The quiet stretched.

'You have to work. For your keep,' Dapper finally said, not looking up.

'No,' Onyx said, quite simply. I could hear the glee in his voice. 'But you can't deny, Dapper, you don't altogether mind my company.'

Dapper blushed.

Please!

'Two weeks,' Dapper said, curt as ever, then looked over to me. 'And you owe me.'

'OK,' I agreed.

'Well,' Onyx clapped his hands, 'aren't we all just so civilised? It's a new thing for me, granted, but entertaining in its own peculiar way,' he marvelled.

'Onyx! You're wasting time. Tell me what's going on,' I snapped, clenching my fists.

'Yes. Of course. You want to get back to your shadow-finder – you do like to torture him. I admire that.' He stood up and started to flounce around the room. I knew he was talking about Lincoln. By this point, I just wanted to smash his face into the wall and from the expression on Zoe's face, I wasn't the only one. I didn't look at Spence. I couldn't meet his eyes right now and Salvatore had moved over to stand with Steph. She was whispering to him, translating, I guessed.

'I have only ever seen it once before. A powerful weapon, though not many of us are willing to take the risk...or the bond.' His nose wrinkled at something. 'I wasn't even sure what it was or its importance when I came across it, it was more speculation than anything... Though after seeing what I saw tonight, it now seems very believable.' He sighed. Typical warm-up. 'It was in the thirteenth century. A young Grigori-turned-spiritual leader. Some even thought him to be the first, and only, Grigori to ever be graced with true vision. Of course, for exiles, his fame made him a particularly important prize and though he was often guarded and deceptively powerful, one exile found a way to get to him.'

Onyx looked at each of us one by one, enjoying that we had no idea what he was talking about. 'The exile appeared to the Grigori as a vision. Used his imagination to put him in a state of confusion and then inflicted wounds that he found...' the corners of his mouth curled, '...appropriately amusing. Afterwards, the exile healed the Grigori and let him go under the belief that he had received a spiritual connection with a heavenly power when in actual fact…' he trailed off as he motioned a hand towards me. I'd forgotten he liked audience participation.

I swallowed nervously. 'He'd done whatever Phoenix has done to me.'

Onyx nodded. 'All that had been achieved was an ongoing physical bond between the Grigori and the exile. The exile, of course, planned to use this new power to help turn the tides, but unfortunately, it was not to be. When the Grigori discovered the deceit, he would not succumb to the exile's demands and endured the pains of the wounds each time they were re-inflicted. It was a harder time then. Religious types were less malleable than they are today.' Another deliberate sigh.

I shook my head involuntarily.

'It had been an ambitious tactic, and if it had worked, would have been an awesome weapon. Even in its limited version, it was.'

'Why?' I asked, feeling my throat tightening.

'Because it still led to the Grigori's death in the end. His injuries gradually drained his powers and the very life from him.'

Steph took a step forward. 'The thirteenth century?'

Onyx raised an eyebrow. 'Yes,' he said, suspiciously, looking at Steph as if noticing her for the first time. I imagined in his exile days Onyx would not have believed in interactions with straight humans, other than for sport.

'You're talking about Saint Francis of Assisi, aren't you? He died after suffering five brutal wounds for just over two years.' Steph looked at me, sickly green. 'He bore the stigmata.' Her eyes were welling.

Onyx was perplexed, as was everyone in the room apart from me. Steph wasn't an out-and-proud brainiac. Onyx clearly hadn't expected someone to spoil his story's denouement.

'Aren't you a very clever human?' he sneered.

'Hang on,' started Zoe. 'This sounds like a load of shit to me. The stigmata? The wounds of the crucifixion? Violet doesn't have those.'

'No, she has my wounds,' Onyx said proudly. 'They're just another version. Assisi's wounds were symbolically inflicted on him first, just as Violet's were, and then healed. By healing the wounds, the exile effectively gives a piece of his immortality to the victim, in this case Grigori, and as Phoenix demonstrated, *What one giveth one may also taketh away.*' Onyx raised his arms and all but took a bow.

'Oh my God,' I whispered to myself. 'He's going to kill me.'

Slowly.

Onyx heard me. 'It appears the likely outcome,' he said, as he lounged back into the sofa, content.

'We kill the Phoenix first. *Si?*' Salvatore asked and Steph nodded.

'You could try. It might work.'

'You lie,' Salvatore said, watching Onyx then turning to Zoe. 'He lies.'

'What aren't you telling us?' Zoe demanded.

'Two Armani shirts, one white with pinstripe, the other charcoal. Slim fit. And…' he ran a hand over his chin, '…an electric shaver. An expensive one.'

'How about I just ram my fist into your face until you

143

tell us everything you know?' Spence suggested, taking a few exaggerated steps towards Onyx.

'Don't bother with that, lad,' said Dapper. 'He'd be happy enough for you to finish him off. You won't get anywhere that way.'

Spence looked at me, but – even now – I still couldn't quite bring myself to look back.

'I'll give them to you tomorrow,' I said, in a daydream.

'Do you think your Lincoln will ever forgive you?' Onyx asked.

'What? He... Phoenix did this. It wasn't me. Lincoln will... He'll understand,' I said, stumbling over the words that I had been trying to tell myself since I saw him walk out of Hades.

'I didn't mean about tonight – though it cannot help your cause.'

I swallowed hard. It wasn't the first time since I'd embraced that Onyx had raised this question. The last time was right before he stabbed me.

'Ah. I see. Worrying you, too? A big thing, that one. Even those with the best intention, the greatest of forbidden love, can struggle to accept another getting to the prize before they do.'

'Shut up, Onyx,' Dapper said. Strangely, Onyx seemed to respond and moved on.

I gave Dapper a thankful glance. I didn't really want to have to explain to the entire room that Onyx was referring to the fact that I'd slept with Phoenix and that had made Lincoln...unhappy.

'Very well. Phoenix has a physical connection to you now. Not only can he bring back the wounds that I so

savagely delivered, he is also the very thing that holds off their recurrence. If something were to happen to Phoenix, if he was killed, or as you like to call it *"returned"*… Well…'
He laid his hands wide.

'I die.'

'It seems inexorably probable.'

'Jesus, Mary and Joseph,' Steph said as Spence and Zoe swore.

'This one – not good,' said Salvatore, shaking his head.

Dapper remained silent.

Onyx smiled, enjoying his version of applause until his eyes fixed on mine. My chest tightened and every breath felt suddenly numbered.

We looked at each other and in that brief moment, when his eyes couldn't quite hold mine – we shared the truth silently between us.

It wasn't just probable.

If Phoenix died – I died.

CHAPTER THIRTEEN

*'A thought, even a possibility, can shatter and
transform us.'*
Friedrich Nietzsche

I hoped a morning of painting would help. Give me some
perspective or at least let me escape for a couple of hours.
But I couldn't even concentrate for long enough to mix the
right colours in my double period of art first thing.

He'd told me he loved me once. It was hurried and
perhaps only part of a game to him, trying to get me away
from Lincoln. I guess it had worked. I'd never felt so
isolated before.

Now, again thanks to Phoenix, I was sure of my own
demise.

After all the events of last night, by the time I got home
it had been late again. My sleep allotments were declining
while my near-death experiences were clearly on the up.
But, of course, it wasn't the lack of sleep that had me so
agitated. It was the lack of something else. *Someone* else.

I had hoped, the whole time we were at Dapper's –

listening to Onyx tell his tale of doom – that Lincoln might come back. That somehow he might realise I would never have kissed Spence willingly. I even held out hope that Magda might have talked some sense into him. Wishful thinking. But Lincoln – he knew me. Surely he would have known I wouldn't be so…

Even though I slept with a dark exile!

And there was my problem – the nagging voice of truth we all have buried deep within. The one that is always there painting with primary colours, not bothering to mix it up.

Onyx was right. *I* had planted all the seeds of doubt that Phoenix was now watering. I may have had my reasons, but that didn't change the fact that Lincoln would probably never forgive me or that the sacrifice required for us to be together would be more than he would ever willingly make for me.

He has his real problem – and I have mine.

I'd sacrificed everything to save Lincoln but right now I feared surrendering his strengths, risking his power, would not be something Lincoln could do. Not so he could be with me.

By the time the bell rang for lunch, I'd barely made a mark on my canvas. As I packed up my art teacher came over to me.

'Violet, you've been distracted lately. I know you have other studies to concentrate on and plenty of social events to attend, however, if you still plan on making the impact I know you can at the Fenton course, you will need to start applying yourself again in art.'

I took a deep breath, deflated and cross with myself.

'I know, Miss. I'll try harder. I really want to do well at the Fenton course.'

'Well, if that's the case, you have work to do,' she said in that voice only teachers can put on, somewhere between parental and guilt-trip. It worked.

In the cafeteria I grabbed a salad and a bread roll and slumped down in my usual spot. When the chair beside me was pulled out and a tray dropped down next to mine, I didn't even look up. I assumed it would be Steph.

'Jeez, Eden – you awake?'

I jumped in my seat and looked up to see Spence laughing away.

'What? What are you doing here?' Then, paranoid, I started looking around. 'You're going to get caught. You can't be here. You're going to get me in trouble! Again!'

He gave me a cheeky wink and his smile widened. 'Glamour.'

I looked around the room again and realised no one else seemed aware of his presence, even though he was not wearing a school uniform and clearly didn't belong there.

'What are you doing here?'

'Apart from nursing a wicked hangover. I came to clear the air,' he said, squaring his shoulders to me. He had no intention of going away.

'Oh.' I blew out an I-don't-want-to-be-here breath.

'Look. A lot of stuff went down last night and I get the feeling of all the awful…if you could take one thing away, it would be the you-and-me-getting-dirty-on-the-dance-floor bit?'

I squinted my eyes at him. 'You certainly have a way with words, Spence.'

He shrugged. 'It's a gift.' He raised his eyebrows and waited. He really wasn't going to go away.

'OK. Look, it's not that I don't... You know. I think you're really nice and all and you were... I mean... It wasn't bad or anything. Crap. I just don't...'

'Like me like that?' he suggested, smiling.

'Yeah.'

'It's OK. I get it. It wasn't exactly my choice either, you know. Don't get me wrong, I'm not feeling violated or anything. You kiss like a maniac – no guy in his right mind would be disappointed after that – I mean—'

'*Spence!*' I cut him off.

'Oh, yeah. Sorry. What I was saying was – it's all good. We're friends. The fact that we've shared one particularly hot kiss isn't going to change that, make it all weird. OK?'

I nodded, relieved that at least one of my concerns wasn't going to develop into a major crisis.

Steph pulled out a chair and sat down on the other side of Spence. 'Hi,' she said to Spence. 'What are you doing here?'

'Hey!' I jumped in. 'How come she can see you?'

'It's a pick-and-choose thing. Right now I'm only providing glamour to those who don't already know me. As far as they're concerned a very inconspicuous – but seriously smokin' – girl is sitting down beside you in a school uniform having lunch.'

'Smokin'?' Steph repeated.

'Hey, some things just happen naturally.' Spence opened his arms. 'It's hard for me to cover up innate hotness, no matter what form I'm in.'

Steph made a gagging motion. 'You do realise this is

a co-ed school. You could have stayed male,' she said.

Spence took a huge bite of his sandwich. 'True, but then it wouldn't have been so easy to stop by the girls' changing room on the way here.' He shrugged.

I started picking at pieces of my bread roll, throwing them at him. Steph picked up her salad bowl and dumped its contents over his head.

It had been good to clear the air with Spence and by the end of the day I started to get myself together and built up towards my next task. Lincoln.

After school, Steph and I detoured via the bank so I could withdraw some money from my dad's Amex account. He'd set it up with joint cards for us both years ago. I paid most of the household bills and did the majority of any shopping so it was just easier if I had access to cash. Dad had told me it was OK to use it to buy a few things here and there, but on the whole I didn't bother. I didn't know how much an Armani shirt and an electric shaver would cost so when Steph suggested I take out a thousand dollars I almost fell over.

'What do you mean a thousand dollars? Are you crazy?' I only really withdrew cash for lunch money and groceries. Coffee and milk don't cost much.

'Listen, sweetie, when it comes to matters of designer clothing, I'm as reliable as they come. You're just lucky that there are sales on – otherwise we'd need more.'

I blew out a breath. If she was telling me it was so – it was so. Still, I couldn't help the aggravation at handing over money so Onyx could get his reward for telling me I might die.

'Are you going to be OK? Do you know what size to get?'

Steph gave me a full-blown eye-roll. 'Honestly, Vi, I could shop with my eyes closed. Anyway, she pulled out a cocktail napkin from her pocket. 'Mr Reminisce-on-the-dark-days gave me all his measurements. I really dislike that guy.'

'Try hate with a vengeance.'

Steph gave me a pitying look. 'Are you sure you want me to go? I can stay with you – come over to Lincoln's – just in case…?'

But this was something I had to do on my own. There was no point arriving with reinforcements – my best chance was to just go myself, try and be completely honest.

'No. You go. We need this stuff. I'll have to deliver it to Onyx by tomorrow or he'll start causing more problems. Why don't you ask Salvatore if he wants to go with you?'

Steph planted a goodbye kiss on my cheek. 'Already done. I'm meeting him at the mall. Um…Vi?' she started, uncharacteristically unsure.

'Yeah?'

'Do you mind if I stay at yours again tonight? Dad's still away and well…Mum's…entertaining.' She looked past me, suddenly distracted by something in the shop window. It was almost believable, if we weren't standing outside a bank.

'Sure, Steph.' Then, deciding that wasn't enough, I added, 'I was going to ask you the same thing. I really don't feel like being alone at the moment so maybe you could just come and stay till Dad gets back? If that's OK with you?' I didn't know what was going on in Steph's home life, but her uncomfortableness said enough.

Steph shifted weight from one foot to the other and shrugged a shoulder. 'Yeah. I could do that.' She finally looked up briefly, pushed the hair back from her forehead and checked her watch. 'Time to fly.' As she walked past, unable to look at me again, she grabbed hold of my hand and we both gave a quick squeeze before letting each other go.

When I walked down Lincoln's street, I couldn't see his four-wheel-drive parked anywhere on the road. The warehouse door was open, which was no surprise as everyone was using it as a drop-in centre lately. I wondered if that was bothering him – if he was feeling put out by everyone else.

Especially since last night.

Griffin was at the dining table, watching as Spence and Zoe practised tactical manoeuvres. The boring stuff, no combat, just exercises. I smiled when I caught the frustrated looks on both of their faces.

Rudyard was overseeing, calling out whenever they made a bad decision and instructing them to go back and start again.

I felt quite smug until I noticed Griffin watching me.

'You're up next,' he said.

I gave him a smart-ass smile.

'Where's Lincoln?'

Griffin's expression tightened. I thought I could see a little frustration in his eyes, too.

'Not here. He and Magda had something to do that couldn't wait,' and there again, I heard a change in his voice. A hint of sarcasm.

'Do you know what's going on?'

'No idea.' Griffin gave himself a little pull-together when he took in my obvious unhappiness. 'Look, we all have things to do at times that are…private. That doesn't mean we want to hurt the people around us or push them away. Sometimes we are just trying to protect them.'

'Griffin?' I began, pulling out a chair and plonking myself beside him. 'Nyla and Rudyard told Linc and me how they're soulmates. How being together made them stronger. Did you ever consider being with—'

'Magda?'

I nodded.

'You have *seen* her, haven't you? Of course I considered it. Who wouldn't?' Then quickly he added, 'I…ah, well. What I meant to say was – she's very beautiful, but that's not everything. Magda and I were never in love. More like brother and sister or best friends at first and now… Well…' But he didn't elaborate. I got the feeling that their partnership had not always been smooth-sailing.

'Would you have tried, if you'd loved her? Would you, you know, have risked your powers?'

He leaned back in his chair. 'That's a big question you're asking.' He frowned. 'The answer is – probably not. I believe in being Grigori, the role I play. It's been hard for me at times – to be from a Seraph when so few are. The responsibility and expectation that comes with being a leader. I'm not always the one I wish I could be – that I should be – but nonetheless, it is my place. If I was

153

to ever show a commitment to something other than my leadership, which could jeopardise the function I have, I would be risking too many lives. I couldn't live with that.'

I nodded. I understood what he was saying but at the same time I couldn't help but think the only reason he admitted it so easily was because what existed between him and Magda never pushed him beyond reason, enticed him beyond the rational.

'Griffin, is Magda from the Seraphim too?' I asked, realising that I didn't really know that much about her.

Other than that I hate her!

'No. No, she's of an Angel.'

'What do you mean? Aren't we all?'

'Yes, but one of the orders is referred to as simply Angel. Technically, it is the tenth order. You didn't pay much attention to that hierarchy chart I drew up for you, did you?'

'Sorry,' I said, suddenly guilty.

He let it slide. 'Her strength is that she can speak telepathically.'

'Wow. So you're from the highest order and she's from the lowest? That must have been hard for her?'

'Well, the order isn't always a reflection of importance, Violet, but yes, at times it has been a challenge for her.'

'I guess speaking telepathically is cool, though. Can she speak to anyone?'

Griffin looked around the room. I could tell this conversation was not one he was enjoying. He pushed his chair up to stand. 'No. She can only speak to others who have the same gift.'

'Oh,' I said, as he gestured to Zoe and Spence and moved closer to observe their game of cat and mouse.

I stayed sitting at the table and watched. My mind was racing with everything Griffin had told me. The only *others* I knew of who could speak telepathically were exiles. Questions kept forming in my mind and I realised that I was just creating more problems and not solving any.

Rudyard stood up. 'That's enough for you two today,' he called out, stopping the grateful-looking Spence and Zoe. Rudyard walked towards the door and started putting on a long trench coat, which looked awkward on him. Like Griffin, he was the type of person who was always destined to grow old. Though he pulled it off better than Griffin and managed an up-to-date wardrobe, he was one of those people you know will look their best in mid-life. I wondered how many more hundreds of years it would take for him to hit middle age.

Rudyard opened the front door and stood aside, just as Nyla walked in. He knew she was coming. That was pretty creepy. I was jealous as hell.

'What's up?' Griffin asked, joining them as I got up, too.

'Magda just called me,' Nyla said, smoothing down her windblown hair. 'She said her source told her where a couple of exiles are holing up. She thinks they're connected to the Scripture. Apparently her source heard them bragging about how they would soon have the key to destroy all Grigori.'

'Sounds like the Scripture,' Griffin agreed.

'Are we hunting?' Rudyard asked.

Griffin grabbed his coat. 'You bet. This is the first good lead we've had. Why didn't Magda call me?'

'She said she tried to, but couldn't get through,' Nyla said.

'Makes sense. I've been on and off the phone all day,' Griffin said, but he didn't sound convinced. I wondered if he knew something I didn't about Magda. And Lincoln, for that matter.

'I'm coming,' I said.

'No, you shouldn't be going out without Lincoln. It's not safe,' Griffin said.

'You're going out without Magda, and Lincoln and Magda are both out without us. I think I'm entitled. Plus, this Scripture is... Well, I want in.'

'OK,' said Griffin. I smiled, loving that he was that sort of guy. The kind that respected guts and people who fought for what they believed in. 'But you'd better get changed. Hurry up!'

I looked down at my school uniform and then ran to the bathroom to put on the spare clothes I had in my bag.

When I emerged in shorts and a T-shirt I heard raised voices from down the corridor. Spence was yelling.

'It's not fair. You just told Violet she can go and her partner's not here!' he complained.

'Yes, but her partner is not far away. If she is hurt we can get her to him. Spence, it's Griffin's call what happens with Violet, but you are under our care and we have to abide by Academy regulation,' Rudyard said.

'You're kidding! I have all the other abilities of strength and speed that everyone else does. I'm not going to get hurt! You can't do this – hold me back forever!'

Before I made it out to the living room I heard the front door slam. Spence had taken off.

Nyla had a hand on Zoe's shoulder. 'Go get him, Zoe. He needs a friend. You're the closest thing he has to a partner at the moment. Help him.'

'Oh, perfect! Just what I need. Another imbecile to babysit. So I suppose that means I don't get to go on the hunt either?'

'Please, Zoe,' Nyla pleaded, looking worriedly towards the door.

'Whatever.'

And just as Spence had stormed out, Zoe yanked the door back open and stubbornly followed. Before the door slammed for a second time, a rush of dried leaves blew through into the living room.

Nyla, Rudyard and Griffin were brushing themselves down as I joined them.

'Zoe?' I asked, assessing the leaf attack.

'Hmm,' Rudyard said, completely unimpressed. 'Using nature as a weapon against us is not a good use of her strengths.'

No. But I could see why she had and was just glad I'd been out of range when she let rip.

CHAPTER FOURTEEN

'The wise man in the storm prays to God, not for
safety from danger, but deliverance from fear.'
Ralph Waldo Emerson

From the car, Griffin tried to call Magda but had no luck. He
threw his phone in the glove box, shutting it with a snap.
I understood his disappointment. It mirrored my own. Not
only had I failed to clear the air with Lincoln, I hadn't even
seen him. I sent him a text. No reply.

We drove for a while and were well out of the city
before I asked Nyla where we were heading.

'To an abandoned farmhouse. Magda said it would
take about ten minutes after we pass the airport.'

When she mentioned the airport, I felt a prickle down
my spine. The kind you get when someone walks over your
grave.

We drove on and when I saw the sign for the turn-
off to the airport I carefully lowered a lid on my senses.
I didn't want everyone to know what I was doing but
felt compelled to investigate, so I tried to ensure I didn't

release my power's mist.

'Violet?' Rudyard began, conversationally.

'Yes,' I said, trying to appear relaxed while also holding my concentration.

'Have I explained my power to you?'

'No, not really.' I couldn't feel anything yet.

'Well, now seems an appropriate time. I'm what you might call a spotter. I can tell the size of someone's strengths, can gauge their power levels and their potential. I can also see power in exiles, can tell what they can do to an extent.'

'Cool.'

'Yes. I am very cool. You know what else I can do?' he pressed.

I was starting to feel something very faint and pushed my senses out a little further.

'No. What?' I asked, distracted.

'I can tell when someone is using their power.'

I stopped breathing.

My senses closed down like a book being snapped shut. I'd been caught red-handed – now I needed a strategy.

I coughed. Delay tactics 101.

'Really?' I replied, my pitch telltale high. I coughed again. 'That's handy. Could you by any chance tell that I was just using *my* senses?'

'As a matter of fact, yes,' he said, smugly. He knew we were now playing a game. I had an awful feeling he was well practised.

'Oh, well that's good. I...umm...was just practising. You know, I don't get out of the city often and whenever I try and use my senses there I always pick up a lot of different stuff.

I thought being out in the country was a good opportunity to see if...'

This was not going well.

I didn't really know why I couldn't just tell them that I thought I sensed something at the airport the other day.

Because I should have checked at the time – but I forgot about it and they'll think I'm a loser if I tell them now. It's probably nothing, anyway.

'And?' Rudyard prompted.

'And,' I swallowed. 'Nothing. I can't sense anything.'

'Right. Well, perhaps you can practise when we get a little closer to where we are going,' he said.

Griffin turned from his driver's position, looked at me and raised a purposeful brow. The we'll-be-talking-about-this-later look. *Excellent.*

Never lie around a truth detector. I was at least grateful that he didn't out me in front of everyone.

We drove past the farmhouse Magda had described. It was small and decrepit. Massive piles of scrap metal, broken glass and general junk littered the front paddocks. Around the property there were no other signs of civilisation. It was a perfect hideout, no one would come here freely and no one lived nearby to notice anything. We could all sense the presence of exiles.

Trying to remain inconspicuous and to buy reconnaissance time, Griffin parked down a dirt track not much further down the road. Before we got out of the car Rudyard suggested I try out my senses. I knew it was a bit of a taunt, but I actually thought it was a good idea.

Much to Nyla and Rudyard's amazement, I was able to narrow it down to three, possibly four, exiles inside the rotted house with one other exile walking the perimeter. We carefully trekked through the bushes and dense shrubbery that surrounded the building. When we reached a mountain of scrap metal, we crouched.

'I'll go take care of the perimeter guard,' Nyla said, sounding a lot more formidable than usual. I half expected Rudyard to argue but he just nodded. 'I'll try and disable him so we still have an element of surprise for the others but if I have to return him, they'll be able to sense me, so be ready.' She took off.

I watched Rudyard for a moment, to see if he was worried. He didn't look it. Instead, he turned to me, taking in my confused state.

'She is a woman, yes, but mostly she's a fierce warrior, Violet. Much greater than I have ever been or will ever be. She has taken down more than double the number of exiles I have in our many years together. And anyway,' he paused, just briefly but enough for me to notice, 'it will do her no favours if I throw myself in the line of fire just to be noble. Our relationship has gone beyond that.' His eyes bore into me as if he were giving me some kind of warning.

All I could think was – *They're perfect*.

We waited for a few minutes, all increasingly anxious. There was a flickering light visible through one of the blackened windows. Possibly a fire or a lamp. Then we saw what could only be described as a showering of colour – like glitter gently illuminating the trees.

'She returned him,' Griffin said, now on red alert.

'She mustn't have had a choice,' Rudyard said, defending Nyla – something I was positive he would do to the end – even though Griffin wasn't questioning her.

Nyla was back in seconds. She crouched down beside me as the front door to the shack opened or kind of fell open. Out came three exiles, but despite the weak light coming from the house, we couldn't see them properly.

'No point hiding, they know we're here,' Nyla said, standing up, completely unafraid. Griffin stood with her as Rudyard and I followed suit a little more hesitantly.

Here we go.

We walked out to the small clearing in front of the rickety porch, avoiding the worst of the broken glass that was scattered in front of the house, a vicious do-not-pass security system.

As we got closer the faces of the exiles became clearer. I gasped before I could stop myself.

'Are you OK?' Rudyard asked.

'I've seen one of them before, at Hades last night,' I said, locking my sights on the ginger-haired exile who had been so casually lounging on the sofa there.

'You were in *hell* last night?' Rudyard asked quietly beside me.

'Yeah, it's a bar. He was there.'

Rudyard nodded, but then tapped Nyla and Griffin on their shoulders.

'Two of them are fear-users – the two on the right. Be careful. The other is no problem.' Then he turned to me. 'You need to put up your defences. They'll try and put your worst fear before your eyes; you have to defend yourself from this. *Now!*'

I nodded and concentrated on putting up my walls, on trying to protect myself and my power. As I did, I could feel the probing start. It was like when Rudyard had looked into my power at the airport, but different. Violent. I had felt this kind of invasion before, from Joel and Onyx. I knew it would take a lot to keep them out. Right now I couldn't face a movie montage of my worst fears. I was already freaked out by the thought of discovering which one would make it to the top of my list.

Griffin took a final step forward. 'We want information. We can get it from you willingly or we can take it from you!'

The exiles didn't respond. I was realising it wasn't that they did not care about their existence, but rather the opposite. They were extreme narcissists. They truly believed in their supremacy and that they could not be beaten. Up until the second after a dagger went through them and it was all too late.

The one to the left – the one I recognised – moved out, towards Nyla. It was tactical, trying to disable her first, thinking she was the smallest, and therefore – the weakest.

Big mistake.

Nyla stepped back, as if she were cautious and brought him in as close as she could to where she stood, then, with freakish speed, she spun and jumped. On the way down, her dagger went straight into the exile's upper thigh. It didn't kill him. But instinct told me that if she'd wanted to she could have. Easily.

The exile dropped to the ground, grabbing his thigh as Nyla simply reached down and ripped the dagger from his leg while he screamed.

'Move again and it goes in your heart.'

The other two exiles, who must have been shocked to see her annihilate their buddy so quickly, barely blinked.

Instead I felt them pushing again at my power. It was like they were turning all the doorknobs and rattling all the windows, looking for a way in.

Griffin kept talking to them, demanding information. They kept refusing, intent on watching me. I was the target – the only one they were trying to infiltrate.

I caught glimpses of images. I rejected the intrusions, tried hard to stay focused, keep the walls up, but I still saw the broken snapshots, pictures sliding past my eyes in a fast-motion blur. But they were definitely there.

First I saw *him*. The one that always seemed to feature at these moments. Even now – with all I have faced, feared, conquered – he still haunts me, accessing that place in the pit of my stomach, which can send terror flooding through my body. The teacher who attacked me, threw me on a wooden desk and ripped at my clothes while pushing his hard calloused fingers into my arms as he forced me down.

I hated that this – that *he* – was somehow a part of my internal structure now, something I could not tear from my being or my history. I saw his face flash by – just a glimpse. But a glimpse was enough.

My hands went to the side of my head as I tried to physically hold myself together. But then…the vision settled on one scene.

It wasn't *him* I was seeing as much as *me*.

Oh no.

I knew where this was going.

I was back in the desert, reliving the moment when I had put his face to the silhouette my dark angel had told me I must kill. I watched now, as the events once again unfolded, separate to me somehow, in another place.

I could see myself crying, begging not to be there. I held the dagger in my hand and pulled it back, ready to make my strike and then watched as the figure morphed into a new shape – me – just as I drove the dagger up into the heart.

There were three of me: the *now me*, watching this vision; the *killer me*, holding the dagger; and the *dead me*, dropping to the ground in a pool of blood, lifeless and... gone.

I vaguely felt something burning in my legs but I couldn't concentrate. I needed to not be here – to not see this. I couldn't go through it again. I drew within and worked furiously, trying to put up my defences. It started to work and then, all of a sudden, as my barriers sprung up, shutting down the images of my past self and the desert, something smashed me across the face.

I opened my eyes, and I was once again in the clearing outside the little farmhouse. I was kneeling on rocks, jagged metal scraps and shattered glass, in the midst of a pool of blood. Nyla was standing above me, a scary combat-ready look on her face. Griffin was crouched at my side, looking more concerned.

He stood and put a hand out. 'You OK?'

'Yeah,' I said, tasting blood in my mouth. I must have bitten down on my tongue at some point. 'They...they were both – I'm sorry, I just wasn't ready,' I said, embarrassed that I had not been able to stop them.

'They were strong, Violet. Very strong – two of them together would have been nearly impossible for any of us to hold back. They weren't going after us – just you,' Rudyard said, as Griffin pulled me up.

'What happened?' I asked, looking around. The two fear exiles were gone.

'Returned. We had no option – fear can kill,' Griffin said.

Oh.

'What about the other one?' I asked, looking over to where Nyla now towered over the less powerful exile.

'That's why I slapped you – sorry. I need your help with this one,' Griffin said, leading me over to where Nyla had repositioned herself to tower over the less-powerful exile.

She gave me a nod. 'All right?' She sounded so different from normal, in complete battle mode.

If it doesn't need to be said right now – don't say it.

'Yep.'

Griffin crouched down beside the exile whose leg was now healed. 'Can you see her?' he asked him, pointing up to me. 'Can you feel her power?'

The exile looked at me and then down to the ground.

'Have you heard about what she can do?' Griffin continued, taunting. 'I bet you have. She can strip you – make you only human; rotting, rancid flesh with no power – no matter what your choice.'

My mouth dropped open as I listened to Griffin verbally torture this exile, but Nyla gave me a look that stopped me interrupting. I knew she was right but still – *Christ.*

'Where is the Grigori Scripture? We know you know. Tell me now or I'll tell her,' he looked up at me again, 'to go ahead and get a little retribution. Get me?'

The exile didn't lift his head, but nodded.

Mother of God.

'Where?' Griffin pressed.

'I can't tell you a specific location – just…how to find it, that's all. But you have to let me go,' the exile said.

'Tell us what you know – everything you know – and I will let you go for tonight,' Griffin said and as he did I could feel him inject truth into his words so the exile would feel assured, but also so that he understood he had to tell us all that he knew.

'OK,' the exile said, standing up.

We all moved back a step, keeping the right striking distance.

'The Scriptures are where all the Rules were first placed,' he said, a small smile creeping into his sour expression.

'What?' I responded, starting to realise what it was that kept making me feel uneasy.

'Where all the Rules went. In the beginning. The Rules – for the three that existed on earth, welcome or not – there were rules and other…instructions, as needed. Find the place of the Rules, find the lost Scriptures.'

I moved forward. Griffin put a hand out to stop me, but I pushed it away. I was closer to the exile than was wise, but I figured he had been sufficiently petrified about what I could do to him and so wouldn't be overly stupid now.

'I'm going to ask you one more question. Griffin over there is going to know if you tell the truth. If you do, you can go. If you don't…'

The exile's eyes darted between us all. I didn't need to turn around to know the threatening looks he would be getting right now – they had my back.

'What?' he growled.

I spoke slowly. I knew what I was about to say was

potentially major. I needed to keep my voice steady even though the very idea of what I might be suggesting was horrific. 'You said there were rules for the three who existed. You said *Scriptures* not Scripture. What else is with the Grigori Scripture?'

His smile broadened. 'He's been waiting for you to figure that out.'

'Who?' I snapped.

'You said one question – which one?'

I swallowed hard. 'The first.'

'Humans found their rules, close to three and a half thousand years ago. The others, one for the Grigori and one for the Exiled, remain in their original place of belonging,' he sighed, 'though not for much longer.' He bowed his head at me, then looked at Griffin.

'That's all he knows, Violet,' Griffin confirmed.

'I'll be on my way then,' he said as he took off running, super-fast. We all just watched, a little dumbstruck.

'God help us,' Griffin spoke quietly. 'We need to find those Scriptures before they do. Now, more than ever.'

'Let's start by getting Violet cleaned up,' Nyla said, putting an arm around me as we started the walk back to where we had left the car.

I hadn't taken much notice until that point, but the cuts on my legs were deep and my knees were starting to swell.

The drive back was quiet. There was a lot to talk about, but right now I couldn't do it and I knew everyone else respected that.

I gave Steph a call to let her know I was on my way home.

'No worries,' she said. 'We caught up with Spence

and Zoe and after the rant ended they filled us in. I came back to your place just in case your dad called. He hasn't yet, but if he does, I'll just say you're in the shower or something.'

'Thanks. Be back there in about half an hour,' I said.

'Are you OK? You sound wasted,' Steph said, concern growing in her tone.

'Yeah. Just exhausted. I'll fill you in when I get home.'

After I hung up, Griffin turned to me. 'Don't you want to go back to Lincoln's? Get those legs healed?'

'Oh…' I looked at my knees. The bleeding had mostly stopped. They'd hurt like hell tomorrow, but it would be the weekend and I just couldn't cope with any more tonight. 'No. It's just a few scratches. They'll heal on their own.'

'If you say so,' he said, not buying it, but not pressing.

As we neared my street, Nyla inched a little closer and spoke quietly. 'Violet, do you want to talk about it?'

I knew what she was asking but even acknowledging the fear the exiles had reawakened was more than I could handle.

'No,' I said, working hard to remain focused on nothing. I'd taken enough visits down memory lane today.

'OK,' she said, realising I wasn't a share–share kind of girl but giving my hand a pat anyway.

Just one more block and then I'm out!

Getting into my building took a while since I had to loiter outside, waiting for the security guy to go for a wander down the halls, so I could slip in unnoticed.

When I finally made it inside my apartment, I closed the door and locked the deadbolt, just like any other day.

I held myself together and opened the door to my bedroom. There, sound asleep in my bed, lay Steph.

I whispered, 'Steph!' checking she was asleep, hoping she wouldn't wake up.

She didn't.

I moved on autopilot back out to the living room, turned on the TV softly to mask what was coming, walked into the kitchen, leaned back against the counter and slid down to the floor, matching the speed of the tears that poured from my eyes. I tucked my knees, sore and swollen, close to my chest and wrapped my arms around them.

For too many hours, I cried silently and screamed inside.

CHAPTER FIFTEEN

*'The terrible thing about the quest for truth is
that you find it.'*
Remy de Gourmont

I woke in the morning, stiff, tender and swollen, curled up in the corner of the couch, to a serious glare from Steph.

'I left you for as long as I could, but Vi – you need a shower,' she handed me a coffee, 'and this.'

I took the mug gratefully. The situation must have been bad for Steph to have tackled the coffee machine. I sat up and took a sip.

'Rough night. What time is it?' I didn't know how much sleep I'd had. The only way I knew there had actually *been* a period of real sleep was the dream.

It had been vivid, almost real. When I'd first opened my eyes I could still almost reach out and touch it, almost bring it back to me, but with every waking moment it drifted further away. I couldn't remember the dream at all now, not one detail, other than that I was sure I needed to and that I had an odd feeling of…loss.

'Ten. I would've left you to sleep but we're supposed to be taking that stuff to Onyx and I figured we should get that done before you're due at class.'

I gave a tired sigh, remembering that I'd agreed to do classes with Nyla and Rudyard on the weekends from midday.

'What happened, anyway?' Steph asked, taking in the state of my still dirty and bloodied legs.

'I fell over.'

She half laughed. 'Am I supposed to believe that?'

'It's true. I was being tormented by two exiles who specialise in the fear department when it happened, but I *did* fall.'

'Bad?' Steph added, unsure how much to ask.

I stood up and quickly grabbed the edge of the couch for support as I handed her the mug with my other hand. 'Bad. I'll go have that shower.'

When I came back into the living room, Steph had tidied up a bit. I didn't say anything, didn't thank her. I knew she wouldn't want that. Instead, I found myself standing at the door to the balcony in the softest, baggiest sweats I could dig up. The ones I usually save for veg-out days. I parted the curtains and slid the door open. *Unlocked. Again.*

I let a morning breeze filter in through the open door and closed my eyes, letting the breeze glide over my face lifting loose strands of hair. I soaked in the promise of a new day and let it deceive me for a selfish moment, before

I closed the door and accepted that it was unlikely today would be any different.

We took a taxi to Hades. I had insisted on walking, even though my legs were hurting more than I would admit. After the first block Steph had made a ridiculous huffing noise and hailed a taxi.

During the day, Hades is pretty low-key. A much older clientele in the restaurant having business lunches. Dapper must have been a good businessman to be able to attract such a range of customers. Surprisingly, it also didn't look too seedy, the way lots of night-time hang-outs do during the day when the lights are up. The scarlet velvet curtains were pulled back, which helped to brighten the place and give a golden glow to the chandeliers that twinkled in the light. Combined with the whitest of white table cloths and crisp shirts of the waiters, the overall effect was very fresh.

Steph and I looked around for Dapper and were directed to the cellar. We went through the staff-only door and down the stairs.

'Get out!' Dapper called as we approached.

'OK,' I said, suddenly nervous we had done the wrong thing. We quickly turned and started heading back up. 'Hang on, hang on. That you, Violet?' Dapper asked, sounding closer.

I stopped halfway up the stairs, my legs on fire, and called back. 'Yes. Sorry, the bar guy told us we could come down.'

'Yeah, yeah, come back. I thought you were Onyx. He's

always trying to slip down here and pilfer stock.'

'Sounds like something he'd do,' Steph said to me, making her way back down the stairs. I didn't follow.

'What are you two doing here, anyway?' Dapper asked, as he opened a case of wine and started loading the bottles onto the floor-to-ceiling racks.

'We have Onyx's shirts and shaver,' I said, still annoyed that I had to pay him for his information.

'Well, you won't find him down here. Check upstairs.'

'Actually…' I started.

Dapper put down the bottle in his hand and took a good look at me. 'Let me guess, you want me to play delivery boy?'

'Come on, Dapper. Look at her. She barely got down these stairs, are you really going to send her on a search mission?' Steph asked, sticking up for me as always.

Dapper glanced down at my legs as if he could see the injuries, despite my loose sweats. 'You find more trouble, did you?'

'A bit.'

'Where's your knight in shining armour?'

'Huh?'

Dapper shook his head at me. 'Lincoln? Your fella who can "*hocus-pocus*" you – fix you all good as new.'

'Oh.' *Thanks for the reminder.* 'I don't know. Look, are you going to take this stuff or not?' I asked, fed up with constantly having to explain myself to everyone.

Dapper put a hand out. 'Give it here.'

Steph handed over the shopping bag.

I was already on my way back up the stairs by that time. I just didn't have the energy today. She caught up with me and called out a thank you to Dapper. She didn't say anything. She knew I couldn't talk it out right now.

Everyone was at Lincoln's by the time we arrived. A feeling of disappointment overwhelmed me. It was great having everyone around and I had never had so many friends, but at the same time, I wasn't used to such a constant invasion. It felt like everywhere I turned, someone else was there. I barely had any time on my own any more. It was all too much.

I went through the motions, involving myself in conversations when necessary. Mostly, the talk revolved around the night before, recapping the story or asking questions. Luckily for me, it seemed no one had gone into the role I had played in too much depth.

I was aware of Lincoln sitting at the dining table with Magda close beside him. At one point I'd made a hesitant move towards him, but he'd seen me coming and turned away so I, pathetically, kept on walking past them to the coffee machine. Spence was rummaging through the fridge, clearly unhappy with its contents.

'Any milk?' I asked, grabbing a mug.

'Milk, yes. Snacks, no,' he said, emerging with the milk and nothing else. He passed the carton to me and must have noticed the tears welling in my eyes.

'Hey, you OK?' he put a hand on my shoulder, but something caught his attention and he dropped it again. 'Oh man, I'm gonna…' He jabbed his thumb over his shoulder and walked away.

I turned around to see Lincoln, arms crossed as he watched Spence move to the sofa. He didn't even look at me.

I took up a spot on my own near my wall, wishing I could slip behind the drop-sheet and disappear. Every time I looked over to Lincoln, Magda was whispering something in his ear, then breaking into sly grins I was sure were meant only for me. She was so smug, sitting there, looking perfect in white jeans and a caramel-coloured sweater. Her clothes were always immaculate and she wore the kind of labels rivalled only by Steph. She was absent-mindedly playing with the sapphire necklace she had been wearing ever since she got back from holidays, apparently some rare and valuable gemstone from Kashmir according to Steph, who'd made a point of knowing these things.

Everyone chatted away as we waited for Griffin to arrive, the last person due. I talked to Nyla for a while but had the feeling she was formulating too many opinions of me so I moved away when I could. My legs were throbbing badly and I felt blood seeping through my pants. I hoped the fabric wasn't sticking to the wounds as the blood dried.

When Griffin finally arrived, he greeted Nyla and Rudyard and then headed straight over to where Magda and Lincoln were huddled. Magda stood, gave him a brief embrace and talked quietly with him. I inched closer but couldn't hear much, other than that she was leaving and it was something she couldn't get out of – though she hadn't seemed keen to go anywhere just a minute ago. She was brusque with Griffin and within moments landed a quick – and annoying – kiss on Lincoln's cheek before she basically flew out the door. I was guessing her abrupt departure was the reason she didn't have the chance to say goodbye to me. *Yeah right.*

'Is everyone here then?' Griffin called out, returning his attention to the room.

We all nodded. He was about to convene a meeting. With the information we gathered last night it was now more important than ever to find those Scriptures. I knew they would have been working on strategies all morning. He was about to lay it out for us – what was going to happen, how it was going to happen. The problem was Griffin didn't have all the info.

'Right, come and sit down,' he went on, readying to start the spiel of a leader. I was glad we had him. The burden he must carry was huge. I was exhausted from just a week of having to deal with these people, I couldn't imagine how difficult it would be for him at times.

Everyone dutifully moved in around the couches, squeezing together. Steph looked cosy tucked in with Salvatore. I smiled at her, noticing as I did that she was looking back at me with a worried expression. Lincoln moved closer too but kept a slight distance from everyone else, remaining at the end of the kitchen bench. It could have just been because there was no room left on the sofas, but I was certain it was more than that.

More to do with staying away from me!

Griffin made himself comfortable in the main armchair and since there was no room left for me I just sat on the floor, which suited me anyway. My legs were on fire and at least there, laying them out straight didn't draw any extra attention.

'OK, I know you were all planning on training today,

177

but instead – we need to work out how we are going to deal with the new information we have,' Griffin began.

Showtime.

I half raised my hand. 'Actually, before you do that, I need to tell you something,' I confessed, taking a deep breath.

'What do you mean, Violet?' Griffin asked.

'I mean. There's more. I...I know who's after the Scriptures.'

I saw Lincoln take a tiny step towards me and then move back to his place as if he wasn't sure what to do – or what he *wanted* to do.

I bit down on my lip. *Stay strong.*

'Phoenix is back.'

'What?!' Lincoln snapped. His eyes narrowed and zeroed in on me.

I knew it was big news, but it still shocked me to see him look at me like that.

'He was at Hades the other night. When we got there,' I shook my head, angry that I had allowed this much to happen, 'I could sense an exile and I checked him out but he wasn't causing any trouble and Dapper reminded me that we'd promised not to fight in his place. The exile from the farmhouse last night – the one who got away – was also at Hades, working for Phoenix.'

'Are you sure? How do you know?' Griffin asked, urgently.

'He used his abilities on me...and Spence.' I looked down. 'He...'

'He made you kiss Spence,' Lincoln answered for me. I looked up and could see the anger drain away as understanding dawned on his face. 'Violet, Phoenix did that?'

'Did you really think I'd just throw myself at her so easily?' Spence jumped in, feigning offence, trying to lighten a moment that couldn't be.

Zoe punched him in the arm.

Lincoln's gaze didn't shift. His green eyes glistened as he continued to stare at me from the other side of the room. I could see the agony in them. And the fear. But now was not the time.

I've got more to tell.

'He wanted to show me that even though our emotional bond was broken, he was still strong enough to influence me and other Grigori. He was giving a display of how powerful he really is. When I confronted him, he showed me something else as well.'

'You spoke to him?' Lincoln asked, now taking that tentative step in my direction.

I braced myself to say it. 'He still has some kind of hold over me.'

'Do you want me to explain?' Spence offered, sensing the tension in the room.

Lincoln shot Spence a look from beneath a furrowed brow. Spence actually seemed to shrink in size.

'No. Even *you* don't know everything,' I replied, keeping my focus on Griffin. It was easier that way. 'When Phoenix healed me, he bonded our life forces. The other night, he... he took the healing away. It was as if Onyx had just stabbed me again.'

'He reproduced old wounds?' Nyla asked.

Lincoln didn't say anything and when I chanced

a quick glance, I couldn't work out if he looked more livid or petrified.

'This is very serious, Violet.'

'I don't need you to tell me that, Griffin,' I snapped.

Griffin nodded. 'You're right. But Phoenix has capabilities we are not fully aware of yet.' He turned to everyone else. 'For the benefit of those who do not know, Phoenix is something of an anomaly. He is the son of an ancient dark exile, Lilith, and also...' he looked down, worried, 'he is the son of man.'

'Doesn't that make him like a Nephlim?' Zoe asked. Nephlim were the result of exile and human breeding. Often they just produced a normal human and sometimes something more, but not as powerful as an exile and generally not as destructive. They weren't common and not usually viewed as a major threat.

Griffin rubbed his eyes. 'No. Phoenix was conceived prior to original sin, before mortality. When he was made, man was of similar power to angel. He was acknowledged by angels as one of their own and existed in their realm before he was cast out. So Phoenix can blend like a human, can almost completely shut off the senses and has a very capable handle on his ability to influence and control emotion.' Griffin looked at me sternly. 'You should've told me the moment he resurfaced.'

I nodded and hated that I'd let him down.

'It was pretty bad. Blood everywhere. I can confidently say we all thought she was going to... You know... Right there on the floor,' Zoe confirmed. She sounded so blasé but she couldn't hide the heavy gulp that followed. Nyla gave her a look that stopped any further contribution.

'When he left, I healed…but…Phoenix is tied to me, physically. If we return him…' I sucked in another breath, struggling to deliver the finale. 'If his physical form dies…'

'It will kill you, too,' Lincoln said, the blankest expression on his pale face.

'Yes.'

The room was soundless. Everyone had a question, something to say – but no one dared. All eyes darted between Lincoln and me. They could feel the energy leaping between the two of us.

Finally, I said, 'I think I know where he is – where they all are.'

'Where?' Griffin and Nyla asked simultaneously.

'The airport.' I shifted my leg and a shooting pain flew up my thigh. I tried to hide the gasp and wondered if there was some glass left in the wound. 'Don't ask me how, I just know.'

'Was that what you were trying to sense last night?' Rudyard asked.

'And why you then lied about it,' Griffin concluded, less impressed.

I just nodded to both. 'Kind of. I sensed something at the airport the other day that I can't explain – I just knew it wasn't right. Then when we arrived at the farmhouse I recognised the exile that we later…questioned.' I tried and failed not to gulp at the memory. 'He was at Hades the other night, just before Phoenix. He must've told Phoenix I was there. Anyway, after seeing him at the farmhouse I knew it was too convenient that they were so close to the airport. Phoenix must've had them hiding out there. I think that was also why they targeted me.'

'What do you mean "targeted" you?' Lincoln asked, increasingly upset by his lack of knowledge.

I felt a bit defensive and was about to say something when Griffin jumped in.

'I tried to call you last night to explain, Linc, but you didn't answer.' Griffin didn't wait for his response and instead turned back to me, absorbing everything I was telling them. 'It makes sense, since you're someone he's fixated on. He would have told them to try and play on your fears. Violet – do we need to know what they showed you? Is this all somehow tied into a fear you have?'

I thought about the question. Though it made me want to curl into a ball, it was fair enough. Everything else seemed to be connected.

But how could they know my innermost fear when even I didn't fully until the moment it was revealed?

'No. It was just a game, it wasn't about the actual fear,' I said, confident I was right.

'Get out!' Lincoln said loudly – bordering on crazy – startling the whole room. He ran his hands through his hair, angrily, as everyone looked at him, frozen.

'Leave!' He marched up to the door and aggressively pulled it open. 'This is my home, I'm happy to have you all here, using it for your needs, but right now… Get out!'

Griffin and I, who knew Lincoln the best, stood. Griffin motioned for everyone else to do the same. One by one, people removed themselves from their seats and made for the door. Griffin paused when he passed Lincoln.

'Take the time you need, Linc. But we need to strategise. We need you on board. We'll continue this meeting at six tonight at Hades. Come and join us when you're ready.'

I started walking towards the door after Griffin left.

'Not you!' Lincoln snapped and when I flinched he quickly apologised. 'Sorry. I'm sorry,' he said, softening his tone, his hand wavering mid-air as if he wanted to reach out to me. 'I didn't mean to… We need to talk.'

I nodded. I was way too tired to argue, so I collapsed onto the sofa and put my aching legs up to rest. If he wanted to yell at me, I was at least going to be comfortable.

Lincoln closed the door after I'd given Steph a reassuring nod and went straight to the kitchen. I didn't bother getting up.

He returned a few minutes later with a bowl of water and some cloths, which he placed on the ground, and handed me a glass of water.

'Thanks,' I said, unsure what else to say.

I sat up a little and as I did he slipped a couple of pillows under my head to hold me up.

'Where are you hurt?' He stared at my legs, not looking at my face. I thought I'd done a good job of covering up the pain. Until that point, I didn't think he'd noticed.

My hands hovered over my knees. Lincoln started from the bottom of my baggy sweats, gently rolling them up.

'Is this OK?' he checked, still not looking at my face.

'Yeah.'

As he got to the area around my left knee, I tried to hide the intake of breath that meant pain. He slowed down, gently holding out the fabric, moving it up and over the joint, only stopping when he was halfway up my thigh, well clear of the injuries.

'The other one?' he asked, looking at my other leg.

I gave another small nod. He let out a heavy breath

through his nose and proceeded to do the same thing, moving the leg of my pants up tenderly until the entire wound was uncovered. When his hand reached the top of my thigh, his fingers grazed the skin and my stomach lurched.

Is it wrong that I can let him still have that effect on me in any situation? Probably.

'Why didn't you come to me?' he asked.

'It was late and I was too tired, Linc.'

'Too tired to deal with me? Is that why you didn't tell me about Phoenix?'

'I would have told you if I'd seen you. I tried to yesterday, but you were out with Magda again. You're never around any more,' I said, trying to hold back the tears.

'Just relax while I fix these,' he said, as he concentrated on drawing on his healing power. I noticed he didn't suggest we try doing it together.

No surprise, I suppose. But it still hurt.

I closed my eyes and leaned back into the soft pillows. I was sure, given half the chance, I'd just fall asleep.

Lincoln's power worked its way through me, seeking out the problem and finding it in my legs. His warm hands were at once strong and gentle as he moved them slowly from my ankle, up my leg before stopping beneath my knees. Everything in me tingled, and it wasn't because of our powers.

I felt the swelling subside and the wounds close over. I sighed with the almost-instant relief, like somehow his healing had submerged my body in a bath of warm creamy honey and I wanted to sink deeper and deeper.

Finished with its work on my legs, Lincoln's power

seemed to assess me again, looking for more injuries to fix. I felt it work its way up through my body and wrap around my heart before melting away.

Could it sense the pain in my heart? Could he?

With my eyes still closed, I felt Lincoln's warm hands leave my legs and a moment later his fingertips brushed the hair off my forehead and slid down my cheek. They were trembling until they cupped the side of my face. I didn't want to open my eyes. I wanted to stay like that forever, feeling the way his hand pressed against my face just enough that somehow, in that one touch, he told me more than he would ever say aloud.

But I had to open my eyes. Had to see him. He was so close I think my heart skipped a few beats.

'Better?' he asked. His green eyes seemed to glow as they took me in and I wondered if it were me sinking into his eyes or him sinking into mine. Either way, it felt a terrible torment to pull my gaze away from him.

I cleared my throat. 'Yeah. Thanks.'

He moved back a little and I resisted the urge to reach out to him, instead looking down at my knees. The wounds were still there but they looked like they were weeks old now. It hadn't been a terrible injury overall – he had almost healed me completely.

'I haven't been there for you. I should have known you wouldn't have…'

He reached down to the bowl beside his knees and dunked a cloth, wringing it out, before running it softly over my legs, cleaning away the blood. The water was perfectly warm.

'When I saw you on that dance floor with Spence it

just looked so…' He shook his head. 'I couldn't go through watching someone else… Not again.'

I didn't know what to say. All I could think was that Onyx had been right. I was never going to be able to fix the damage I had caused to Lincoln by spending that time with Phoenix.

'You know – I'm feeling much better,' I said awkwardly, standing up. 'Since it's just you and me here now, how about some training?' I mustered a small smile. 'Believe it or not, with all the extra help, I feel like I get less done these days,' I carried on, desperate to do anything other than have this talk.

Lincoln, seeing my point or maybe feeling the same way, looked hopeful. 'Are you sure you're up to it?'

I nodded, jumping up and down a couple of times, testing my legs. 'Yep, all good.'

'OK then.'

We moved into the big open space and after turning on some music, Zoe's sparring mix, we didn't waste time getting into it. I was surprised to realise I had managed to pick up a few things, mostly from watching Spence in action, and I enjoyed trying out a few moves that Lincoln hadn't taught me. I actually caught him by surprise a couple of times.

'New tricks,' he said.

But like all good competitors, he didn't just take it. He came back at me, reminding me how strong he really is, how fast and capable in any fight.

'You need to move higher with that kick, take it from your hip,' he instructed me on the move.

I nodded and tried the same move, this time better.

He gave a small nod of approval and we kept going, both of us in our element. Fighting and training – we did that well. I revelled in the simplicity of it.

Lincoln moved like Nyla, tactically superb. In the years to come he would become such a master warrior, it would be near impossible for any lone exile to challenge him. I was glad of that. Glad for him… Sad for me.

At that, other thoughts started breaking through my barriers. How could I ever expect him to explore the possibility that we could be together? If I was the cause of weakening his power, taking away his strength, how would he defend himself so easily? How could he ever forgive me for taking that chance?

While I wallowed, Lincoln set me up and took me down easily. He put his hand out.

'Come on, Vi. If you want to train, train properly. You're fighting like you did with Spence the other day. What's the problem?'

The way he said it… No, the way he *looked* at me when he said it, as if I was pathetic, as if my efforts were derisory.

When he pulled me up I used the hold I had on his hand and drew him closer as I crouched down and swung a foot out and round, taking his legs from under him. He fell flat on his back as I slapped a hand to my mouth. It had caused more impact than I'd planned.

'Point taken,' Lincoln said, smiling as he put a hand out for me to help him up.

I grabbed it and he pulled me back down to the ground with him. It knocked the wind out of me and I had to suck in a few deep breaths. I wasn't the only one with ragged breathing.

'One good turn deserves another,' he said, his eyes looking at me the way they shouldn't. The way I wanted them to, always. But lying half on top of him, instead of returning his smile or responding with banter…

'Are you in love with Magda?' I blurted out without thinking.

Lincoln's eyes went wide and then looked away. He was thinking fast. I rolled away from him.

'That's why you followed…' His head went back in realisation. 'Oh, into a hotel. It must have looked… And I was so mad with you. Violet —' he sat up.

'It's OK,' I said quickly, sitting up, too. 'If you are, I mean. It's not as if I have any claim on you. I can't be…We can't be… So you should be able to… I just need to know.'

'Violet, it's not like that. Magda's been helping me with…something,' he pleaded.

'Well, there's a reason you trust her, want her by your side and not me. I'm not an idiot and I…I heard you two talking in your room when she first came back. You said you didn't want me to know, that it would hurt me. Is she pregnant?'

What is with me and the verbal diarrhoea?

Lincoln was silent for a moment. I couldn't bear to look at him but then I felt him shaking and looked up in time to see him burst into laughter and roll around on the ground.

'Oh. I'm glad you find this all so funny!' I said, totally grumpy now. I made a move to get up, but he rolled back towards me quickly and wrapped an arm around my waist holding me there.

'Wait. Sorry. It's just – it's not like that with Magda.

And if she *is* pregnant, which I doubt very much, it is not by me. That's physically impossible, Vi!' He tried, but couldn't hold back a few last chuckles.

Yeah, yeah, hilarious.

'Hey?' he snapped, sobering. 'Is that why you were off your game in training, why Spence took you down so fast?'

'It wasn't *that* fast,' I said, still sour.

'That just proves my point,' he said as he shuffled away from me.

'What does that mean?'

'Nothing. I just don't want to be a cause of distraction for you.'

It was like he went into some other world when he spoke like that. Quietly. Lately, he was so insular. It wasn't like him.

'Well,' I continued, trying to shake off his cryptic words. 'What *were* you and Magda talking about then?' I was not ready to give in.

Lincoln sat up on the floor, crossing his legs and I did the same. He studied me for a while and finally sighed.

'While she was away, she came across a small group of exiles. Over the course of her holiday she gradually took them out. Anyway, one of them was a telepath so she was also able to probe into some of his thoughts. It turned out he worked for an exile called Nahilius.'

'That's who that jock-exile who killed all the homeless people warned you about. You said he was no concern.' I didn't hide my suspicious tone.

'He won't be, soon.' He dropped his head and when he spoke again his voice was different. 'Nahilius is the exile who went after my mum. Magda made the exile she was hunting tell her where Nahilius was, which was here. When she got back, that's what she was telling me.'

'Well, why couldn't you tell me that?' I asked, not ready to let go of the hurt.

'Because, if cancer hadn't killed my mum, *he* would have. He ruined her, Vi, ruined her last months alive, took everything she'd worked for and I couldn't save her until it was too late. I swore I'd make him pay and I promised myself I'd never let anyone else I love be hurt by him.' He stopped, like he'd already said too much.

'But you let Magda help you?'

'Yes.'

'Because you trust her?' I added through the lump in my throat. Trust was the basis of love. The terrible idea stirred that perhaps he didn't even realise he was in love with her.

He shook his head. 'Yes, but don't make it out to be something it isn't. And anyway...'

He stopped again, mid-sentence.

The silence between the two of us said everything.

And it doesn't matter because we can never be together anyway.

My heart sank and I wanted to bolt, but instead I took a deep breath and tried my best to look at him, even if I couldn't hold his eyes.

'Tell me everything then. What do you know about Nahilius? Do you know where he is?' I asked, hoping that at least we were finally communicating.

Lincoln looked around the room and then back to me and I could actually see it happening – he was locking up... and there was nothing I could do.

'I'm close. That's all you need to know.'

But I had to try.

I moved forward till we were only inches apart. I put a hand on his arm, petrified he'd swat me away. In one touch I tried, the way he seemed to be able to, to say all the things I couldn't bear to say aloud – couldn't bear to hear rejected.

'Linc, don't shut me out. Please. I know you want to stop Nahilius and protect everyone at the same time, but you can let me help.' And then I couldn't stop myself, my hand travelled up to the side of his face and as I held it there I felt the energy between us and the searing heat of desire engulf me.

I was so close I could smell him, that soapy clean smell he always had, mixed in with the light sweat that reminded me I was with a man. Heat radiated from him and I wanted to be wrapped tight within his arms, but sitting there on the ground beside him, I could see he'd already put up the walls.

And in the end, I have to, too.

My eyes cast down and I let my hand slide from his face, but before the last finger broke contact he caught my hand in his, held it there – no, *pressed* it into his cheek. I looked up, our eyes locked and for one brief moment of indulgence before he let go, before my hand dropped to the ground, I was sure.

Sure, beyond all doubt.

He was my 'other'.

CHAPTER SIXTEEN

'The course of true love never did run smooth.'
William Shakespeare

It's not a small thing, knowing that in this world you have a true match. It's hard to keep a level head and avoid hyperventilating when everything inside you is exploding with new truth. Harder still to look at the person, the *soul*, your perfect complement, knowing he can't be yours and you cannot ask him to be. Ever.

Lincoln had disappeared to have a shower and change. I was pretty sure his main motivation was to get away from me. I didn't blame him. Sometimes the air between us felt so thick it was barely breathable.

My wall, the one Lincoln had given me to paint, remained covered by a huge drop-sheet. I'd been working on it off and on. I wasn't much further than a double coat of primer and a huge awkward streak of green that I knew I'd probably have to return to white. Before he'd finally agreed to let me paint the wall, things had been so different. I was human, to start with. I wasn't perfect. But I was just me, baggage and all. Now, everything had changed. I wasn't sure what was left of that person – or who had taken her place.

I stared blankly at the wall and decided I wouldn't touch it again until I was sure of what needed to be there. Until I knew who it was painting the wall.

Lincoln's phone buzzed on the kitchen table.

I walked over and grabbed it as I called out to him.

No answer.

I looked at the screen, alight with a new text message. I hadn't intended to read it, but it was already half visible. And…I could see who it was from.

Have a good lead. City Comm Realty. If we don't strike now, they'll—

The message ended there. To see more I'd have to open it and then Lincoln would know I'd been snooping. Why would Magda be tracking down a real estate company?

The distinctive click of Lincoln's bedroom door startled me into action. I quickly replaced his phone, exactly where it had been before, angling it slightly towards the edge of the table, and darted back to my wall, where I pretended to be readjusting the drop-sheet. I heard him walking down the hall, heard his footsteps slow and stop outside the spare bedroom. The room with all his mother's belongings locked away. He never goes in there but can't bear to part with the sorry possessions that only remind him of what is no longer.

'Hey,' he said, walking into the living area and then behind the breakfast bar. He opened the fridge.

I was still tugging awkwardly on the sheet, scared to look at him.

'You hungry?'

'No. I'm fine. I…I think your phone buzzed.'

I listened as he closed the fridge, went to his phone and pressed a few buttons. I turned to face him in time to see him slide it into his pocket.

He fake-stretched and made a show of checking his watch. 'I didn't realise how late it was. I have to get going,' he said, messing around with things, putting them away – he didn't want to talk with me any more. He grabbed his keys and wallet. He was barely making a show of being discreet, desperate to get out the door. Back to Magda.

It was as if everything that had just happened between us no longer mattered. *We* didn't rate high enough, even though I was sure he'd felt the connection between us, too. Somewhere in those thoughts my frustration built to anger.

Why is it that every time I discover something new about myself, it only makes everything harder?

'What are you doing, Linc?' I asked, the tone of my voice alerting both of us to my temper. I put my hands down on the opposite side of the breakfast bar and stared straight at him. 'Where are you going?'

'It's just a thing I organised earlier.' Lincoln's eyes darted around the room.

'You're avoiding talking to me? I think I deserve to know what's going on.' And it was true.

Lincoln ignored me at first and I thought he was going to snap back at me, but he just dropped his head.

'I made a promise to you, so I'm not going to lie, but I have to go out and I want that to be OK with you.'

'And what if it's not?' I replied, daring him. I couldn't help it, I hated knowing he was choosing Magda over me again.

'I've had to trust you in the past, Violet.'

He used my full name – never good. I looked intently at my feet.

'I could ask you questions that are hard for you to answer,' he pressed, 'but I respect that if you think we should discuss something, you'll tell me.'

He was skirting around something, turning this back on me somehow, and I could feel my anger morphing into panic.

'Well, don't let me hold you back. Say whatever you want. *Ask* whatever you want.'

His eyes snapped up briefly but, as if he couldn't stop them, as if he couldn't hold my gaze, they dropped again. When he spoke it seemed like it came from a faraway place.

'Are you glad Phoenix is back?'

My throat tightened instantly. I could feel a rising blush, which I desperately wanted to smother. I bit down hard on the inside of my lower lip.

'No,' I said in a too-meek voice. 'Of course not,' I added, trying to compensate.

Lincoln jolted and backed away from me a few steps.

'It would be understandable if you were... I mean, you two were...close.'

'He was controlling my emotions,' I said quietly through gritted teeth. Were we really having this conversation? *Now?*

He sighed, 'Yeah, he has all the control. Even now. He can hurt you and it doesn't matter how strong I am,

I can't...' He stopped himself, or maybe it was the break in his voice.

We both stood awkwardly for a moment until he shook his head, gave a kind of tormented half-laugh and scooped up one of the leftover glasses of water only to smash it on the ground.

'He'll always be there! Phoenix is a part of you and I can never change that!' He fisted his hands and I could see he was trying to calm himself down.

I felt myself flinching with fear. Not of him, but for him. My lower lip trembled and I tried to compose myself as I watched him fall apart in a particularly stoic manner.

'This doesn't even sound like you. Can you hear yourself?' I asked.

It was like someone had been feeding him all these new thoughts, in addition to the ones already put there by Onyx. I was betting I knew who, too. Magda worked every situation to her favour.

Lincoln looked at his watch and clicked his jaw to the side.

'I have to go, Vi. This is something I need to take care of and I can't be late to meet with Magda.'

'So you're meeting Magda,' I said as casually as I could.

'You read my phone,' he said, resigned, but I could still see the touch of anger.

'No,' I said, nonchalantly. Actually, pathetically high-pitched. I scrunched up my face, not sure what to do with myself. I was a terrible liar.

He half smiled, returning to himself a bit. 'Yes, I'm meeting Magda.'

I wasn't getting anywhere arguing with him so

I took a calming breath trying to lighten my mood, too. 'Nahilius?'

He nodded, but didn't want to say more. At least he was being honest about it.

'And you only want to go with Magda?'

'It would be best that way,' he said calmly, trying to keep the peace, but I could tell how anxious he was to leave.

I wanted to beg him to stay or at least take me with him. My stomach knotted, fighting with my mind, almost forcing me forward, pushing me towards him. But I didn't move. I wanted him to trust me and confide in me the way he did with Magda.

I'd do anything for you.

Somehow, that very thought reminded me... I couldn't ask *anything* of him. He wasn't mine and I could never expect him to risk losing his strength, his powers as a Grigori, just so that he could be with me. It didn't matter that I'd have done it for him in a heartbeat.

'I thought we were partners,' I said, trying to keep an even tone.

'We are. I just... I can't fight at my best with you at the moment.' Lincoln ran a hand through his hair and looked towards the door again. An escape looked mighty appealing to me too after that comment.

'Right then,' I mumbled, burying my chin in my shoulder.

His expression broke and seemed to soften. 'Please try and understand – it will all be over soon and then you'll be... I know I've been distracted, but once this is over, I'll be better for it – better for you...as your partner.'

I stared down at my feet and then headed over to start

picking up the pieces of glass scattered across the floor. 'OK, Linc. I'll stay out of it.'

'Thank you,' he said, surprised. He walked up to the door and put on his coat. 'Don't worry about that. I'll clean up later.'

'Actually, I . . I don't need to be at Hades for a bit. I'm happy to stay and clean up – if you don't mind?'

His shoulders dropped, relieved I'd made it so easy for him. 'Sure. You know where the spare key is. Just lock up on your way out.' He grabbed a backpack and opened the door.

'Lincoln!' I called. 'What about meeting Griffin and the rest of us at Hades?'

'We'll meet up with you guys there if we can. If not, Magda will get the low-down from Griffin.'

I stared at him in disbelief.

Is he really so obsessed he's going to miss his chance to hunt Phoenix?

He smiled. 'Don't worry. Griffin won't go after them tonight – he'll want to do surveillance first,' he said, as if he'd read my mind.

His eyes fixed on mine for a moment before he closed the door. Beautiful green eyes – yet steely. I had not seen them like that before. All emotion under tight lock and key.

I was desperate to reach him but he was further away than ever.

I watched the front door for a long time after he had closed it behind him. How had things come to this? Lincoln was managing me. We'd had our fair share of arguments, so tension was not something we weren't accustomed to, but this was different. He was just shutting down, locking me out. He was cold and distant, as if everything we had between us, our friendship alone – no longer registered. He was so desperate to get his revenge on Nahilius, nothing else mattered. I was starting to think that he was willing to pay just about any price to get it.

'Well, not me,' I said out loud.

I might have told Lincoln I would stay out of it, but lie-detecting wasn't one of his strengths. For all his imploring me to stand aside, it really came down to one question; if it were me, if the roles were reversed, would Lincoln let *me* go off on some renegade mission if he had a strong feeling I was headed for nothing but trouble and regret?

Not on your life!

And neither would I.

When things were at their worst, when I have needed someone to be there for me – it has always been Lincoln. Until recently, it didn't matter what it was – training, protection, hell…even a balanced diet – *he* had been the person I'd talked to, who'd backed me up. He was everything to me.

I was damned if I was going to sit back and take this shit. The whole thing with Nahilius had given him twisted blood. Since Magda had come back from her holiday, Lincoln had changed – he was losing himself.

I needed caffeine. There was still an hour or so until I was supposed to meet up with the others at Hades. I made a coffee, sat at the breakfast bar and drank it slowly while I re-evaluated everything that had happened over the last week. By the time I started on my third cup, I'd come up with a number of theories and only one thing I knew for sure – I needed help.

Steph arrived a half-hour later.

'Hey,' she said, walking in and seeing that I was alone. She'd changed since the morning and looked great, her hair perfectly styled in the edgy spritzy look she had mastered and she was wearing skinny jeans and a green vintage top. Her best colour. She'd obviously been planning something much more interesting than hanging out with me. I felt guilty, but I couldn't do this without her.

'You look better,' she said, noticing I wasn't limping. 'What's so urgent? Salvatore and I were at the mall. He needs new jeans.'

'Jeans can wait. I need your brains.'

'And you only just realised,' she said, smiling. 'What's up?'

I rolled my eyes and then explained everything that had happened, and how Lincoln had been acting so awfully since he started pursuing Nahilius.

She was surprised to hear that Nahilius had infiltrated his mother's company and I was glad that it stirred her interest, because the more intrigued she was, the more likely it was that my plan was going to work.

'So basically, this all goes back to Nahilius, to what happened to his mother,' I summarised.

'I hear you. Corporate evil. But what is it you want me to do?'

'Linc wants me out of this. He only trusts Magda, for some stupid reason, and I told him I wouldn't get involved, but...'

'You plan on sticking your big nose in anyway?'

'Damn straight,' I said, collapsing into a chair. 'If we can find Nahilius before they do then I can help Linc finish this properly. I'm scared that if he finds Nahilius with Magda... he'll do something he'll regret.'

Steph went to the fridge and helped herself to a Coke. She took her time, considering everything I had told her. After she'd positioned herself across from me at the dining table and taken a sip of her drink, she looked up and squirmed.

'What?' I demanded, automatically defensive.

'No offence or anything, but what's he going to regret? I mean, don't you guys have a 007 licence to kill exiles, anyway?'

'It's not like that, Steph!' I snapped. 'Sorry, it's just... There's a difference between getting into combat with an exile and giving them a choice, and hunting one down solely for vengeance, with only one plan. We're supposed to give them a chance, Steph, and the way Lincoln was talking...'

'Got it. Where do I start?' Steph asked, all jokes halted. The knot in my stomach eased and I exhaled a few tight breaths before I filled her in on what I needed – which mostly involved gluing Steph to a computer and the library for the next couple of days.

'Done. I'll let you know when I find something,' she said, while opening random kitchen cupboards, prying. 'You realise he's too clean for a guy?' she said, pointing to the spice rack.

I half smiled. 'Thanks, Steph, I don't know where I'd be without you.'

'You'd be in need of a manicure and in a great big mess, is where you'd be.'

'If it's any consolation I think Salvatore is going to be pretty busy for a while now, too,' I said.

'I figured. Anyway, being stuck with Zoe for a bit without me as a buffer will be good for him.'

'You mean, good for you.'

She shrugged and gave me her devious grin, which quickly faded to sombre. 'You guys are hunting Phoenix, aren't you?'

'I think that's what Griffin will want. It won't be tonight, though, according to Lincoln.'

'Well, you better get going. Sal was headed straight there when I left him.'

I checked my watch. *Crap*, it was getting late. I ran through the warehouse, turning off the lights.

'Thanks Steph, I owe you big-time,' I said as we left Lincoln's. 'Call me if you find anything.'

'No guarantees – I've never tried to locate otherworldly creatures on the internet before. It might not work.'

'I know, I accepted with a sigh. But I had to try.'

'Be careful out there, OK?' she said, giving me a serious-Steph look.

'I will.'

'Salvatore said he can sense lies around – he just can't see where they're coming from.'

Probably me.

'And can you make sure Zoe isn't too much of a bitch to Salvatore?'

'Really?' I asked, raising one eyebrow at her.

Steph re-evaluated. 'No. Let her be a bitch,' she said,

giving her best conspiratorial wink.

'That's my girl,' I said, glad to see Steph hadn't had a dramatic personality change like Lincoln.

Steph didn't mind if Zoe and Salvatore became closer – she wanted it for him – but deep down, we felt the same way: girls don't need to make any other girls close to their men. *Come on.*

All in all, I was pleased with myself. I was sick of just letting things happen and then dealing with the aftermath. I wanted to be a step ahead for a change and I had a feeling having a semi-genius in my corner was about to be a big help. Plus, there was another upside. With Steph on-board helping out, she was also away from the action and out of the firing line… For now.

During my brisk walk to Hades, my hand kept going to the pocket where I had slipped Lincoln's spare key. For some reason, I knew having it with me was important. Something back at his place had made me stay behind so I could get that key. It didn't make a lot of sense, but thinking about it as I walked I couldn't help but wonder if someone else was interfering.

And then there was the second part to that thought – light or dark?

CHAPTER SEVENTEEN

'The resolution to avoid evil is seldom framed till the evil is so far advanced as to make avoidance impossible.'
Thomas Hardy

The meeting at Hades went pretty much as expected. We all sat around a big table at the back of the restaurant section. Nyla and Rudyard ordered lots of food that none of us – except Spence and Salvatore – wanted, but it kept Dapper's agitation at bay. He wasn't as grumpy as usual. He was definitely softening some, though it was on a knife-edge.

Griffin had brought half a dozen local Grigori along with him. I'd been getting to know everyone gradually over the past month. He had people working in all precincts of the city – mostly they were self-sufficient, weeding out individual exiles and following up on intel and leads that he had filtered. Griffin acted as the central hub. Some Grigori got titbits of information from exiles they returned that could uncover another group. They would pass this intel back to Griffin, who would then allocate the nearest Grigori to the task.

So far, Lincoln and I hadn't been given a territory. Partly because we'd been too busy with chasing up the Scriptures, partly because I think Griffin likes working closely with Lincoln and partly…probably…Griffin didn't trust me on my follow-through yet.

And he was right.

Until I could prove I wasn't a liability – in other words, until I could draw my dagger and use it without compunction – I wasn't ready. Griffin teamed everyone up – pairs with pairs. Nyla and Rudyard headed out with Samuel and Kaitlin. They were going after more intel on the Scriptures. If we could find the location of the mysterious Scriptures, we would find Phoenix. I got the feeling it was messy work from what Griffin said – or didn't. They were going after a small pack of exiles in Samuel and Kaitlin's precinct – a mix of light and dark who they believed were under Phoenix's command.

It was now the consensus that Phoenix had taken over where Joel and Onyx had left off, which meant volatile groups of mixed exiles, light and dark, were now most likely under his charge, thanks to the help of two particularly viscous exiles, Gressil and Olivier. What he'd had to do to win that control was something none of us wanted to brainstorm.

Zoe and Salvatore were sent out with two Grigori I'd never met before – Archer and Beth. But while we were waiting for Griffin to get started they made small talk with me. I tried to nod politely after I told them I was an artist and they responded by telling me about the time they met

Michelangelo. They were in Florence and apparently he'd just been commissioned to start work on a new statue that was later named *David*. *David* was sculpted by Michelangelo at the beginning of the sixteenth century!

Suddenly I was very nervous. I mean, how do you talk to people that have been around for more than *five hundred* years? The weirdest thing, of course, was that they didn't even look close to thirty.

Zoe, unfazed, leapt right into conversation with them. She didn't seem to struggle to find something to talk about and from the looks of Archer and Beth; they were not surprised by anything she said. I guess when you never really age you just learn to move with the times.

Griffin arranged for them to go to the farmhouse and scout around as much as they could without getting within sensing range of the airport, which wouldn't be easy. He didn't want to tip off Phoenix that we knew where he was. Griffin was planning on gathering more reserves before anything like that happened.

He'd heard from Magda and it seemed clear from Griffin's subsequent abruptness that both Magda and Lincoln were MIA for the night. When I came to think of it, Magda had been around even less than Lincoln.

Finally, Spence and I were put on a different kind of recon. Since the airport was currently out-of-bounds, Griffin wanted us to go to an aircraft factory. He was hoping that I might be able to sense something there that might help identify a pattern that could help locate Phoenix. We knew from my reaction at the airport there was a good chance he may be hiding on a plane of some description and I agreed it was worth a shot. Spence, on the other hand, was piqued.

'Great. So while everyone else is off doing real recon, we're going to see if we can *sense* a *plane*. Excellent,' he grumbled.

As far as I was concerned it worked out perfectly. We hadn't been paired up with anyone else and now the only person I had to deal with was Spence, which was manageable for what I had in mind.

When we all started heading out, Griffin gave me a look that told me he knew I was up to something, but he either decided I was entitled to a few secrets or just didn't want to know, because after a few appeasing words to Dapper, he left.

'So, I guess you and I have the night off?' Spence said, still sounding sour as he watched the last of the Grigori filter out the main door of Hades.

'Not exactly,' I said, shooting him a guilty look.

Spence's face lit up and he gave me a toothy grin. 'Never a dull moment with you, Eden. I don't know how I ever survived without you in my life.'

I couldn't hide the look of alarm.

'Don't flatter yourself,' he said, grinning as if he could see right through me. 'It's the fight action I'm interested in right now. I thought we got that straight.'

'Sorry…I just…'

'Don't want to give me the wrong idea. Forget it, Eden – I know where we stand and just so you know, I'm a one-woman kind of guy and I like it the same way in return. As much as I would be in it to win it with you I'm really not interested in getting in line.'

'OK, OK. Let's just drop it,' I said, cringing.

Spence smiled, he won this round, but I still wasn't fully

convinced. I knew from experience – getting caught up in Phoenix's emotional thrall could be incredibly confusing.

'Well,' I mustered a smile, pushing aside my concerns for now, 'if you're looking for all things out of the ordinary – I'm your girl,' I said, not quite as enthusiastic as Spence was that this was now my life.

'Count me in,' Spence said without hesitation.

'Don't you even want to know—?'

'Nope. I'm in.'

'Great,' I said, slapping a hand on his back. Then I pulled out some cash and passed it to Spence. 'You're going to need that glamour of yours – and steer clear of Dapper, he can see right through it.'

'Yeah – crafty bugger, isn't he?'

I nodded. 'Just stay down the other end of the bar. We need bourbon – Onyx's brand.'

His excitement dropped a gear. 'I was kind of hoping more for torture than bribery.'

'You'll have to run and catch up with Nyla for that one. Torturing Onyx isn't going to work.'

And I don't want to have to torture anyone, ever!

Spence obligingly made his way to the bar. I knew he wouldn't have too much trouble when I spotted Dapper busily chatting away with customers on one of the sofas. Sure enough, he returned in a few minutes, two bottles of bourbon in his hands.

He gave me a wink and then waggled his eyebrows. 'You sure you don't want to just hit the town with these?'

'Absolutely sure,' I said, already walking towards the stairs. Something told me Onyx was key to all this.

Onyx's door was ajar. I was surprised to see the studio

was now in relatively good order. Onyx himself looked much cleaner than he had when we first saw him on the street. It didn't inspire the best feeling, unfortunately. Sitting on his sofa, feet on the small glass coffee table and wearing what was no doubt one of the shirts I had paid for and Steph had selected, reminded me of how he used to look – when he was stark-raving mad and, oh yeah, evil as all hell.

'Still alive then?' Onyx remarked as we walked in, barely looking up. He was watching TV.

'Catching up on *Gossip Girl*, huh?' I asked, noticing his viewing selection.

'Yes. Chuck is a very entertaining human. At first I was sure he was an exile, but he lacks follow-through. I imagine the show is somehow inspired or influenced by an exile, though,' he said, totally at ease despite the absurdity of the conversation. His eyes flashed up to me and then across to Spence, who was standing beside me. It was easy to tell the moment he registered the two bottles of bourbon. He picked up the remote and turned off the TV.

'You've brought me a gift.'

'Yes. And when I get the information I came for it's all yours,' I said, crossing my arms and giving off as much 'tough' as I could muster.

Onyx spread his arms wide. 'Well, what do you want to know? I must admit, even I am intrigued to know where your little adventures are headed. Who would have thought you would be so keen for more knowledge since the last I gave you... Well, it wasn't exactly cheery, was it?'

I did my best to ignore him – rewarding Onyx's goading never fared well for me. 'I want to know about an exile called Nahilius?'

'Nahilius. Yes, I know of him. Seedy immortal, used to be a Cherubim of light.' His lip curled. 'Why do you want to know about him? Surely you have bigger fish to fry?' He raised his eyebrows suggestively. He knew I didn't need the reminder that I had an almighty exile after me.

'Funny that, I'd forgotten,' I said, sounding every bit the petulant adolescent I missed being so much. 'It's none of your business why – if you want the bourbon, just tell me.'

Spence nudged me from behind and whispered, 'Maybe we should show him we're serious.'

I spun and stared at him.

'OK, sorry to interrupt,' he said.

I turned back to Onyx. 'So?'

'So, little rainbow, it's very simple. You are terrible at negotiating – I have tortured, maimed, killed for less and enjoyed it. There was a time when it was more effort for me to *not* kill than *to* kill. You are standing in front of me and I have no powers left but I can see that same desperate human need you have – it's pathetic and even with no supernatural enhancement, I've still got more "nasty" than you. You want to know, you tell me why.'

'You're an asshole.'

'Thank you, it's something that took an eternity to perfect.'

I turned, determined to leave, but stopped and turned back before I'd even taken a step. Onyx knew something and if there was any chance of finding this exile, he was it.

After all, you have jumped off a cliff and given up your life as you knew it for Lincoln – surely you can endure a bully?

I stared at the ceiling, while I took a few deep breaths.

'OK,' I said, looking back to Onyx, trying to ignore the overly smug look on his face. I walked to the centre of his room and sat in the chair opposite him. I was damned if I was going to be left standing awkwardly in the doorway. Onyx was right, I had to stop letting other people rule me. Spence, following my lead, took a seat on the only other chair, a dingy kitchen stool, positioned between the kitchenette and the living area – no man's land. He looked ridiculous.

'Nahilius hurt Lincoln's mother years ago. Lincoln heard he's back in town and he's going after him. I want to help.' I tried to stay neutral, not give away too much in my tone, nervously clutching at my hands, twisting my fingers.

'Still saving the one you love, little rainbow? What is it you are most worried about – that he will never find Nahilius and put this revenge to rest? Or that he *will* find him?'

I stared at my hands.

'I see. You want to get there first. And what is your plan if you *do* find him first? Will you kill him for your Lincoln? Can *you* do that?'

Spence jumped off his stool from behind me. 'I've had this shit!'

Before I could stop him, he threw himself on top of Onyx, hauling him off the sofa and throwing him, face first, to the ground. Onyx, reduced to mere human strength, went down like a feather pillow. He could offer Spence no resistance.

'I've got your measure. I've been watching you tell your stories, ask your stupid questions and you know what? You may not care about Violet or anyone else, but

I don't buy the crap about you not caring for yourself. Selfishness like yours only comes from one place – self frikin' love!'

'Spence!' I yelled, worried I was about to lose my only chance.

'I got this, Vi,' he answered, flashing me a quick smile.
Shitshitshit.

Spence pulled Onyx's arm behind him, hard. I was sure it was about to break. His face was smushed into the seagrass matting, his cheeks bulging at the sides as Spence's knee ground heavily into the space between Onyx's shoulderblades. I could see his face going beet red as he closed his eyes tight with the pain and groaned.

I took a step forward to intervene. Just as I did, Onyx cried out.

'OK! Get off me,' forcing the muffled words out.

'You going to tell her what she needs to know?' Spence asked, completely calm now. In control.

Onyx didn't respond. Spence pushed harder and I flinched, torn between staying put to get the information I so badly needed and stepping in. Need outweighed my sense of right and wrong.

Finally, Onyx caved. 'Yes, yes. Get off!'

Spence looked at me. For gratitude or permission – I wasn't sure. I gave him a nod. He eased off Onyx, giving him a last dig with a trailing knee. I just watched while he went through the motions and eased himself back onto the stool. Onyx pulled himself up gingerly.

Spence had helped me big-time. Just like Nyla, he had the ability to zone in and simply get the job at hand done. On this occasion it had worked in my favour but I had an uneasy feeling that that might not always be the case.

Onyx kept his back to us as he straightened his shirt and combed his fingers through his now not-so-styled hair. When he turned to face me he held his head high, despite it being dotted with the carpet's imprint, and tried to maintain some dignity as he limped back to the sofa. He ignored Spence.

After an uncomfortable silence, he cleared his throat. 'Nahilius is a weapon. Alone, he is not to be feared. It is not him you should be seeking.' Onyx did not hold my eyes, did not look for my reaction.

I tucked a few loose strands of hair behind my ear. 'Onyx…English please.'

'A weapon is ineffective without an operator.'

I stared at him blankly.

'I honestly can't believe someone who is so dense at times was sharp enough to undo me.' He shook his head to himself, muttering something else. Clearly all the insanity hadn't left him when he became human – or maybe it was gradually leaving him.

'He's a gun for hire. Nahilius wouldn't know how to act alone even if he wanted to. He is one of the tempted. In the angel realm, there are angels who are more dominant than others. There are divisions between light and dark, the way you have divisions between political parties or races. As a result, naturally there are those who are leaders, those who follow, those who persuade and those who are persuaded. The ones who are so weak they can be persuaded have no true belief system. They can be made to do many things.'

'Even exile?' I asked, starting to grasp where this might

be going. I spotted a box of tissues near the TV and jumped up to get them.

'Yes, finally, some almost intelligent words. The angels that are persuaded are more often than not subjugated by means of temptation. An angel like Nahilius would have been lured into serving another angel – when that angel decided to exile he would have recruited Nahilius, tempted him with material riches and had him chosen exile to serve his purposes on earth.'

I offered the tissues to Onyx, who abruptly snatched them from my hold and started wiping at his bloodied nose.

'So who does he work for?'

'Well, that's the very interesting part. Nahilius is a modern exile, preferring to use technology and financial structures to hide within. He has an instinctive aptitude for survival. You see, his leader was killed by one of your lot half a century ago. Nahilius has become somewhat of an entrepreneur since then.'

Onyx pepped up. He was getting back into the swing of things. 'He's a freelancer – working for the highest bidder, so to speak – and not only for exiles. I don't know who he's working for – but I can guess.' He practically sang the last words.

Here we go.

'Look, Onyx, I need to find him. As you so kindly pointed out I do have some other problems I need to be dealing with and it would be great if I could have Lincoln back with me. So OK, if it makes you happy to hear, then yes, I admit I want to stop him before he makes a huge mistake, so tell me what it's going to cost. I'll buy you more bourbon, shirts, whatever. But you *will* tell me,' I looked over to Spence, 'or I'll tell Spence he can have it out with you and frankly, I don't think you need to be a mind-reader to know he wouldn't really have a problem with that.'

I turned back to Onyx, whose eyes were now transfixed by Spence. Spence had been right, Onyx was starting to care about his life, even if it was only human.

'You have to think the way we do,' Onyx said, flipping a hand out and then frowning a little. 'The way *they* do,' he corrected. 'Right now, you have big problems. Instead of focusing on where this is all coming from, focus on the main one for a moment – usually things will lead back to that.'

My main problem was easy. Phoenix was going to find the Scriptures before me and when he did, there would be nothing I could do about it because he had the power to kill me.

'Phoenix.'

Onyx nodded. 'I imagine that this little issue Lincoln is having has worked quite well to divert his attentions away from the Scriptures... And you.'

As he spoke, I realised he had been the first one I'd heard refer to the Scriptures in plural. He'd always known there were two. A reminder that he wasn't divulging more than needed at any time.

'It's perfect,' Onyx continued. 'Lincoln is off seeking revenge instead of helping you find a way to stop Phoenix. It's distracting you almost as much as him and best of all, separating you both physically and emotionally. Lincoln is your best shot at trying to heal you if Phoenix reinstates your wounds...' He paused, considering something. 'I have to say this is not a good sign for you. I wondered if, in the end, Phoenix would really be willing to destroy you, his love for you seemed real, but it appears you were successful in disintegrating that love completely and in return he is apparently ready to ensure that when he defeats you it will be...'

'For good,' I finished.

Onyx smiled, but for once I didn't think his heart was truly in it. He was too busy dabbing his bleeding nose and watching Spence out of the corner of his eye.

He was right, though. As soon as he said it, it made sense. Of course this was Phoenix and of course he wanted to drive a wedge between Lincoln and me. Weaken us.

And you walked right into it!

I wanted to slap myself. He must be laughing so hard at how easy it was to separate us, how easily I just let Lincoln go off on these renegade missions instead of focusing on the Scriptures, how easily Lincoln was derailed and turned from his responsibilities.

Of all things, this – the exile that had hurt his mother – was the only thing that could spoil him so effectively, have him turn his back on his obligations. Lincoln had an excuse – he was blinded by his love for his mum and his need for closure – but what the hell was mine? I should have seen this coming.

'Now, if you don't mind, could you please instruct your brawn to hand over my payment and go away?'

'Spence, give him the bourbon. Thank you, Onyx.' I nodded at him and he looked away.

Spence put the bottles on the coffee table and I could tell he was even less pleased than I was about having to pay him for information.

As we walked out Onyx spoke again, 'I know someone who might know where he is. I'll let you know.'

I didn't turn around, I just paused in the doorway. 'Thank you.'

Spence and I left Hades without talking after I'd stopped to let Dapper know that Onyx could do with an ice-pack. When we hit the pavement Spence was all pumped up.

'Do you think he'll send through the address tonight?' he asked.

In the dark, the night air was cool and made me feel unprotected and somehow all alone, despite my company. I turned a wary look to Spence. 'Not tonight. I have to get home before Dad calls and anyway I'm too tired for anything else. If I get the address, we can go tomorrow.'

Spence's shoulders sagged forward.

'I promise I'll let you know. I won't go without you,' I assured him.

He smiled. Spence still hadn't asked for the full story about Nahilius. It occurred to me he didn't care. As long as there was the potential for a fight, he was in.

'Um, Spence, can we keep this to ourselves for now?'

'You won't catch me telling anyone,' he said. And I knew he wouldn't. Spence wouldn't risk missing out.

Another good thing to remember!

CHAPTER EIGHTEEN

'Anger and jealousy can no more bear to lose sight of their objects than love.'
George Eliot

The phone was ringing when I opened the door.

'Hello? Hello?' I called into the receiver after lunging to get it before it stopped.

'Hello?' I said, again.

'Vi, it's me. Where have you been?'

'Oh, hi, Dad. I was out with Sp— Steph. We were at the library.'

'Uh huh.'

'Dad, seriously. If you don't believe me, call Steph – she's probably still there.' Lying just isn't something that sits well with me, so the fact that I seemed to be lying to everyone in my life at the moment *and* was turning out to be pretty damn good at it was disturbing. For whatever reason to whatever person, it never feels right. I've felt like that my whole life, always thinking it was something I had inherited from my mother. *Until I discovered she was the biggest liar of all!*

'OK, OK – so you were at the library. Sweetheart, I was worried about you. I've called the apartment a few times today and you haven't been home. I tried the other night as well, but you weren't there. Is there anything you want to tell me?'

'Like what?'

'I don't know. How's Lincoln?' Dad asked, trying out the question.

'He's OK. You know, same as always.'

'Are you two still…friends?' he asked, a lilt in his voice.

'Yes,' I deadpanned.

'*Just* friends?'

'Dad,' I warned.

'OK. But you're OK then?'

'I'm fine. How's your trip going?'

'Same as always, sweetheart. Somehow Caroline has managed to arrange meetings with almost every client the company has.' Beneath the obvious exhaustion I noticed something that sounded a lot like endearment. If I hadn't known Dad as well as I did I would've wondered if something were going on between him and his PA. Dad sighed. 'I miss you. I'm trying to rearrange the schedule, with any luck I'll see you in a few days.'

Talking to Dad, I had an idea – a memory really – of the dreams I'd had. Until now, they had seemed so unreal I'd just brushed them off as weird, but with everything that was happening, I realised for the first time that maybe they were the clue I had needed.

'Sure. Dad?'

'Yes.'

'When you met Mum, when you lived in New York

– did she ever mention any friends she had there? Um…
Did she ever mention anyone's name…like Nyla or
Rudyard?'

'No, not that I remember. Your mum didn't have many
connections when we met. She had only recently moved
from a small town to New York. Why?'

See! My mum, biggest liar of all.

'No reason, I just met this nice old couple the other
day… They were from New York and thought I looked
familiar. I wondered if maybe they were recognising Mum.'

'Oh,' I could hear Dad choking up. People always told
me how much I looked like Mum. Apart from Dad's hazel
eyes, I was supposed to be a lot like her. 'Well…I doubt
they knew her.'

'Yeah, I'm sure you're right. Have a good trip, Dad.'

'Sure, honey. Call me if you need anything and
remember – no one at the apartment except Steph and if
you need anything…'

'I know, I know – the Richardsons are just next door.'

When Dad hung up, I paused, holding the phone,
trying desperately to think back to the dream. I don't know
why I'd thought of it at that moment, or why I hadn't tried
to figure it out before now.

Every time I'd woken from the dreams I'd been so sure
that they were real. The first time, shivering and sore, as
if the raining ice had chilled me to the bone and bruised
my skin. The other times, feeling the dream and its contents
slipping out of my grasp but always left with a lingering
sadness and sense of burden. I was certain my angel
maker had shown me the dreams but then – like so many
others – I'd let myself forget. Till now. I couldn't remember

everything but I could hear his words. The warning.

'A traitor,' I whispered.

Desperate to clear my head, I ran myself a bath and soaked for a small eternity. I had to let out the cold water three times to top up with more hot. It was comforting to lie there and think quietly. I couldn't remember the last time I'd done this. I let my hair out of its ponytail, released it into the water and slid back. The long strands explored the water, snaking around my neck and chest. As the warmth of the water reached through my skin and into my core I felt some part of myself – a part I had not allowed to surface in a long time – awaken. Silent tears started to trickle from my eyes. I let them. They were not tears of panic, or even despair – just tears, tears of quiet, tears for me.

Eventually I let my head slide right down the back of the bath. My loose hair floated in the warm water, which enveloped me in a world of both amplified sounds and quietness. I held my breath and let my lips part slightly so I could feel the water move inside my mouth. I waited, and waited. I waited for the burn – the urgent need for air. But being Grigori meant it was a slower process than it once was. I could hold my breath for a lot longer now.

It was a relief to be alone. Even if I was crying and submerged, I still felt a peaceful calm. My hands slid along the ceramic of the bath and then to the place on my stomach where Onyx had rammed his silver sword. I tried not to – but my thoughts went to *him*. I couldn't stop them – the memories. As much as I wanted to deny it, there was a part of me that would be forever linked to Phoenix and it had nothing to do with his physical hold over me.

A surge of emotion flooded through me as my lungs started to burn with hot ice and when morning and evening flashed across my closed eyes, I knew the burning in my lungs was not for oxygen. It was everywhere. I bolted upright, gasping for air, my eyes darting frantically about as a gust of chilling wind hit me in the face.

'Son of a bitch!' I jumped out of the bath and wrapped a towel around me as I charged out of the bathroom.

'Phoenix!' I yelled to the empty apartment. 'I know it's you!'

Worst of all, just as I had felt his blast of intense emotion before he left, I knew it was a result of the initial feelings he had felt coming from me.

I secured the apartment as tightly as I could, once again finding the sliding door to the balcony unlocked. I checked everything, pulling across the safety latches on the main door and checking the deadbolts on all the windows.

Like that can stop him.

It was more about the active process than anything else.

I considered calling Steph, but she'd been ordered by her mother back home for a night and what was she going to do if Phoenix returned anyway? I was stronger without having to defend her as well. I'd already dragged Steph into this world more often than I was comfortable with.

I *wanted* to call Lincoln, but I could just imagine that conversation: *Yeah, so Phoenix was in my apartment while I was in the bath and thinking of him. I'm pretty sure he felt everything I was feeling. Do you think you could come play protector for me?* I don't think so.

With no one to turn to, I hauled my giant-sized quilt out to the sofa and slept, if you can call it that, in the living room.

Phoenix was gone, but not far.

I realised now, he never was.

I couldn't sense him as easily as I could other exiles. His human part gave him a valuable camouflage and he could mask his presence much more effectively. I didn't know if I was more disappointed or embarrassed that I had been refusing to acknowledge the truth, but despite his subtlety I had definitely been feeling him. Never as close as this before, but he'd been there.

Watching. Waiting.

I now had little doubt. I had felt his intensity in that one burst of emotion, felt his desperate need to eliminate me. Any glimmer of hope that might have once been there – that somehow Phoenix would change, would be that guy I first got to know – was gone.

Phoenix will kill me.

Or, I'll kill him.

CHAPTER NINETEEN

*'He cast upon them the fierceness of his anger, wrath,
and indignation, and trouble, by sending evil angels
among them.'*
Psalm 78:49 (King James Bible)

Spence and I had been walking around the aircraft factory for hours. It wasn't my idea of a joyous Sunday. There was nothing so far that had resembled the mottled feeling the senses had given me at the airport. It was no surprise. Despite Spence's mumblings he was right when he said we weren't metal detectors. The senses are designed to pinpoint exiles, not aircraft carriers.

I was about to grab Spence, who'd decided to make the most of the excursion and was now having a splendid time checking out all the machinery, when I felt the senses. The type that cause no confusion and were definitely not directing me to an aeroplane.

The flavour of apple watered in my mouth, seeping through my cheeks and onto my tongue. Morning and evening – the raw beauty of their power slid in and out of my vision as I smelled bouquets of syrupy flowers, sickly, like concentrated honeysuckle.

I welcomed the senses, which were now a part of me that I could, in a way, communicate with. I could hear the sound of wings flapping furiously as if struggling to reach me before colliding into trees. Of all the senses, this was the one that always evoked the most emotion in me. Lincoln had explained to me that the sound of the wings – light and dark for doves and ravens – represents the battle for life, the ongoing effort necessary for any living force to survive. The collision of branches and leaves symbolises the 'everything' that must be faced and defeated if a living force is to continue. It's the choice to go on.

The final sensation, a humming energy of cool heat, moved through my entire body, travelling to each end and then beyond. It enveloped me and then released me just as smoothly, ensuring that every part of me was now attuned to what lay ahead.

I acknowledged all of the senses and allowed them to flow through me, do their job, and then I let them go. It was so much easier than it had once been and each time I felt them, I had more control.

I looked towards Spence, who had not sensed the exile yet. Even if he had felt an inkling – I wouldn't have been surprised if he missed it – he was male, after all, *and* in an aircraft hangar. He was in boy-toy heaven.

'Spence,' I said. He turned from an engrossing conversation with one of the mechanics and looked at me blankly. He wasn't going to make this easy.

'Ah, Spence. I think we should go look over there,'

I said, trying to give him the we've-got-a-problem look. He missed it completely.

'Oh, OK. You head over, I'll be there in a minute,' he said, brushing me off and making the mechanic smile.

Great.

I put on a big cheesy grin for the mechanic, who was clearly enjoying the show, then I turned it on Spence.

'Come on, Spency. Why don't you come over here and I'll give you an apple for being such a good boy?' I said sarcastically.

Spence's eyes grew wide as he realised what I was saying. I was willing to bet at that moment his little taste buds were suddenly getting all appleicious. His eyes darted between me and the mechanic, like a fool. If I wasn't trying to concentrate so hard on locating our problem I might have laughed at him.

He stumbled through a departure speech which only translated to the mechanic that he was under my thumb. The man teased him as Spence tripped over himself to catch up with me.

'Nice,' I said, as he fell into step with me.

'Give me a break. I didn't know.'

'Really? I never would've guessed. Now concentrate. I don't want to get jumped by a dozen exiles at the moment.'

'A *dozen*! Really?'

I rolled my eyes, but of course the idea of a dozen exiles had Spence almost jumping for joy.

'No. Not *really* – I can only sense one…but that doesn't mean… Look, things have been odd and when it comes to Phoenix – I can't be sure of anything.'

Other than that he wants me dead.

'Got it,' Spence said, giving me a mock salute. I hoped it was his way of finishing the games and getting serious.

We walked around the back of a small passenger plane and crouched under the wing. There were no mechanics in this area, but no exile either.

'In there,' Spence said, nodding towards the next massive maintenance room.

My mouth was dry as I followed. I had a bad feeling and I didn't like being on a hunt without Lincoln.

'OK,' I whispered.

I thought about telling Spence, explaining to him the problems I'd been having with my dagger. It was hard to admit my failings, especially a problem even I didn't fully understand. We both knew if there was an exile on the other side of the wall it would come down to a fight. Could I really ask Spence to go in there with me, after telling him I wasn't sure that when it came to pulling my dagger, I wouldn't malfunction?

'Let's go,' I said, making my decision and moving forward. I'd work on being a better person another time.

Spence moved like a pro – probably an advantage of living in the Academy and training every day to be Grigori. I was a little more awkward, forgetting to always check behind and not positioning myself in the most defensive positions. But I watched Spence and tried to follow his spy tactics.

We hid on our side of the doorway, which led into a massive area of military planes. Everywhere else we had been housed commercial aeroplanes or private jets. This room was filled with planes of a telltale army green colour and some even bore the splotchy camouflage design.

A guy was walking around the largest of the planes, taking notes in a book. He had sandy-coloured hair that went down to his shoulders and looked young – too young. Everyone else in the factory looked at least thirty. They were probably all qualified personnel. Most workers would have had engineering degrees of some sort and getting that kind of stuff took time. This guy, who looked no more than eighteen or nineteen, had on a white lab coat and was flicking through the plane's outer control box as if he really knew what he was doing.

Spence gave me a knowing look and I nodded. This was our guy. I was willing to bet that to anyone else he would look different, older and less striking, but we could see past the illusion.

Spence turned to me and mouthed, 'Just one?'

I was about to nod when I felt something else. It was very faint and didn't feel like the senses normally did. It was like I was experiencing a kind of lethargic version of them. I put a hand up in the air to stop Spence launching into combat. He gave me an impatient look. I raised one finger, pleadingly. He nodded.

As we watched the exile press some more buttons, the front of the aircraft started to open, the entire nose lifting into the air. Spence's eyes lit up with delight. I knew something about it opening from the front like that had impressed him. I was starting to think he may not have been the best person to bring along.

'Whoa!' I gasped, before I could stop myself. The senses hit me so fast I had to brace a hand on the wall. I looked over to Spence between flashes of morning and evening and could tell he was feeling it too. We looked back to the plane and out walked another exile from inside. Tall, like many of them but he was also very slender with slick black hair. He looked like a stereotypical lanky villain.

The two exiles started to talk.

'All done,' said the lab-coat one.

'Yes. This will work – the titanium is all in place. We can send it out once we've loaded it with supplies. Where's this one going?'

The first one shrugged. 'Don't know yet. They won't tell us till the last minute, you know that.'

The tall exile harrumphed, 'Yeah, yeah. Get it finished off this month so we can get going on the next one.'

'Won't be a problem. The mechanics here don't know *what* they're doing. They just bring in the military planes, do the work in a daze and then they leave. We even use them to fix 'em up and they don't remember a thing! No one comes in here otherwise – morons don't think the room exists. It's the perfect set-up,' said the exile, laughing wickedly.

Horrified, I looked over to Spence. Correction, I looked over to where Spence was *supposed* to be…and wasn't. My eyes darted around frantically until I found him crouched under the tail of a nearby army plane. He was waving me over.

This is so not going to end well.

I scurried across the floor, crouching as low as I could and trying desperately not to make any more noise than necessary. It wouldn't be long until they sensed us. In fact, I was surprised they hadn't already.

I stopped beside Spence, who was almost laughing out loud at my commando effort.

'Shut up,' I whispered. 'Why are we hiding under this ugly plane anyway?'

It hadn't brought us any closer, just to another viewpoint the same distance away.

He looked at me like I was an idiot. 'It's a better vantage. We can come up behind them from here. And by the way, don't diss the plane. This is a B1 Bomber, you have to treat it with respect.'

'Ah, Spence...I hate to burst your bubble but this thing doesn't even look like it can fly.'

'*Ah, Vi!* It has no wings yet. When this baby is finished it will be the baddest thing in the sky,' Spence whispered, putting a reverential hand on the underside of the aircraft and bowing his head in praise.

Give me a break!

'OK, all hail the wingless plane. Let's go.' Knowing that we only had seconds left until the exiles sensed us, there was no point trying to surprise them.

I stood up and started to move towards them. Spence followed. I was glad I wasn't relying solely on the element of surprise when my phone beeped with a message.

Both exiles spun round with super speed.

'Jeez!' I said sarcastically, 'I thought you guys were never going to notice us.'

Good one, Vi. Piss off the already mentally unstable exiles!

'And *I* thought today was going to be boring,' the tall exile said as he flung himself towards me.

I knew he was going to do it. One thing about exiles, they don't hesitate, but even so, I was thrown off-balance by the sheer speed of the onslaught.

Spence launched into action against the sandy-haired

guy. The sounds of punches and kicks popped and echoed throughout the large cement room along with the squeak and screech of rubber-soled shoes on the painted cement floor.

The tall exile got in a few early hits when I was caught off-guard but it didn't take long for me to find a good rhythm. I might have been having a problem finishing them off, but overpowering them and generally beating them in a contest of strength and ability, came naturally.

I drew the exile in, allowing him to think he was getting the better of me. It meant I had to take a few solid punches to the gut and one to the side of my face, but I absorbed them and he was getting cocky. As soon as I saw my opening I was in, he launched a wide arm at me, leaving the rest of his body unguarded. My foot was in the air before I even thought about it and kicking hard into his chest.

There was a time, a more human time, when I would never have been able to make a move like that – not in speed or agility. Today, it was just about making it happen.

The exile went down. He wouldn't be there for long.

This is my chance.

My hand went to my concealed weapon. As it did, the exile looked up at me and his eyes widened as his nostrils flared. Something was wrong – very wrong… He was scared.

I paused, confused. Exiles do not get scared, not like this, anyway. They fight tooth and nail until the very last moment – he wouldn't think I'd beaten him just because I was reaching for my dagger.

His shock transferred to me and our mutual surprise gave him enough time to scurry to his feet and scramble back. His eyes were fixed on me – switching from one wrist to the other.

I smiled. Tough. 'You know who I am, don't you?'

'I know enough to know you're as good as dead,' he said, still backing away.

'Come on – don't tell me you're scared,' I teased.

I noticed the other exile shoot a glance towards us – he obviously wasn't expecting this turn of events either. Spence used full advantage and hurled his entire body on top of him in an overly dramatic but effective move that was becoming something of a trademark for Spence.

I smirked at my target and raised my eyebrows, daring him.

His mouth twitched at the corner. I could tell he wanted to go on the attack, but he restrained himself, moving away with each step I took towards him.

At my back I felt the glow of Spence's power and heard him yell out the usual spiel – offering the exile a choice. No surprise, the exile told him to eat shit.

The tall exile in front of me had full view and I could tell his instinct was to retaliate. He didn't much care for the other exile but he liked the idea of inflicting pain on us. That was obvious.

My phone beeped again. I was distracted for a second and then…I was foggy, like all logic dropped out of my mind for a moment and I couldn't quite remember what I…was. It was just a second, then all the doors in my mind re-opened and I was myself again. But it was enough. The exile had disappeared.

'Hey, why'd you let him go?' Spence asked from beside me.

'I…I didn't. He must have used some kind of mojo on me. One second I had his number, the next I was…I don't know – and then he was gone and you were beside me.'

'Memory?'

'I think so. He only got through my defences for a moment – I wasn't keeping my guard up,' I said, now cross with myself. I should have been better prepared but I'd been concentrating on the physical instead of the internal.

A rookie mistake, Vi.

'Don't beat yourself up, you did something right if he was running away.'

But that was just the point, I hadn't. And one more thing I realised, this wasn't the first exile I'd seen flee. Outnumbered or not, the exile at the farmhouse had taken off, too. But it just wasn't in their make-up to run.

'Hmm,' I said, not up to speculating with Spence right now. Instead, I fished my phone out of my pocket. Onyx would be delighted when he found out his text caused me so much trouble. 'It's the address for Nahilius.'

'This day just gets better and better.'

'Spence… You need a hobby.' I scrolled down my phone to the next message. It was from Griffin.

We have a lead on the Scriptures. Can't find Lincoln or Magda, let them know if you hear from them. Everyone at Hades now!

'Shit,' I said under my breath.

'Bad news?'

'No, good maybe. Just bad timing. We have to get back to Hades,' I said as I walked towards the plane from which the exile had come. We were running out of time and there was still so much to do.

'But what about Nahilius?' Spence persisted.

I spun, close to falling off the emotional ledge I was already balancing on so precariously.

'Do you think I don't want to go after Nahilius? Do you think I don't want to help Lincoln? I can't be everywhere at once, Spence!' I yelled.

Spence looked down and didn't respond. I turned around again and proceeded into the mouth of the plane, getting back to business.

Push it aside, Vi. Remember – no quitting!

'Somehow, when the exile was inside here, I couldn't sense him as well.'

That's why I couldn't sense them at the airport.

'Yeah, I couldn't sense him at all,' Spence admitted, a little deflated.

'What kind of plane is this?' I asked Spence.

'This *plane*? Oh, Violet, how can you not know what this is? I mean, this isn't a *plane,* this is an artwork. *This* is a moment in time, an extreme piece of machinery that will—'

'Spence!' I cut him off.

'You have no appreciation,' he said, now glum. 'It's an Antonov, the biggest military transport plane in the world. You need a tank in a hurry, this is your baby!' He over-emphasised every word with supportive hand gestures.

'Do you need a moment alone with the plane?' I asked, on the verge of being sick.

'Umm…no. It's OK,' he said. I think he actually thought I was being genuine.

We walked inside. The inner shell was covered in silver metal panelling.

'This is new,' Spence said, inspecting the panelling. 'It's everywhere.' He disappeared into the cockpit. 'Even up here!' he yelled. 'And there are shutters that pull down over the windows as well!'

'It's what they were talking about...' I said, joining him. 'It's titanium. Somehow it distorts the senses. It's why I couldn't sense them clearly at the airport and why that exile seemed to appear out of nowhere. They must be in one of these planes.'

'Well, that narrows things down considerably. Antanov planes are few and far between. I'd be surprised if there was more than one at the airport, though...' he trailed off.

'What?'

'This is a military plane, which means it'll be in a restricted area. It won't be easy.'

'Lucky I have someone around who can pull off a wicked disguise then,' I said.

'Too true, Eden,' Spence said with a wink.

I sent Spence to meet up with everyone at Hades, telling him I needed to run home first and I would meet him there.

Once I was on my own I called Steph – she was at the library, so I jumped in a taxi.

I found her sitting at one of the big communal tables though I noticed no one else was sharing the space. It was strewn with books, which surrounded her laptop. Steph had claimed the whole area for herself.

I took in what, to me, was a windstorm of papers, highlighted photocopies and newspaper clippings and felt more exhausted than ever. It looked like it would be difficult to make any sense of the material and impossible to actually *get* to it all. But I should have had more faith. Steph is, after all, a genius of sorts. Not to mention her super-handy photographic memory she never willingly flaunts.

'Dare I ask?' I queried nervously, worried that she would snap at me. This workload definitely went above and beyond the normal call of friendship.

Steph barely looked up from a newspaper clipping she was reading. 'Well, let's just say the guy doesn't have a Facebook page. It's not that it's difficult so much as there is not any one piece of significant information about him. Only a few words here and there. I've had to trace him through other people I think he has done this kind of corporate stuff to – you know, other victims.'

'Wow, I never would have thought to do that.' *Or known how.*

'The bottom line is, I'm not getting very far. All I can really tell you is that he's been around – involved in a whole heap of extremely profitable companies and by the time he leaves or disappears they're going under or already bankrupt. There always seems to be some scandal with the owner or a major financial controller – Skase, Conrad Black; he's been everywhere. Someone else always ends up getting the blame and later, there seems to be a lot of mysterious deaths. One guy even jumped off the back of his yacht – Maxwell, I think, or something like that. It's like the stuff you see on TV when a shonky businessman gets blamed for overpaying himself and stealing money on the side, but when it comes down to it the authorities can never actually find where he stashed the money and six months later you hear he had a sudden heart attack or similar.'

'Oh my God,' I said.

'Yeah, and while there's always a fall guy, I think the one actually getting away with the money is—'

'Nahilius,' I finished for her.

'Exactly. The problem is I can't find much about Lincoln's mother here. The company was all run privately, and pre-internet, which makes it hard.'

I remembered that Lincoln kept all his mum's old company documents in his spare bedroom at the warehouse. It was basically stacked to the roof with boxes. I felt for the key in my pocket.

Someone *had* interfered.

'Why don't you just tell me or something?' I said, looking up.

'Vi? Honey, how are we on planet earth?' Steph asked, watching me.

'Oh, sorry. It's just, I had an idea and I get the feeling I wasn't the first one to have it.'

'Seriously?' she said, catching on. 'Messages from above? Christ, Vi, you better watch out who you tell this stuff to. Even the God Squad might find some of your bag weird.'

I collapsed into the chair beside her. 'I find it insane.'

She nudged me from the side. 'You know, you don't have to carry the cross on your own.'

I looked at her blankly. I got the gist – still.

'You need to simplify. You're trying to save everyone,

but the thing is, you can't be everywhere at once and no one expects you to be.'

'I know, but Phoenix is going to get the Scriptures if we don't get there first. Griffin reckons he knows where they are which means…'

'You have to go after them instead of going after Lincoln?'

I dropped my head and tried to hold back the tears. Steph put a hand on my shoulder.

'Sweetie, you're no good to anyone like this. You're just going through the motions. You love him, anyone can see that and frankly, you're better with him anyway. If you have to go up against Phoenix, do you really want to do that without Lincoln by your side?'

With that, there was no stopping the flood. I started breaking into snotty sobs. Letting the first tear out is always the mistake.

'It's horrible. Loving him. Especially when…he doesn't love me, Steph. You don't love someone you don't trust. He trusts Magda.'

'Bullshit! I mean, the guy's being a dick, let's face it. He should be working with you and trying to get the Scriptures, but we both know why he's going after Nahilius.'

'We do?'

She gave me a gentle push. 'What would *you* want to do – if you knew someone had hurt your dad and was potentially lethal to anyone he came across? What would *you* do if you finally let yourself care enough about someone again and the one that had taken everything from you once before returned?'

'I…I don't understand.'

'Yes you *do*, Vi. You just don't want to admit it because then you'll know exactly what you're going to do.'

We were both silent for a bit. Steph passed me a tissue to mop up the leakages. I thought back to the exile in the alley who told Lincoln that Nahilius was coming for what was his.

When I finally thought I might be able to open my mouth without letting Niagara Falls return, I took in a few hiccupped breaths and tried to let them out slowly, through quivering lips.

'He doesn't want to be hurt again. He doesn't want Nahilius to take the person he cares about the most.'

'And?' Steph pushed.

'And that's why he didn't want me involved,' I said, trying to calm my heart that was now racing. Part horrified, part excited.

'Because?'

'Because… He cares about me the most.'

'*Because* he loves your ass in the epic sense!' Steph said, giving me a little job-well-done pat on the back. This was as far as her deep and meaningful would extend. 'Right,' she said, standing and starting to pack books away. 'What's the plan?'

CHAPTER TWENTY

'And as soon as he came near the camp...Moses' anger
burned hot, and he threw the tablets out of his hands
and broke them at the foot of the mountain.'
Exodus 32:19

The God Squad, as Steph was still tagging them, were
sitting at what was becoming the usual table in Hades.

When I'd walked in I was surprised to see Onyx at
the bar chatting to one of the bar staff – semi-civil. He was
dressed in pants and a black shirt and he was clean, recently
shaven and though he was sipping on what I was sure was
straight bourbon I was also quite sure he wasn't drunk.
Every time I saw him lately, he looked more...human.
Still flawed in many ways, he was definitely less insane
and though I wouldn't ever want to test the boundaries he
seemed less sinister. Now, well... Now he was just mean.

Right on cue, as I walked by he gave me an icy stare
and looked me up and down.

'Ha, no wonder you seem to be partnerless these days.
Wardrobe counts, especially when your face looks like

that.' He snapped his fingers in my face.

'Go to hell, Onyx,' I said, not stopping.

'Already there thanks to you,' he called after me. I ignored him.

Griffin was deep in conversation with Nyla and Rudyard when I approached. I got the distinct impression from the look on his face that I wasn't invited to be part of the secret whispers. Neither was Zoe, Spence or Salvatore, who were all jammed down the far end of the table, playing with coasters. I'm pretty sure it was a drinking game – the one where you balance the coaster on the edge of the table and have to flick it up in the air and catch it on the spin in one, otherwise you drink.

Steph and I had tried it one night, but never got past the first attempt. It probably wasn't the best game to play when we'd already had too much to drink and didn't know what we were doing. We ended up in hysterical laughter. Steph, who can't hold her alcohol at all, actually fell off her chair and stayed under the table laughing until we got kicked out of the seedy little bar where underage kids could get away with drinking. I can't even remember how we discovered it, but Steph made the place famous at our school and now it's where everyone hangs out.

Except us, we're stuck in Hades.

I felt a twinge of guilt. I'd been asking so much of Steph. Just because *I* was bound to this life didn't mean she had to be. I wouldn't be surprised if she ended up hating me. I made a mental note to do something really thoughtful for her to say thank you.

What gift really says – Thank you for tracking down the insane exiled angel that is tormenting Lincoln?

'Hey,' I said, pulling out the chair beside Zoe.

Zoe and Salvatore exchanged a glance when they saw me.

'What? What now?' I asked. But I already knew it wasn't good news. They kept looking at each other, as if waiting to see who would draw the short straw. Zoe hitched a shoulder and flung her hands on the table. Her wristbands made a blunt whacking sound on impact.

'We went to the farmhouse with Beth and Archer and it was all cleared out. We couldn't really sense anything but definitely felt something odd as we got closer to the airport. Anyway, there wasn't much else we could do without tipping them off so we got back early and decided to see if we could fit in a training session over at Lincoln's...'

Zoe looked down nervously.

'And?' I prompted, while dreading where this might be going.

'Well, when we got there the door was open so we just kinda walked right in – we didn't think to knock.'

Salvatore coughed loudly. Zoe rolled her eyes. 'I didn't think to knock,' she corrected, giving Salvatore a cold glare. 'I mean, everyone's just been coming and going from there so I didn't expect to interrupt...'

Oh no, please God, don't do this to me.

Spence shifted in his seat – he was dreading the same thing I was, he knew how much it would hurt me. I bit down hard on the inside of my cheek and stared at the spot just over Zoe's shoulder.

'Was he with Magda?'

'Yeah,' she said, but then taking in the look on my face

and the trepidation on Spence's she straightened in her chair and started waving a hand in the air.

'Oh... Whoa – I don't mean...yuck! I didn't walk in on them naked or anything... Yuck! Now I'm going to have freaky mental images all night!'

'Then what?' Spence and I asked together.

'They were loading up,' Zoe said with a shrug, as if compared to the alternative this was now simple.

I had no idea what she meant and looked around to the others. Salvatore shimmied closer in his chair.

'They were armouring themselves. Guns in fact,' he said in his Italian English.

What was Magda thinking? Is she really that desperate to get her claws into Lincoln that she would drive him to murder?

'Do you...' I swallowed through a suddenly dry mouth. 'Do you guys know what happens to an exile if they're shot?'

'It doesn't return them, I know that much,' Spence said.

'I think it's meant to hurt like hell, not kill them but it's a kind of torture,' Zoe offered. 'Some Grigori use them – guns – to help get the upper hand, but it's frowned upon.'

'Cowardly,' Salvatore said.

I shot him a fierce look.

'I am sorry, Violet. This may have been the not right wordings.'

And yet, I had a feeling it was exactly what he meant. As much as I wanted to defend Lincoln, I couldn't.

Griffin, Nyla and Rudyard chose this point to move down to where we were sitting.

'Sorry to keep you waiting. We were just trying to double-check our research. We believe we know where the

Scriptures are.' Griffin looked at me. 'Are you OK? Spence filled us in on the plane situation.'

'Yeah. I'm good,' I lied, knowing he would let me.

Even when you can tell someone isn't being honest, you have to pick your times, decide when you will and won't pull them up on it. This was one of the *won't*s.

'Is it commonly known that titanium does something to shield exiles against our senses?' I asked, embarrassed for not knowing more.

Griffin sat down beside me. 'No. It's not general knowledge and we had no idea it could be harnessed in this way.'

'So *you* knew about it?' I asked, wondering how many other things weren't 'general knowledge'.

Griffin spun a glass of Coke in his hand. 'I knew. But up until today we believed the only people who knew were Grigori leaders.'

'So how did Phoenix figure it out?' Spence piped up before I could ask.

'I'm not sure,' Griffin said plainly. Then he looked about and his expression turned quizzical. 'Where're Lincoln and Magda?'

I shrugged and tried to play it cool. 'Your guess is as good as mine, boss,' which was as close to the truth as I could get.

'Well, we can't wait for them,' Griffin said, shaking his head but not really surprised.

'Back to the Scriptures,' Zoe said, impatiently. 'Where are they?'

Nyla, Rudyard and Griffin all looked at one another and then back to us.

'Jordan,' Nyla said.

'Jordan?' we all repeated simultaneously.

'The country?' Spence added.

Griffin nodded and then gestured to Rudyard to speak.

Rudyard cleared his throat. 'Yes, Jordan. We believe the Rules the exile we captured at the farmhouse was referring to are the Ten Commandments.'

My mouth wasn't the only one to drop open and all but hit the table.

Rudyard smiled, looking positively thrilled at the reaction to the developments. 'I know it's a lot to get your head around. We believe that when Moses received the Ten Commandments almost three and a half thousand years ago, he in fact received two sets of three stone tablets. On one set were the Ten Commandments as we know them, while the second was to be held for subsequent discovery by the Grigori, and the third was for exiles. When Moses realised humans were not the only inhabitants of the earth and that exiled angels existed, and even more concerning, that angels existed in the angel realm in both light and dark capacity, he was enraged. He smashed a complete set of tablets and never revealed anything more than the Ten Commandments for humans. For humans the second tablet with the Ten Commandments was uncovered and stored away. What remained were hidden for safekeeping and eventually translated into scripture, only to be revealed by their own kind. We believe that the Scriptures for Grigori and exiles are in this same place – concealed somehow – waiting to be discovered.'

'And that's in Jordan?' Zoe asked again.

'Yes, we think Moses was buried in a tomb beneath his

place of death and that some time after this, the Scriptures were placed in that tomb, too. A prophet, Jeremiah, was sent on an angelic quest with the Ark of the Covenant, within which the Scriptures were concealed. Jeremiah was charged with delivering the Ark and its contents back to their original owner. If our information is correct, he took the Ark to Jordan.'

'It is a very old legend, not one widely told. Over time, the legend has been almost completely lost,' Griffin added.

'Yes,' agreed Rudyard, placing an ancient-looking leather-bound book on the table and opening to a yellowed page. 'Allow me to read a small passage from the Second Book of Maccabees,' he cleared his throat.

'*The prophet, Jeremiah, having received an oracle, commanded that the tabernacle and the ark go with him, he went forth into the mountain, where Moses climbed up, and saw the heritage of God. And when Jeremiah came thither, he found an hollow cave, wherein he laid the tabernacle and the ark, and the altar of incense, and so stopped the door. And some of those that followed him came up to mark the way, but they could not find it.*

'*When Jeremiah learned of it, he blamed them, saying: As for that place, it shall be unknown until the time that God gather his people again together, and receive them unto mercy.*'

'Well, I have no idea what that meant,' Zoe said, slouching back in her chair.

'We believe the Ark of the Covenant may be hidden in the tomb of Moses, which is in Jordan.'

'So we're going to Jordan,' I echoed.

Rudyard nodded.

'Well, it's about time something went in our favour,' Zoe said.

I got the feeling I wasn't the only one who agreed with her wholeheartedly.

'So,' Griffin said, clapping his hands together to get everyone's attention. 'We need to get organised. Dapper overheard some exiles in here last night, they were talking about flying out tonight, so we have to assume it's Phoenix. I've got Archer and Beth taking care of things here. Violet, you need to clear things with your dad somehow – we need you on this trip.'

I nodded. Finding a way around Dad was the least of my concerns.

'Nyla and Rudyard are heading straight to the airport to get a plane organised and the rest of us need to be there in two hours. Since we now know that Phoenix has a military plane we have to assume that if he is going to Jordan himself he will be flying into the military airfield in Amman. The Academy is owed a few favours so Nyla is confident she'll be able to get us a military plane, too.'

Nyla and Rudyard stood up simultaneously to leave, their hands unwittingly intertwining, and at that moment I felt like standing up and putting my foot right through their beautiful connection.

'Spence,' Nyla said, standing over him. 'You will stay here. I'm sorry but this trip is too dangerous – we don't know what's ahead.'

Contrary to his tight-fisted hand, Spence surprised everyone by looking up at Nyla and Rudyard and smiling. 'No problem,' he said. 'Have a good trip – bring me back a souvenir.'

Nyla and Rudyard almost fell over. 'Well, that's...very grown up of you,' Rudyard said. But as they walked out the door and Spence gave them another smile and a wave, I could see the doubt on their faces.

Spence was up to something, but right now I couldn't have cared less.

Everyone else stood up and started to get organised, planning trips back to the hotel and to get supplies. I left them to it. Instead, I zeroed in on Griffin.

'I'm going to get Lincoln,' I said in a way that didn't leave room for negotiation.

'We don't have time, Violet.' He barely looked up from his papers. 'I've left them a message. If they miss our flight they can get a commercial plane.'

'No can do, Griff. Lincoln's not himself and if I leave him in Magda's hands any longer it's gonna be all bad.'

'What are you talking about? They're trying to wrap up an old case. Don't get jealous over silly things,' he said, shaking his head at me, trying to fob me off.

But I didn't have the time, or the patience right now. 'Griffin, open your eyes! Lincoln and Magda have been off on some covert op since she got back. You have no idea what they're doing and Magda never hangs around long enough to give you any more information than the bare necessities. They've gone after Nahilius!'

At the mention of Nahilius' name, Griffin's eyes grew wide the way they always did when something major was dropped in his lap. He steadied himself, putting a hand on the back of a chair. Of course, the second he learned of anything that he hadn't already been fully aware of he blamed himself.

'It's not your fault,' I tried to reassure him. 'They've been sneaking around behind everyone's backs, but the thing is I think Lincoln is losing perspective and I also think that Phoenix is the one doing this. He wants to keep Lincoln and me apart.'

Griffin opened his mouth to speak, but I didn't let him.

'I know you think we don't have time to wait for them but I'm not going without him. I can't leave him – not now, not when I know he needs me.' I grabbed the backpack I'd stashed under the table.

'Go,' Griffin said.

'I'll be at the airport in two hours. I promise.'

I wasn't sure what Griffin said, something about watching my back. I didn't wait around. The clock was ticking. If I was going to get to Lincoln it had to be now. I knew he must have known where Nahilius was staying. As I walked out of Hades I spotted Onyx unpacking a case of vodka. 'You stealing or helping?' I asked, not slowing.

'Haven't decided yet,' he said. 'How about you?'

I smiled. 'Just going to get what's mine! Thanks for the info – I owe you one.'

I was halfway through the door and expected to hear a demand for more bourbon, but there was nothing. He was probably working out a shopping list.

I ran a few streets, keeping an eye out for an empty taxi. Finally, I spotted one and jumped in. Just as I shouted out the address of Nahilius' hotel and reached to pull the door closed, Spence flew in beside me.

'You promised,' he said, closing the door behind him.

Shit. 'Spence, I'm sorry, but things have changed. They have guns. For all I know so does Nahilius. I can't risk it – you might get hurt.'

'Damn it, Eden! I heard you give the address to the

driver. I know where you're going. Don't make me pay for my own taxi.'

Here's the thing about priorities. When your main one is on the line you find yourself doing things you would usually put in the 'questionable' box. Normally, I wouldn't risk Spence's life just to help my own cause; normally, I would kick up a fuss and try to negotiate my way out of this; normally... But nothing was normal about this situation and well... Priorities.

'OK,' I conceded. 'But if you get dead, it's on you.'

'Hey,' he shrugged, 'I wouldn't have it any other way.' He buckled up and smiled with victory.

I'd deal with my conscience later.

CHAPTER TWENTY-ONE

'Well! Evil to some is always good to others.'
Jane Austen

When the taxi pulled into the kerb, Spence and I all but scrambled out the windows, heaving for fresh air.

The driver and his taxi stank. The combination of garlic-charged body odour festering for hours on end in terry-towelling seat covers with no air conditioning, was pungent. From the moment Spence closed the door we'd been holding back the gag reflex as we tried desperately to stick our heads out the small openings the jammed windows permitted.

Stumbling onto the footpath, my head was spinning with a combination of car sickness and repulsion.

Spence took in a few deep breaths. 'Wow, that was...' he scrunched his face while flapping his T-shirt – aerating.

'Yeah,' I said, gasping for a few cleansing intakes of fresh air, too.

Spence waited patiently while I took a moment to right myself. I hate riding in the back of cars at the best of times.

'OK,' I said eventually as I stood straight and started to register my surroundings. 'We must be close. I can sense exiles.'

Spence nodded and looked around. He couldn't sense anything yet.

We were outside the hotel Onyx had directed us to. The Luxe Grand, a five-star hotel with all the trimmings. Standing to attention in crisp white shirts beneath tailored grey waistcoats, were three doormen – one to open car doors, one to take any luggage and one to open the hotel doors for guests. It had the clichéd red carpet out the front edged with gold pillars and heavy velvet rope. It sent out a simple message – *If you can't afford to be here, go away.*

Spence and I paused. I heard him scoff under his breath. He was in the same pair of baggy jeans he always wore when he wasn't in training gear and a faded green T-shirt – as opposed to his faded blue T-shirt. Spence wasn't well-off. I looked down at my own very average ensemble – black cargos and black long-sleeve T-shirt. At least we weren't wearing flip-flops.

We spared each other a glance, both thinking the same thing, and shrugged simultaneously before moving towards the red-carpet entrance.

The doormen each gave us a snooty up-and-down look, but we didn't stop. We needed to get up to Nahilius's room. Unfortunately, Onyx's text had only said 'top floor'. No room number.

We powered through the lobby not wanting to draw any more attention to ourselves than we already had, and bee-lined for the lifts, deciding to take a chance that Onyx was right. *And that he wasn't setting us up!*

The top floor, which turned out to be the twenty-sixth, consisted of two penthouse suites. Spence and I pressed the number in the lift and waited.

Nothing happened.

'It's got one of those swipey things for the top floors,' Spence said, pointing to the electronic swipe machine, which was not dissimilar to the one I have outside my apartment building.

'How are we going to get one of those?' I asked, feeling everything was against us.

Spence looked over to the reception area and then to where a maid was busy tidying up some of the lobby tables. He pulled out his mobile phone then dashed over to one of the coffee tables and grabbed a hotel notepad. He dialled a number and, after a short delay, he coughed and started talking in a deep voice.

'Yes. Hello, I'm staying in the penthouse on twenty-six. I've been in meetings all day and am on my way back to the hotel now. I'd like someone to go up and check that the air conditioning is on. Last time I walked in it was unacceptable.' Then he just ended the call.

I held my hands up as I walked towards him. 'I don't understand,' I said.

But then Spence dragged me back to the lifts. 'Just wait,' he said with a wink.

One minute later, a maid came rushing towards the lifts and pressed the up button. Spence, who had a hand on my shoulder, put a finger to his mouth to tell me not to speak. It was then that I realised, he had us under a glamour.

The lift bell sounded and the maid ducked through its doors. We were close behind. Inside, she swiped her key card and pressed the number twenty-six. Finally – I got it. I also saw what kind of glamour Spence had used – nothing. Literally, when I looked in the mirror I couldn't see anything other than the maid. No wonder Spence wanted me to stay silent.

Who needs an invisibility cloak when you've got a Spence?

The ride took a lifetime. I didn't breathe I was so scared of exposing us. Finally, the lift stopped and the doors slid silently open. Level twenty-six.

We snuck out and waited in the hall as the maid went up to one of the two doors and knocked. Spence hadn't clarified which penthouse he was 'staying' in – it was perfect. She was going to have to check both.

The door opened and a scantily-clad woman answered the door.

'Da?' she said, in what I thought was a Russian accent.

'Madam, I'm sorry but I'm just checking to see that your air conditioning is running to your satisfaction?'

The woman, who was dressed in a clingy leopard-print dress, looked at the maid like she were something she'd stepped in. Spence was shaking a little and I elbowed him to stop him from laughing out loud.

''Tis fine,' the woman said.

'Certainly, madam, sorry for the interruption,' the maid said, backing away and giving a little curtsey as she did. I had no idea how much a night in the penthouse cost, but judging from the woman and the sheer amount of jewellery she was draped in, I was willing to bet it was a lot.

Spence and I flattened ourselves against the wall as the maid moved over to the other door, now flustered. This was it. If Onyx was right, Nahilius could be behind this door. My stomach jumped into my throat as we watched the maid give three polite knocks.

Waiting.

Will Nahilius be able to see through the glamour?

Waiting.

I felt for my dagger and wondered if today would be the day.

Waiting.

No answer. He wasn't in.

The maid tugged on the swipe key hanging from one of those coil key rings around her waist and opened the door.

Spence and I quietly glided through the door before it closed. We watched silently as the maid checked the air-conditioning unit, pressed a few buttons and again waited.

We gave each other a look. *What was she waiting for?* But then, the air conditioning made a sound and kicked in. We felt a breeze of cool air, which gave me a different type of chill, filter into the room. The maid nodded to herself, checked the digital control monitor one more time, and left.

Spence took his hand off my shoulder. I knew the moment he did the glamour would lift, but I didn't feel anything as it happened. Weird.

'Holy crap!' Spence said, taking in the gigantic suite we were standing in. I mean, you think you've seen penthouses before, on TV and stuff, but this was something else altogether. It was three times the size of my apartment easily and was only one bedroom.

The living area was a new kind of huge – it had a plunge pool right in the middle – Steph would have freaked. Or maybe just felt at home.

Spence charged from one end to the other, stopping

only to pull out his phone again. I was about to ask, when I saw him start to line it up and take photos.

'Spence, we really don't have time.'

He just shrugged and put away the phone. 'Well, he's not here. Where to now?'

'I don't know.' I hadn't thought beyond getting here. I looked around, confused. 'I could've sworn I sensed an exile – I still can.'

'You've got a pretty wide range and this is a dense area. You could be sensing other exiles nearby.'

He was right and it wouldn't be the first time. But still, I couldn't shake the feeling. Something was off.

I called Steph. My only hope was that she might have found a lead.

'Hey,' Steph said, answering on the second ring. 'I was just about to call you.'

'Please tell me you have something, Steph. I'm nearly out of time,' I said, feeling as desperate as I sounded.

'It's not much, but I found one thing. It's the building Lincoln's mum owned. It's abandoned now but from what I can see it was one of the main assets of her business. The deeds for the property were set aside before she died. I'm guessing somehow Nahilius got her to sign it over to him.'

'And?' I prompted.

'Well, I did a search and the building went on the open market a few weeks ago. I think he's trying to sell it while he's here.'

I remembered the text message on Lincoln's phone. 'City Comm Realty?' I'd given Steph the name, but we'd had nothing to link it to at the time.

'You got it.'

'Where?' It was the best shot we had.

I moved to the window as Steph was talking and looked down at all the people crowding the city footpaths far below, the cars streaming by. No one knew what was really going on in this world. It's funny, but at that moment more than any other, I knew that if I couldn't find my way back to Lincoln then both of us were going to be very lonely. It wasn't about *being together* it was about sharing this life together, about being the partners we were destined to be.

I realised, too, that I'd always begrudged it. Even when I'd stood on that cliff, it crossed my mind before I jumped – that by becoming Grigori, by becoming his partner, I was not only helping him but also ensuring that we'd never be together.

Thinking of him directly, I had a surge of nearness. Lincoln was close. My body reacted, my *power* reacted, knowing he wasn't far. It was like I was starving for him. The human *and* the angel. *How could that be?*

Steph rattled out the address and as she did, the craziness of it all settled in and her words slowly registered. My eyes looked up and across the road to what was now an abandoned building.

The senses erupted within, encouraged by knowledge, my angelic part now on the hunt.

'Oh. My. God.'

'What?' Steph asked on the other end of the phone just as Spence said it from right beside me.

'It's across the road,' I replied, answering them both. 'They're across the damn road.'

I could have cursed myself for not trying to pinpoint the senses when we first arrived at the hotel. I could have blamed myself for not using my connection to Lincoln earlier. I could have felt responsible for putting Spence in direct danger as I charged into the hotel lift with him desperate to get to Lincoln in time. I *could* have done a lot of things.

Instead, I thought of the time that Lincoln had asked me to tell him I loved him. My mind went back to that terrible day when I first became Grigori, to healing him and feeling completely connected to, and yet disconnected from, him. Everything was wrong for us that day – but it was the one day he'd told me the most. The day he'd confessed he cared. That, like me, he'd fantasised about us being together. I could almost hear his words.

'*I planned everything – the dinner, the candles, the lilies.*'

Since we'd sorted everything out after I became Grigori, we'd settled on just being friends – it was the only option – but Lincoln had always kept a vase of lilies in the warehouse. Always white – my favourite. When Griffin had commented one day, Lincoln just smiled and told him they brightened the place. But he'd glanced at me, his eyes green and perfect, glistening with something that we both knew deep down was our secret.

There were lots of things I should have been thinking. Tactical thoughts would have been sensible, but in that lift and running through that lobby, full of pretentious rich people who would never get it, everything came down to one simple thing – there was no limit to what I was willing to do for him.

No limit whatsoever.

In the lobby, I pushed past the businessman who

thought the world revolved around him as he paced in the middle of the walkway on his mobile phone. I jumped over the Louis Vuitton luggage that had been dumped near the entrance and I didn't even spare a glance for Spence. I threw all of my strength – which was way too much – into the front entryway doors before the designated doorman even reached for the handle and flung myself through them into the street as the shattered glass fell to the ground behind me.

Franticness overtook. I wasn't going to let Lincoln do this – especially if part of him felt like he was doing it to protect me.

The doorman yelled at me to stop. I was too fast.

I understood this choice better than anyone. It's not that I regret the decisions I've made but if I'd had another choice... It would have been nice to have had another option.

The visions that had tormented me at that old farmhouse taunted me again. The decisions that were made in that desert when I embraced. The choices that haunted me in my dreams and plagued me when awake.

It seemed so obvious now – of course, it was my greatest fear.

I was hurling myself into the road, dodging traffic on a busy six-lane street as I remembered how I'd rammed my own dagger into myself. How sharp the point had been, how easily it sliced into my flesh, how easily *I* forced it in. I had struck myself down with that killing blow and it wasn't the question but rather the answer that disturbed me. A car honked, another swerved and all I could think was –

I'll never know.

I'll never really know who I killed that day.

It was agony, to admit there was a part of me that honestly believed I really *did* kill part of myself – my humanity. As I became more and more powerful as Grigori I feared my humanity slipped further and further away and that frightened the crap out of me.

I would not, would not, *would not* let that happen to Lincoln.

I reached the other side of the road and gasped desperately for air. I wasn't tired at all but I felt as if my insides had seized and my lungs had compressed with the terrible truth. I had no idea who I was.

I straightened, took one final gasp and then I pulled myself together.

Remember the rules, Vi – no quitting, no running!

Spence leapt into position beside me, cars honking like mad. He didn't speak. What was the point? He knew we were going in. Nothing in this world was going to stop me and he was along for the ride. No invitation issued or required.

I wasn't about to let Lincoln do something that might make him later question his beautiful humanity, the very light that shines out of him at all times. I simply wouldn't allow it. There were no limits any more – nothing I wouldn't do to protect that – because I knew.

I wouldn't quit on Lincoln.

CHAPTER TWENTY-TWO

*'Knowing your own darkness is the best method for
dealing with the darkness of other people.'*
Carl Jung

The front door to the building, or rather, the massive piece
of rotted, flaking, plywood that was covering the entryway
had already been partially ripped off and was hanging
loosely from the last few nails.

I could sense the exiles clearly now. We pushed aside
the makeshift door and entered. I paused to focus my
senses.

'What now?' Spence whispered.

'They're upstairs,' I said, without breaking concentration.

They were directly above us. I drew into my power, not
just my senses but beyond.

It was like the night in Hades when I'd felt Onyx and
Joel coming, like what I had started to feel at the airport – as
if some element of myself, not physical, was being lifted off
the ground.

I became somehow separate from myself. Able to go anywhere I wanted with just a thought. My senses moved through walls, rooms and ceilings – capable. *Powerful.* I moved upstairs, faster than my body could carry me, and found them. A group of exiles. Lincoln and Magda. They were already fighting.

I came back to myself, and felt disoriented. A sensation not dissimilar to the car sickness I'd felt earlier overwhelmed me, momentarily.

Spence was right up in my face and I had to step back to reinstate the required distance. His brow was furrowed. He was looking at me like some kind of puzzle he couldn't work out.

Join the club.

'There are four of them.' But I knew more than that – I knew for example, that three of them had been angels of dark, but that the other must have been Nahilius, since he had been an angel of light. I recognised one as the exile we'd let go that night at the farmhouse. It was strange. I couldn't see him, recognise him by his look or characteristics, it was more of an internal signature.

It was all connected. This was my proof. Phoenix. Somehow he was calling the shots. The thing I didn't understand was – *how*? Surely everything couldn't have just fallen into place for him so perfectly?

'Spence, they're already fighting. Magda has two, Lincoln is fighting the other two, one of them being Nahilius. Listen,' I grabbed his shoulder, 'none of them are all that powerful – this is weird. I mean, Phoenix is behind all of this – why didn't he send exiles who would be more of a threat?'

'Maybe they have weapons, too?' Spence suggested. But I couldn't see that.

'Maybe.'

'So? How do you want to play this?'

Sacrifice is a funny thing. Sometimes the less time we have to think about something, the more we're willing to do. Maybe if I'd had the luxury of time and consideration I would have made a different decision. I'll never know.

I didn't tell Spence everything, just the part he would play. It's not that I particularly thought he'd have a problem with it but, well, I didn't want him to jump the gun.

'Let's go,' I said, already moving.

We ran up the stairs and into the open first level. The floor had been stripped bare – right down to the concrete. Stray electrical wiring hung from the ceiling. Everything of any kind of value had been taken and the rest, it appeared from the piles of ash that were all over the floor, had been burned to keep squatters warm in the winter.

Buildings like this don't stay vacant for long in the city.

There was nowhere to hide, no partitioning walls or desks to scramble under, so Spence and I ran right into the middle of the action.

We moved straight past the two exiles Magda was fighting off without pause. She didn't stop fighting, or let down her guard, but she saw us. And I saw her register… surprise.

Spence and I kept moving forward, sticking to the plan.

Spence threw himself into the fight with the exile who was grappling with Lincoln, which left Lincoln with only Nahilius to concentrate on. Lincoln moved in on Nahilius, who was clearly outmatched. I was surprised to see how battle-shy this infamous exile was. Maybe when he'd had the help of the other exile he had a chance at holding off his opponent but now it was one on one and Nahilius had no game.

It could have been because Lincoln's force was unrelenting as he threw solid fist after fist into Nahilius's face – and by the state of the other exiles, had already been there, done that – but I had not seen such lame fighting from an exile before.

I was just getting centred when Lincoln screamed something. I think it was, 'Magda!' but I can't be sure because it was overruled by a God-awful crack and boom that reverberated through the building.

Gunfire isn't a sound normally associated with fighting exiles, so it threw everyone. We all paused – a super-fast intake of what had just happened. Magda had shot one of the exiles she was fighting.

It was crazy to think all of this had taken place within a few seconds of Spence and me coming up the stairs.

I heard Lincoln yell, 'Get out of here!'

I assumed the order was for me. I ignored it.

The exile who had been shot – in the throat, of all horrific places – writhed on the floor, screaming, while gurgling on his own blood.

It was wrong. Magda could've returned him, instead she'd chosen this torture.

Grigori exist to get rid of exiles. We have to take whatever steps are necessary to protect human life, to guard free will and hopefully not get killed in the process, but nowhere in the job description does it say torture and maim. That's what exiles do. It is one of the all-important distinctions. Griffin had told me that very thing.

Magda had just crossed the line.

Blood flowed from the exile's neck freely for a few moments before it stopped. He was already healing, but that didn't make it OK.

I refocused on the job at hand. Lincoln was still pounding into Nahilius, who surprised me by getting in a few hits to Lincoln as well.

Magda screamed out, 'Shoot him!', and Lincoln's hand went to his waist. I could see his dagger and the handle to what must have been another gun poking out from his jeans. He pulled out his dagger.

'Get out, Violet!' Lincoln growled at me.

But I was exactly where I needed to be.

Gun or dagger, it made little difference. I looked over to Spence, who had the upper hand in his fight but I could see he was getting carried away.

'Spence! Hurry up!' I yelled.

An instant later, Spence grabbed the exile's arm and twisted it behind his back. He yelled to the exile to make a choice but didn't wait more than the time it took him to secure the physical lock required to release his power for an answer, before he drove his dagger into the exile's lower back and up. Just like that, Spence's exile disappeared. Simply gone.

It was now or never.

I released my power and crossed my fingers.

An amethyst mist – not unlike billions of tiny airborne crystals – lifted from me and dusted the room. Each minuscule crystal rotated smoothly, searching out all corners and then dissolving the moment it made contact.

I heard Spence gasp. It had to have been him. Lincoln and Magda had seen my mist before.

I didn't stop or lose concentration, I just kept pushing it out, until I had each exile in my control. My eyes focused on the room and the mist settled, though a small showering of it remained around me, following my every movement. It was part of me.

The exiles were frozen. Paralysed, but aware of what was happening. I started to take small steps towards Lincoln.

Before any of us could move further, Magda plunged her dagger into the exile she was fighting, the one she hadn't shot. It was the one from the farmhouse and while I felt no love lost, I still thought he should have been entitled to his choice. Magda hadn't given him a second glance.

Lincoln looked at me when I took another small step in his direction, then to Nahilius. One hand in a white-knuckled grip around his dagger, the other hand fisted tightly. Magda screamed out again for Lincoln to kill Nahilius and when Lincoln glanced at her I took my chance.

I lunged forward at top speed and my fist went right into Lincoln's face.

Normally, a move like this was not advisable. Lincoln is near unbeatable and even on a bad day he'd see it coming. But this wasn't a bad day – it was his worst. Channelling all my force into that one hit, the impact was enough to throw him off-balance. I didn't waste the advantage of surprise and swiftly moved in with another hit to his face. I didn't think – I just did it.

The dagger dropped from his hand and he collapsed to his knees.

One more, Vi. Make it good.

Lincoln's eyes, full of surprise, lifted to meet mine as I pivoted around and swung my foot across his face. The impact was full force again and he went down completely.

'What the hell are you doing?' Magda screamed, but by the time I looked over to her, Spence was already holding her back. Just.

'Nice gun, Magda,' I said. 'You plan on shooting me, too?'

Magda looked at me with shock, then down to the hand that was still holding the gun, now pointed at me. She lowered her arm and tried to shrug Spence off. Bless him, he just kept holding on.

'Lincoln is *my* partner.' My eyes were flitting between her and Lincoln. 'Now back up, unless you're going to use that thing,' I said, looking at her gun again.

She jolted free of Spence's hold, who let her this time, and walked a few steps away.

I turned back to Lincoln and knelt beside him. He was coming round. I didn't have long.

I called on my power again, hoping I'd be able to keep my hold on the remaining exiles while also doing this. I focused on the healing element and sent it out to Lincoln, feeling the power travel into him. I sent it to his heart. I hoped that just as his powers had sought out the pain in my heart the other day my power might be able to do the same and even ease some of the pain in his.

I needed to bring him back to me.

My will worked its way through him, touching his heart and even deeper, to the fibre of his soul. But it was waiting for something. To strip away some of Lincoln's fear and pain, I also needed to fill the void, send something to take its place. There were so many reasons why I shouldn't, good reasons, too, but in the end it was easy.

I sent him love.

I pulled the gun from his waistband and slid it over to Spence, who stopped it with his foot.

Lincoln opened his eyes. I took his dagger in my hand.

'Violet. What's… What's going on? You knocked me out,' he said, sounding perplexed.

I smiled sadly. 'Linc, we all have to make choices.' My hand instinctively went to his face, soothing him. 'They're not always easy. Now you get to make yours.'

I stood, all business now. 'But this is how it's going to work.'

'I don't understand.'

I walked towards Nahilius, who remained silent. He was watching what was going on, eyes darting between where Lincoln and I were to Magda and Spence. He could move a little, and talk, too, if he wanted to – but he didn't. I could almost see his mind working, looking between everyone, searching for the weak link.

'If you want to kill him, you're going to have to ask me to do it,' I said, raising my hand to show I was armed with his dagger.

'Violet, you don't know what you're doing. Don't be ridiculous.' He started to get up.

'If you get up off the floor, I'll kill him,' I said, trying not to flinch at my own words.

'This isn't your battle,' he snapped at me, but he didn't get up off the ground.

'I would rather it was me than you.'

'How can you say that?'

'Because, Linc, I need you to make the good decision.'

His green eyes locked on mine. 'You healed me, didn't you?' His hand went to his heart. 'The tightness…the…'

'Pain. I didn't heal it, I just eased it…and, and you're an idiot. You don't have to carry all of this on your own,' I said, a combination of hurt and anger seeping into my words.

Holding the dagger out, my arm started to tremble. I was growing weak from keeping the exiles at bay and healing Lincoln.

'Coming from you, that's—' he started, but I cut him off.

'I'm not going to let you do this.' I forced the shaking to stop and showed him nothing but resolve.

He let out a small cry. 'He'll kill you!' he crackled through less than a whisper, barely audible. 'I can't survive it.'

I wanted to drop to the ground, crawl over and cradle him in my arms. Tell him everything would be OK. But that would be a lie. I didn't know if things would ever be OK, for any of us. And somehow, I knew trying to explain to him that Nahilius wasn't the problem wouldn't help. I bit down hard on the inside of my lip. I bit until I drew blood and felt the sting. I forced the control and stood my ground.

'If you kill him, it will change you. Forever. Trust me…' I stared into the nothingness, that place that I could go. 'I know.'

He looked to the ground. 'That's a price I'm willing to pay.'

I shook my head at him, desperation mixed with stubbornness taking over. 'Well, I'm not!'

Lincoln, increasingly confused, looked from Nahilius to me. He was suffering so badly. The cruel burden of inherent protector weighing him down.

My only chance was to turn things around, give him a way to save us both.

'You're not the only one who will pay the price for this decision. Don't you get it? Since the trials... Since... that day,' I struggled to hold my voice as I fought back the memories trying to invade. 'The only time I find myself – *me* – is in you.'

Truth stung my eyes and I quickly blinked the tears away and forced fresh ones back.

Now is not the time for leakages.

'If you do this, you'll be gone and what will happen to me?'

Please, let this work.

'You don't need me to know who you are,' he said, quietly, not able to look at me.

'Of course I do. When one soul is lost, how can it ever find itself again if not in its—'

'Counterpart,' he finished, astonished. He was looking at me now, the cogs turning behind his vivid-green eyes.

'Yes,' I confessed, relieved yet terrified I was admitting what I knew.

We were silent, both wondering where to go from here. Confusion built in Lincoln's face, as he battled an internal war.

'Lincoln,' Magda said smoothly. 'Violet is young. She doesn't understand. Nahilius won't stop and you won't get another shot at this. Are you really willing to take that chance?' Her voice was honey sweet, and more dangerous than any bee sting.

Lincoln's eyes were darting around the room, frantically. He would do what he believed was best. He would protect me at all costs, I knew that now. Just as I would him.

'I will not hunt you,' Nahilius said, surprising everyone.

He looked like he wanted to say more, but my arm was shaking badly now. I was out of time. I mustered all the strength I could and turned on Lincoln again. 'Decide. If you don't make up your mind in five seconds, I'll kill him.'

Please, please, please let this work.

It was the only option. If it had to be one of us, I would rather it was me. I was already broken.

'One…two…three—'

'Wait!' Lincoln screamed. 'No, Violet. Don't!' He dropped his head and lowered his voice. 'I don't want this.'

I let out the breath I was holding and relaxed my arm, still fighting to keep my hold over the other exiles.

He stood. 'I'm so sorry.'

I took a step towards him, my shoulders dropping with relief, but flinched when from behind me, Nahilius screamed, 'No!'

Even spinning around at inhuman speed didn't get me there in time to see or stop any of it. All I saw was Magda standing behind Nahilius, the tip of her dagger coming through his chest.

'Bitch!' Nahilius moaned, staring straight at me as he fell to his knees, but before they hit the ground, he was gone.

I was startled by the venom in the one word intended for me until I realised I had no right to be. I had held him in that immobile state, threatened his life, then, when I was finished with him, had done nothing but turn my back in time for his end.

I am a bitch.

Spence watched, hands stuck mid-air, mouth open. He didn't know what to do. I couldn't blame him, nor did I. We'd wanted to stop them using guns and Lincoln killing Nahilius for the wrong reasons. We hadn't considered things beyond that. It's not like we were planning to send the exiles off at the end with a pat on the back.

It was Lincoln who walked over and stood on the spot Nahilius no longer inhabited.

'Magda, you had no right.'

But Magda stood tall as she sheathed her dagger. 'I had every right, Lincoln. I helped you do this in your way and let you make the call, but he's an exile and that's our job. I'm not sorry for that.' She stormed away towards the stairs. 'I'll be downstairs when you two are done with your reunion.'

Spence chose this moment to walk over to the final exile, who had been wordlessly recovering on the ground from his gunshot wound. He glanced at me quickly. He wasn't asking permission – Magda was right, this was our job description – he was checking that I wouldn't object, which I didn't.

It was over quickly.

Lincoln and I watched on silently.

'Um…' Spence said, looking awkward. 'I think I'll go hold Maggy's hand. She seems a bit wound up.' He was giving us space.

Lincoln pulled me in for a hug as soon as Spence was out of sight. 'I feel like I haven't seen you in ages.'

'You haven't.'

'I guess not. I'm sorry,' he said, his words thick with emotion as he held me close, breathing deeply. I could have sworn he was breathing me in. 'I couldn't let him get to you.'

'I know. It's over now.'

He pulled back from the embrace. 'Hey, you didn't... You know... When you healed me...you didn't have to—' but he didn't get a chance to finish. It's too hard to talk when someone is kissing you.

It was wrong, totally.

But it was right, completely.

Our souls were connected. I realised when I reached within my power to help heal Lincoln's heart that I shouldn't be able to do this. Phoenix may be able to have a physical connection with me, even tamper with my emotions, but all of that was related to the senses – to external forces. The soul is the only part that is eternal, that transcends the fabric and goes beyond, into the tiniest fibres of our very existence. My soul belonged to Lincoln as his belonged to mine. Did that make everything OK? Open the doors to happily ever after? Of course not. There would never be a guarantee, just a feeling, and that wasn't enough. Not for the risk.

But I kissed him anyway. I opened my power to him. Not for healing purposes, but for a brief liberation. I was nervous he'd pull away and I felt him hesitate for a moment, but then just as my power had opened to him his power flooded into me. Finally, we could no longer deny the truth to each other.

Even if it is just for this moment. It's perfect.

I pulled away from him, but kept my arms around his waist. Not wanting to break contact yet. For once, things were as they should be. He knew I loved him, I knew he loved me.

We didn't say it wouldn't last. That there was too much at stake. And we didn't pretend it wasn't real. One stolen moment that would punish me later. Painfully.

It was a sentence I was prepared to serve.

CHAPTER TWENTY-THREE

On the way to the airport, Spence and I filled Magda and Lincoln in on everything. They knew some from what Griffin had told them, but hadn't heard the latest updates about the plane or the destination.

'I can't believe you went to that aircraft hangar without me,' Lincoln said. But he was only concerned, not accusatory. I was struggling to follow, anyway. Lucid thoughts were hard to hold on to. He was still holding my hand, his thumb running over it back and forth, gently. I couldn't stop counting. I was up to sixty-three. Sixty-four.

'It all comes back to Phoenix,' I said, my voice catching. The lies and omissions had to stop. Lincoln could handle it and he deserved the truth, 'It was Phoenix who brought back Nahilius.'

Magda swung around from the front seat with surprise, before landing a sour look on me.

Jesus, she hates me to the extreme.

Lincoln was shocked, too, but I kept going.

'He set it up to distract you. He wanted to separate us.'

Lincoln's free hand fisted tightly. I heard his breathing deepen, the way it does when he's fuming about something. Of all people to use Nahilius against him, Phoenix was the worst. In the end, Lincoln just nodded. He got it. I wasn't going to rub it in.

We drove the rest of the way in silence. Spence was texting on his phone, constantly, and Magda didn't acknowledge us again, but I knew she'd heard everything. I was guessing she was pissed off it wasn't her holding Lincoln's hand right now.

Can't say I felt bad for her though.

As we neared the airport, Lincoln squeezed my hand and shuffled the tiny bit closer to me that the back seat would allow.

'Thank you, Vi,' he whispered.

It wasn't only him that swallowed hard. I knew what he was saying – how big it was. Saving someone from doing something so horrific, something they would never have been able to come back from – I knew how much it meant. I was glad I could save him. It felt a little like rescuing myself, too.

The taxi pulled up outside departures and we all got out, except for Spence. He was still busy typing away on his phone.

'You guys go on. I'll see you when you get back,' he said, barely looking up.

Magda had already walked on ahead, not concerned at all with what any of us did right now.

Sulking, much?

When Spence realised we hadn't moved on, he looked up and gave us a cheesy grin.

'It's fine. Seriously. I get it: no partner, no ticket. It's OK, I hear Jordan sucks, anyway.' He pulled the taxi door closed and went back to his phone. 'See you guys later,' he said through the open window.

The car drove off and Lincoln, still holding my hand, started to walk towards the entrance to the departures area.

'You think he's really going to let this go?'

'Not a chance,' I answered.

But before we could start to speculate as to what Spence was up to my phone rang. I would have to let go of Lincoln's hand to pull it out. I didn't want to. Once the connection was broken... I knew this wasn't forever and wished I could hold on a little longer. But then, Lincoln let go of me.

'I think that's you,' he said, smiling as my heart sank thinking that it seemed so easy for him.

I guess that's that.

'Hello?' I said.

'Violet, tell me you've got them,' Griffin said.

'Yeah, we're at the airport – where do we go?'

'You'll have to run, we're already on the runway and they want to take off. Don't go through the commercial terminal. Come around the southern end of the building and through the security gates there. There's a uniformed soldier there, Lieutenant Marks, who'll get you through. Don't say anything to anyone.'

'Do we need passports?' I said, suddenly panicking I'd made a critical error.

'No. Just get to Marks fast and you'll be OK. Hurry!'

I was already running, with Lincoln beside me keeping pace. We couldn't see Magda – she had gone on ahead into the commercial building.

After a couple of minutes of running way too fast for normal humans, we spotted the security gates and had to slow to a walk – there were more people around. We picked the official who had to be Lieutenant Marks, since he was uniformed and already looking straight at us. As soon as we reached the gates, he said something to the security officers, who then nodded at us. Marks waved us in and was already jogging towards the runway. We followed suit.

When we hit the open tarmac, Marks pointed to a large green plane that had at least a dozen military personnel standing guard around it and was stationary on the runway. After a quick nod, he started back in the opposite direction.

Lincoln took the lead and we ran to the back end of the plane, which was still open. Griffin was standing there with a guy dressed head to toe in camouflage greens.

'You the last two?' the army guy called out over the roar of the engines.

'No!' Lincoln yelled back. 'One more on the way!'

We looked behind us, but could see no sign of Magda.

The soldier looked back to Griffin. 'Sorry, but we have to go or we'll lose our slot! Your friend will have to get on a later flight. We have a transport plane headed to Jordan tomorrow – any stragglers can get on that.'

Griffin clearly wanted to argue, but the army guy was too busy pushing us all towards the stairs as a military truck was driven up the ramp.

'That's all of 'em!' yelled the driver as he jumped out and started back down the ramp. 'You're good to go!'

The soldier ushered us further inside and hollered into his radio.

'All clear for take-off! Doors up!'

Then he gave Griffin a salute, which Griffin aptly mirrored in response, and disappeared up towards the front of the plane.

When the doors closed things became much easier to hear.

'Right,' said Griffin, looking at Lincoln and me, and then down. We were no longer holding hands but somehow, without noticing we'd moved so close, we were touching from shoulder to elbow. 'You'd better tell me what the hell's been going on,' he said, as we followed him through to the upstairs section of the double-decker plane.

It was amazing, not as big as the Antanov Phoenix had been using, but it was still cool. Spence would have been in heaven. The cargo area was pretty standard, but upstairs was more similar to a commercial plane, though the seats were a lot bigger and there were desks scattered between them. Griffin stopped at the first set of seats arranged like a four-seater booth. Everyone else was already on the plane, seated and buckled. Nyla and Rudyard were opposite, Zoe and Salvatore back a couple of rows behind them.

Lincoln and I filled Griffin in on what had happened with Nahilius. I became nervous when I had to mention the guns, but Lincoln stepped in and explained. He took responsibility for everything and didn't skip over anything. He really was feeling himself again – always the martyr.

Griffin honed in on the most significant issue instantly. 'So Magda has guns these days,' he said, in a flat tone.

Poor Griffin. He looked exhausted. He'd been running all over town trying to organise us as well as the entire city. Magda should have been helping him, not putting a gun in Lincoln's hands.

'Griff, this is on me. Don't blame Magda. I was out of control. She was only trying to help me,' Lincoln confessed, bowing his head in shame. I fought the urge to contribute my opinion on the matter.

'Yes, well, we'll deal with that later. Let's just get to Jordan and find these Scriptures.'

Griffin pulled a file from his bag and sat down. From the looks of it, he wanted to be left alone.

'Buckle up for take-off,' a male voice said over the PA. It was weird to hear what sounded like an order instead of a polite airline flight attendant.

Lincoln took my hand again and I exhaled, as if sated by just one touch. He pulled me towards the back of the plane. When we passed Rudyard, he put his hand out and grabbed my free wrist.

'Are you sure?' he said to Lincoln as much as to me.

My eyes grew wide, my mouth quickly dry. I was about to explain, to say that we knew it was too risky, when I looked at Lincoln. He was smiling.

'We're hungry, Rudy, we'll talk later,' Lincoln said and started to pull me towards him again. Rudyard kept hold of my wrist. He didn't say anything, he just held it for that extra moment, squeezed a bit tighter and then slowly let me go with a thoughtful smile that I couldn't decipher.

Lincoln stopped at the larder at the end of the cabin and

handed me a banana I knew was for him and crisps I knew were for me. I was somewhere between astonished, elated and...petrified. Lincoln looked happy. He grabbed a couple of bottles of water and we settled into the back seats behind Zoe and Salvatore, who after each saying a quick hello, left us in peace.

Is this possible? Does Lincoln mean to keep his hold on me for more than just now?

I went through the motions, buckling up and eating my crisps in a daze, trying to work it all out. We were soulmates – I was almost sure of it. But as always, there was that voice, the one that pulls everything apart, whispering in my ear.

Are you sure enough? Sure enough to let him risk his power?
I stared out the window. *Damn.*

Phoenix was probably on his way to Jordan, too. No one had sensed him or any other exiles at the airport – they'd gone somewhere. It was never going to be easy. We were Grigori – angel warriors who dealt with the angel realm's cast-offs, the egotistical riff-raff – but now, for the first time, there was a possibility we could face it together. Partners in every way.

If you're right. And if you're wrong, he'll never forgive you.

Lincoln snacked on his banana, stealing one of my crisps every now and then, and we chatted for a while. I tried, unsuccessfully, to focus when he asked me how my dad was doing on his trip, which only reminded me I needed to call him. We talked about how I would miss school and that it was good Steph could help me catch up. As we sat there, in a military aeroplane on our way to fight exiles for Scriptures that have been lost so long they're almost forgotten completely, Lincoln told me about a rock-climbing trip he'd seen advertised. He thought we could go together and use it for training.

I don't know when I fell asleep, only that his arms stayed wrapped around me the entire time. For the first time I could remember, when I dreamed the sun shone brightly and the world was as it should be. A dream.

In the end, though, we all wake up... Don't we?

Lincoln had to coax me awake when we landed. I was surprised that I hadn't woken up when we touched down.

'Where are we?' I asked, groggy.

'Jordan. You slept through the refuel,' Lincoln said.

I guess I was more exhausted than I'd realised.

'Did you get any sleep?' I asked, taking big gulps of water, sure I had awful morning breath.

He gave a small shake of his head. 'Doesn't mean I wasn't dreaming, though.' He smoothed my hair down at the back.

I must have looked hideous.

'You look beautiful,' he said, smiling.

'Ha ha.'

'You do. You're most beautiful just after you've woken up. It's always my favourite time, when we go for a run in the morning and I get to see you first thing.' He kept playing with my hair.

I got the feeling he was relishing saying these things out loud. Liberated. There were a lot of things I wished I could say out loud.

But I couldn't. So, I hit him in the arm instead and he laughed.

Zoe and Salvatore were hauling bags out of the cargo area when we headed down the stairs.

''Bout time you two joined us, we aren't your pack-horses, you know,' Zoe said, stomping around tossing bags to Salvatore. I think she was actually aiming for a very sensitive area.

'Ah...Zoe, we didn't bring any bags with us,' I said, throwing her a bitch smile Steph would have been proud of.

'We packed for you!' She catapulted a duffle bag at my head so fast I had to duck.

Lincoln caught it. 'Easy, Zoe,' he said, catching the second bag that came zooming towards us, but he was laughing.

Nyla and Rudyard walked past with their bags and Griffin was soon loading them into the minibus, waiting on the tarmac.

Lincoln carried both of our bags and we headed out of the plane, but as soon as I hit the outside air, I felt something strange. Not strange, exactly, it was the senses, but they were...raw!

Apple sliced into my tongue. I dropped Lincoln's hand, which had somehow ended up in mine again.

'Vi?' I heard him say before the birds circled so close to me I could practically feel them swoop and the branches were whipping so manically I was sure they were lashing me.

My hands were at my face – trying to stave off the overpowering scent of flowers, like fleshy stems left in water long after they had perished – and tried to hold back the intense visions of morning and evening as they melted in and out of each other, working with the cool heat that now flowed through me; ice for bones and lava for blood.

Someone was dragging me back into the plane.

'Violet. It's me.' He held me tightly from behind and spoke right into my ear. 'I'm here. I'm going to help you, give the senses to me,' he said smoothly. 'OK?'

I couldn't answer, I could only scream, but Lincoln wasn't waiting, anyway. He spun me in his hands and – as he'd done once before – crashed through the senses, finding his way to me through a kiss. It happened quicker this time than it had before. We knew what we could do together, we trusted it. We trusted each other.

I fed the senses to him and one by one they moved through me, into him and beyond. My vision returned. I could breathe in Lincoln's sun-baked smell, that hint of honey that came when he was using his power on me, and taste his lips on mine.

He pulled me close and kissed my cheek. 'I got you,' he whispered, sounding drained.

'Do I have really bad breath?' I asked shakily, saying the first thing that came to mind.

He gave a low chuckle which sounded a lot like relief. 'All I could taste was apple,' he reassured me. I was pretty certain he was lying, but I squeezed him tight.

'Something's out there.' I couldn't hold back the tremble in my voice.

'I gathered. Exiles?'

'Exile,' I clarified. 'And not like anything I've felt before.' And yet, the moment I said it aloud, I couldn't stop the feeling I wasn't entirely right. I had felt something similar before – I just had no idea when or where. I shivered.

'It was old. When the senses hit me, it felt like they were only meant for me. Did you feel anything?'

'No, not until I was feeling them through you.'

'None of us did,' said Nyla, who was standing back a bit with the others.

'But I know what you mean,' Lincoln said, still holding me. 'They had an edge to them.'

'Yeah – like the senses had been locked away for a really long time, like they'd built up all this pressure and had gotten old and musty. When they reached me, they just exploded.'

Nyla looked at Rudyard. They were worried. *Not a good sign.*

'Violet, we need to get to the hotel. We can't defend ourselves here. Can you try going outside again?' Nyla asked, as Rudyard pushed the others ahead.

I looked at Lincoln nervously.

'I won't leave your side.' He took my shaking hand, holding it firm to give me strength.

I nodded.

'Come on!' called Griffin from the tarmac, holding open the doors to the minibus.

We all headed out. Lincoln on one side of me, Nyla on the other, but this time when I walked outside it was different.

'Nothing,' I said, though I couldn't relax.

'Keep your defences up, just in case,' Nyla said.

Once we were all piled into the minibus we started making our way to the hotel.

Salvatore leaned over his seat in front of me and passed me a bottle of water.

'Thanks,' I said, even though I wished he hadn't. My hands were shaking badly and now everyone could see.

Lincoln sat back a bit, giving me space. He knew not to smother me when I was like this – that I hated feeling like I was too weak to look after myself. Nyla didn't do the same, but the death-stare she got when she started patting my arm stopped her in her tracks.

Honestly, I'm not a dog.

'Where are we going anyway?' I asked as we drove past a sign saying Amman, keen to move the focus of attention away from me. I knew they were all waiting for answers, but I didn't have them and I was starting to feel claustrophobic.

Griffin turned to face us from the front, where he was studying a map with Rudyard.

'We're going to a Grigori safe-house in the mountains, outside the city of Madaba. Grigori own hotels all over the world, like the one where Nyla and Rudyard are staying. It's the safest place for us, but…'

'Here we go,' Zoe said, voicing exactly what I was thinking.

'. . . they are a different breed of Grigori. This is a sacred place and the local Grigori see themselves as guardians of the land. You will have to try and understand and respect their ways, otherwise they will not help us.'

'I am not understanding,' Salvatore said, sitting forward in his seat. 'This different breeding?'

I did. 'Religious, right?'

'Devout,' Griffin said.

'OK,' Salvatore said, nodding as he pulled a chain out from under the collar of his shirt. Somehow, I doubted a small gold cross was going to make much difference.

As the conversation petered out I turned my attention to the army guy driving the minibus and another army officer, a female, sitting next to him. They had a pretty full-on commando look, the guy big and scary, the girl smaller but compensating with a serious armoury hanging off her. They had the don't-even-look-at-me message sounding loud and clear.

Lincoln was talking with Salvatore. Well, trying. Zoe looked back and caught me staring at the commando guy.

'Nice, huh? I got dibs,' she whispered.

'You can have him, but what's the deal? How come they're helping us?'

She put her feet up on the seat in front and popped a few m&m's, which she had dug out of her backpack, into her mouth.

'Rudyard told them exiles were tampering with their aircraft. There are Grigori all through the military.'

'Why?'

'You need to read a book or something! They figured out a long time ago that exiles would go for the power jobs and one way to get there is to go through the army ranks. Plus, that's how they can get their hands on all the fun toys. Anyway, it draws too much attention when civilians like you and me run in with daggers raised, so Grigori have people stationed within all military sectors, who deal with exiles along the way. Cool, huh?'

'I guess,' I said, gripping the handrail as we drove over a bumpy patch.

'What's the plan once we get there?' Lincoln called out to Griffin.

'We need to talk with the local Grigori. They're expecting us, but they don't know exactly *why*. We thought it best to keep everything as quiet as possible until we were here. This is a big thing. Where we want to go is a sacred place. It may not be easy.'

Like any of this ever is!

We reached the city of Madaba and kept driving through. I'd never been to Jordan before, I'd never really been anywhere. It was fascinating. I pushed down the window the tiny amount it would allow. Searing heat blasted through the opening, dry and crisp. The town was busy and not what I would have expected. The streets were full of cars and small trucks that were open at the back with locals sitting on the edges, feet dangling. The whole city was the colour of desert sand, all the buildings stone or concrete and not more than a few storeys high. Every now and then we would pass something more modern, made of brick – usually a hotel – but they just looked out of place.

Everything was kind of monochrome. Even the signage was predominantly dark brown with white words written in Arabic and some other languages I didn't recognise. The only ones in plain English? The bright red Coca-Cola signs.

'Madaba is famous for its mosaics,' Rudyard said, looking back at us. 'There is an entire school here dedicated to restoring and preserving the mosaic discoveries that have been made in recent history.'

I loved mosaics. I'd done a study on them in art last year. Somehow, though, I was betting we wouldn't be doing much sightseeing.

We drove on in silence, but as we reached the edge of the city, I tasted apple. Oddly, I didn't feel the other senses. I looked out the window, trying to see what or who I was sensing. We drove past the last corner building and a man in faded brown robes stood hunched over, all alone. As our minibus rattled by, he raised his head. He was wearing a hood so I couldn't see his face, but I could have sworn I felt his eyes on me.

Before I could even think to say anything to the others – before I had any idea what it was I *would* say – we turned the corner and hit open road again. I looked back to see the man in the robes had followed us around the corner and watched as we drove away. I stared through the dirty glass, watching Madaba and the stranger disappear as the lingering flavour of bruised apple slowly dissolved in my mouth.

'Oh. Come. On!' Zoe called out, breaking me from my trance.

I swung around to see her pushing her way to get to the front of the minibus. Obviously, I'd missed something. Nyla and Rudyard were laughing hysterically.

'You need to appreciate all types of music, Zoe,' Rudyard said, blocking her path to where Griffin was guarding the stereo controls.

'Here – I brought my iPod. You can pick any song from it, any song at all – just turn off that crap you're listening to. I swear, you people have to move with the times!'

Griffin turned up the volume. He was playing some old

song I recognised but didn't know the name of. It was one I could remember being tortured with as a kid when Dad actually had control over the radio. I fully agreed with Zoe. Even Salvatore seemed offended by the music selection.

Zoe slumped back into her chair, muttering something about how she should whip up a sandstorm. I just leaned my head against the window, which was warm and uncomfortable, matching the feeling from the vinyl seat coverings, which had stuck to my thighs. I had little doubt that wherever we were headed in the mountains was going to be a bare-minimum kind of place.

My mind drifted again as we continued through the desert. It was impossible *not* to think of the last time I had been in a place like this. Death felt dangerously close. At least I wasn't alone this time. Then again, *this* time I knew who was waiting for me and I had no idea what I was going to do about him.

Or, what he was planning to do about me.

CHAPTER TWENTY-FOUR

*'Those who hate most fervently, must have once loved
deeply; those who want to deny the world, must have
once embraced what they now set on fire.'*
Kurt Tucholsky

'Wow.'

I don't know who else said it. It sounded like a chorus though – maybe all of us.

Well, when I'm wrong, I'm *totally* wrong.

'Are you sure this is where we're staying?' I asked, standing in front of the most incredible building that I'd ever laid eyes on. Nestled in the gigantic stone mountains with waterfalls cascading behind it, the entire place – *palace* is the only word for it – was built of heavy sandstone blocks and crowned with domed rooftops. It was somewhere between Aladdin's Palace and Steph's ideal getaway.

'Steph is going to flip,' I said, thinking of her.

Salvatore nodded, looking around confused. I followed his gaze.

The only thing there wasn't, was people.

'I'll go find someone,' Griffin said, heading towards the massive wooden entry doors.

Lincoln gave my shoulder a squeeze.

'Hang on. I'll come with you,' he said, running after Griffin.

He was finally letting us be what I'd always dreamed of. So why was I freaking out?

Once he and Griffin had gone through the main doors, the rest of us slowly followed with the bags. When we made it into the main lobby area, again, I was amazed at how beautiful it was. We were in the middle of nowhere and yet here was this spectacular hideaway.

We dumped the bags just as Griffin and Lincoln walked over with a man and a woman both wearing a similar kind of outfit. Not exactly robes, like the ones I had seen covering some of the women in the town, more like baggy yoga-wear or something. Black wide cotton pants that finished above the ankle, revealing the almost matching sandals underneath and a wide-cut top with half-length sleeves in the same fabric. I didn't know if it was a culture thing, a religious thing or just…comfy.

'This is Azeem and Ermina. They are Grigori partners and the owners of the hotel. Azeem is of a Seraph.'

Azeem was freakishly tall and well built. Everything about him seemed huge, and when he put his hand out in offering, everyone else's seemed to get swallowed in his hold. Ermina was the opposite, petite in every way.

We all said hello and understood that since Azeem was of the Seraphim, Griffin had just introduced us to the leader in these parts.

'We are not open for normal business at the moment.

We have been taking a break from the public – some time for prayer. We are not due to re-open until next month. The hotel is almost entirely locked up but we have arranged for the northern wing to be opened for you. You will find everything you need there and meals will be served in the dining area,' Azeem said, in a deep, rounded voice.

Rudyard gave a small bow of respect. 'Thank you, Azeem. We are sorry to impose and will not be here for long.'

'It is no trouble, though we *would* like to know your intentions.'

Nyla stepped forward. 'We'd be happy to discuss this and hope we may then ask for your assistance. Perhaps we could get settled and then have a walk through your security systems first, though.'

Always thinking tactically, Nyla was going to make sure we were safe first. I had to admire her direct approach.

Azeem and Ermina exchanged a glance and for a moment I thought we might have a problem but then they nodded.

'Ermina will show you to your rooms and then I will arrange for a tour,' Azeem confirmed.

When it came to picking rooms, panic set in. I couldn't look at Lincoln. Griffin took the first, then, as we walked down the hall, Ermina allocated suites one by one. I was impressed she'd remembered all of our names from the brief introductions. She presented so meekly, especially for a Grigori. If I hadn't known better – looking at her fragile frame, mousy hair and small features – I would have thought a gust of wind could take her down.

Griffin walked into his room but just before he closed his door, he gave me a look. I was sure he wanted to say something, but seemed to restrain himself.

Yes, it's immature. Yes, it's *completely* inappropriate. Yes, my mind should have been out of the gutter. But when Zoe ducked into her room, departing by giving me a sly grin, I was burning hot.

The remarkable thing is how much quick thinking can happen in a short walk down a corridor. After Zoe disappeared, Salvatore was allocated the next room.

Will Lincoln say something? Suggest we share a room? Do I have an answer?

Lincoln seemed so sure all of a sudden, but was that just because everything had gotten so crazy? *Maybe he wasn't himself.* And with that, came another sickening thought. Maybe, when I'd healed him, sent him my love, it overshadowed his real feelings. Maybe he was just mirroring my own feelings. That I put there. Was that even possible?

There was so much I still didn't know.

On Ermina's instruction, Rudyard took the next room and then Nyla the one after. They had no qualms about being together and letting everyone know it, so I wondered why they did this. Nyla looked at me and I waited to see if she would say something. But she just gave me a knowing smile, which made me blush, as she closed her door.

Ermina opened the next door. 'Lincoln, this will be your residence,' she said.

Lincoln walked over and then looked back at me. Why

was I panicking so much? When I started fidgeting and tucked a few strands of hair behind my ear, he smiled warmly and came back to me. I was so on edge I flinched when he brushed a hand across my cheek, igniting my desire. He leaned close and I couldn't help but gravitate towards him.

'Remember, Vi,' he turned us slightly so his back was to Ermina and he mouthed the next word with raised eyebrows, 'devout.'

Then his look changed. A whole lot more intense, private. I was still panicking, knowing that while Ermina couldn't see Lincoln's face, she had full view of mine.

Lincoln smiled, obviously pleased with my reaction, before he turned and went into his room without looking back.

Ermina watched me with a strange, distinctly disapproving expression, which morphed into a stern look when she opened the next door on the other side of the hall.

'Violet, this will be your residence throughout your stay.'

I nodded and started to take a step forward, but from the glare she gave me, I knew to stop.

'We are in a time of prayer. Unless you are married to someone here, we expect you will not enter another person's private chambers.'

That's why Nyla had been smiling. It seemed totally obvious now but I'd had my mind in another place. A little warning might have been nice – they clearly knew the rules.

'Of course,' I said, nodding profusely. 'I'm...um...I'm Catholic.' As if that were supposed to mean something. As soon as I said it, I wanted to die.

Ermina cleared her throat. I had definitely started off on the wrong foot with her. I decided on a fast exit and gave her my best attempt at a respectful bow before scooting into my room.

I waited, like a statue, back to the door, listening for footsteps. Once I was sure she was gone I took a few deep breaths to try and stave off the hyperventilation that was brewing and banged my head against the wall.

The suite was a continuation of the beauty we had already seen. I thought of Dad, how he would love a building like this. As an architect, he would see its many merits. Then I thought of Steph. She was going to kill me when she found out the kind of place we were staying. I actually wished for a moment she was there – before I remembered *why* we were there.

I'd barely unpacked my bag and splashed some water on my face when I heard a knock. I went to the door and opened it, still patting my face dry, but no one was there.

I heard the knock again and this time looked around to see where it was coming from. There was an internal door. When I opened it, Nyla was on the other side.

'You could've warned me,' I said, taking in her smug smile as she leaned against the doorway. In spite of the satisfaction, she really did have the air of an ancient goddess.

'You'll know for next time,' she said, still grinning.

Great, another person that gets their kicks at my expense.

'Did you come to gloat?'

'No. I'm headed off to do a security lap. Thought you might come in handy. Interested?'

'Sure.'

She tilted her head towards the door, 'Let's go.'

'Just us?'

She nodded. 'It's easier. Men always get in the way.'

I followed her back down the hall, the same way we'd come in. The hotel was huge and it was unsettling to be in a place designed to house so many when it was empty. The corridors all looked identical. I was glad Nyla seemed to know where she was going.

'I can see you love him,' she suddenly said, from nowhere.

I didn't know what to say, so I changed direction. 'Did my mum love my dad?'

She nodded once, definitely. 'She was a procrastinator. Never thought herself worthy of anything good. When she met James, she tried to talk herself out of it – you know…' she said, honing in on me with a knowing look that made me want to run away. 'She was worried about bringing him into this world. But your dad, he just kept coming back and, well, she loved him. In the end, love will rule the mind.'

I felt relieved to hear this. I had wondered since discovering my mother was Grigori if she were still the person I'd imagined. Dad misses her so much – he'll never get over her. I didn't want that to have been for nothing. It didn't make all the rest OK, the lies and betrayal, but it was something.

'Is that what happened with you and Rudyard?'

Nyla smiled and steered us towards the hallway that veered to the right.

'Our choice was simple. There was no other option.'

I envied her.

'Do me a favour, Violet?'

I gave a non-committal shrug. The truth was, although I liked Nyla, I still didn't *know* her. My instinct was to trust her. Zoe and Spence clearly did. But I'd been wrong before.

'Ask all the questions you need to ask. Understand the consequences before making your choice. Every choice has a price.'

'I don't understand. What price?' From what I could see, Nyla and Rudyard had it all.

We walked through a door that took us outside and both had to squint into the afternoon sun. Azeem was waiting.

Nyla put a hand on my shoulder, which made me feel a bit squeamish. She acted like she knew me well and it made me uncomfortable.

'Rudy and I will explain everything later.' She smiled. 'We have plenty of time.'

I nodded, moving casually away from her touch.

Azeem showed us the impressive security system that comprised a network of modern surveillance cameras and two more traditional watch-towers, which were manned around the clock.

When Nyla asked me, I pushed out my senses and tried to feel the close surrounds and a little beyond. She didn't want me to go too far, preferring that I learned to control my scope and just see if there was anything we needed to know about.

I travelled the immediate area, seeking out anything that could activate my senses.

I felt them instantly.

His unique signature.

Waiting for me.

'Are you picking up on anything?' Nyla asked, while Azeem pointed out their look-out stations.

Apple first, as always, with just a hint of something else that made it so…moreish. Musk, maybe. Then the flowers. He smelled like musk and jasmine.

I knew he wanted to see me, knew he could disappear faster than we could reach him. If I told Nyla, he'd leave.

When I hesitated, she raised an eyebrow.

'Nothing,' I said, finally responding and Nyla, after a suspicious pause, trustingly accepted my lie. I felt even worse.

'OK,' she said to Azeem, and they started to walk back towards the hotel.

'I'm…going to have a look around if that's OK. I… saw a pool on the way in. Do you mind if I go have a look?' I asked, fidgeting, sure it was obvious I was up to something.

'Certainly,' Azeem replied. 'If you would like to swim, there are towels by the pool deck. The waters are the natural supply from the springs – I hope you like it hot,' he said, giving me a small nod and walking back to the main building.

Nyla gave me a quizzical look. I held her stare and smiled back as reassuringly as I could. She followed Azeem.

I made for the cascading waterfalls, grateful at least that my lies had me moving in the direction I really needed to go.

The mountains, formed of pure stone like they had been carved into shape, were incredible. I could even see why Azeem and Ermina were so devout in their religion –

if I lived in a place like this, maybe I'd have had faith, too. Maybe.

The senses intensified as I neared one of the smaller waterfalls. It was strange sensing him like this. Knowing he was calling me. Even stranger that I was going to him, aware of the power he had over me. There was no point running from him. It was too late for that.

I found a trail that was carved into the mountain and started the climb. I fought the nauseousness as I climbed higher and clamped my hands into tight fists, letting my nails dig harshly into my skin to distract me from the déjà vu of being surrounded by cliffs.

As I neared where I knew he would be, water spritzed over me, the wayward sprays from the waterfall, and I spotted the path that led behind it. So many things went through my mind. So many memories. I wondered if he was putting them there. Then, I wondered if he was thinking them, too. My hand moved to my waist and my fingers wrapped around the hilt of my dagger. It would be no use to me here. For one thing, Phoenix was a better fighter than me. And he knew it.

I followed the path into an opening behind the flow of water coming from above. I expected it to be noisy and wet. Oddly, it was quiet and dry.

He stood on the far side, a few metres away. Despite the heat he was wearing jeans and a fitted dark denim jacket. He rested easy on the rocks.

I expected him to say something cruel, or make some snide remark. I expected to say something myself, but neither one of us spoke. It was worse. His chocolate eyes were bitter and cold. I finally realised that no matter what had been, no matter how real either his feelings or mine…

He's going to do this.

And I'm not going to let him.

Our eyes locked and his seemed to warm a little. But it was only to share in a brief moment of acceptance…and regret. It wasn't going to change anything.

'I see you and your people found their way here safely,' he said.

'You actually sound like you're glad.'

'I wouldn't have made it so easy for them if I hadn't wanted you here.'

He was playing with me. 'Right. We came for the Scriptures.'

'Who do you think led you here?' he asked, his smile a little tilted. Secrets hidden within.

'We found the old stories, Phoenix, we know where to look,' I pushed.

'I know. I all but opened the books and put them under your noses. You never would have found the location if it weren't for me.'

The penny dropped. 'The exiles at the farmhouse.'

He just continued smiling.

'That's why they were really there – so they could tell us about the Rules. Why? You don't want to help us.' I knew that much.

'No, but it seems I might need you after all,' he said, his tone becoming bitter.

'Why all the games, Phoenix? Why did you do it?'

'You have yourself to thank for that. You showed me there is only one place for me in this world. I'd been fooling myself, granted. I'll not make the same mistake twice.' He was suddenly interested in the cave wall, picking at a piece of stone, avoiding looking at me.

'I meant Lincoln. I know you were the one who sent Nahilius.'

He shrugged, not surprised or worried that I'd figured it out. 'It was mutual benefit. I see he made it here, anyway. I take it Nahilius is downward-bound.'

I didn't answer.

'Still afraid to admit what you are?' He smiled. 'Never did like the Cherubim.'

I shook my head in disbelief, grasping what he was telling me. The exiles he'd given to Nahilius had all been Cherubs, as was Nahilius. I remembered Phoenix had some kind of grudge against them.

'You knew he'd be able to beat those exiles you sent after him. You wanted him to do it.' I couldn't hold back the anger, pulsing out of me, or the look of disgust.

'It was a win, win,' he said, now holding my glare.

'You make me sick.'

He took a step towards me, staring right through me. 'I make you many things,' he said, his voice travelling the length of me. I tried to ignore it, not be affected. But when he took the next step he opened a channel to himself.

'Don't,' I said, putting up my defences and mentally pushing him out. I was shaking with a frightening sensation of want. Then fear of want.

'Do you think I need the *power* to reach you?' He half laughed. 'Do you think I don't know how your thoughts drift to that night, to when you were in my arms?'

'I'm with Lincoln,' I blurted out, surprising myself as

much as Phoenix. He took a step back, his jaw clenched. I had said the wrong thing.

'You're lying,' he growled. 'If you were with him you'd be weakened and you're not.' His eyes grew wide when I hesitated. 'Oh,' he said.

I bit down on my lip.

'My plan brought you together, you just haven't...'

'It's none of your business!' Why was it that everyone seemed to know so much about my love life just from looking at me?

'Wait. It doesn't make...' He stopped.

I held my breath when his eyes churned with fury.

'You think you're kindred souls, don't you?' he snapped, taking those few steps back towards me until he was just centimetres away. 'Don't you?' he repeated, this time darkly bleeding into me as much compulsion to answer him as he could.

'Yes,' I replied, for a moment under his spell.

He was silent as he contemplated my response. Finally, he straightened.

'Well, it makes sense you'd be willing to sacrifice your life again for him. I admit, though, I'm surprised you'd be willing to sacrifice *his* life, for you.'

'What are you talking about?'

He laughed lightly, though his brow was still furrowed. 'Still diving in head first without all the information. That naivety of yours really is going to get you – or someone else – into trouble, Violet.'

'Are you finished?' I asked, turning to walk away.

'Tell your people I'll give them the morning, but the Scriptures will reveal themselves to me come tomorrow evening. If you want any chance to get hold of them you'll be in place then.'

I walked away but felt the push. One step, two steps.

Move, move.

And I did, I kept going, I didn't stop. But for just a second, I couldn't resist. I dropped my guard and sucked in what he was sending. An explosion of lust. A feeling of unfettered bliss just as I'd remembered. My eyes rolled back in wicked delight as I forced my feet forward and stopped them turning back to him.

Like a damn junkie!

I snuck back into the north wing of the hotel, grateful to spot Zoe.

'Hey,' I called out, running to catch up with her. 'Where are you going?'

'Everyone's meeting with Azeem and some local Grigori. I guess we'll fill them in and find out if they can help us.'

'Oh.'

'You OK? You look wasted.'

'Yeah. Umm…I think I might skip this one. Can you tell Griffin and Lincoln that I was too exhausted. I'll be in my room if anyone needs me.'

'Sure. I'll stop by and get you on the way to dinner if you want?' she offered.

'Thanks,' I called after her as she hurried off. She didn't want to miss any action. Pity she'd already missed today's main event.

By the end of tonight I was going to have to explain to everyone that I'd wandered off to have a little one-on-one time with Phoenix. But before that came the harder task.

I was going to have to explain it to myself.

When I made it back to my room, I really was exhausted. I had no idea what was going on with my body clock or what time it was. I turned on the shower, undressed and sat in the bath with the water pelting down and random tears falling.

My life is not how I imagined it would be. In some ways, I was starting to like being a Grigori. I mean the power was great. The strength alone gave me confidence I'd never had before, and knowing I could sense beings before they arrived was a bonus, too. The obvious downside was that I knew a whole lot more bad was coming my way. And Phoenix.

I tried to keep things black and white, but – as everyone is always telling me – nothing ever is. I *loved* Lincoln – absolutely, totally, jump-off-a-cliff for him loved him – even when I'd shared that time with Phoenix. But…

There is always a *but*.

Phoenix and I had been friends. *Really* good friends. When I felt like there was no one else, he was there. I know now that he had been lying to me through a lot of it and I could never forgive him for forcing me to choose life as a Grigori when he could have healed Lincoln himself. Of course if he *had* healed Lincoln he would have probably had the power over Lincoln that he now held over me and…I was doubtful he'd have procrastinated for too long about reinstating Lincoln's wounds.

And, I couldn't help it, there was a part of me that was drawn to Phoenix. I've told myself it's just his abilities, his pull of seduction and floods of lust, that he influences me and controls my emotions, but it's more than that. I was unhealthily aware of those things yet still unable to resist. And as bad as this might sound – it wasn't even *him* so much as his *power* to make it all go away.

He's the ultimate escape.

For someone who has spent a long time denying herself the right to run or quit or anything of the sort, Phoenix was like the biggest wagon I could ever fall off.

I'd turned wrinkly and the water was starting to run cold when I heard a knock on the door. I jumped up and wrapped a towel around me, expecting to see Zoe on the other side of the door collecting me for dinner. When I opened it, it wasn't Zoe standing there.

'What are you doing here?' I asked.

'Did I or did I not help you make your plan work with Lincoln?'

'Yes,' I said slowly.

'Have I or have I not backed you up on a number of cases of questionable judgement lately?'

'I guess.'

'Well, it's time for payback. Where do I sleep?' Spence said, pushing past me and walking right into my room. 'Nice towel, by the way – I'm not big on wearing clothes in my room either. This is going to work out well.' He dumped his bag on the bed, unzipped it and started unpacking.

'Whoa! Hang on. How did you get here? I mean – hang on!' I said, ducking back into the bathroom and wrapping a bathrobe around me before I reappeared. 'OK, explain,' I demanded.

Spence leapt onto the bed and reclined, putting his hands behind his head. 'It was genius, really. I stowed away on the army truck they loaded onto the plane at the last minute. I had the truck waiting for me round the back of the airport. While you lot were all comfy upstairs, I rummaged through Rudyard's bag and found the address for the hotel. Took me a while to get here, had to get a local bus and then hitch part of the way, plus get past the security, which took a while, but here I am. Did you miss me?'

I should have protested but instead I collapsed next to him.

'Yes,' I said, realising how much it was true. Spence was crazy, unpredictable and had a serious death wish at times, but I wasn't his keeper and right now I really needed someone to talk to. 'You are going to die when I tell you what's been going on.'

'Like I've said before...' he began, making strained noises as he reached over me to grab a bottle of water, 'never a dull moment with you, Eden.' He cracked the lid open, took a sip and sighed dramatically. 'Spill.'

CHAPTER TWENTY-FIVE

'Thou art to me a delicious torment.'
Ralph Waldo Emerson

'Hey, you get there OK?' Steph asked, sounding worried.

'Yeah. And thanks to you, we got to Lincoln in time, too,' I said, hovering by the window that looked out over one of the hot springs...and more mountains. The mobile reception wasn't great in my room.

'No problem. I take it he made the plane, then.'

'Yeah, we all did, even Spence, though no one else knows that little gem of information yet.'

'Is Magda there?' she asked.

'Actually, no. She didn't make the flight. Why?'

'Oh, just wondering. I, umm...I've been looking through some more of Lincoln's mother's company details.'

'Why? Steph relax! Lincoln's OK and Nahilius is gone, Magda returned him.' There was silence on the other end. 'Steph?'

'Yeah, sorry, it's just there's something that doesn't add

up. I've still got Lincoln's spare key, I was going to go back there after school.'

'I guess, if you want. Just don't mess anything up.'

I could hear her smile. 'He won't even know I was there. When do you think you'll be back?'

'Couple of days.'

There was a knock on the door. 'Dinner!' Zoe called out.

'Steph, that's Zoe, I've gotta go. I'll say hi to Salvatore for you and give you a call as soon as I can.'

'OK. Stay alive.'

'Working on it.'

Zoe banged on the door again.

'Send Zoe my warmest,' she said sarcastically, before hanging up.

Spence walked out of the bathroom, showered, changed and looking ready for anything. He'd probably used all the clean towels. He struck a pose, hands on hips hero-style. 'Let's do this.'

I rolled my eyes. '*You* do this. Don't speak like there's an "*us*" involved. I've got enough to answer for tonight without having to explain how you stowed away.'

'Point,' he said pulling the door wide open and greeting Zoe with a massive smile.

'Holy crap! You're dead,' Zoe said, smiling like the fun had just begun.

The dining room was – no surprises – beautiful. All of the tables and chairs were wooden, of a heavy design and made it look somewhere between an ode to all things natural and harmonious, and a tavern. By the time Zoe and I walked into the room, everyone was there. The scene struck a chord, the room full of part-angel warriors wearing silver leather wristbands made by angels, readying for the unknown.

My eyes found Lincoln's and my entire being relaxed. As I watched, he seemed to exhale as well, and my heart forgot itself and skipped a beat.

About two seconds later, Lincoln's eyes, along with everyone else's, turned to Spence, who was standing behind me. I was quite sure I shared their look of surprise. Only I wasn't looking at Spence.

Magda.

How the hell did she get here?

Everything had felt so much easier without her around. But there she was, tucked in close to Lincoln, looking devastatingly perfect. The rest of us were dishevelled and exhausted, but Magda looked fresh in a recently pressed white sleeveless shirt and perfectly blow-dried golden hair. She was looking straight at me, an annoying smile playing on her lips as she fondled the sapphire on her necklace.

Zoe, the great friend she is, took a seat and pretended she'd been none the wiser. I couldn't leave Spence standing there alone, so I just awkwardly hung beside him.

Rudyard looked at Nyla and then back to Spence. I was waiting for the eruption, for the massive blow-out that was almost guaranteed. But Rudyard just picked up his fork and stuffed something that looked like it was wrapped in leaves into his mouth.

Nyla picked up some flat-bread and broke it in half. 'Hello, Spence,' she said, between mouthfuls.

'Hello, Nyla,' Spence said, gulping.

Griffin and Lincoln were exchanging glances and then I couldn't help but feel guilty when I saw Lincoln look back at me. I wished I'd been able to tell him about this somehow. But then he gave me a crooked smile. I didn't know what to make of it. My eyes kept darting to Magda, I couldn't really muster my own smile right now. Interestingly, I noticed Salvatore was looking at Magda with similar confusion. I wondered what problem he had with her.

'Did you enjoy your trip?' Nyla asked, still munching on her bread and reaching for the wine.

'I...um... It was fine.'

Poor Spence. This wasn't going to plan. I knew he'd been expecting a big blow-up, where he could just stand his ground, throw a hissy fit and storm out.

'Rudy and I once did a stake-out in one of those military trucks. They can be awfully uncomfortable. Are you sure you're OK?'

Busted.

'How did you...? I mean, yes. I'm good.'

Nyla took a sip of wine and passed the carafe to Rudyard, who proceeded to pour himself a glass. Every movement between them looked like some kind of perfect dance.

'And tell me, Spence, how did you get here from the airport?' Nyla asked, remaining tauntingly calm.

'I...umm... Bus, and then I caught a ride to a few miles out. I walked the rest of the way.'

'And the security – how did you get past the security?'

'Oh, well...I...I used a glamour,' Spence said, increasingly nervous.

'Hmm. You must be hungry. Are you hungry, Spence?'

This was torture.

'I'm OK,' Spence said.

'Get a bite to eat while you were in Violet's room, did you?'

Holy crap! Look at the ground, look at the ground, be *invisible.*

'I umm… Violet didn't know I was coming.'

'No. *She* didn't,' Nyla said.

Nyla and Rudyard smiled at each other and then raised their glasses to Griffin. 'You were right.'

Griffin looked up at Spence. He was on the verge of laughter. 'You can't lie to me, kid. We were onto you from the moment we told you you couldn't come.'

Not the most encouraging news, given the secrets I was juggling.

'But then – why? Why didn't you stop me?'

Griffin shrugged. 'We can try and protect you but in the end you have to make your own choices.'

'Griffin reminded us, Spence, that that's what it's all about, after all. We can advise you and – while we are right and you are wrong – we decided in the end if you were determined enough to find a way into the battle, we may as well let you be of use,' Rudyard explained.

'So…I'm not in trouble?' Spence asked, looking seriously suspicious.

'Oh, you're in trouble,' Nyla said, now a little more stern. 'You'll be stuck with double theory classes for the next month and, trust me, a world of pain awaits you in prac training, since I'll be your new sparring partner. But for now, you're here, so rest, eat, catch up on the intel and be ready. You came looking for a fight,' she took a sip of wine, 'congratulations – I believe you're going to get one. But not from us.'

Lincoln pulled out the seat beside him. I didn't need asking twice and quickly sat down.

'Did you know?' I asked quietly, suddenly wondering if everyone had been in on it.

'Griffin just told me before dinner,' he whispered back. His breath was warm and as he spoke the hairs on the back of my neck spiked and a shiver ran through my body. 'Should I be jealous?'

I was suddenly nervous – or guilty. I knew he was talking about Spence, but that wasn't the cause of the guilt.

'We need to talk,' I whispered, before standing and walking to the corner of the room. Lincoln followed.

'What's happened?' he asked as soon as we stopped.

'It's not Spence – I'm not, you must know...'

'I know. Tell me,' he cut me off.

'What's Magda doing here?' I asked, unable to hold it back.

'Oh, she caught a commercial flight and arrived a few hours after us. Azeem sent a car to collect her, she got here about an hour ago.'

Then, before I could stop myself, I had to have a dig. 'What is it with her and that necklace anyway? Does she really have to parade how rich she is here?'

Lincoln looked over at her as if only noticing this now. 'I don't know.' He shrugged. 'It's a family heirloom or something. She used to wear it all the time.'

I took a few calming breaths – I was being immature.

She had every right to be here, but I was still angry at her for putting that gun in Lincoln's hands and for always looking like she'd just stepped out of a salon and…other things.

'Vi?'

'Oh… Sorry.' I was supposed to be telling him something. I took another deep breath and gripped my hands tight. 'I saw Phoenix.' And before Lincoln could launch into whatever panicked conversation he was about to, I put my hand up. 'Let me explain.'

He nodded, but his hands went into his hair before he threw them back down. He wasn't happy. Not that I expected him to be cheering.

'I sensed him earlier, when I went out to do a security check with Nyla. I knew he was waiting for me and I knew he wouldn't hurt me.'

I didn't know how to say this – to admit to everything and then I realised…I couldn't. I'd rather pay for my sins later.

'I was just his messenger, that's all, but before I told everyone else, I wanted to give you the heads-up.'

'No more secrets, hey?' he said with a worried smile.

'Yeah,' I said, hating the fact that a better person would have told him everything.

Lincoln wrapped a hand around the back of my neck and drew me in, kissing my forehead. 'Thanks.'

I wanted to throw myself in front of a train.

His hand moved down and wrapped around my waist as he walked me back to everyone.

'Griffin, Violet saw Phoenix – he has a message.'

Just when I was expecting Griffin to launch into

a demand for a full play-by-play, he simply turned his attention to me.

'What do we need to know?'

The entire table was focused on me. Everyone thinking something different. Judging me. I wanted to crawl into a hole.

'He said to do what we need to do but by tomorrow night he will have the Scriptures and if we want any chance of getting our hands on them, we'll meet him there in the evening. I think he needs us somehow to get them.'

'Makes sense if he isn't worried about us finding them before him. They must be protected somehow,' Griffin said.

'One other thing – he's been playing us the whole time. He gave us that information about the location on purpose. He wanted us to be here now.'

'Only more proof that he needs us.'

'Maybe we would be better off just leaving, then?' Salvatore suggested.

I wished I could agree.

'We are Grigori, Salvatore. We do not have the luxury of leaving things up to chance,' Nyla said.

Salvatore nodded and averted his eyes, ashamed for even considering it.

Griffin stood up. 'Azeem has a team who are going to take us to the place of Moses' final resting in the morning. We hope to discover indicators there that might show us the way to the Scriptures. Spence, a room has been made up for you – Ermina will show you to it after you have eaten. Everyone rest up, we leave at 5 am.' He threw his napkin down and looked over at Ermina, who was standing in the doorway to the kitchen. 'Thank you, Ermina. Dinner was superb,' he said with a nod and then he looked at Lincoln and me. 'I'll see you two in my room in thirty minutes.' It was not a request.

We both nodded. I guess he did have more questions and I was instantly nervous. I might be able to omit certain things when talking to Lincoln but with Griffin it was another story.

Magda didn't even say hello to me. She spoke at some point to everyone else at the table but never once did she acknowledge me. I guess I didn't say anything to her either – but still. The only thing that made me feel better was the odd looks Salvatore kept giving her. There was definitely something about her that he didn't like. Maybe Steph had said something to him.

Good, one down six to go.

Thinking of Steph made me think of my normal life, which made me think of Dad. Which made me panic.

'I have to go, I have to call my dad,' I said to everyone, quickly pushing my chair back and making loud scraping noises on the ground. 'Sorry,' I said, turning to Ermina, remembering my manners. 'Thank you very much for dinner.'

I hurried out and down the hall towards my room. I was due to call Dad. Transferring the home phone to my mobile wasn't a trick that was likely to work too well in Jordan so my only hope was to call Dad myself. Steph had stopped by my house and left the phone off the hook. We figured if Dad tried to call there he'd just get the engaged signal and think

I was gossiping to her. He didn't have the commitment to keep ringing. Either way, I was hoping if I called him first he wouldn't bother trying to call home at all.

When I got into my room, I grabbed my phone.

'Shit,' I said to myself, noticing how low the battery was getting.

I punched in Dad's number and while I was waiting for him to answer, Lincoln walked through the open door and sat down on the end of my bed. I put a finger to my lips. He nodded and remained silent.

'James Eden,' Dad answered.

'Dad, it's me.'

'Hi, sweetheart. Your number didn't come up on the phone. Where are you?'

'I took my caller ID off earlier,' I said too quickly. 'I was umm, playing a prank on Steph.'

'Oh, sure. Is everything OK?' He sounded busy and I could hear papers being shuffled about.

'Yeah, fine. I just missed you and thought I'd call,' I said, staying in the good corner of the room for reception, hoping he wouldn't be able to tell I wasn't at home. I turned my back to Lincoln and ran my finger along the window sill, trying to stay focused on the conversation with Dad instead of the fact that Lincoln was *sitting on my bed*!

'That's nice, sweetheart. I miss you, too, I can't wait to get home. We're almost all done here so I'm trying to get on an earlier flight. I could be home in a couple of days.'

Shit.

'That's…great news.'

'Are you sure everything is OK? You know the Richardsons—' I cut him off.

'I know, I know, Dad – are right next door if I need anything.'

'OK,' he said with a small laugh. 'Just look after yourself. I worry about you. Have you been seeing much of Lincoln?'

'Oh. I, umm…' Lincoln kept looking in the other direction, but he was too still, I was sure he would know what we were talking about. 'Umm… Yeah, a bit.'

'Well, you be careful. You know…Steph is the only one that has permission to stay overni—'

I cut him off again. 'Dad! I know. Look, I have to go.'

'I'll call you tomorrow,' Dad said.

'OK, bye.' I hung up. Mission accomplished – *for today, anyway*.

I put my phone down and rummaged through my bag in the hope that someone might have bothered to throw in my charger. No such luck.

'So,' Lincoln said, a smile creeping to his lips. 'Why does Steph get permission to stay over?'

'Because, she can be trusted,' I said, throwing a pillow at him.

'Hey, what's that for?'

'Eavesdropping!' But before I got the word out, Lincoln was right in front of me, his arms wrapping snugly around my waist.

'I can't help it if I have supernatural hearing.' He sighed deliberately. 'You know I didn't actually come up here to listen to you talk to your dad.'

My insides exploded despite the lingering bitterness of guilt nestled within. Lincoln moved a hand up my arm and across my face.

'Do you know how many times I've…'

I wanted to say, *What*? I mean, damn it, I wanted to know this stuff. But my mouth had gone so dry I couldn't speak. Everywhere his hands went felt like awakening that part of my body for the first time.

'A lot,' he said. As if somehow I knew exactly what he was going to say and this was the answer. 'You know – I should tell you. When you and I have kissed before, it's been different.' His hands kept moving over me and I was struggling to remain upright let alone focus on the words.

This was too much multi-tasking.

'Except for that time on your birthday, I don't count any of the other kisses. I mean we've already established that healing kisses don't count, right?' he asked, the edges of his mouth turning up. I needed to turn the air con on.

'Uh-huh,' was all I could manage.

'Uh-huh,' he mimicked, but much lower. *Much* sexier.

Bloody hell, he was enjoying this.

'And then there was earlier, but that doesn't really count either. I wasn't myself and I think that kiss should be written off as, warm-up. That OK with you?' His smile increased ever so slightly.

'Ah-hem,' I think I mumbled.

'Good. And when I really think back to it that kiss on your birthday was…amazing but we did get cut short, didn't we?' His fingers moved down my neck and along my collarbone.

I nodded. Mumbling now beyond me.

'So unless you have an injury that I don't know about, if I was to kiss you now, in some ways it would be our first *real* kiss.'

I stopped breathing.

'Do you, have any...' his lips were barely moving as they got closer and closer to mine.

Pull it together, Vi, you're shaking!

'. . . injuries that need healing, Violet?' His lips grazed mine as they spoke my name.

I didn't answer, but – thank the heavens – he didn't wait. His lips, delicious as ever, found safe landing on mine and the second they did, my frozen state melted in the absolute steaminess between us.

I don't know how much time passed. It felt like moments. But somehow my legs had found their way around Lincoln's waist and my back was against the wall. For once, neither one of us pulled away. Even when we smashed into the bookshelf and it cracked in two. If anything, it made the whole thing better.

Our powers found their way to each other. We didn't ask it of them, it just happened. A natural progression and yet more confirmation that this was what was meant to be. And somehow through it all, my soul found his and they reached for one another like fingers stretching desperately, almost – but not quite – touching.

My breathing quickened, as did his. We both pulled back at the same time. 'We should...'

'Stop,' I finished for him.

'Yeah,' he said, heavily.

We both knew that a few seconds more and clothing would be coming off.

And the problem is?

But then I remembered. There *was* a problem. I straightened my top and moved to the far side of the room.

'Griffin will be waiting for us,' I said.

'That's true,' he said, cocking an eyebrow at the distance I'd just put between us.

I started for the door, trying to steady my wobbly legs as I dodged the piles of books that had fallen to the ground.

'Ermina is not going to be happy with you,' he said, not trying to stop the chuckle that followed.

Like I give a damn!

All moral dilemmas aside, *that* was the most amazing kiss I'd ever had.

Lincoln and I sat on the sofa in Griffin's room while he asked me a million questions about Phoenix.

I told him most of everything and avoided anything that could lead to me having to admit that I'd let Phoenix bleed emotion into me. I told him how I'd followed the senses to the opening behind one of the waterfalls – how Phoenix had said he'd been waiting for us to arrive. How he had admitted he'd been responsible for sending Lincoln after Nahilius.

'But, I don't understand. Magda told you that she found out about Nahilius while she was away,' Griffin said to Lincoln, seeming more interested in this than anything else.

'Yeah. Phoenix probably arranged that, too,' Lincoln said, brushing it off. 'And it almost worked. If Violet hadn't made it to me in time I would have done something I just...' His tone dropped. 'Something I couldn't have lived with.'

Griffin shook his head as he paced the room, confused. Anxious.

'Violet, there's something you're not telling us. I'm sorry, normally I try not to pry into people's lives, but right now I cannot afford to be tactful. You're not giving the entire truth.'

There was only one way around Griffin's ability. You had to *believe* what you were saying. It was the flaw in his strength – he could see truth from a person, so if they didn't believe in what they were saying it was clear to him, but if they *believed* in it, even if they were wrong, he was fooled.

'Griffin, the truth is I…I don't know if I can…' I dropped my head, embarrassed to cry over Phoenix.

Lincoln tried to console me even though it must have been hard for him. 'It's OK, Vi. Did you think we all expected you to return Phoenix? It's not a possibility at the moment, anyway. Not until we can break his connection with you.'

I pushed aside the thought that baited me, the fear that there were some connections that may never be broken.

'Lincoln's right. If we fight tomorrow, we will find a way to stop him without returning him,' Griffin said.

I kept my head down and nodded. I held on to the truth in my words rather than my lies by omission and I didn't risk looking at Griffin. I tried not to let my thoughts drift – whether it was about the connection or not, could I really stand by and let him be returned?

'So,' Griffin said, changing tone and sounding uncomfortable. 'You two…'

Lincoln stood and I followed. It was definitely a good time to exit.

'The subject of *we two* is not open for discussion right now.'

'Right, then your choice is made,' Griffin said, sounding worried, even defeated. Good to see he was so thrilled by the idea of us actually being happy.

'Either way, Griffin – we're not currently inviting outside opinions!' Lincoln called out as we continued walking into the hall.

'5 am tomorrow!' Griffin yelled after us.

Lincoln walked me to my room but didn't come in. 'I think it'd be best if I...'

'Went back to your own room,' I said, smiling.

'You need to sleep,' he said.

I *was* exhausted. 'You too.'

'Anyway, Ermina probably patrols the halls at night.' He was so right. As much as I wanted him to come in I knew if he did he wouldn't be leaving and, apart from already having one broken bookshelf to explain, I wasn't sure that I could be trusted.

He kissed me lightly on the cheek and then pulled me close. 'I love you, Violet Eden.'

My mouth wasn't dry now and I knew exactly what I wanted to say.

I prayed to God – prayed in that moment, desperately, that there might *be* a God and that that God might be listening and willing to do one thing for me that would actually reflect well on him.

Please, please, please, let there be enough of my soul left to give.

As, once again, the fear that I gave up something very vital in that desert plagued me.

'Heart and soul,' I whispered.

CHAPTER TWENTY-SIX

'I tell you the truth, you shall see heaven open,
and the angels of God ascending and descending on the
Son of Man.'
John 1:51

By six o'clock the next morning, we were back in Madaba's city centre and there was only one thing on my mind. Coffee.

You'd think I would have already had several, I'd been up since dawn, but Ermina doesn't believe in it and looked at me like I was the devil's progeny when I told her that every hotel needed a seriously large espresso machine.

Lincoln had dragged me onto the minibus, promising he'd find me coffee as soon as we reached the city. But we'd been there twenty minutes and I was still caffeine-free – not a state that agreed with me. The last thing I needed was another one of my addictions dangled in front of me, while I endured a killer headache from the withdrawals.

Finally Salvatore, who shared my love of coffee, found a little cafe – if you could call it that. Anyway, it served coffee. While Zoe, Magda and Nyla walked down the street with Azeem to wait for his local Grigori, Salvatore and I ducked into 'Ayola'.

We were given a choice – Turkish coffee or Nescafé. Salvatore had to snap me out of my stunned state. He ordered Turkish coffees for both of us since they were short and fast. Griffin and Rudyard hadn't looked impressed by our detour so he figured they'd be the best option. They just didn't understand that I couldn't function without a hit.

The coffee was disgusting. It tasted gritty and bitter with a very strong flavour of cardamom. But I was dedicated to the cause and desperate for my headache to go away so I closed my eyes and downed it. Salvatore, who couldn't manage and left his coffee untouched, gave me a nod of respect. I suppose it takes an Italian to understand that kind of dedication to the bean.

When we walked out of the coffee shop, I felt something shift. A distinctive alteration. The air was thinner, the gravity unstable. I slowed, struggling to understand the change. Salvatore walked on, none the wiser. My senses were everywhere. I half expected to look around and be surrounded by exiles.

'Linc!' I called out.

He only had time to spin around and face me before he stalled.

Everything stilled.

A kind of amplified noiselessness surrounded me that reminded me of putting a seashell to my ear. My heavy, frantic breathing echoed like a tornado. I felt hurt each time my stomach rose up into my chest and plummeted back down to my gut. *Not good.*

'Lincoln!' I yelled again, but it was futile.

No one else reacted when the sands started to roll in. I wondered if I was losing my mind, if somehow the memories of my time in the desert had driven me completely insane. I watched, unable to walk or run, though I wasn't sure if the inability was enforced by another or just human nature. The dust storm settled and cleared my view to a man who had not been standing in front of me a moment before.

I fought for feeling in my legs, I needed to be sure I could move them if it came to a fight. The thing about angels is, you just never know. Especially, I suspected, when it came to this one.

'Hello, Nox,' I said.

'Hello, Violet,' he said, keeping a clear distance from me.

I knew it wasn't that he was scared of me, more that I repulsed him somehow.

'You have been busy since we last met. Are you enjoying your new path?'

I remembered how he had asked me about Phoenix when I'd embraced. 'You knew this would happen. You knew that Phoenix would turn on me, didn't you?' I responded, suddenly angry that angels had the power to play these games, that they seemed to enjoy manipulating humans like pawns on a chessboard.

He raised his chin, before adjusting his silver cufflinks. His suit was different from the one he'd worn last time. This one was more like a tuxedo, with tapered shiny seams. His shoulder-length, sandy-blond hair was slicked back.

'I did not put any of it into effect, if that is what you are suggesting.'

'Right, like I'd believe that!' I wanted to call out to Lincoln again. It was sickening to know he was so close and yet so far.

'Do you think it matters what you believe? Do you think it could change the reasoning or fact of any situation? I have presented many paths to you, Violet, I will present many more. I do not find value in lying to you.'

'Why didn't you tell me about Phoenix?'

He ran a hand over his jawline, the way men do after they've shaved. He just seemed intrigued. 'You discovered it at the right time, in the right way – that is all you need to know.'

'Great.' I'd forgotten how annoying my angel guides were. 'Where are we, anyway?' I asked, looking around. I could still see Lincoln, maybe ten metres away, and Salvatore nearby, but they were completely unaware of me. Nox wasn't exactly here either. When I looked closely, his feet, still in those patent-leather black shoes, were in the sand of his desert. He was here but not at the same time and behind him, something was moving. Clear swirls of something indefinable, almost translucent, that blurred like drifting sunspots.

'We are exactly where we were a moment ago.'

'Nox. How are we talking to each other and why can't anyone else see us?'

'Realms are just layers. There are many layers, any one layer is at any time close to another. Right now your realm and my realm are like a pair of fragile curtains blowing in the breeze through an open window, moving just enough that at one point they touch.'

'Our realms are overlapping,' I said, trying to understand.

'Very good. For a time, in this place, the realms are touching.'

'You can do that?'

'It is not without difficulties, and I had to pay a price,' he said, now unhappy. Why Nox had bothered to pay anything in order to see me made me very nervous.

'Why can no one else see?' I asked as I silently willed Lincoln to find me.

'Time has been altered. It would not be good if everyone else could see these things. I can see them because I am a guide, linked to both realities as much as any angel – elect or malign – is now permitted.'

'And me?'

He nodded, showing some vague form of fascination. 'I admit, I did not know if you would be able to see me. It is part of the reason for my journey.'

'So it was a test?'

'Yes. And no.'

'Why? I thought you guys knew everything.'

'We do,' he said, shortly.

'Everything but that which comes from above you,' I said, remembering what Griffin had explained to me once before.

'How's your conscience, Violet?' Nox sneered, now angry.

'Why did you come here?' I retorted quickly, knowing to stand my ground. I hadn't meant to anger him but now that I had, I decided it would be a bad idea to back down.

Nox tilted his head to the side, examining me, but also

looking beyond, momentarily, to the city and its people. He was acutely aware of his surroundings, though he didn't want to show it. He was fascinated by humanity. No, he was enthralled by possessions. 'I have a question and a message.'

'Let me guess, question first.'

He smiled. 'Are you ready to take his life?'

I wet my lips, unnerved to once again be in a desert with an angel of dark. 'I thought I would only be returning him? If I kill Phoenix's physical form his spirit still goes back to the angel realm, doesn't it?'

'Little girl, I am not asking you about your exile. I am asking about the one who mirrors your soul?'

I gasped. 'It's true, then, we are soulmates?'

'You didn't need me to tell you that. Now give me my answer, we are running out of time.'

'But I don't understand. I...I would never hurt Lincoln.'

'And yet, your decision says you would. Darkness and lessons lie ahead – I will be watching closely to see where that will of yours takes you.'

'That's it?'

'Yes.'

'Well, where's Uri? Is he here, too?' I asked, not sure if I wanted him to be or not.

'In his way. He sent the message. He is anchoring the realms so that I can move between.' He smiled deliberately. 'We tossed a coin. He lost.' Nox looked disdainful for a moment and I thought he wouldn't tell me what Uri's message was, but then he spoke. 'I am supposed to remind you of his words about surrender. Goodbye.'

I couldn't remember what they were.

The sands picked up again and I knew I only had seconds. 'Nox! Wait! I need to know what happened that day, that night, in the desert! Please!'

I heard him laugh but that was all.

The world around me started moving. Lincoln rushed towards me, 'What? Is it the senses? I can't feel anything.' He was looking around on full alert.

I couldn't answer him. I couldn't do anything. The angel realm or whatever it was, the desert that the guides came from, had just overlapped with my reality. I didn't know if I would ever have the same feeling of gravity after experiencing the strange sensation of being in two places and yet neither at the same time.

'Violet!' Lincoln said, shaking my shoulders. 'Snap out of it!'

I blinked. 'Sorry.' I was about to tell him what had happened. Was about to explain how he'd just stopped, how *time* had stopped, when a familiar feeling came over me. This time it wasn't only me.

'Violet. I can sense it, there's an exile here.'

I nodded. 'It's the same one I sensed when we arrived.' I was speaking on autopilot. I knew I should be onto it, but all I could think about was Nox, how I'd just missed my chance to find out. I wanted to scream. No, I wanted to hit someone.

My eyes darted everywhere, but all I could see was a man in a dirty brown robe walking down the other side of the street. When he was directly opposite us, he turned towards us and stopped. I waited for him to look up. He didn't.

In the blink of an eye, he was gone. 'Did he just

disappear?' I asked, letting my frustration get the better of me. 'Jesus.'

'No, but just as old.' I spun around. Rudyard had come up beside me. To say he looked pale didn't cover it.

'You sensed him?' I asked.

'We all did and you were right, Violet, he is very old indeed. And he is very, very powerful.'

'What is he? He didn't feel like a normal exile – something was off,' Lincoln said.

'I have no idea. We are in an ancient place. There are things here we cannot begin to comprehend,' Rudyard said.

'Yeah, well, no offence but the sooner we get out of here the better. I've had it with being everyone's play-thing,' I said, running my hands through my hair and starting to put up my walls. Lincoln looked at me, a question in his eyes. He knew he'd missed something.

With everything that had been happening, I'd been letting everyone down more and more – new friends, people to confide in, Lincoln, it was all making me lax and that just wasn't good enough.

Things were pushing at the edges, scary things were playing games with me and I was letting it all spiral out of control. Something had to give.

Lincoln put a hand on my shoulder. I stepped away, breaking contact. I knew he was doing it to show he was there for me, but right now I was too confused. I needed to get back some control. When his hand dropped away he didn't say anything and part of me wanted to holler and invoke teenager change-of-mind rights. But I didn't, I just turned away.

CHAPTER TWENTY-SEVEN

'On reaching the mountaintop we came to a church...
I saw a slightly raised place about the size of a normal
tomb. I asked about it and the holy man replied,
"Holy Moses was buried here by Angels."'
Writings of Egeria

Azeem and his other Grigori drove us out in once-were-white four-wheel-drives now covered in dirt and desert dust to a place called Mount Nebo, about twenty minutes from Madaba.

The whole journey my mind bounced between the moments.

How can all of this be happening? Am I losing my mind? When will Phoenix finally kill me?

And through it all, the growing feeling that something very significant was about to happen. I was missing something.

It was beyond me, beyond Phoenix and Lincoln. It was beyond us all.

Since I'd arrived in Jordan and sensed that exile, I've

known it. Just as I knew the day I stood on top of that cliff that my life was about to change forever, so too I knew the man in those robes was another 'cliff'.

I struggled to breathe through an ever-tightening chest and my eyes stung with a detonation of pure fear. What the hell was going on?

Spence was sitting beside me. I was glad Lincoln had decided to travel in the lead car. He'd gone into warrior mode and wanted to be up front just in case. I was happy to ride with Spence, Zoe, Salvatore and Azeem and just tune out for a while. I was especially glad Magda was in the other car – I couldn't deal with her death-stares right now.

When we pulled to a stop, Azeem jumped out and held the door open. 'Welcome to Mount Nebo, the final resting place of Moses,' he said.

I was the last out.

'We must walk from here,' Azeem said, taking my hand to help me from the car. 'The others have already begun.'

I looked up to see a hill. Lincoln and the first car-load were already on foot and halfway to the top. There was a road leading up but we were on the wrong side of some fairly serious gates and I was betting 'open sesame' wouldn't work.

Spence, Zoe and Salvatore marched on, keen to catch up with the action. I walked more slowly with Azeem.

'You carry the burden of one many years more than you,' he said as we walked.

'Yeah. I'm taking it all up front so that later in life I can lay back on a banana chair and drink mojitos.'

'An armour of humour is not a strong defence.'

'I know,' I admitted. 'But right now, it's all I've got.'

'That is not true, you are never alone,' Azeem said, looking to the sky.

'I don't really believe in… I'm not sure what I believe.'

'We would all believe in God if he served our every whim. Belief is not about an easy life or even truth. Belief is something you have regardless.'

I wished I could nod and say something spiritually appropriate, but…no. We were nearing the top and an enormous sculpture came into view, which sent a shiver down my spine.

'The cross?' I enquired, looking up at the impressive cross that looked like it was made of bronze, the figure of a serpent wrapped around it. It made me think of Lilith. In some stories she is thought to be the serpent of Eden. It's a visual that doesn't leave you.

'When Moses brought the people on pilgrimage from Egypt in hope of the Promised Land, they turned on him and on God. Starving and dying, they questioned why they had been brought to this desert and wilderness only to die. On this, God sent poisonous serpents to bite them and many died. When Moses prayed to God to save the people, he was told to make a serpent and put it on a pole. Everyone who had been bitten and looked upon it was saved.'

'And this is the God you believe in?'

Azeem gave a small smile. 'I admit, it is not the most inspiring of stories.'

Now it wasn't just the sculpture that reminded me of Lilith. That story sounded like something that would come from her book of tales, too. I was learning more and more, nothing was as clear-cut as I would have liked it. Nothing was wholly good or evil, it seemed. And if there was a God,

I wasn't sure he was any better than the worst of us.

We were nearing the top. I stopped and turned to Azeem. 'Azeem, I... When I embraced and became Grigori, I had to do something.'

'A test of will,' he said, nodding.

'I had to kill an image that I chose.' I couldn't find the words to express how that silhouette had turned into me.

'And now you feel remorse,' he said compassionately.

'Kind of – I don't regret it, it's just, the image that I chose...is there any chance I could have actually...'

'Violet,' he put his gigantic hand on my shoulder, 'I don't have your answers. I can see you are haunted by this. Choices often reveal consequences in many ways. But what you are looking for I cannot give you.'

'But I'm not looking for something, I...I just want to know...'

'Of course, you are searching. You seek forgiveness and this is something I cannot give. You will have to look beyond this place of dirt and rock.'

He was back on the God thing.

I didn't want to offend him, tell him that right now, I wasn't finding much comfort in the possibility that God might actually exist. I settled for, 'I'll think about it.'

'This is a good place to start.' He continued along the path and picked up the pace. 'Come on, we're almost there.'

The mountain, actually more of a hill, was not spectacular. It was large, but not like the rock formations that surrounded the hotel with waterfalls. It was simple, and though you could see work had been done to restore the area – small trees and green shrubs to break up the continuum of barren land, a small path that was well maintained – it wasn't until we reached the very top that I realised why it was such a special place.

The views.

Azeem pointed towards a mass of water. 'West, the Dead Sea,' and then raised his hand higher, signalling beyond, 'and the Promised Land.'

'Jerusalem,' Griffin said, now standing beside us.

'Wow,' I said, meaning it wholeheartedly.

Azeem turned, 'South is the Crusader Castles, north, the Seven Hills of Amman, and east, the Jordanian Desert to the wastes of Saudi Arabia.' Then he walked us in a full circle around the perimeter of the chapel that rested at the top of the rise. It was old but also surprisingly modern in design. Nyla took in my reaction.

'The original chapel is within the walls of this one,' Nyla explained.

'The outer shell was built to protect it. But even the one within is no more than sixteen or seventeen hundred years old. It is mostly a tourist destination now and normally open every day,' Azeem added.

'Why not today?' I asked.

'We have asked a favour. We did not think it wise to have you all here among tourists.'

I couldn't have agreed more.

Lincoln and Spence appeared from the back of the building. Spence had a handful of small rocks he was throwing into the patchy shrubbery. Lincoln looked frustrated.

'How are we going to find anything here? This construction is too recent. Griffin, this looks like a dead end.'

'No,' Griffin said. He was standing out the front of the chapel, studying every stone, every groove. 'There has to be something here. The story tells us that Moses was buried within the mountain, and later Jeremiah returned with the Ark and left it where Moses was buried.'

'We should look inside,' Rudyard said.

'I am afraid Lincoln is right. You will not find what you are looking for inside. We have searched every inch of the chapel for hidden passages or markers.' Azeem gestured to his men. 'I fear this may be a wasted trip for you.'

'If Moses was buried in this mountain, it's likely some sort of tomb was created,' Griffin said.

'I am not disagreeing with you, friend. It *is* likely that there is a tomb directly under the chapel. But short of pulling down the mountain, we cannot be sure and, well, for some time we have considered that perhaps this may be for the best. If the wrong people or *beings* were to get their hands on the remains of Moses and whatever else may rest with him, it would not be good.'

'Well, they're coming, Azeem,' Griffin said, now irritated. 'And if *we* don't find it, believe me, they will.'

This is why I have a problem with religion. People do too many things in the name of belief, or worse, use it to prevent others from exploring alternative possibilities. I walked to the back of the chapel and saw a narrow overgrown path that led down the back of the hillside.

'Why is that path there?' I asked one of Azeem's Grigori, who was standing nearby.

'It used to be the path to the top – pilgrims would trek from Jerusalem. Now the roads have taken its place,' he said, looking back to where the others were milling about.

It gave me an idea and I ran back to the front of the chapel. 'Rudyard, do you have that thing you read to us at Hades? The Mac-whatever.'

He raised his eyebrows. 'I am assuming you are referring to the Second Book of Maccabees.'

'Yeah.'

He reached into his well-organised backpack and pulled out the old leather-bound book, opening it to the right page before passing it to me.

'Thanks,' I said, reading as I walked back around the chapel.

'Don't suppose you'd care to enlighten any of us?' he called out.

'Just an idea,' I yelled back, not stopping.

A few paces later, I turned. Everyone was casually shuffling behind me. Lincoln came to my side and shrugged.

'No one else has had an idea.'

'Oh,' I gulped, suddenly feeling like I was on display.

I headed down the old forgotten path, my shoes catching on dried roots that carpeted the ground. Once I got a third of the way down, I stopped and turned back to face the hilltop.

Here's the thing about observation, it is open to so many interpretations. At the first and most basic level – visual – we see, we believe. Even this level is sub-standard for the average human. We have four other main senses that influence us. If we smell something burning, for example, but see nothing on fire, most people will investigate to find the source.

After the senses comes instinct. Griffin had been teaching me in our classes that humans are confused by this concept and therefore, on the whole, are unable to harness the power of intuition. Instinct requires self-belief, something humans, who are all too aware of their own shortcomings, often fail to find.

From instinct we move to the higher end. Imagination and manipulation. Angels have dominion over these.

But in the end, observation will always come down to the final, unique factor – perception. Any one person's point of view will provide their own individual perspective, influenced by the accumulation of their own life's millions of moments. What one person would do if they saw the one they loved gunned down in front of them is completely different from what another would do. Whether it's real or imagination doesn't matter. The only thing that is certain is that an individual's response sets off a chain of events that change everything for that person, forever. The power of angels – and this is why there must be both light and dark – is to filter perception.

'Here,' I said, letting the part in me that wasn't human take the reins.

'What?' Lincoln asked, baffled.

I pointed to the plateaus on the mountain face and the trees that offered seclusion. 'Doesn't that look like the perfect place for a cave?'

'I guess, but, Vi, there are no caves here – no sign of an old opening. I don't understand where you're going with this.'

'Jeremiah was on some kind of angelic mission, wasn't he?' I asked, the sun catching in my eyes.

'Apparently,' Lincoln said, taking off his cap and putting it on me.

'So he may have been able to see things that the normal person couldn't. Maybe even things only angels could see, right?'

Lincoln wiped his face, tired, and looked at me dubiously. 'I suppose.'

I huffed, and moved closer to him, sharing the book. 'Look,' I said, pointing to the passage. '"*And when Jeremiah came thither, he found an hollow CAVE, wherein he laid the tabernacle, and the ark, and the altar of incense, and SO*",' I emphasised, '"*STOPPED THE DOOR. And some of those that followed him came to mark the way, BUT*",' I looked at him to finish, '"*THEY could not find it.*"'

'There's a cave!' Lincoln called out to the others who'd been waiting at the top of the hill, watching us.

Spence and Zoe raced down with the others not far behind.

'Where is it?' Zoe asked, looking up and down, all around.

'We don't know,' I admitted, hoping I wasn't leading everyone down a dead end.

Once everyone had joined us, Lincoln explained to the group of astonished faces that were all now positive that there was a cave in this mountain.

'Rudyard,' Griffin said, 'I think you can help.'

'Shoot,' Rudyard replied.

'Can you sense power here? You'll need to try and focus it at the mountain and find its source.'

Rudyard crouched to the ground, touching it with both hands.

He waited.

Eventually, he stood and sighed. 'I can't be a hundred

per cent, but a different energy certainly comes from that direction.' He pointed to the right.

'OK, my turn,' Griffin said, as we all silently looked at each other, trying to figure out what was going on.

Griffin didn't take long, though. He just walked a little to the right and then back. 'The true mountain has definitely been disturbed and Rudy is right, it comes from over there, but like him I can't pinpoint the spot.'

Griffin put his head down, thinking. Everyone gave him time. 'Right,' he said, as if not really sure. 'Zoe, your turn.'

'About damn time. What's your pleasure?' she asked, beaming.

'*Lift* the mountain.'

'What?' everyone chorused.

Zoe just looked from Griffin to the mountain, back to Griffin, then back to the mountain. 'How high?' she asked, as the mouths of the rest of us fell open.

Griffin smiled. 'Just move it. If I'm right and the glamour holds, it won't move. If you can shift the mountain and part of it remains still—'

'The cave will be showing,' Salvatore finished, looking impressed. He really was doing well at keeping up and I wasn't the only one who noticed. I think Zoe, who usually appears completely immune to Salvatore, actually became aware of him.

She closed her eyes and we all waited. Well, until Spence cracked. 'You right, Zo?'

'Shut up! Even Mother Nature would need a moment for this one. I need to concentrate,' she snapped.

So we waited again. And waited. It must have been about ten minutes, but then…the earth started to move.

Azeem and his men, still at the top of the mountain, dropped to their knees. But there was little point unless they were praying to the almighty Zoe.

We all crouched to the ground to hold our footing. And marvelled.

Rocks began to move from side to side – it was only slight, but in sync. The trees – the entire mountain – rocked. Zoe had nature moving as one. Dancing.

'There!' Lincoln yelled.

'Yes!' cried Nyla, standing up, swaying like a magical creature, surfing the mountain.

One small area remained still. The mountain moved around it, but that one part showed no sign of life. It was the perfect size – an opening.

'OK, Zoe, you can stop!' Griffin roared over the sound of the live mountain.

Zoe stood and opened her eyes. The mountain became still, everything exactly where it had been. Everyone else stood slowly, in awe of what we had just witnessed. Salvatore bowed his head.

'Zoe, *complimenti.*'

She couldn't hide the smile as she swatted him away. 'I. Don't. Speak. Italian!' she said, marching towards the place we were all now headed.

'Zoe, that was remarkable,' Rudyard said. With this she couldn't hold back a full-blown smile.

'We're proud of you, Zoe,' Nyla said, so warmly her words struck a chord in my heart. I realised they were like a family and when Zoe beamed back at Nyla, she gave the kind of smile a daughter would give a mother. I realised something else, too. That's why Nyla unnerved me so much.

Nyla linked hands with Rudyard and they walked on.

Could I have that one day?

When it came to stepping up to the area that had not moved, it was Nyla and Lincoln who were first off the ranks. They felt around, trying to pull at rocks and dirt, but anything that was removed seemed somehow instantly replaced. It was useless.

'It's solid, or something. It regenerates itself,' Lincoln said, still persisting, pulling at more rocks.

'Everything is under a glamour,' Nyla said, walking back to us. 'We cannot break through it with force,' she clarified, even as we all watched Lincoln throwing boulders at the opening.

Ideas were put forward, the best of which was to try and tunnel in from another place.

But if Phoenix knew how to get in, there must be a way. He must have known we could get in, too.

I took a tentative step towards the opening, scared, as if it might swallow me whole. I placed a hand on the glamour. It felt like touching dirt and rock.

I drew on my power – worked it up within and then released it over the glamour, willing it to fade. My mist poured from me straight to the opening, concentrating solely on the facade. It knew what I asked of it.

The mist gripped its target, fixed onto it like billions of tiny droplets, and ate into the opening, working its way down to the ground.

'Well… That was effective,' Griffin said, mesmerised. Before us stood a cave leading to a long tunnel, alight with what must have been ever-burning torches.

Eternal fire.

CHAPTER TWENTY-EIGHT

'There are no days in life so memorable as those which vibrated to some stroke of the imagination.'
Ralph Waldo Emerson

We followed Azeem and his men as they led the way into the tunnel. I wondered why only the male Grigori had joined us on the trip. The only female Grigori I'd seen, other than Ermina, had been in the look-out posts back at the hotel.

Spence came up beside me. 'Da da da dah-dah, da da da dah-dahh, da da da dah, da da da dah, da da da-dahh.'

'*Star Wars*?'

'Crap. I was going for *Indiana Jones*,' he said. 'This place is wicked.'

I wanted to agree but I had a different feeling and it had me on edge. I couldn't place it, something stale, almost. I took off Lincoln's cap and stopped walking. Spence's attention had already drifted elsewhere and no one else noticed. I let them walk on ahead and turned back to the opening. Something was definitely not...

Then I realised what I should have sensed as soon as we entered the tunnel. Though on a much lesser scale, it was that same musty feeling I'd had when I'd felt the senses on our arrival.

The sun beamed into the ominous tunnel and as I walked back towards the opening I saw the robed exile standing there, bathed in bright light, head bowed beneath a hooded drape.

Waiting for me.

'Friend or foe?' I said, stopping a few metres away from him.

'Neither.'

His voice was young but tired, very tired.

'You're an exile, aren't you?' I asked, suddenly unsure.

'I made my choice, yes.' And yet somehow I didn't feel like it was really an answer.

'Who are you?' I took another step towards him. He didn't seem concerned.

'A messenger.'

'What do you want?'

His head moved to the side. I thought he was going to look at me, but then he stilled again. 'Nothing. I want for nothing.'

'Then what are you doing here?' I asked, confused.

'Wanting. Nothing.'

'Right...'

Escape from the institute much?

'What's your name?' I tried, starting to feel impatient.

'You can call me Jude,' he said, still not revealing himself. I wondered if something horrific lay beneath the robes, if he were wounded or scarred.

'OK, Jude. Do you know where the Scriptures are?'

He nodded once. 'You must see the room which goes beyond your eyes.'

Why the hell does everyone have to be so cryptic all the time? It's like it's some angel/exile criteria.

He turned to leave.

'Why are you so familiar?' I asked, still unable to shake the feeling that I knew this exile somehow.

'I was famous once,' he said, and though I still couldn't see his face, he sounded oddly amused.

When I caught up with everyone else again, they were piling into a small room. Azeem's Grigori were walking back past me.

'Where are they going?' I asked.

'To guard out front,' Azeem said.

'Oh,' I responded, briefly considering telling them about Jude but deciding not to. He was gone.

'This is truly remarkable,' Nyla was saying as I walked into the room they were all gawking at.

Lincoln came to my side. 'Where did you go?'

I didn't think anyone had noticed. 'I'll tell you later,' I whispered.

Along with everything else.

He raised an eyebrow but let it go.

I looked around the room, really just a dirt floor and cracked stone walls covered in paintings and symbols that looked thousands of years old, which were precisely what made it so remarkable.

'This is an amazing discovery,' Azeem said, 'but I cannot see anything in here to help you. It is possible this is the – or a – pre-chamber to Moses' tomb, but I cannot see where it would lead,' he said, circling the room, running his hand along the walls.

'We have to allow ourselves to see it,' I whispered to myself, repeating Jude's words. 'Oh my God! I know what to do.'

I looked at Lincoln. 'It's like the front, but more. This place – it's made by angels.'

'Glamour?' Lincoln asked, trying to keep up.

I shook my head, 'Imagination.'

The two things seem the same but glamour is external, a trick of the eye. Imagination is within us, a perception. To reveal it, our own imaginations have to be open to new interpretation.

And before anyone could ask, I released my power into the room. A blanket of amethyst mist floated over everything and began to work its way through the apparent barriers. This room was a defence, just another layer.

The intensity of my power built and built and started to encircle the room, rebounding off the walls until the mist became its own windstorm. Everyone hit the deck.

I pushed it out, pushed it to break down the entire fabric of what was surrounding us. It looked real. If we tried to walk through it our legs would not take us and if we put our hands to the wall our minds would tell us it was solid. But it was not.

I felt the sweat start to bead on my forehead and the strength flow rapidly from my body. I wasn't controlling this well. I started to see the room break away, but only in my peripheral vision. When I tried to see what was beyond, I couldn't.

I wasn't strong enough.

But I didn't need to be. Without looking I threw my open hand out to the side. He caught it firmly. The room started to fill with new colours and his grip tightened. I knew the mist – though multicoloured like everyone else's, it contained the most vibrant green, just like his eyes. I was still weakening but squeezed Lincoln's hand back as together we demanded the veil be lifted.

I'm not quite sure what happened next, just that everything went dark and I was going down.

The next thing I felt was someone kicking the soles of my shoes. I was lying down.

I opened my eyes. I was on the ground, head in Lincoln's lap. I looked down, Spence was lining up to kick me again. I moved my foot just in time.

'You know, I really think everyone needs to assess the way they treat their fellow Grigori – especially when they're unconscious.'

'This coming from the girl who decked her man a couple of days ago!' Spence said, arms wide as if he didn't understand the difference.

I blushed. Pathetic as it was, lying in Lincoln's lap and having someone else call him *my man*, was embarrassing. Lincoln was pretending to look elsewhere for a moment. But he was biting back a smile.

'Eden, you've got some heavy mojo, I'll give you that, but ya got no staying power. Come on!' Spence said, throwing a hand out to me.

'Take your time,' Lincoln said, smoothing the hair back

from my sweaty face and sending a sharp look in Spence's direction. 'That *was* some major stuff back there.'

He was right. I was absolutely spent, but I sat up anyway and let Spence pull me up. This wasn't the time for feebleness.

I took in my surroundings. We were in a completely new room. Well, actually it was a very, very old room. Everyone else was slowly moving around the space, studying the symbols on the walls.

Azeem was kneeling on the ground.

'Is he praying?' I asked Lincoln. He nodded. Azeem was committed, I'd give him that.

On one wall there was a painting of Mount Nebo and it looked like a sheer curtain had been lowered over the entire mountain. The next wall showed the curtain partly covering a wooden box with a golden top comprising two majestic birds, perched, wings outstretched. On the third wall, there were three figures in human form. One was painted bright, one shadowy dark, and one... faded, almost translucent. The three figures, each wearing a small silver crown, stood around a large chalice, which rested on a very long stem. All three of them had an arm extended and were bleeding from the wrist into the cup. The other hand rested on the shoulder of the one to their left so they were all connected. I cast my gaze to the last wall – it was completely faded or had never been painted.

Nyla and Rudyard were standing very close, holding hands and whispering.

'This one is not good news,' Salvatore said, from behind me. I spun to see what he was talking about and found myself staring at the same thing that had everyone's unwavering attention.

'You think?' Zoe snipped at Salvatore, throwing a hand to the chalice that balanced on a long wooden stem, just as it did in the painting.

'Stop being a bitch,' Magda spoke up, contributing her first words for the day.

'What? You got a patent on it or something?' Zoe returned, her anger causing sand to swirl at her feet.

I was starting to feel woozy again.

Magda looked down at Zoe's miniature sandstorm. 'You wouldn't get it off the ground,' she warned.

'Lady, I could build a sand castle around you before you even knew what was happening,' Zoe said, taking a step forward, daring Magda.

Maybe I did get up too quickly.

Magda was about to say something else, when Griffin stepped between them. 'Stop it!' he yelled, staring at Magda. She looked away, her hand going to the sapphire around her neck as if it would somehow protect her.

My head was spinning. Zoe looked like she was about to say something else, but she stopped when I lost my balance and fell to one knee.

'We need to get Violet back to the hotel and I think we all need to get out of this place. Now,' Griffin ordered.

He came to my side as Lincoln helped me stand.

'I'm OK,' I tried, but they just ignored me.

So much for being strong.

'Let me guess, Violet needs you both to rescue her now,' Magda said under her breath as she charged out of the room and into the tunnels.

'What's her problem?' I asked weakly, trying to understand once and for all what her issue was.

'She… She's just tired,' Griffin said. But I wasn't buying that any more. By the look on Griffin's face, neither was he.

As we all walked out I noticed Salvatore stayed very close to Zoe, who was still fuming, almost protectively.

CHAPTER TWENTY-NINE

*'Love is the only fire that is hot enough to melt the iron
obstinacy of a creature's will.'*
Alexander Maclaren

I woke up disoriented to find myself in my bed at the hotel,
then startled when I registered someone was beside me.

'It's just me,' Lincoln said soothingly, closing the book
he'd been reading.

'Hey,' I said, sounding croaky. I'd been dreaming
a familiar dream. The same one I'd had often now.
I concentrated and tried to hold onto it, draw it back to
me. But once again, the moment I could almost touch it,
it seemed to dissolve completely. The only thing left in its
wake was the same feeling of isolation and sadness and
the smell of lilies. White.

Lincoln was smiling, studying me. He twisted around,
leaning on his elbow. The way he manoeuvred himself,
carried his weight and breathed in through his nose and
out again slowly – I was suddenly very aware we were in,
or at least *on*, the same bed together.

'How are you feeling?'

Paranoid.

I returned his smile, though mine wasn't so easy, and tried to push aside the feeling that I was missing something big. 'Better, I think. What happened? Last I remember we were getting in the cars.'

'You passed out when you were climbing in, almost took Azeem out with you,' he said.

I couldn't stop staring at him. His hair was damp and he'd changed into pants and a light blue shirt, sleeves rolled up so I could see the blond hairs on his bronzed arms. He looked divine.

He raised an eyebrow.

'Oh,' was the best I could muster while trying to stop my wandering eyes.

'No one else could have done what you did back there. How did you know it was imagination?'

I heard the words but the way he spoke – quietly, intimately – made it feel like he was saying a lot more. Goosebumps ran down my arms, prompting a domino effect as arm hairs stood to attention.

He reached over and opened a bottle of water for me.

'Thanks,' I said, taking a sip. 'I saw that exile. The one in the robes, he was waiting for us when we went into the caves.'

He nodded, putting two and two together. 'So that's where you disappeared to.'

'Yeah. There's something weird about him. He knows stuff and I know he's old, even for an exile, but there's something else. He isn't like the others. He's not inclined to fight and I'm not afraid of him in the same way.'

Lincoln looked concerned. 'Don't be fooled, we have no idea what his powers are,' he warned. The comment was loaded. Clearly, I'd been fooled before.

'That room, those caves...it was all created by angels so that normal humans would never discover it. That place was only meant for us to find,' I said, feeling shivers of a different kind.

'Us *and* exiles,' Lincoln corrected. 'They can see past the imagination of angels, too.'

'Yeah,' I said, taking a deep breath. I didn't know how long I'd slept but it wasn't enough. 'What time is it?'

'Almost five.'

I sat up urgently. My stomach turned – I still wasn't at my best. 'We have to go. Phoenix is going to be there in a couple of hours. I can't believe you let me sleep this long!'

'Relax. We have time and you needed to rest. Everyone is meeting downstairs in an hour.'

'Oh,' I said, unable to resist falling back on the bed.

'You know, this isn't how I imagined the first time you would wake up beside me,' Lincoln said, smiling *that* smile.

I was about to launch into one of my mental mind checks, remind myself of all of the dangers. Lincoln for some reason had decided not to hold back any more. He'd seemed so sure since what happened with Nahilius. I'd had my doubts. But then I remembered what Nox had said. He'd confirmed it. We were soulmates.

This was what I wanted.

There was nothing to hold us back.

I thought of Nyla and Rudyard and smiled as I fantasised about how that could be Lincoln and me.

Lifetimes of being together – free to love each other completely.

But then another line of thought had my smile fading fast, as Lincoln watched on, amused. I was sure I had panda eyes, bad breath and terrible hair.

He probably wants to run screaming.

I sat up. 'Sorry,' I said, quickly throwing the sheet off and standing up.

Kill me!

I wasn't wearing my cargos, just undies. 'Ah...' I started, feeling a rising flush, totally at a loss as to what to do. I didn't want to shriek, but...O. M. G. I was standing there in front of my soulmate in my green Incredible Hulk undies!

Lincoln was holding back a smile and his eyes stayed on my very bare legs. I guess it was better than focusing on my burning red face.

'I swear, I didn't do that,' he said, hands up in surrender. 'Zoe brought you in and got you settled.'

'Well, thanks for the warning,' I said, grabbing a towel from the cupboard shelf and wrapping it around my waist.

'You got up kind of quick. Anyway, I'm part angel, not saint,' he said, his voice thicker than usual and his smile twisting. He was getting way too comfy keeping those green eyes fixed on me, which would have been OK, if I wasn't a fumbling mess.

I darted towards the bathroom.

'Where are you going?'

'Shower!' I called back. Then, realising he'd probably take that as his cue to leave, I made a decision. 'Wait there, I'll be back out in a minute.' I closed the door before he could answer. It was time to level the playing field if I wanted to maintain any control.

I gave myself a smile in the mirror.

Let's see who has the upper hand now!

Then my smile turned to a grimace. I looked horrific. My hair was all but in dreadlocks, my eyes had tired dark circles under them and there were random smudges of dirt on my neck and shoulders. I desperately wished I had Steph's little make-up bag of everything handy.

I turned on the water and stripped off my singlet and underwear. I had a fast cold shower, just wetting my hair enough to control the craziness before jumping out again. I used what I *did* have, which was pretty much just eyeliner, mascara and lip gloss. I gave my hair a quick towel dry and then flicked it back a few times. On my way to the door, I strategically wrapped the short white towel around me, letting it drape at the back. It covered the important parts.

Lincoln was standing by the window. He was looking out but he knew I was back in the room. I could tell by the way he stilled.

'That's much better,' I said, combing my hair with my fingers.

'That's…good,' Lincoln said, not turning around.

'Linc, what's wrong?' I asked, innocently.

'Nothing.' He cleared his throat. 'I just thought…I didn't want you to feel uncomfortable.'

The truth. I was *totally* uncomfortable. I mean, it wasn't about being close to him, that was easy, especially now that I knew we could – but this stuff…Well, I hadn't done anything like this before.

'Me? I'm not uncomfortable at all. Why? Are you?'

Hold it together, hold it together.

I was sure he must have heard the tremble in my voice.

He didn't respond. But he did turn around and when he did, it was worth it.

Seriously, big-time worth it.

He tried not to drift, he tried to hold my eyes, but he couldn't and when they travelled down the length of my body my mission had been well and truly accomplished. Just in case, I put the cherry on the cake.

'Oh, there it is,' I said, spinning around to the bedside table to get my brush. My towel was draped at the back so it dropped all the way to the top of my butt. It didn't show any more than a backless dress would, but it's different when the only thing between you and stark nakedness is a loose sheet of cloth.

I turned back just in time to catch the corners of Lincoln's mouth go up.

'You do realise I'm coming over there, don't you?'

'No. Why?' I replied, but I was already laughing.

He took a few steps and by that stage he couldn't move fast enough. Just as he reached me there was a knock at the door. Zoe called out.

'Everyone's getting ready to go. You guys OK?'

'Yep,' we called out in unison.

'Right,' Zoe said, sounding like someone who knew exactly what we were doing.

'At least it wasn't Ermina,' I said. But Lincoln *really* wasn't interested. His lips found mine and though we had to go, nothing was going to stop us from sharing this moment. He pulled me close and the towel dropped from my back as my hands wrapped around him. His touch glided gently over the contours of my shoulders and down the sides of my body and suddenly there were a million places I wanted them to be and I knew his hands wanted to be there too.

Instead, they reached down and picked up the dangling towel, gently rewrapping it over my back then running his hands down, smoothing it over. Always the gentleman.

'You know that what you just did is a form of very serious torture,' he said, his voice more enrapturing than ever before. I watched him, hypnotised as he reached out and ran a hand through my wet hair.

'You deserved it.'

He half laughed. 'I don't know that I will ever do anything in my life remarkable enough to make me deserve you, but I promise you, Violet, I will try every day for the rest of my life.' He took a step back and took in the sight of me in a way that made my insides flip. 'When we get home, I plan on showing you just how amazing we really can be together.'

Why is it he has the ability to say these amazing things at times like these?

Once again, I could hardly breathe. Honestly, who was I kidding? I couldn't control this thing between us, I'd be his slave if he asked it of me.

There was another bang at the door. 'Rudyard's coming,' Zoe whispered through the crack.

'Go!' I said to Lincoln. 'I'll meet you down there.'

He didn't need telling twice. Neither one of us was up for a discussion with Rudyard about the seriousness of this choice we were making.

When I got downstairs, I spotted Lincoln first on the far side of the room – my eyes would find him anywhere first. He was already looking at me, smiling.

'Oh, for Christ's sake!' Magda, who I hadn't noticed standing alone near the entryway, said between a series of huffs. She gestured towards my still-wet hair. 'For someone who needed everyone to carry her back here, you look awfully...fresh.'

'You know what, Magda, I feel sorry for you. You have the most amazing Grigori partner and he's been carrying the whole load, covering up for you, doing your job even when he can barely find the time to do everything he has to. Why don't you just try being helpful for a change?'

She moved in close to me, so no one could hear. Salvatore was behind her, watching us.

'Just remember who Lincoln came to when he needed someone. You think you and he have a chance? Well, you don't. You're sparkly and new right now, but he'll see through that soon enough – then he'll see what you really are.'

My eyes widened. Her words splintered through my defences too easily.

She smiled, encouraged by my reaction. 'Do you think of him often? Fantasise about being wrapped in his arms? Do you tell Lincoln about what it was like to share a bed with Phoenix?'

'Shut up,' I said.

'Didn't think so. It must be hard, impossible even, to

forget,' she taunted. 'Phoenix is, after all, the son of lust and seduction. No wonder Lincoln needed to go after Nahilius. He was probably desperate to regain some dignity.'

I glared at her and tried not to back away. 'You know, you're not looking so great, Magda. Jealousy doesn't work for you.'

She leaned in, close to my ear. 'You think you're Lincoln's soulmate? Come on. How could you ever think a soul as tainted as yours could be a match for his?'

'I…I…' I was trying desperately to hold back the tears. I wanted to hit her and before I knew what had happened, I had. I slapped her across the face.

She stumbled back a step, then I saw her smile as she added a couple more steps.

Please.

Griffin was at Magda's side in an instant. Lincoln was at mine, but he wasn't happy. I could almost see the lingering high from our earlier towel moment disintegrate into nothing.

'What happened?' Lincoln asked, looking between Magda and me. I could see him drawing his own conclusion before I'd even had a chance to explain.

'She… She…' but what was I going to say? I could see the smile in Magda's eyes as she held a hand to her face like a beaten woman. I hadn't hit her that hard. Anything I said was just going to sound childish. I dropped my head.

'Violet, I don't care what petty arguments you and Magda are having, we don't lash out at our own like this. She's my partner – striking out at her is a strike to me.'

Griffin's words were like a return slap to my face. I thought for a moment Lincoln might defend me as Griffin had Magda, but he stayed silent. Magda walked out in Griffin's hold.

'Everyone load up!' Griffin called behind him.

'Lincoln, I... She started it,' I tried to explain.

'Violet, it doesn't matter.' He shook his head, disappointed with me, and my heart sank.

I could almost hear Magda laughing at me, taunting me... *With a soul as tainted as yours.*

'You shouldn't have hit her.'

'I barely touched her,' I said quietly.

He shook his head at me again and followed the others.

Salvatore walked out beside me. 'Carefully, Miss Violet. Carefully, carefully, *per favore.*'

Zoe raced up behind us and draped an arm around my shoulders. 'Don't worry, babe. I had your back. She had that coming.'

Yeah, Zoe had my back. From the furthest point across the room!

CHAPTER THIRTY

'Without darkness, nothing comes to birth,
As without light, nothing flowers.'
May Sarton

'They are not here yet,' Azeem said when we arrived back at Mount Nebo.

His Grigori, the men anyway, had been patrolling and scouting all afternoon. When I had asked, Rudyard explained that even though the female Grigori were very powerful, their beliefs still overrode their entitlements. The women Grigori were confined to securing the home perimeters and healing. It had left me baffled.

No exiles had come near the caves. It wasn't exactly encouraging to hear. Not because I thought they wouldn't come – more that I knew they would. And I had a strong suspicion that Jude was not far away. But that was just intuition, I couldn't sense anything.

The mountain had a different feeling in the evening. The air surrounding me felt thick despite the cool breeze. Dusk was falling and there was a clear view to the horizon in all directions. It looked as if the flesh-coloured clouds with dark grey tops were rising from the ground encircling us, suffocating the last of the sun's golden glow with shadow. Closing in.

'How are you feeling?' Lincoln asked. Again.

'I'm fine,' I said, a little sharp. I was still angry about the Magda situation. And I *was* tired, but it wasn't going to help admitting to it. He kept his attention on me, wanting me to say more. I pretended I was interested in something to the side and angled myself away from him.

Griffin herded us all down the back of the mountain. He had decided, even though we might be walking into a trap, it was better if we were in the tomb. It was now completely dark and I heard Spence swearing every few steps as he tripped.

'If it's a tomb, how come there's no coffin?' I asked, putting a few steps between Lincoln and me.

'It is likely Moses was laid within the earth,' Azeem answered.

I felt uncomfortable around Azeem now, like I should speak up on Ermina's behalf or something. You know, feminism and all. But then again, Ermina hadn't done anything to suggest she wasn't happy with the way things were. Maybe it only seemed backwards to me.

The entrance to the tunnel was easily visible this time, as if now our eyes had seen the truth, they would not again be deceived. I hoped the same would apply inside the cave, but the rules here seemed to be a bit different. The tunnel glowed with the eternal golden flames, which burned silently from torches dotted at intervals. I noticed no one else was particularly fascinated by the perpetual flames like I was. There was probably some class at the Academy that covered it. I surprised myself with a small smile as I envisaged turning a page in one of my textbooks to see a chapter named Fire That Ignites, But *Never* Burns. For the first time, I wondered if I'd made the right decision vetoing my education at the Academy.

Azeem's men remained outside at their posts, though Azeem joined us. By the way he watched us, I got the impression he was more concerned with preserving the site than anything else. That is, until I saw him pull out a machete from beneath his robes.

'That work?' Lincoln said.

'We are each given the tools of our culture. This is mine.'

'I didn't know the machete was ever an Arab weapon,' Lincoln said.

Azeem spun the heavy blade like it was a butter knife. 'I was not always from these parts.' He smiled a different smile from his standard – more tooth showing, catching the firelight. It sent a shiver down my spine.

'Impressive,' Lincoln said with a nod.

'Yes,' agreed Azeem, looking ahead.

I'd be impressed when I saw him put it to good use.

Not that I can comment, I thought, unconsciously brushing my hand across the hilt of my own dormant dagger.

The tunnels had the same musty smell and there was a new energy within the walls that I couldn't quite identify.

When we piled into Moses' tomb room I let out a small gasp. Unlike the entrance to the cave, in here the room and all its imaginations had restored themselves. Once again we were in the smaller space that looked completely real, even though we knew it wasn't.

'I thought once we knew what to look past, we could do it?' Zoe said.

Everyone was looking around the room in awe, as if seeing it for the first time.

'We usually can,' said Nyla. Spence took a running jump at one of the walls, slamming his shoulder in the process. It was futile, so I was a little annoyed when I saw Salvatore line up and do the exact same thing.

'It's because the room is not under the typical glamour of exiles,' I said, unable to hide my frustration.

'Explain please, Violet,' Rudyard said, in a teacher's voice not unlike how Griffin's could be.

'This room was created by angels to hide its contents. Only when Grigori or exiles are here will the room be revealed. Each time we leave, the layer of imagination is reinstated.'

Griffin, who'd clearly worked this much out himself, only nodded. 'Violet, do you think you can?'

I looked around the room again, feeling something I couldn't see but knew wasn't the same as before. I resisted the urge to wrap my arms around myself and shiver.

I hoped it would be easier second time round.

Lincoln took my hand. 'Together,' he said, squeezing my hand tight.

'OK.'

I took a moment to centre myself. No one pushed, not even Spence. I pulled within myself and sent my will into the room. It *was* easier this time. My power, the frosting of amethyst, rolled over the room, followed closely by Lincoln's many colours led by green.

The metallic markings around my wrists began to churn rapidly. The walls that surrounded the room started to evaporate, first in my peripheral vision and then everywhere. The weight of the mask seemed easier to shift, as if recognising our return custom.

As the last of the pretence faded away, I had to close my eyes. The senses bombarded me in my fragile state. I swayed. Lincoln had a hand at my back instantly, steadying me.

'Senses,' was all I could manage.

'I know,' he said, as I fought the urge to collapse and opened my eyes. Jude was sitting in the corner of the room. He had been there all along, *within* the glamour.

'Oh.'

Azeem already had his machete out and pointed at a side angle to Jude's neck. I was about to say something, ask Jude how he'd hidden within the angelic facade, when I heard clapping.

I spun, more slowly than I wanted, to see Phoenix standing at the entryway, a platoon of exiles behind him.

'You're truly inspiring, Violet. It took me a week locked in this damn room to finally break it down and you did it in just minutes,' Phoenix said. His eyes were frighteningly devoid of emotion.

I stood tall and was grateful that Lincoln was quick to take his hand from my back. Phoenix noticed anyway. For a moment I thought I saw the smallest flash of something, concern perhaps. Whatever it was, it was quickly covered as he moved into the room. His presence commanded such attention it was unnerving. He didn't even seem to try, unlike Onyx and all his theatrics. For Phoenix it was… natural.

He took up one side with his followers, while we took the other, standing behind Griffin. Jude remained in his corner, Azeem's very large blade still resting at his neckline. Jude seemed unfazed. In fact he had not even lifted his head, which remained covered under a hood.

'What of my men outside?' Azeem asked with a megaphone volume.

'Some are probably dead, others might live,' said a very stoic exile who stood directly behind Phoenix. There were twelve of them including Phoenix, outnumbering the ten of us. Jude was an unknown. *Neither friend nor foe.*

Phoenix merely shrugged.

How can he be this? How can he be attacking us like this?

I didn't understand. I mean, I got the bit about him being dark and hating me, even wanting to kill me. But why was he so intent on getting the Grigori Scripture? It just didn't fit.

I was missing something.

'That is,' Phoenix said, 'dependent on how quickly you can get help to them.' He was smiling. 'I take it you have figured out what is required.'

Griffin took a small step towards the centre of the room, fearless. 'An exile of light, one of dark and a Grigori,' he answered.

'Yes, but not just any. To lift the veil a prince in each is required. A leader.'

I looked back at the paintings on the wall. That was why each was wearing a small crown.

'Well, I believe you have a problem then,' said Griffin. 'You might have exiles of light in your fold, but there is certainly no leader among them.'

A few of the exiles, obviously of light, sneered at Griffin. But he was right. None exuded enough supremacy.

'Griffin, you always were too slow,' Phoenix said. He turned, seemingly distracted, to me. 'You're weak,' he said, as if angry with me about it.

'Strong enough to deal with you,' I said, pushing my shoulders back.

The corner of his mouth twitched. 'Good.' He switched his attention to Lincoln. 'Still think you can protect her?' He laughed and raised a hand. 'No matter,' he said, before Lincoln could answer.

I could sense Lincoln stiffen beside me. He was biting his tongue.

There were small movements happening everywhere as people adjusted, moving to get the best line on the exiles they were going to fight. I could see Nyla and Rudyard strategically positioning themselves at the far end where the most vicious exiles were crowded. I spotted the two who Griffin's intel told us were now Phoenix's right and left – Gressil and Olivier. I could see why he'd selected them. Just the sight of them put my hairs on end, and it had nothing to do with their massive stature in height and build. It was something else, seeping out from beneath the surface. Something altogether eager and…evil.

Nyla appeared unfazed. She would tackle the extra numbers and Rudyard would have her back.

Spence made a move towards Nyla and Rudyard. I caught his eye and I shook my head at him, but of course, he kept inching his way up there anyway. Lincoln stayed down with me and Magda was at our end too. Griffin held his place in the middle, Zoe and Salvatore flanking him.

'I presumed you'd be here, Jude,' Phoenix said. 'Still waiting for something to trade for your return?'

Jude remained silent. But raw power emanated from him. He was not afraid of Phoenix. Of any of us.

'Jude is a leader,' I said, starting to understand.

'Yes, the oldest remaining exile of light,' Phoenix said. 'Here is your chance to play a part in history that is of your own making, Jude.'

Jude stood and pulled down the hood of his robes. Azeem looked to Griffin, who nodded. Azeem lowered his machete and allowed Jude to pass. He walked to the centre of the room and raised his arm over the chalice. He looked no more than thirty years old and he was...beautiful...in a most indescribably painful way.

His dark hair, wispy thin and tattered, fell to his shoulders. His eyes were baby blue and crystal clear beneath thick eyelashes. His high cheekbones and slender features begged for some form of contact. I was tempted to reach out to him and I had to force back my suddenly weightless arm that was so drawn to him. I saw some of the others actually take a step towards him before forcing themselves back.

I imagined that he would have the power to lure the love of many and the arsenal to punish their trust with devastating accuracy. And yet, until this point, he had remained hidden beneath his robes, had withheld his enigmatic strength and power as if – and I was almost certain about this – he had no desire to use it.

'And now we just need the Grigori leader,' Phoenix said, also stepping forward to stand before the chalice.

'I cannot permit it,' Griffin said.

Phoenix just smiled as if Griffin was doing and saying all the things he'd expected.

'Tsk, tsk.' He turned his attention back to me. 'Must I force blood from you so soon?'

The spot in my stomach where Onyx had stabbed me, the place Phoenix now had control over, tingled with fear.

'Very well!' Phoenix said, irritated. I braced myself.

'Stop!' Griffin said, taking a step forward. 'I'll do it.'

Phoenix laughed. 'You misunderstand yet again.' He swung his hand around the room encased in paintings. 'I need your *true* leader.'

'Griffin is of a Seraph, you will not find a truer leader,' Rudyard said.

'Of the Seraphim, yes. But your *true* leader? No.' Phoenix directed his attention back to me. 'And you already know that, don't you, lover?' Phoenix said, looking towards Lincoln at his last word, gloating.

'*She* is not our leader,' Magda said, sounding horrified. No, mortified.

'Oh, but she is. Like I am born through a unique binding and have chosen darkness. Like Jude has been abandoned by the light on his own say-so in order to deceive deception itself – we are both unique. Violet is more powerful than any Grigori who has come before, her very arrival awakened the possibility for this discovery. Violet,' he threw his arms wide and raised his voice. 'Violet, is of the Graced!'

'I... What does that mean?' I asked, looking at Phoenix then to Lincoln, who seemed...stunned. 'What does that mean?' I screamed at everyone, who stood shocked or dumbstruck or, in the case of Magda, like she was about to implode.

'It means, lover – that you are the first human to have ever been parented by one of the Sole. As a Grigori, you outrank everyone.' His expression broke. I couldn't tell if it was triumph or sadness.

'But...I...I...' I looked around the room. Even the other exiles seemed rocked by Phoenix's revelation. Except Gressil. He looked like he was struggling to restrain himself. Clearly the idea of taking me on got his rocks off.

Lucky me!

Then I did the maths and half laughed. I was such an idiot. I'd actually thought that maybe he... And then I realised something else.

'That was why the exile at the airline factory ran away from me. And at the farmhouse. I couldn't figure it out.' I shook my head, angry with myself. 'That's why you didn't just kill me at Hades. You needed me for this.'

Phoenix moved from one foot to the other and swept a hand quickly across his face, covering his eyes for just a moment. 'Onyx and Joel were on the right track but they hadn't found the caves yet. It was only a matter of time, but if they'd had it their way they would have killed you and destroyed the very key to the Scriptures.'

I looked at Griffin, who had taken a step back, level with everyone else. For some reason that hurt more than anything else.

'Griffin,' I said, 'it's your call. Tell me what to do.'

'I don't think you have a choice,' he said with a nod.

I knew he was right. These things always ended with

me not having a choice. 'Great,' I sighed. 'So I guess that means I have to divvy up in the blood donor stakes?' I looked back to Phoenix. 'What happens when we get the Scriptures?'

He raised his eyebrows and gave another indecipherable smile. 'We can all sit down calmly and discuss donating them to the world history museum.'

I deserved that.

We would do what we always did. We'd fight.

Jude, I noticed, remained silent with his wrist over the chalice, which – now that I knew I had to bleed into it – looked really bloody big.

'Anyone have a dagger handy?' Phoenix asked.

'I do,' said Azeem, raising his machete.

Phoenix looked unnerved for the first time since he arrived and I didn't hold back my smile.

I pulled out my dagger and tried to ignore the feeling that always came when I touched it. The one that made me feel so sick, because…it felt right. A part of me.

Phoenix looked at the painting again, pointing to the hands on each of the shoulders. 'Sheer bleeds dark, dark bleeds light, light bleeds sheer.' He looked back to me, then to the dagger, then he raised his wrist above the chalice. 'You'll need to keep the dagger in there or I'll heal too quickly. Think you can manage that?'

'Oh, I think I can manage that,' I said, as I punctured the veins in his wrist with the sharp tip. His chocolate eyes penetrated mine and suddenly I wanted to pull away. My mouth was dry and I wanted to escape, but I couldn't. Phoenix rotated his wrist so the inside was facing me and blood started to trickle down. His eyes never left mine.

All too soon the blood was slowing, his skin already healing around the blade and we still had a long way to go.

'Twist it,' Phoenix said, with a slight twitch of his lip. It hurt.

I didn't deliberate for too long. Hell, he'd left me bleeding out like a pig the other day. I twisted the dagger in his wrist, re-opening the wound, all the while unable to take my eyes from him. He barely reacted, just a slight narrowing of his eyes, not unlike the time I'd seen him eat a chilli. Like then, I couldn't tell if it was self-control or because he actually enjoyed it.

Blood flowed into the chalice, while Phoenix continued to watch me intently. I tried to look away from him, tried not to think the thoughts I was thinking. But, even in this moment of violence, somehow he invoked something so illicit in me that I was breathing a different kind of heavy.

I could feel him compelling me to keep looking at him. I knew he was feeling it too. I couldn't turn my eyes away, even though I was sure the entire room of exiles and Grigori knew exactly what I was thinking at that moment. And Lincoln was behind me.

'That's enough,' said Jude, not even raising his head.

Phoenix turned his wrist upwards again, in a way that caused the dagger to bite into him one last time. I quickly pulled it out and tried desperately to slow my breathing.

Jude's hand went out.

'May I?' Phoenix said, smiling a little but not able to hide the intensity in his eyes, too.

I handed him my dagger. His own wrist was now already healed.

'Ready?' he asked Jude, but he didn't wait for an answer. Instead, he raised the weapon, point down, and looked right into my eyes as he thrust it through Jude's wrist until the base of the hilt stopped it going any further and the majority of the blade had gone right through to the other side.

I made a sound, but couldn't speak as my heart thumped loudly over everything else and adrenalin surged through me. I feared I was going to be sick. The room started to spin and I felt the blood drain from my face.

'Girl!' Jude yelled at me just in time. My trance broke and I managed to look away from Phoenix and from Jude's wrist so that I only heard the scraping sound that came when Phoenix twisted the blade against the bone.

Through such a deep wound, he bled quickly into the chalice and then Phoenix withdrew the blade, wiped it and passed it on to Jude.

I watched the cut on Jude's wrist quickly heal as if it had never been there. Was it miraculous? Imagination? Was anything real?

'Just you, now,' Phoenix said, his voice almost breaking.

'Violet,' Lincoln said quietly, from behind me. He was doing everything to hold himself together, too. 'You don't have to do this.'

'Yes,' I glanced back at Phoenix. I felt like he understood this better than anyone, 'I do. I always do.'

'Jude, don't cut her too deep. She'll bleed freely much faster than you,' Lincoln pleaded.

Jude nodded, but didn't say anything.

Com-for-ting! Don't be weak. Remember the rules, Vi. Don't run, don't quit.

I raised my wrist over the chalice that was now two-thirds full. My whole arm was shaking.

Damn it.

Jude looked up and into my eyes. He really was a beautiful creature, not just handsome but with a loveliness I couldn't describe.

'It is better to be quick,' he said, and on his last word I saw the flash of silver that was my dagger as he sliced my wrist open and, I was sure, hit every major vein. But that wasn't all he hit. I saw instantly the blood pour from the markings around my wrist, causing the power within them to generate and swirl like mercury.

Then, the pain hit and I suppressed a scream and bit down hard. But I was too slow to stop my other hand that flew rigidly into the air, searching for something to hold onto.

Phoenix grabbed it, and squeezed hard. He held me still and I let him. He gripped tighter and tighter until it hurt and it was all I could feel, and – for just a moment, I was sure – he was helping me, distracting me. As if…he cared.

Blood flowed from my right wrist.

When I heard Rudyard gasp and someone else, Azeem, I think, whisper, 'Dear God in heaven,' I pulled my eyes away from Phoenix and looked to my wrist.

The blood that flowed was glistening with tiny sparkles of silver. Part of whatever marked my wrists was also flowing into the chalice, which was now almost full and its contents started to swirl in the cup. When it was close to the brim, Phoenix's hold on me softened. I glanced at him and swore I saw a look of concern. He knew I had caught it and in response he straightened and reached out, moving my bleeding arm away from the chalice roughly. He ran his hand over the wound, smearing the blood up my arm, as he looked at Lincoln.

'You know she feels it,' he said, taking in a deep breath. 'It's almost too easy.' He looked back at me as I yanked my arms away from him. 'What? You don't want me to heal that for you?' He smiled his empty smile, pushing all the buttons he intended.

'Step back,' Jude said. I didn't need telling twice and Phoenix didn't seem to either. We both leapt back to our opposite sides of the room, while Jude stood at the top.

I resumed my position beside Lincoln. He didn't look at me, he just grabbed my bleeding arm and started trying to heal it.

'It's OK,' I said. 'Just stop the bleeding.'

He nodded, pretending to concentrate on my arm. It was fair enough. He wasn't the only one who needed a moment.

The blood in the chalice continued to swirl. I was starting to think nothing else was going to happen when the cup itself started to…dissolve.

We watched with wide eyes, everyone except Jude, who'd repositioned his cloak and hood. The chalice disappeared, along with the long wooden stem it had rested upon. At first I thought the blood was actually reacting with it, like acid, eating away at the wood. But as I watched the blood swirling, now suspended in mid-air above us, I realised, this was just another level of imagination.

The ground beneath where the chalice had been started to distort and then, in the blink of an eye, the liquid suspended overhead dropped and splashed onto the floor, seeping into the sand so it looked like the earth was oozing blood.

Slowly, the red sand bubbled up to form a large box. It hovered a few inches above ground level, unsupported, until suddenly it dropped back to the ground with a whooshing sound. There was no trace of blood and left in its place a wooden box with two gold birds – no angels – wings outstretched, on top. For a moment it was ablaze with fire and light, but then, just as quickly, it wasn't.

Azeem dropped to his knees again. Salvatore grabbed the small cross around his neck and many of the exiles took a step back.

The box sprung open from a middle seam, the two golden angels dropped to the side and there, lying within the box, were two tightly rolled parchments, bound in a silver ring imprinted with the same intricate feathered design as the Grigori boxes and wristbands.

That was all I had time to see, that and hear someone else scream: 'The Scriptures!'

But I didn't know who it was, and there was nothing I could do about it anyway.

I was dying.

CHAPTER THIRTY-ONE

'For their feet run to evil, and they
make haste to shed blood'
Proverbs 1:16

Blood poured relentlessly from the wounds that Onyx once gave me and that Phoenix now owned. He stood above me as I fought for my life. Battle surrounded us but Phoenix was uninterested. He remained focused, watching the wound, not looking at my face.

Everyone was fighting. It was déjà vu – just like that night at Hades – only this time, I wasn't strong enough to do anything. I was instantly at the worst point of the injury. I had a few minutes at best. He had planned it perfectly.

Lincoln was fighting two, maybe three, of them. He was so focused, landing lethal blow after blow as he positioned himself between the oncoming exiles and me. Protector to the end.

The exiles attacked him from all sides. Overcoming them seemed an impossible feat and yet he was magnificent, superior in speed and strength, it was as if he could anticipate their every move. I couldn't help but be frightened for him when I saw a series of strikes to his face, but he didn't slow. He would not fall.

He took out the exile to his right. When his dagger plunged into his heart – it was the stoic exile, who had spoken earlier – it cleared his view to me. Our eyes locked just long enough for me to see the terror register in his as he realised what was happening and for him to scream at me, 'Hold on!' before he was fending off a frontal attack.

My entire body burned with pain. Organs fighting for survival but on the brink of letting me go. I saw random out-spills of power that meant exiles were being returned. I saw the flash of a large weapon flying through the air – it could only have been Azeem's machete. Sounds of flesh hitting and slamming into flesh filled the room, screams of pain and vengeance equally shrill.

When I saw Gressil approach, and the look in his eyes, I found I could still tense.

He'll kill me easily, quickly.

But Phoenix had other ideas. Just as Gressil came near enough to strike, Phoenix took a step closer to me and released an indisputable growl. I was his. Much to his chagrin Gressil backed away, just in time to collide with Azeem.

I looked up at Phoenix. I think he loved me once.

Is this all that comes of love? Is this because I couldn't love him back?

He was concentrating intently on the battle. He was trying to look relaxed, as if everything was going to plan, but he was playing with the cuff of his shirt. He did that when he was worried. His eyes darted up and fixed on mine and in that instant I could see his regret and I realised the worry was for me.

'You don't have to do this, you know,' I whispered.

He looked around the room and then back at me. A hint of alarm breaking through his otherwise calm exterior. The battle was taking longer than he'd planned. Just then, the strangest thing happened. He gave me his emotion. For just the blink of an eye – a blink of mercy – I *felt* his need. My scream filled the room with a sound of pain I didn't believe possible. I looked to him again, and somehow knew we shared this reality of terrible choice, vengeful motivation and of all things lost, most of all friendship and love.

The rest happened so quickly.

I saw Magda behind him, she was lunging away from the exile she had just returned, dagger in hand, determination plastered all over her face. Phoenix didn't turn from me, but his eyes grew wide as if instinctively he knew.

The wounds within me started to close.

I gasped as I saw her leap into the air, dagger raised and pointed towards Phoenix's heart. In a blur from the left, something collided with Magda's dagger.

Lincoln.

He'd leapt in front of her, taking the impact in his shoulder. He fell hard to the ground.

No!

Screams sounded from the other side of the room. There was an explosion of rainbow mist, from more than one direction, then a cracking sound reverberated followed by what could only be described as white light.

'Out!' Phoenix yelled. His remaining exiles disappeared

380

with super speed and he followed, leaving a trail of lightly falling desert dust in his wake.

Lincoln was crawling to my side. 'Violet, Violet.'

He dropped beside me, Magda's dagger still embedded in his right shoulder. He pulled it out and dropped it, cringing with pain. His blood mingled with mine in the pool I was lying in.

I was already healing now that Phoenix had gone. In fact, I was almost certain I'd started healing before he'd even left. Lincoln heaved himself onto his elbow and leaned over me. I could tell he was hurting but also knew he would be OK. He reefed my top up to reveal the final stage of the wound healing. A small sound, a cry of relief, fell from his mouth. When we took in the sight of each other, we both exhaled.

'Thank God,' he said, putting a hand on me, which I grabbed tightly. I didn't tell him that despite everyone's hails I was pretty sure God wasn't in this room with us.

I pushed myself up to sit and that was when the impact of what had just happened hit me.

Lincoln was beside me, Magda standing nearby – in shock or something. Zoe and Salvatore were kneeling over something – someone. In the other corner of the room, Griffin was barely restraining Nyla while Azeem knelt over…

Oh no!

He was kneeling over Rudyard and if I hadn't known instantly from the painful wash of the senses that leeched wickedly into my body – the aftermath of exile vengeance – the deathly wail that came from Nyla that moment could leave no doubt.

A scream that held more than life and death, for it also held her soul, as everything she was departed this world with the one she was bonded to forever.

When one soul mirrors another…what would it do if it had nothing to reflect?

Silence followed her cry. It was the last sound that would be heard from her. She crumpled to the ground, nothing but living flesh held together only by Griffin's arms. My eyes, running with tears, found Lincoln's, and they shared the very same sorrow and deep grief.

I knelt and put my hands on Lincoln's shoulder.

Focus on what you can do, Vi.

I healed his wounds, knowing my power well enough now that I no longer needed to harness it through a kiss. Lincoln recovered quickly and ran to kneel beside Azeem, while I scrambled on my hands and knees, weak from so much blood-loss, to where Zoe and Salvatore were kneeling over who I now knew had to be Spence.

Blood almost covered my entire body. By the time I reached Spence, the desert dust coated my arms and legs, while my wrist throbbed badly where the gash, although no longer bleeding, was still fresh.

'Jesus,' said Zoe as she made room for me. 'How the hell are you still alive?'

It was a damn fine question. I ignored it.

Spence was unconscious and bleeding from the head.

'What happened?' My hands shook as they hovered over him, afraid to touch and make things worse.

'Too many, too vicious,' Salvatore said. 'He was Gladiator, but Rudyard fell to the Gressil, and so Nyla fell. This made too many.'

Zoe was shaking her head in disbelief and shock. 'We couldn't get to him. I saw him being thrown against the wall. They were crowding to finish him off. Azeem took out one and then Phoenix called them off. Guess he had what he wanted.'

Spence was barely breathing. Magda came over and crouched beside him. She silently moved her hands through his hair, but Salvatore grabbed her arm.

She spun to look at him, but he held her stare and her arm. 'I need to check the wound,' Magda said.

Salvatore glanced at me. I didn't know what he was asking.

'Let her look, Sal,' Zoe said calmly. It was the first time I'd heard her call him Sal. He nodded and removed his arm.

Magda felt behind Spence's head and then checked his pulse.

She looked up at me, and then beyond. Lincoln had joined us. 'How is he?' he said to me. I shrugged.

'He's dying,' Magda said quietly. 'He has a punctured lung and the head wounds are severe. I'd guess he's bleeding internally. If we move him, it won't work and... we can't get anyone in here to him.'

This was my fault. I'd let him come along, hidden him in my room, let him get dragged in to all my dramas. He wouldn't have even been there in the first place if I hadn't refused to go to the Academy.

Zoe was crying. Actually, she was snotting up a storm.

I inched closer to Spence, then instinctively put a hand on either side of his face. There had to be some good in all this power. I had to be able to do more than just kill.

'Not you. Not today,' I told us both.

I closed my eyes and ignored whoever it was who tried to pull me back. I was super strong. If I wanted to stay here, I would stay. I found my centre and focused on Spence. On my friend who had paid me out, gotten me drunk and had no ulterior motive. I dug into my power and then beyond and forced my will upon him.

'Live, Spence,' I whispered. My left wrist tingled with power and my right one burned with pain but I kept going, pushing my influence into him. Commanding it.

Little by little, it seeped through my hands and into his wounds. The healing began.

It wasn't like healing Lincoln, it wasn't as simple, or pleasant. I pushed through my own faded strength and demanded more of myself. Spence groaned.

Someone said, 'It's working.'

I pushed harder. It almost felt as if my hands were inside his head pushing it back together. Spence's eyes shot open, bloodshot and looking like they were bursting under pressure. He screamed, and screamed…and screamed. I opened my eyes and held his stare.

'Hold on,' I told us both. But the pain was immense and he grabbed for my hands, pulling them, crushing them. I felt my fingers, maybe three or four, snap and break. Lincoln was on top of Spence in an instant, holding him down as he screamed, restraining his hands while I kept going with my healing.

Eventually, the screaming stopped. He was wounded still, a gash on the side of his head, but it was closed. Internally he'd been righted. I began to sink down and Lincoln leapt off Spence in time to catch me. He held me from behind. His arms wrapped around me, his hands closing over mine, healing the breaks. I felt his mouth on the top of my head, buried in my hair. It hurt more than anything had ever hurt before.

It's over. It's all over.

'Thanks, Eden,' said Spence, as Zoe helped him sit up against the wall. 'I owe you one.'

I gave a small smile, happy he was alive, but all too aware that on the other side of the room was a problem I couldn't fix.

'Lincoln,' Magda said, coming up beside us as we stood. 'Are you...OK?'

'What were you thinking, Magda?' he snapped. 'Everyone knew Phoenix was off-limits – if you killed him, you would've killed Violet!'

'I... He was already killing her. She was almost dead, Linc. You were fighting, everything was happening so fast. I knew you'd want me to try and save her. I...I thought it was the only way. I thought if I took him down, they'd all leave and we could try and save her.' Tears fell from her eyes.

Before Lincoln could respond, Azeem stood and a hollow silence fell over all of us. Carrying Rudyard in his large arms, he walked back through the caves. Griffin followed, cradling Nyla, who was alive yet, at the same time, just as dead. I swallowed hard.

We all walked behind, Zoe and Salvatore helping Spence, who was still a little shaky.

'What happened to the Scriptures?' Spence asked, as if any of us really cared just then.

'Jude took off with one early in the piece,' Lincoln said. 'That was the last I saw.'

'Phoenix snatched the other one on his way out,' Zoe said.

'Great. So it was all for nothing,' I said, feeling sour as we followed the others out like a bloody funeral procession. We left the box in the middle of the room. Somehow we either weren't willing to take it – given the price that had been paid – or we figured it wasn't meant for us. I just didn't care.

'Not for Phoenix. He got what he came for,' Spence said.

'Not everything he came for,' Lincoln said, looking at me.

CHAPTER THIRTY-TWO

'Ever has it been that love knows not its own depth
until the hour of separation.'
Khalil Gibran

I sat in one of the military vehicles, inside the plane we had arrived on. Spence was beside me in the driver's seat, Zoe and Salvatore were in the back. Zoe had cried herself to sleep.

This time when we had boarded the plane, the army guys were different. There were a number of them on-board but they left us alone, not interested in getting us to take our designated seats. Buckle up. We had casualties. I guess camaraderie comes from death.

Lincoln and Magda were pacing around the front of the plane. None of us was willing to go down the back end – where Rudyard's body was closed up in a military transport coffin. And going upstairs wasn't an option.

Long stretches of silence made it worse. Even the noise of the engine didn't cut through it. I think we were all hoping to hear her scream or something, but there was never a sound. Griffin had been up there with her for hours, but Nyla was catatonic. Completely and utterly broken.

Lincoln couldn't even look at me. Not that I knew for sure – I couldn't look at him either.

It's all such a foggy haze now. After getting down from the mountain, Azeem had called in reinforcements. Four of his Grigori had been badly injured but, surprisingly, all were still alive. A clean-up crew arrived and set about covering everything up so come morning the tourists wouldn't know.

My eyes stung with tears again. I blinked them back and concentrated on chipping away at the already cracked plastic panelling with my bloodied and dirty fingernails. My fingers still hurt where Spence had crushed them. I pressed harder and focused on the relief of physical pain.

Spence was staring out the front windshield, deep in thought. Almost dying tends to humble a person.

We saw feet coming down the stairs and all sat up a little, the sounds of fabric shifting and the car creaking seemed amplified. Lincoln went over to meet Griffin. I noticed Magda didn't join him. She was lost in thought. Perhaps it was grief – she'd known Nyla and Rudyard for as long as Griffin.

The windows were wound down so we could hear. When we saw Griffin's face, we all slumped. He looked… how someone does when they know there is no hope. He glanced at us, sitting in the stupid truck. Useless.

Spence and Salvatore got out, needing to do something. I stayed where I was. I couldn't… It was selfish. Awfully selfish, but I couldn't stand beside Lincoln and be told what

I knew Griffin was going to say. Hell, I'd felt it back in the cave.

'Her soul is shattered. She's alive,' he shook his head and coughed out a small cry. 'Trapped inside her own... I can't reach her. No one ever will.'

I looked out the window in the opposite direction. I couldn't watch and I wished I couldn't hear.

Don't cry. Don't cry. Breathe. Concentrate. Breathe. One, two, three. Remember how this goes, remember you can do this. When everything falls apart, when everything is strangled and taken from you and nothing is left, not even the tiniest glimmer –

I ran my hands over my face, pulled back my hair and swallowed through the lump in my throat that I knew was there to stay.

Remember the rules. Don't back down. Don't run. Don't quit. And now, remember the new rule...Don't dream silly dreams.

At some point, Spence and Salvatore got back in the truck. Lincoln went upstairs to try and help Griffin. I think in the end he may have found it less torturous to be up in Nyla's hell than down with me.

Magda stayed away from us, which was at least a small blessing. Silence dragged on and on. Someone passed me a bottle of water. I hugged it until fatigue finally overtook the numbness and I fell asleep.

My paintbrush glided over the canvas. The colour flowing and changing without me even trying – an effortless spiral of illuminating colour.

I forced my hand to stop. The painting before me started to bleed tears of grey.

I dropped the brush and looked over to the window, where I knew he would be looking out. He was the same – tall, handsome, overly strong jaw and distant. Inhuman. More interested in the outside world than being confined to my art studio. But it was my dream so I guess that meant the territory belonged to me.

'Are you my Angel parent?' I asked.

He nodded once.

'Who are you?' I pressed, going through the motions. He had told me to call him Lochmet – warrior – but I knew that wasn't his real name.

'That is not important.'

'Are you one of the Sole?'

'Yes.'

His answer threw me. I hadn't expected anything so direct.

'Can you tell me who you are?'

'First, you must know who you are – and you must see what is right in front of you.'

He watched something through the window and it was surreal to see that what he was gazing upon was not the true view from my city apartment. Though it was raining like it usually did in my dreams, he was looking over an open field with a tall forest in the distance. Perhaps this wasn't only my dream.

'Is this about Jude? Did you know him?'

'He was my dearest friend for a time.'

'Why did he exile?'

'For balance. Sometimes, the things that are required of us are beyond our comprehension and even when we have fulfilled our destiny…it can be hard to recognise if we have done so with a clear conscience.'

'I don't understand.'

He sighed, for the first time showing emotion. It was sadness or even…a type of acceptance. 'Humanity requires simplicity. A villain in every story appeals to the most basic human feeling, mistrust. There was a time when direction was necessary, a certain form of proof for comfort. To achieve this we had to provide defeat in some, in others, triumph against all odds.'

'Why?' I asked, still struggling to see where this was going.

'Because the only human emotion more inherent than mistrust is the need for victory.'

'You sent me those other dreams, didn't you? They were about Jude, weren't they?' I asked, remembering flashbacks from dreams I had not been able to hold onto.

'In a way.'

'He's stuck here, isn't he?' I pressed, starting to feel a kind of sickness in my gut.

'He is waiting. Beware, Violet, trouble follows.'

I didn't even have a sarcastic retort. Mostly because I knew he was telling the truth. I looked back to my canvas – it was completely grey now, all the colour covered over. I glanced to the window again.

He was gone. Despite my unanswered questions, I was relieved.

I walked to the corner of my art studio, relishing the solitude. I crumpled to the floor and allowed myself the private freedom to cry. And cry. And cry.

I woke with a jolt when the plane touched the ground. My eyes shot open and locked instantly with Lincoln's.

He was sitting on one of the landing seats along the side, watching me.

I quickly wiped my eyes to break the contact. They were wet. I cursed myself.

By the time I looked back, Lincoln had moved away.

Spence and Salvatore made stretching noises as they unfolded themselves from the truck. A group of army guys came from the cockpit area and bowed their heads as they passed us. They headed straight for the coffin and stood in front of it respectfully.

'We have to get off,' I said to Zoe, not bothering to ask how she was. There was only one answer to that question.

She grabbed her backpack and kicked open her door. 'You sense anything?'

I concentrated. 'No.'

She shrugged, trying to hide the relief. 'Pity.'

I mustered a small smile, which she returned.

When we walked down the ramp from the back of the plane, two Grigori were waiting for us. Zoe, Salvatore and Spence went over and started speaking with them. I hung back until Spence called me to join them. They were from the Academy in New York. They were here to take Rudyard back.

And Nyla.

I felt sick as I watched the army guys wheel Rudyard's pale wooden coffin down the ramp. They had him on a goddamned trolley. I felt even worse when I watched Griffin carrying Nyla.

Rudyard got the better deal.

The Grigori – I forget their names, although they introduced themselves and I think I even shook their hands – had a private jet waiting. Griffin wouldn't hand over Nyla. He insisted on carrying her onto the plane and getting her settled.

The Grigori told Zoe, Salvatore and Spence that they would be returning to collect them and all of Nyla and Rudyard's belongings in two days. Everyone just nodded.

Lincoln stayed with Griffin, who was a mess after handing over Nyla, walking him to a waiting taxi. Magda went with them. The rest of us piled into another taxi. Phoenix wasn't at the airport. None of them were.

'I think we should have a memorial. You know, something here – to say goodbye,' Zoe said.

I nodded. It was a good idea. Rudyard should be remembered.

'He had no regrets. Rudyard, I mean,' Zoe said. 'I remember once in one of his classes, he said if he were to die in battle he would die fulfilled.'

I couldn't help but wonder if he would agree now. Given the state in which he'd left Nyla.

'He also used to say, "We fight the fights that need fighting. Sometimes we win but when we lose and should we die, others will fight in our name, because only one thing is certain for Grigori – we must fight,"' Spence said, impersonating Rudyard endearingly.

'He was right,' I said.

Zoe jingled a set of keys I recognised in the air. 'Lincoln gave me his keys. They're taking Griffin via his place first. He needs a shower and has to check on the local Grigori. Lincoln said we could let ourselves in.'

Spence called out the address to the driver, who nodded

and drove on. I ignored the fact that Lincoln had left without a word and that he hadn't passed this information through me, like he once would have. That was before.

I fished out my mobile phone, but it was long dead. 'Hey, Salvatore, have you spoken to Steph lately?'

Salvatore nodded. 'I telephone her before boarded aeroplane. She was worried for you. Frantic... Said I was not to take my eyes from you. She is waiting at Mr Lincoln's houses.'

'Thanks,' I said, suddenly grateful Lincoln and Griffin weren't going to get there first. I had a feeling Steph would have used the spare key to let herself in.

I was right. As soon as we put the key in the lock, Steph was pulling the door open from the inside.

She pushed past everyone, including Salvatore, and grabbed me. Her slender frame hugged me so tight I was scared I would actually allow myself to feel it. But the numbness stayed with me. Protected me.

'Thank God you're OK,' Steph said.

How could I explain to her I wasn't.

'Sal told me what happened. About Rudyard.' She looked down. 'And Nyla,' she added quietly.

'I think I should have a shower,' I said, subtly moving out of Steph's hold. If anyone could break me right now, it was her. I dug my mobile out of my pocket and put it on Lincoln's charger in the kitchen as I walked by. It even gutted me that we had the same phone.

'Vi, I...I can't believe I have to do this to you,' Steph

said, as she followed me and sucked in a deep breath. 'I mean, I totally want you to hibernate, you know, do your thing. I don't want to be part of the problem, but…I found something and I think…I *know*, you have to see.'

I just nodded and followed her down the hall towards the spare room. Spence moved to follow us but Steph gave him a look and he turned back to the living room.

'You've been busy,' I said, taking in the chaos that was Lincoln's spare room. Boxes were open everywhere and papers piled up in what I imagined were all chronological or alphabetical or numerical order or something else incredibly intelligent that would be way beyond me yet totally normal for Steph. Then I realised something else.

'Steph, Lincoln never even comes into this room himself. He's going to freak.'

'Violet, honey.' She braced a hand on my shoulder. 'I know you've been to hell and back. I do. I really get it and I don't even know how you're holding it together, but right now I need you to look at some pieces of paper and follow what I'm about to tell you.'

'Whatever this is, can't it wait?'

'That's the thing, sweetie…'

I looked up.

Steph shook her head.

Perfect.

I sat on the floor and Steph sat beside me. She picked up the first piece of paper that showed me bank records – transfers from Lincoln's mum's company, big lump sums going into some account. Then she showed me more of the same and a piece of paper that showed the bank account where the transfers had gone.

'Are you following?' Steph asked, watching me, reminding me that somehow all of this mattered.

'Big money transfers from her company to this account and I take it this account is somehow linked to Nahilius, right?'

'Right,' she said, sifting through the papers in her next pile.

'Steph,' I started to complain, but she shoved another piece of paper under my face and pointed to a line at the bottom. It was another bank transfer sheet. This one had funds, almost as large, going from Nahilius's bogus account to another.

My eyes widened as I looked at the piece of paper. 'Do you know who this account belongs to?' I asked, starting to understand.

Steph pulled a piece of paper out of her pocket. 'I had to hack into the computer files of the bank's main server and could be going for a long vacation in jail very soon, but...' she waved the piece of paper.

'You know who Nahilius was working for?'

Trust Steph to delve deeper than anyone else had dared to consider.

She nodded. 'And I want you to promise me that after you look at this, no matter what – no matter what you want to do – you have to swear you will not leave this room until I say you can.'

'Steph, stop messing around,' I snapped.

'Promise.'

'I'm not promising anything, give me the damn paper or I'll stand up and take it from you.'

Steph stared at me, I stared back and wondered if

I actually had it in me. She didn't budge.

'Steph!' I yelled.

'I love you, Violet, so no. Not until you promise.' She held strong but I saw her cringing just a little, her fingers clenched tightly to the paper. She was scared of me.

I recoiled. 'Oh my God, Steph, I'm sorry. I… Everything is so messed up.'

'I get it. Don't think I haven't worked it out, Vi. I know the moment Nyla lost Rudyard, you lost… I'm sorry. And I feel like a cow having to do this to you but I know if you promise me, you will do it and I know you can't look at this piece of paper until you promise me.'

I threw my head back and looked at the ceiling. 'OK. I promise.' I stood up and Steph unfolded the piece of paper.

'I've got a new name for Mr Burke's list of great betrayers,' Steph said, as I read the words that made so many things click into place.

I scrunched the paper in my hand and bit down hard. 'I'm gonna kill—' but Steph cut me off.

'Not until I tell you, you can leave the room,' she said, crossing her arms.

CHAPTER THIRTY-THREE

*'Suppose you struggle through to the good and
find that it also is dreadful?'*
C. S. Lewis

Steph let me be for the first half-hour. I sat on the ground, staring at the piece of paper, trying to put all the pieces together. Steph went about putting all the other paperwork back into boxes, leaving a few key documents in a small pile. Eventually, she sat beside me and helped me try to fill in the gaps. Every now and then, I'd leap to my feet and charge for the door, furious and needing to do something. Each time, Steph pulled out the 'You swore' card and I'd slump back to the ground.

After we had gone over about as much as I could handle, I groaned. 'Lincoln will be back soon. Maybe we should go out.'

Steph just headed back to the last of the boxes after passing me her laptop.

'Why don't you read over my chem notes first? You have a few classes to catch up on.'

I wanted to throw the computer against the wall. I couldn't give a toss about chemistry. But Steph wasn't going to give, so I opened the file and stared at the screen. I opened the wrong notes and up popped the ones from last week.

Gradually, as I read through our class work on precious stones and their characteristics, my curiosity grew.

'Are you connected to the Net?' I asked.

'Yep,' Steph said, lugging a heavy box up onto a few that were already stacked.

I found what I was looking for quickly. For some reason I wasn't surprised. Miss Stallad's excitement at giving a class that had just *popped* into her mind that morning now made perfect sense.

They'd been leaving clues everywhere.

I sighed with crazy frustration and felt like such a puppet.

'Damn angels.' My head fell back against the wall, looking up to the ceiling. 'Why do you have to play all these games? Why couldn't you just tell me?' I might've been able to do something different, save Rudy.

'Vi, any chance you might be able to fill in those of us without a direct link?' Steph said, hands on hips.

So I did.

I heard the front door. Lincoln, Magda and Griffin had arrived. Steph had now had me locked in the spare room for almost two hours. It surprised me no one had come in. They were probably giving me space – or themselves.

This shouldn't have been possible.

I stood up. 'Steph, I'm OK. We have to go out otherwise Lincoln is going to come down here and see you've been through all his mum's stuff.'

A look of panic flashed across her face, but she held her ground.

'Are you sure you're OK?'

I took a deep breath. I *needed* to be OK right now. 'Yes.'

Steph stood up and opened the door. 'OK, maybe you should go have that shower now. I brought over a change of clothes for you. I didn't know if you'd have anything. They're in the bathroom.'

'Thanks, Steph,' I said, giving her a quick hug.

'It's OK – I stayed at your place last night anyway.'

'I didn't mean for the clothes.'

'I know,' she said with a smile as we left the room.

Steph pulled the door shut quietly behind us. I darted across the hall and hovered just inside the bathroom door. I could hear everyone talking, but I just couldn't face them yet, I needed a few minutes alone.

Spence had been down to the corner store and Zoe was offering round glasses of orange juice. Griffin was on the phone, getting back to business. I heard someone start walking my way so I quickly closed the bathroom door and turned on the shower. Then I heard another door close. Lincoln's bedroom.

I stripped, got in the shower and couldn't even stand. I just sat in the corner and leaned against the tiles as the water washed off dried blood and dirt that had remained hidden beneath my sweats. I rested the side of my head against the wall, knowing that Lincoln's room was on the other side.

I listened to the banging.

Drawers being pulled out and slammed back. His cupboard door – I'd heard that one slam before, I didn't know how it was still on its hinges. Then I heard a thud nearby and then a smaller one almost exactly level with my head. It was a thin wall.

I imagined Lincoln there on the other side of the wall, sitting in the corner of his room. I put my hand to the wall and let it slide down the wet tiles.

There would always be a wall.

Even so, I eventually dragged myself out of the shower and changed into the black jeans and red T-shirt Steph had left for me. One thing I knew about Lincoln, he had to say it out loud.

I knocked on his door and opened it. My heart clenched. He was sitting on the floor, exactly where I had imagined he'd be. He didn't even bother getting up.

I sat opposite him on the edge of his bed and looked at my feet.

'How's Griff?' I asked, my voice crackly.

'You know Griff. Blames himself.'

I nodded.

'You were amazing back there. The way you healed Spence. You… You're amazing,' he said, stopping himself from saying something else.

'You too. I saw you take down at least three of them

and then… Thanks by the way. I don't…um…I don't think I ever said so.' In all the commotion I hadn't even thanked him for saving my life.

'I'm so useless to you, when Phoenix hurts you.' He dropped his head into his hands. 'I can't help, I can't stop it and it kills me. The idea of you in pain, hurting so badly – I'd do anything.'

'I know.'

'We're soulmates, Vi. I know you've had your doubts, but I'm sure of it,' he said, glancing at me for just a moment.

'I know,' I whispered.

'No wonder Rudyard and Nyla wanted us to know everything.' He slammed a fist into the wall. 'I could never do that to you. Risk leaving you like that.'

'I know. Me too.' And even though running my heart through a shredder would have hurt less, it was true. I couldn't commit Lincoln to a future like Nyla's, knowing that Phoenix had a physical hold over me that meant he could kill me at any time. There was no way I'd risk bonding my soul with Lincoln's and then stealing his away when I died.

He stood and came over to sit beside me. My entire body ached, craving to reach out and touch him.

'I don't know how to do this, but I know there's no other way.'

'We just keep fighting. Like Rudyard says – said – that's what Grigori do,' I said, letting the numbness in, wanting it to surround me.

'Yeah,' he agreed, nodding sadly. His hand moved towards me instinctively before he stopped it and stood up.

He walked towards the door. 'I should go check up on everyone.'

'Wait. Linc, there's something I need to tell you,' I said, standing too, bracing myself.

But he already had his head out the door, and we could both hear the raised voices.

'Something's going on,' he said.

What's new?

I followed him out of his room and down the hall.

'What's happened?' Lincoln asked Spence when we reached the living room.

'Got me. Zoe and Salvatore were over in the corner talking and then, all of a sudden, Salvatore just lost it. I think he's frustrated by the communication problem.'

'Oh,' said Lincoln, as if it didn't matter.

But knowing everything I now knew and watching how Salvatore, Zoe and Steph were all whispering hurriedly, I got that feeling. The bad one.

I looked over at Griffin. Magda was speaking, looking like she was collecting her bag to leave. Steph must have said something Salvatore didn't like because he was shaking his head, getting more and more upset. Zoe was just looking confused.

'What is going on over there?' Griffin asked, distracted from his conversation.

Salvatore stepped forward. 'I am sorry for these troubles, Mr Griffin. I am trying to give explanation. I must tell these things I know.'

Griffin nodded, seeing Salvatore's distress. 'Stephanie, would you mind translating for Salvatore?' Griffin requested.

Steph looked at me, worried. I gave her a resigned shrug. Lincoln saw and shot me a questioning look.

'I think you're about to find out,' I mumbled.

Did everything have to happen like this?

'OK,' Steph said.

Salvatore spoke to Steph in Italian. Nothing he said seemed to shock her that much. I didn't take it as a good sign.

When he had finished she looked back at me nervously, then licked her lips.

Shit.

'OK. Salvatore, as you all know, has the strength to detect lies. Unlike your gift, Griffin...' She swallowed, she was freaking out.

Shit shit shit.

'Salvatore's looks for the threads that interconnect and then lead to more. He says it's sometimes like looking at a fine strand that is out of place,' Steph continued, talking as much with her flailing hands as with her mouth, 'weaving in and out of many larger pieces of fabric, holding them together. When that thread, no matter how small, comes away, it can unravel the rest.'

'Yes, Stephanie, we understand his gift. Could you please get to the point?' Griffin asked, losing patience.

'Yes. Um...Salvatore has a question for Magda.' She swallowed again, hesitantly.

Magda didn't say anything. Instead she just looked around like this was all a waste of valuable time.

'Well, what is it?' Griffin asked.

'He would like to know...why she lied back at the tomb. He believes – thinks, really – that when she told Lincoln she tried to kill Phoenix to save Violet's life, she was lying.'

'Well.' Griffin looked at Salvatore. 'I'm sorry, Salvatore, but that just isn't possible. Magda wouldn't lie about something like that. She has no reason to and anyway I would have seen the absence of truth if she had, and I didn't.'

Salvatore said something to Steph, who finally seemed to be getting back some of her Stephness.

'Salvatore says you're wrong. He believes Magda has a way of clouding truth. She's protecting herself and attracting trust in others. He says you're too close to her to see past it, but he's been seeing it for some time now and he's sure.'

'This is ridiculous,' Magda said, looking around the room, convincingly. 'I don't have any protection against my own Grigori partner. Lincoln, surely you don't believe this?'

Lincoln looked at me and then to Salvatore. 'I'm sure you have your reasons, Salvatore, but it has been an incredibly traumatic time for everyone. We have no reason to doubt Magda…or Griffin's abilities for that matter.'

Salvatore shook his head, frustrated. Zoe stepped up beside him. 'Listen, I'd be the first to admit he can be backward, but if he says she's lying, she's lying.'

Steph took out the piece of paper from her pocket that I had earlier scrunched up. She smoothed it out, looked to me and, after I nodded, she walked up to Magda and gave it to her.

Magda snatched the scrap from Steph's hand and as she took in what it was and what it meant, her eyes grew wide. Panic.

'Take off your necklace, Magda,' I said, stepping forward, putting a quick hand on Steph to lead her back to Salvatore and Zoe.

She looked at me like she wanted to rip my throat out. Funny, I felt exactly the same way about her.

'No,' she said, looking to Griffin again. 'This is crazy.'

'As you can see, Steph has been *really* busy. She doesn't like to boast or anything, but she's a genius. I told her about a conversation I'd had with Onyx. He'd explained how Nahilius was only a gun for hire. I mean, I thought that meant he was working for Phoenix. In a way he was, not that Nahilius knew it, though. He actually believed he'd come back here to sell that building and get the money, didn't he?'

'I have no idea what story you are trying to concoct. Are you that desperate for attention?' She looked at Griffin. 'She has a problem, Griff.'

I took a step towards Magda. 'I'm not the one with the problem, Magda. I'm not the one who gave Phoenix the information about titanium, I'm not the one who betrayed all Grigori by giving exiles a new defence against us.'

'Violet,' Griffin warned, moving to stand beside Magda.

'Do you know what makes sapphires blue, Griffin?' I asked, pushing harder. 'Titanium,' I answered without waiting. 'The same metal exiles now know can confuse our senses. You discovered it, didn't you, Magda? Being Griffin's partner has had its advantages and you figured out a way to harness them for your benefit. It must've been years ago when you first hunted down that necklace.'

Magda started to take a small step back but I was too

quick. I reached out and ripped the chain from her neck, hoping it hurt her.

Magda's hands went to her throat in shock.

I half laughed, even though none of this was funny. 'Kashmir sapphires are the rarest because they are the richest blue. You know, I Googled them – only a few have ever been discovered. Some believe they even attract divine favour and…can weave truth.'

'Violet, stop this,' Griffin said, but I could see the wheels turning, his mind going into overdrive.

'I'm sorry, Griffin,' and I really was, 'but I can't.'

'Ask her now, Lincoln. Ask her why she tried to return Phoenix,' Steph said.

Lincoln looked from me to Magda to Steph, then Salvatore and finally back to me. In the end, he would trust me.

'Why did you do it?' he asked Magda.

'I told you why. I did it to save her.'

Griffin dropped his glass of orange juice. He could see her lies. 'Oh, Magda. You wanted to kill her?' Griffin said.

Lincoln's mouth was open. He was stunned.

'Actually, she wanted to kill Phoenix and me. Me, to get me away from you,' I said to Lincoln. 'And Phoenix because after getting rid of Nahilius, she was covering her tracks.'

'I don't understand,' Lincoln said, probably willing it not to be true.

'This is crazy. She's trying to turn everyone against me!' Magda started up again.

'Stop!' Griffin yelled so loud, she jumped. 'Stop lying. I knew that damn necklace did something. I knew it. I let you get away with things, covered up for you, hoped you would find your way. I never thought you were this…evil. Do you have any idea how many lives you have destroyed? How many you have endangered by giving over the knowledge of titanium?'

'Steph went through all the boxes of your mum's company documents,' I said to Lincoln, who, by his mortified expression, I gathered was quickly starting to piece it all together. 'Onyx told me Nahilius was working for someone. I thought it was Phoenix, but it was never *Nahilius* working with Phoenix. Steph found records, the bank transfers from your mum's company to Nahilius and then almost as much transferred out of his account into another unnamed account. The piece of paper Magda is holding shows that she is the owner of that account.'

'No,' Griffin said, shaking his head at the unforgiving truth.

Lincoln looked from me to Magda, his jaw clenched tight. 'You were working with Phoenix?'

'He forced me!' Magda said quickly.

Lincoln half smiled as he shook his head. 'No shadows, Magda. I'd be able to see if you were under his influence.'

Magda was silent, but frantic.

'Since you came back from holiday you've been working with him. You brought Nahilius back, used him to drive a wedge between Violet and me so Phoenix could get to her. I trusted you.'

'Lincoln, it's not what you think. I didn't know you back then, I… When I realised who you were, that you were going to become Grigori, I pulled Nahilius out of your mother's company and I told him to disappear. I *saved* her.'

'You killed my mother!' Lincoln screamed.

Everyone was silent.

'Why, Magda?' Griffin finally asked, the words breaking.

Magda walked towards the door but then seemed to reconsider and turned back on him.

'Because *you* have all the power. You could've made us great, but you could never see the possibilities. It was all about the damn cause.' She tossed her head towards Lincoln, her eyes were actually welling. 'Because I would've done anything for you to look at me the way you...' She shot me a poisonous look. '*You* ruined everything!'

She was moving at full speed. I barely had time to react when her hand reached my neck and she flung me back onto the dining table. But Lincoln was faster and was there in an instant. He thrust her off me with one hand and such force that she flew through the air until she slammed into the far wall.

Lincoln helped me up. Gentle hands. Only touching where necessary and yet every spot where we were connected still burned.

'I'm OK,' I said, giving him permission to move away from me.

Magda was back on her feet. She looked as if she was about to pounce again.

'You think you have everyone fooled!' she screamed at me. 'But your true colours will show soon enough.'

Griffin moved in on Magda slowly. His head bowed. When he stood right in front of her, his hand went out in a snap and braced her neck as she had mine. He pushed her back into the wall she'd just collided with and heaved her into the air, his arm fully extended.

I held my breath as I saw the muscles in his arm flexing tight, the expression on Magda's face exposing her pain. She couldn't breathe and he was close to crushing her windpipe altogether.

'A strike to Violet is a strike to me,' he said, echoing the words he'd said to me when I'd slapped Magda. 'Give me a reason not to squeeze.'

Magda put both hands on Griffin's shoulders, as if consolingly. He must have let his guard down for a moment, because when her knee flew up to hit him under the chin, he released his grip on her and she landed on the floor.

'Sure thing, Griff,' she snarled, making for the door again.

Spence and Salvatore beat her there and stood in her way, but Griffin gave a small wave of his hand and they stood aside.

Magda smiled at Griffin. 'You're too weak. And when you try to figure all this out and keep stumbling on the big questions, remember – the answer is the very thing you fight so hard for.' She took the handle, pulled it open and paused without looking back, just long enough to say two words.

'Free will.'

CHAPTER THIRTY-FOUR

*'The sin both of men and of angels, was rendered
possible by the fact that God gave us free will.'*
C. S. Lewis

I don't know who found the bottle of vodka. I didn't care. No one did. Hard liquor was probably a bad idea, but one by one we took our seats and Spence started to pour.

Looking at us all, slumped around the dining table, it was clear – not one of us had escaped the last few days unscathed. I couldn't remember when we'd last slept. I didn't even know what time of day it was – only that it was now dark.

'To Rudy,' Spence said.

We all raised our glasses and drank. My throat burned and I relished the distraction. Spence refilled the cups one by one.

'And Nyla,' Griffin said.

And though we didn't want to admit to it, we didn't want to deny it either. We raised our glasses and gulped down the poisonous truth.

To Nyla.

'What now?' Zoe asked.

'We fight,' Lincoln and I said in unison without looking at each other.

'I'm sorry, Violet, and Lincoln. I knew Magda was up to something but I swear, I never thought...' He couldn't finish.

'We know, Griffin,' I said, wanting to reassure him.

'None of us did,' Lincoln added.

'I owe you an apology too, Salvatore.' They gave each other a nod. 'And a debt of gratitude to you, Stephanie.'

No one said much after that for a while, just mumbled here and there. Every now and then another penny would drop.

'The exiles in the alley who killed the homeless?' Lincoln said.

I nodded. 'I think Phoenix provided them and Magda sent them. I'm gathering there was never a group of exiles who she took out on her holiday, probably just one exile and she didn't take him out.'

'Phoenix,' Lincoln said, clenching his jaw.

Another stretch of silence until Griffin had a lightning-bolt moment. 'That's why she would never stay long around me! She was scared the sapphire's influence wouldn't hold.'

We all just nodded as the theory sank in. It explained a lot of her quick exits when Griffin arrived.

And finally.

'She wanted me to kill Nahilius. She knew it would change me forever, make me doubt everything,' Lincoln said quietly.

I didn't need to respond. I'd figured the same thing. That Magda wanted Lincoln to do it so he would feel so isolated from everyone else, especially me, that he would turn to her. When her plan backfired, she killed Nahilius to silence him. I took little comfort in the realisation that it wasn't me Nahilius had called a bitch.

'Violet, you lead us now,' Griffin said as Spence lined up more shots. 'Phoenix was right. You are from a Sole Angel, the highest rank. That makes you our leader.'

I looked around the table expecting, and ready to welcome, intervention. But no one argued.

'No. It just gives me a right to choose. I don't want to lead, Griffin. I have school and *you're* our leader. If I'm ranked highest, then I get to say who's in charge, and that's you.'

I held out my glass and then drank. Lincoln did the same, followed by everyone else supporting my decision. Finally, Griffin nodded.

'For now,' he said and drank.

'While we're getting things sorted,' Spence piped up, 'I, um…I've made some decisions of my own.'

'Let's hear 'em,' Griffin said, his country accent now thick under the influence of alcohol. He was resigned to anything at this stage.

'I'm not going back to New York. I'm staying here.'

When we all just looked at him, he shrugged. 'Well, I've got no parents waiting for me and I'm not very well going to leave the one person who can heal me until my partner comes of age, am I? And anyway, I'd like a chance to return the favour,' he said, shooting me a genuine smile. 'That is, of course, if that's OK with everyone,' he added, looking at Lincoln then glancing at me. After everything that had happened, he was giving Lincoln the chance to tell him to get lost.

I think Lincoln appreciated the gesture although I was sure it stuck him like a pin. I know it did me.

'You can stay here,' Lincoln offered. 'I'll clear out the spare room.'

I shot Lincoln a look. I never thought he'd clear out that room.

'It's time,' he said, answering my unspoken question. I was glad for him.

'We're going to apply for permission to return as well,' Zoe said. 'We want to be here to help fight what's coming but first we need to go back and check on Nyla and debrief everyone at the Academy. It's only right.'

We all nodded.

Griffin took another drink. I think he was taking two for every one of ours.

Lincoln's phone rang. He answered as he got up and walked away from the table. While he was talking, Steph used her own version of best-friend telepathy with me – a series of raised eyebrows, head tilts and one mouthed 'O-K'.

I nodded to them all.

'That was Dapper,' Lincoln said when he returned. 'He's been trying to get hold of you for a while,' he said to me.

'Oh.' I stood and went over to my phone still on the charger. I made a show of turning it on and shoved it in my pocket. I heard the voicemail bell chime a few times. I'd check the messages later.

'We have to go to Hades,' he said.

'Look, honestly, Dapper can deal with Onyx or throw him out on the street,' Griffin said.

Lincoln kept moving and shrugged on a coat. He wedged open the door with his foot, waiting for us all to get up. 'It's not Onyx. Let's go.'

And like good little soldiers, we all got up and followed.

CHAPTER THIRTY-FIVE

'The star that leads the way is your star . . .
You will exceed all of them for you will have sacrificed
the man that clothes me.'

It may as well have been a lifetime ago, those moments Lincoln and I shared in Jordan. In some ways, I wished they'd never happened.

OK, that was a lie.

The city seemed different, foreign to me somehow. I was so exhausted, but still my legs carried me on. Nothing would ever be the same. Even the air felt different. Jordan had changed me, irreversibly.

Maybe it was for the best. Maybe I needed to be given a dose of harsh reality. Somewhere along the way, I'd obviously lost sight, forgotten to protect myself and keep control of things. Now I would pay the price.

Lincoln walked up ahead with Spence, flanking Griffin in case he tumbled over. Poor Griffin. He carried us all, felt responsible for leading us and now, after everything that happened in Jordan, to have discovered Magda had played such a terrible part… This was one thing for which I knew he'd blame himself for a long time, even though he shouldn't.

This was only the start. I didn't just feel doom settling around me now. It had moved in, taken possession. Lincoln looked over his shoulder, caught my eye and turned back. I wanted to scream.

Steph, who had been chatting to Salvatore, slowed her pace to meet mine. She linked our arms together like she'd done so many times before. Still my best friend.

'Would you like me to say something that will distract you?' she said.

'Sure.'

'Your dad's coming home tomorrow.'

I sighed. 'Wow, I guess he managed to cut his trip short after all,' I said, knowing I must have missed a number of calls from him. Probably the messages my phone had beeped with earlier.

'Yeah, well, on the upside, I spoke to him last night, told him you were out getting takeaway. He sounded worried, but by the time I'd finished yabbering on about all the stuff we've been doing, he was fine.'

Thank God for Steph. And Dad, he just made it too easy, but right now I couldn't complain.

'On the downside?' I asked, knowing there was more.

'He saw the Amex bill and didn't buy the story I gave him about you needing a thousand dollars' worth of urgent school supplies. He said he'd be expecting an explanation. I suggest starting with "I'm not on drugs!"'

I shrugged. It wasn't ideal, but I could manage that. I was sure I could produce a few utility bills he hadn't been following and make up a few extra expenses. It was the least of my worries.

'Are you staying over?' I asked.

Steph hesitated, 'If… You know, if that's OK.'

'Things still crappy at home?'

'Sort of.'

'Maybe we could go get an early breakfast at the mall before school?' I said, reinforcing that she was welcome to stay at mine. I really wanted to just sleep for weeks but it would be nice to do something normal and I owed her a good talk. She clearly had things to fill me in on.

Steph nodded and gave me a nudge. It was all that was needed with us.

We turned the corner, the burnt orange doors to Hades shining at the end of the road.

I felt him as if the senses rose up from the ground, wafted like a heatwave. My grip on Steph's arm tightened. His senses made me anxious, they were so powerful. But they weren't at full force. He was holding back, just letting me know.

Jude.

The others all seemed to become more alert as we reached the entrance to the club. Either sensing him too or just intuition. Griffin seemed to sober himself and stand to attention.

There was a brief pause before we all moved into the heaving bar. I had just enough time to say, 'Upstairs,' before the doors opened and music blasted out from inside.

We moved through the crowd, towards the unmarked door that led upstairs. Patrons of Hades were dancing, drinking, flirting. We must have looked like a pretty weird sight to all of them. As a group, we didn't exactly look like we were out to party.

I prepared myself for anything. Jude had abilities that stretched so much further than he had shown. I didn't know what he was capable of.

When we reached the bar I spotted Onyx. He was wearing jeans and a white shirt. I'd never seen him in jeans before. He looked...stable. And that wasn't all, he was working, serving a blonde girl from behind the bar and he looked like he was actually taking some kind of pride in it. That's not to say I didn't notice the large glass of what I guessed was bourbon or whisky sitting by the register.

He spotted me after he gave the girl her drink and change, and his eyes narrowed. Strangely, I was comforted that he hadn't changed completely. He cocked his head towards the door that headed upstairs, letting me know to follow him as he walked on his side of the bar.

He opened the door and leaned on it as one by one we all filed into the narrow stairway.

'This will be interesting,' Onyx said as I passed.

'Do you know who he is?' I asked.

He smiled his old wicked smile, but somehow it had less bite now. 'He's the villain.'

Fragments of my dream floated back to me as I remembered my angel maker showing me flashes of the past, of decisions made. Jude's choices.

'Why did he come here?' I asked Onyx.

'He's been watching you for some time, I'd say, waiting,' Onyx said, again his words striking a chord with me.

Griffin knocked on Dapper's door.

'Come in,' called Dapper from inside.

The senses were now strong, the flavour of apple seemed to mix with a foul aroma.

'Ew, that's putrid. What is it?' I couldn't help asking.

Griffin and Lincoln, as specialists in sensing the floral combinations exiles exude, were also wrinkling their noses.

'*Dracunculus vulgaris*,' Griffin said. 'A stunning flower that smells of rotted meat.'

We walked in and found Jude sitting on a stool at Dapper's minibar. His robes still the same dirty brown, still covering his face, his whole frame hunched over.

Dapper stood behind the small wooden bar, looking nervous, not taking his eyes from Jude.

'I don't think I was clear when I told you lot not to bring your troubles here,' he said calmly, as if worried he might stir his unwanted guest.

Since I was the only one who had spoken with him in the past, I felt I had to say something.

'Jude…' I started, unsure. 'Why are you here?'

He didn't answer. I looked to Griffin, he just opened his hands a little. But then Jude started to move. I saw Lincoln's hand go to his dagger while Jude's went to his hood and he revealed his beautiful face. This time I was prepared and stopped my hands floating towards him.

Reaching into the sides of his robe, Jude revealed something else. The Scripture, the one he'd taken from Jordan. He raised his head, his baby blue eyes looking softly at mine as he held the parchment out to me.

'You're just giving it to us?' I asked, worried to take it in case it was some kind of trap.

He nodded once.

'What do you want in return?' I asked, trying to concentrate as more images from my dreams flooded back to me. All the pain, the guilt, the responsibility.

'Nothing,' he replied.

'What about Phoenix?'

His head tilted. 'He thought he had found my weakness. He had not.'

'You were supposed to give him the Scripture in return for something.'

He nodded again. 'He will know by now that I have not kept my end of the arrangement. It will not take long for him to know where I am.'

I looked around the room, everyone seemed unsure of what to do. Lincoln's hand still hovered near his dagger. Steph looked completely baffled and Salvatore had a firm arm around her. He must have had to restrain her at some point from approaching Jude. Even Onyx seemed wary, standing at the back of the room, though I also saw him keeping one eye on Spence. I wondered if he was still a little apprehensive in his presence too.

But I wasn't scared. Images of my dream continued to flow as if the door had been unlocked. I could see it, feel it.

'How long have you been in the world realm?' I asked.

The corners of his mouth made a minuscule movement. Did he know I was working it out?

'A little over two thousand years.'

His eyes went to the Scripture and then back to me. I took a step towards him, towards the thing that had cost so much already.

'You are betraying your own.'

'Sometimes it is necessary, even when others cannot see.'

Because we need a villain.

He stood. I heard the others shuffle nervously behind me. I took the Scripture in one hand, and closed the final step between us. I leaned in slowly and he let me. My other hand took hold of my cold hard destiny.

This was it. The moment.

And I was right, Jude *was* another cliff. I remembered how Uri had explained it in the desert. Now, it was true again.

It was simply a matter of the right question being laid before you so that you could, in turn, make the right choice.

My grip tightened around the dagger. This was the same as leaping and I knew, once I did this, I'd never be able to go back. And then the words of my angel maker floated through my mind, words from my dream. I'd assumed he was speaking of Jude, but now I wasn't so sure.

We all have the capacity to find the will – even when that which we must do terrifies us most.

Jude's cheek was soft, and untouched for so very long. I kissed him. Once.

'Thank you, Judas,' I whispered as I pulled back and drove the dagger into him, returning him for judgement.

His kind eyes met mine. An eternity of sacrifice showed. A tortured solitude.

'Thank you, Keshet,' he said, using the same title both my angel maker and mother had given me as his hand reached out towards me gently. Before his fingers touched my face they disappeared, along with the rest of him. And though he was gone, I was sure I still felt him the moment he would have connected with me.

I hoped he got the nothingness he had craved.

'Did you just say *Judas*?' Dapper asked.

'Uh-huh,' I answered, looking down at my hands. In one, an ancient Scripture, in the other, a dagger. *My dagger.*

'Oh. Just checking.' Dapper started pouring himself a drink.

'So it is true,' Onyx said from the back of the room, moving forward now.

'Which part?' Lincoln asked, sounding out of breath.

'Keshet,' Onyx said, looking at me.

'The rainbow,' I said, distracted. Bewildered.

I just killed Judas.

Dapper, who seemed to be relaxing a bit now that Jude was gone, put down his drink. 'It's why your aura is always different,' he marvelled, reminding us of his ability to identify auras. 'Kind of a contradiction – Grigori power usually comes out all multicoloured, but Grigori auras are always just the one colour. It can be different shades for different people, but always just one and, on top of that, a lining of gold. Violet, here – she's, well, she's like a rainbow with streaks of gold all over the place.'

'I hate to ask the obvious, but what the hell does all that mean?' Spence spat out.

'It means,' Lincoln started, as if saying it hurt him, 'she can connect the realms.'

I didn't really understand, but I knew he was right and that somehow, my mother had always known. It was why she'd sacrificed herself, why she'd named me Violet.

Onyx moved over to the bar and motioned for Dapper

423

to pour him a large glass of whatever he was having. Whisky, I think. Salvatore and Steph collapsed onto the chaise while Zoe made herself comfortable on Dapper's shag rug. Griffin and Lincoln joined me on the other side of the minibar.

I took a deep breath and unfurled the Scripture.

The blood drained from my face. My vision blurred.

'What?' Griffin prompted.

My eyes welled with tears of pure fright. 'Does anyone know what Tartarus is?' I asked, in barely a whisper.

'The pits of this realm,' Dapper said, as Onyx took a massive gulp of his drink and offered a much plainer explanation.

'Hell.'

My hands shook, holding the Scripture that was not meant for us. 'This is not the Grigori Scripture. It's…it's…'

My heart started to race, my mouth went dry. The large bold outline of a triangle in the middle with small symbols at each point haunted me to the core. Below that, two sections of text. The words were not decipherable, but they didn't need to be. Instinct told me what this was.

'I know why Phoenix wanted the Scriptures. It was never about the Grigori list.' My hands shook so much Lincoln had to take the parchment from me.

'What is it?' Griffin asked, now looking over Lincoln's shoulder at the Scripture.

'Writing. Diagrams. It's in another language but… I think it's…instructions.' I stared into the room, full of my friends – Grigori warriors, Steph, even Onyx and Dapper. I feared for us all and could think of only one person who would know what to do. But Mum was already dead.

'To return one of the damned,' Lincoln said. 'Phoenix wants to bring someone back from hell.'

'Who?' Spence asked, irritated he was missing something.

Lincoln's ghost-white face now mirrored mine and even when I looked at Onyx I could see he wasn't exactly a shade of good health either. Together, we gave Spence his answer.

'Lilith.'

'And so,' Griffin sighed, 'we have what he wants and he has the lists.'

My phone beeped in my pocket and I pulled it out with still-quivering hands. I already knew it would be him. There was no running, no quitting – he wouldn't let me, and somehow that helped. A kind of resignation came over me.

I stood a little taller, not so tired any more. I stared at the text message as my hands stopped shaking.

Interested in a trade...lover?

The star that leads the way is your star...
You will exceed all of them for you will have sacrificed
the man that clothes me.
The Lost Gospel of Judas

ice

ACKNOWLEDGEMENTS

Writing really is only part of the process. There have been so many people that have played a part in bringing this series together. None more so than my agent and friend, Selwa Anthony, whose guidance, know-how and support has been invaluable. I am honoured to be one of her authors and cannot express how grateful I am to be in such safe, sure hands.

Thank you to my stellar publishers, in particular, Fiona Hazard and the very savvy Vanessa Radnidge for putting up with the countless phone calls and umming and ahhing over every tiny little detail. Thank you for caring just as much as I do! Special thanks to my wonderful editor, Kate Ballard, who has taken meticulous care to improve and develop the manuscript. To work with a team, which includes many more, who are so passionate about the series, makes the entire process incredibly exciting.

Thanks to designers, Xou Creative, who have done a superb job on the cover and photographer, Branislav, and the beautiful Kasandra for being so flexible and fitting in the last-minute photo shoots!

To my friends who have helped so much; Peita Daly, for all of her PR expertise and encouragement; Harriet Henderson for the many hours of phone support and for being one of my most trusted early readers; Grant Henderson for putting together the perfect author website; and Ben Eaton, for his amazing generosity (and the mighty trimmer!). I am so grateful to you all.

To the rest of my friends and family, you know who you are and how much I value all of your love and support.

Matt, you astound me on a daily basis with your never-ending support and complete faith in me. Thank you for being the husband you are to me and the father you are to our gorgeous girls. To say I love you just seems so insufficient...but it's true! xx